SIMON & SCHUSTER

New York

London

Toronto

Sydney

Tokyo

Singapore

THE Marzipan Pigeon

ALYSSA DONATI

SIMON & SCHUSTER
ROCKEFELLER CENTER
1230 AVENUE OF THE AMERICAS
NEW YORK, NEW YORK 10020

SIMON & SCHUSTER AND COLOPHON ARE
REGISTERED TRADEMARKS OF SIMON & SCHUSTER INC.
DESIGNED BY PEI LOI KOAY
MANUFACTURED IN THE UNITED STATES OF AMERICA

1 3 5 7 9 10 8 6 4 2

LIBRARY OF CONGRESS CATALOGING-IN-PUBLICATION
DATA
DONATI, ALYSSA.
THE MARZIPAN PIGEON / ALYSSA DONATI.
P.   CM.
1. CITY AND TOWN LIFE—NEW YORK (N.Y.)—FICTION. 2.
YOUNG ADULTS—NEW YORK (N.Y.)—FICTION.   I. TITLE.
PS3554.046922M37 1994
813'.54—DC20   93-48134
                                      CIP

ISBN: 0-671-86889-6

For my

mother and father

Chapter 1

Minty was my friend. Minty used to paint the marzipan pigeons on the roof. It wasn't like he was schizophrenic or anything; he just liked the damn birds. He used to crawl out the kitchen window and climb up the fire escape of our building with all these canvases pinched under his arm and these warped tubes of paint brimming over his pockets. Surrounded by the sleek rage of Manhattan, he would begin. Dipping a frazzled brush into dollops of blazing black and shotgun yellow, he would hold the brush suspended for a moment while his hands and eyes merged. And then, a flick of the wrist and that brush would come alive. He would lead it dancing over the raw white canvas until there was no space. Until the pigeons were spilling over the edges and dripping into the tar. My God, he was beautiful, terribly beautiful. His stained hands fluttering against the sky. The sun's copper remnants shattering in his eyes.

Just as dusk expelled its last ginger fusion, he would return, aligning his damp canvases against the wall in the living room, sipping a pink lady with too much grenadine. Occasionally he would slip into the bathroom to absorb the Warhol print over the john. He had this thing for Warhol, this terrific thing. He used to say Warhol was the king of the scene. I certainly didn't think he was any king. Maybe a voyeur, but no great goddamn king. Besides, he's dead.

It's 1 A.M.

A gunshot slaps the air; a rat squirms beneath the overstuffed, leaking garbage bags at Sixty-fourth and Lex. An old woman is lost in the twenty-four-hour Food Emporium (she can't remember if her bedroom is in the produce or dairy section). A bum is trying to sell a frostbitten dove outside Palladium, while the jet-set, shoeshined Wall Street success slips into his Mercedes outside Regine's. He's got two sparkling whores hanging off his sleeves like cuff links. They have AIDS, but he won't know about it till 1997. A doorman sits in the lobby of a Park Avenue building, hunched over a portable TV watching David Letterman. Some lunatic zookeeper is chasing Letterman around the studio with a giant lizard. The doorman smiles, but not really. In a West Side bar, a foxy ash-blond waitress is flirting with two fraternity brats from Florida State. These guys can't decide whether to rape her or order another round. They can't decide whether to transfer to Southern California or break out and form a heavy-metal band. They both lust to be rock stars. To be sex symbols. I've got a good seat tonight. I can see it all front and center.

Downtown it's Savage. Downtown crazy outrageous, enhanced by extraterrestrials you thought you'd encounter only in a Spielberg movie. It's a long night's journey into day—the aliens gravitate toward the line that's been forming since nine-thirty outside Savage, the shrine where the bouncer is messing up minds. He likes to watch the hopefuls hope and the beggars beg.

Minty does neither; he simply grabs my hand and saunters up

to the border. Not even Darth Vader would dare fuck with this golden man, and in less than a second he is opening the gates to hell. Inside, the fire has begun to burn, the tangerine light of the underworld draped over the natives, bouncing off their white-hot brains and red-hot souls. My eyes reach down to the floor. Thousands of cigarette butts are being diced and stabbed by stiletto heels. What a goddamn mess.

Mint has my hand, he is leading me to one of the corner tables. There he lights up and orders us drinks. Just to have him next to me . . . it turns my bones to quicksand, it crushes my heart like dark, sweet berries. The pandemonium is louder. A strawberry blonde is coming our way. I've seen her before. She's like a fucking bomb, exploding all over the scene. She's right in front of us now. She is wearing funky rubber hot pants, hoop earrings the size of hubcaps, and a blouse that appears to be made out of cheesecloth. Her aqua eyes are framed by ropes of thick black lashes.

Slowly and sensuously, she leans over the table until she is face-to-face with Mint. "Hey, Minty, wanna dance?"

Jesus, her voice is like the ear-piercing whine of a power drill. Mint blasts out of his seat and drags her out onto the dance floor until they are crosshatched with pulsing beams, fragmented in the kaleidoscope. I try not to stare at them, but it's like trying not to piss when you've had a keg of beer. So I just sit there and watch him invade her body and mumble some supersexy garbage in her ear.

So I'm sitting there and I hate that shit, because whenever you're sitting alone in a joint like that, about half a dozen morons come over to seduce you. And I swear I haven't been sitting there for more than sixty seconds when the first moron spots me from the bar. I know this one. His name is Giorgio. He's this terribly haughty Eurofag from Milan who doesn't do a damn thing but arrange parties and go around filming everybody with a camcorder. He's the biggest asshole I've ever seen. Always in a tux. He could be going to a ball game and he'd still wear a tux. He gets a very big hard-on from seeing his snapshot in the society pages of *Women's Wear Daily*. The worst part is his drug habit. The guy is a madman coke addict, and every time he's next to you, you can hear those damn vials rattling in his pockets like ice cubes in the bottom of a glass.

So he sees me, and I know it's too late for me to scram because he's already swaggering over to my table. Boy, does he look stupid. He has hair down to his cummerbund and always wears earrings. The sad part is, he doesn't have the faintest idea how stupid he looks. Just as I expected, he has that video camera with him. He sets it down on the table and slides into the seat next to me and says, "Oh, baby! You know you so beautiful. *Sè così bèlla!* How many times I tella you? Whya you stay with sucha badda man?" He's referring to Mint, who by now is almost stuck in the power drill's bountiful cleavage. "*Perché, tesòro?* Whya, baby?" These European guys always think the accent's an aphrodisiac, that a woman's just going to drop her pants the minute she hears it. Well, I couldn't care less. I can't stand his accent and I want him to disappear. Only Eurotrash never disappears. They're like Pampers in a landfill.

I haven't given him the time of day. I haven't said two words to him, and he keeps right on. He starts to tell me about some nude photo collage he's done of some high-society tart, and then the imbecile actually has the nerve to start filming me. He picks up his camcorder and shoves the lens in my face and starts shouting out all these directions like, "Eh, come ona, Salty, looka over here . . ." as if he's such a pro. As if he thinks he's somewhere up there with Sir David Lean, for christsakes. Boy, do I want to sock him. I want to sock him so much my hand begins to ache. I'm about to get up and go to the bathroom to get away from him, but then I notice Mint and the bimbo coming back to the table.

Mint slides back into his seat and to my horror pulls the creature in the scuba pants right down on his lap.

All I can think of is that I have the opportunity to make Mint jealous, so I don't budge. I'm suddenly wildly amused by Giorgio. I start to flood his lens with an array of poses. I chuckle mechanically at his dreary wit, and when he puts down the camcorder I force myself to look at him as if he were the man of my dreams. I steer my focus into his polluted, muddy-brown eyes. His eyelids slouch wearily like blinds yanked halfway down over a window. The more I look at him, the more vulgar he becomes. He's wearing some kind of maraschino-cherry lip gloss, and it's sort of smeared down his chin. And then, of course, there is that hair, that long gangly mane of hair, and the incoherent English hemorrhaging out of him is almost worse than the Power Drill, who mobilizes in my peripheral vision like a car on the freeway.

I wonder how many times in my life I've suffered with some slob to try to make Mint turn his head and drop his drink and snatch me into his arms. Only it's a hopeless attempt, since he is, and always has been, oblivious of my suitors. It's worse than hell doing that. Like a hooker rocking the bedsprings for a simple crumpled roll of dough that disintegrates into her pimp's hands. There is no reward. You're lucky if you break even. If it's not the pimp, it's going to be somebody else. If you're a real legal-minded bastard, it's going to be the IRS who takes it and cuts it all in half, and someday it's going to be the guy on the corner in black leather with the switchblade who makes off with Uncle Henry's engraved solid-gold watch and today's paycheck. You never get rid of the pain of feeling cheated, so you make it work for you. You adopt it like a street kid who follows you around popping gum until one day you wake up and you just don't give a shit anymore. Your whole body's swollen up inside from all the blows you've taken, and all you want to do is collapse in the ring and let the other guy walk away with the title. You stand there wavering, just waiting for that one supersonic blow that's going to choke your eyes up with blood and let you descend.

So I remain entranced by Giorgio, furtively looking over at Mint every couple of seconds to see if he's noticed my spurious devotion to this foreign fuck. He's begun to bounce the bimbo on his knee. And then she and Mint stand up, and Mint leans over and tells me that he's going to split and he'll catch me later. Act 1 is over.

As soon as they're out of sight I dismantle my character and shift myself away from Giorgio, who by now is convinced that I'm madly in love with him. Astonished that I'm leaving, he grabs my arm with his monstrous nicotine-stained fingers and utters, "But, baby, where you going?"

"Oh, for christsakes, let go of me!" I roar, and yank myself out of his grip. I walk away as fast as I can, but I can hear him shouting my name, and when I turn my head it's just as I suspected. He is plowing through the crowds after me. I can't see his body 'cause there are too many people ahead of him, but I can see that big bulky camera moving toward me with its dismal red light flashing. The imbecile is actually trying to film me as he chases me.

I decide to cut onto the dance floor to lose Giorgio. I know I'll lose him because it's so jam-packed out there. And I do. I lose him. But like a fool, I've migrated to the very center of hell. All these prismatic streaks of light keep flashing and receding, everything is splitting into a thousand dizzy fragments. Arms and eyes and hands keep flying toward me like burning shrapnel and I fear I'll never escape. Then I see a crack, a tiny tear in the great wall of flesh, and I lunge forward. And as I emerge dripping from the Technicolor waves, I stagger through the steaming gates to freedom.

Jesus Christ, it's almost morning. I can make this distinction because the moon's night shift is nearly over. And this sunlight starts oozing all over everybody like a goddamn egg yolk and I start to notice the zit somebody tried to cover up with Erace, and the real color of the bouncer's wig. It's red. As red as Jerked Chicken Callaloo and ugly as hell.

Minty never worries about how I get home alone on the streets. It isn't that he doesn't care; he knows I can handle myself. I start walking, since there isn't a cab to be found. I'm just another refugee of the night, hauling myself into the morning light. I wearily remind myself that I've survived.

On my high heels I totter like a newborn colt in the barn. It's gonna take me a fucking hour to get to the deli on the corner, but I can make it! I'm as tough as hell. Tears begin to cascade from my eyes. I'm as tough as hell—*bullshit.* Without my angel, I'm just a fucking unloaded gun. I can give the appearance of the guy who doesn't feel, but in actuality I'm rotting like fruit in the yard. I wipe one of the tears futilely. I know that at this very moment Minty's butt-naked on top of that strawberry whore—her funky rubber hot pants have blown out the window, and she's reaching for a condom. She has a leaning tower of Trojans that could last her a lifetime, or maybe a week. Everything is out of focus. The deli up ahead is beginning to resemble a human skull. Its bone-white canopy and linear boxes define the peeled head of a corpse.

One of the Koreans has noticed me coming now. It's just another morning on China Beach. I'm heading for the border, stepping into enemy territory, gonna beg 'em for a pack of smokes and a Tab. Boy, am I a healthy motherfucker. They're going to find me in the coroner's office with kamikaze holes in my lungs and saccharine vandalizing my arteries. Ever since I've known Mint, I've been a self-destructive, radioactive bastard; statistically I'm twenty-three, realistically eighty. And it's all his fault. Only he has the power to say if I'm desirable or not. But he never says it. And therefore I don't exist. He's the only tangible evidence I have, but he's not around. I'm alone and terrified before the jury and the judge. The Living People versus Salty: Case 962,478. My attorney glances at my hopeless soul. There's nothing he can do for me anymore. The People are getting restless. I'm going to burn at the stake because my witness is fucking the girl in the tight mesh blouse. I'm so bitter. I'd like to blow up the world and just before that I'd do all the drugs I never did and lay all the men I never did and tan all the skin I never did.

I just want to go home, I just want to curl up in bed with my squeaky stuffed bear with the chewed ear. We're two of a kind. Both inanimate objects with no living proof.

Good-bye, Sunday . . . I hate you.

Chapter 2

When I woke up Monday morning, Mint was making breakfast. I suppose I ought to tell you that Mint and I shared an apartment. My parents died when I was very young, and that's kind of why Mint and I grew up together. But it's a helluva long story and I'd rather not go into it right now.

Anyhow, as I was saying, Mint was making breakfast. As I lay there listening to the rattling pans and the gnawing grind of the juicer, it all started coming back to me. The horror of Saturday evening at Savage. I dreaded having to get up and parade into that kitchen with this phony-baloney bullshit smile plastered on my face. Summoning courage to face him, I got up slowly and headed toward the kitchen. From a substantial distance, I could see him—a human flash of gold rummaging through the cabinets, his peroxide-white flesh fusing all background objects into a muddy shadow.

I started into the kitchen. The closer I came to him, the more distressed I became. I was on my own, again.

"Hey, Mint, long time no see." I felt that smile begin to tear my lips upward, and Mint, completely oblivious of my forced good humor, turned briskly and hugged me. His grasp was that of a child to a parent.

"Boy, we both were knocked out yesterday."

"Yeah, I know. When did you get home?" I asked.

"Oh, God, I guess around eleven yesterday morning. I just passed right out and slept all the way through until now. What about you?"

What about me? Now I was going to have to really start the bullshit. Who did I meet? Where did I go? I blurted out, "Giorgio and I stayed at Savage till about four-thirty and then Billy showed up and asked if I wanted to go have breakfast. So we went to this coffee shop and hung out for a while. I got in around ten, I guess."

"Sounds good." Minty smiled and went on gathering spoons and forks from the drawer, completely unaffected by the possibility that I might have stayed out so late with someone of the male race. Suddenly I was stabbed with the revelation that Billy, some guy we both knew, might talk to Mint and tell him he never even saw me. Oh, fuck, I was losing my composure, my false pretense; I was sinking further and further into this hideous predicament.

I know he's going to talk to Billy, I thought. I'll be stuck in the muck like Nixon, trying to crawl out only to be blinded by thousands of lights and microphones. My DNA was whirling out of control. Think, Jesus, just think. What can you say? You didn't tell him which Billy it was—didn't make any reference to his unmistakable persona. That's it! You can tell him it was another Billy. It was Billy the Kid. Billy of Baton Rouge, the French journalist; it was Baseball Billy, Biologist Billy. . . . The muck was beginning to dissolve. The press was piling back into its vans, the motors roaring.

"Want a croissant?" Mint broke into my inner confusion, and I realized I was starving. The acid was decomposing my stomach walls.

"God, yes! Anything and everything." I walked over to the stove, and he stuck a warm, flaky piece of it in my mouth; the fleeting velvet-smooth texture of his hand brushed my lips, and I did all I could to stop myself from keeling over backward at his touch. Drooling like Pavlov's dog at his every movement. There was no movement he performed without perfection. Just the slight shift of his weight onto one leg or the sensual lift of his acid green irises—that's about all it took, and in no fucking time I was right back in that courtroom establishing my existence. The pin-striped defense attorney picking up momentum, sloshing back and forth to the jury, to the judge; his arms waving in a futile attempt at some kind of justice, proving I was alive. Justice is bullshit. There's no such thing as justice—it's got a good solid ring to it, but it's just another illusion. They might find the goddamn cure for cancer, but nobody's ever gonna get to the bottom of justice. Nobody's going to save your ass.

Mint and I ate our breakfast on the roof. Mint was telling me about the cabdriver who took him home yesterday. "He was muttering some crap about Gandhi, wearing a turban and a toga and a nose ring. Jesus, he was from the wrong century. He thinks he's come to save all the guys in the city from eternal sin or something. So Eve ate the bloody apple, it's too late to change the world." The sun squirted an orange-gold ray through the clouds and it broke across his flesh like citrine. "I mean, nuts like that need treatment, Salt. And what the hell has he done for the world, anyway? Nothing. Not a thing." Minty looked up into the sky with this dead-serious expression on his face. I didn't understand why he was so worked up about this cabdriver. I mean, I thought it was kind of funny. In New York you're always running into some maniac who's going to tell you he's Joan of Arc or something. But Mint, he always got worked up about it.

"Those guys are completely innocuous. It's a joke, Mint. It's no big deal," I said after a couple of seconds. But he didn't say anything. He just kept staring at the sky like there was something going on up there.

Wordlessly I ran my eyes over him, and as I did I found myself returning to Savage: the melodrama, the futuristic zombies, the pulsing, the grinding; it all came raging back to me like a hateful film. I heard a glass breaking and crunching under someone's shoe . . . a transvestite zoomed into focus, his lips shining around a purple fruit . . . the projector shuddered—and suddenly Minty was blinking on the screen. He was back with the bimbo. Her thick voluptuous thighs were spreading over his like apricot preserve. Her huge phony breasts were squashed against his chest. I thought I would throw up. Jesus, it was vivid. Not grainy and muddled like most memories. It was 3-D and fucking cubist. I saw them from every angle, every side, twisting on that dance floor, and I was as nauseated as hell. I finally got a hold of myself, and as the credits started to roll, Mint came back to me.

He hadn't even noticed my disappearance. He was still gazing up, his face blazing like phosphorus against an ocean of sky. God, his color mesmerized me. My sun-drenched darling was all I desired, only failed to possess.

If he only knew—oh, God, if he only knew how desperately I wished to crawl into the warm white fire of his arms. If he only knew how every night my body curled and ached around my pillow, pretending it was him.

"Minty . . ."

"Hm?" His eyes swept down into mine, and I was stung by their blindness.

"Nothing," I said, "nothing."

That evening Mint dragged me to O'Riley's, a bar on the Upper East Side in the Seventies. I wasn't too fond of the joint, but

Mint got a real kick out of it. He said it didn't feel like a bar, that
he liked it because it always felt like a party given by a bunch of
close friends. But I think he liked it because all the younger kids
there idolized him. The minute he walked through the door,
every girl in the place would quit yacking to gawk at him. It was
just so monotonous. Shadows were always bobbing all over the
walls and the jukebox was always cranking out "American Pie."
Jesus, was I sick of that "American Pie." No matter what night it
was, some sixties freak would always stick a quarter in the juke
and pick out that song. Everybody was so superficial, too. Private-school girls with fake IDs who thought they were movie
stars set fire to their hair, and the guys were just full of attitude.
You tried to have a conversation with them, and all they could
talk about was doing some slut in the can. No kidding. Speaking
of the can, you'd never believe what a horror show that was.
Firstly, you could barely get into it. They might just as well have
called the joint "The Can," since that's where everybody was.
Herds of gossiping, giggling girls darting back and forth, mashing
themselves in there for a whole half an hour, all of them fighting
for the mirror like a bunch of savages. God, you should have seen
the makeup on these kids. If I were a guy, I'd be fuckin' terrified
to bring one of these chicks back to my pad. Honest to God. Because the guy doesn't know what's under all the crap. And then
the next morning he wakes up and looks over at the chick, who's
still snoring, and all her crap has rubbed off on the pillow. He's
got some chick he's never seen before and a pillow full of crap. It
was just too much for me. Minty and I had been coming to O'Riley's forever, and now I really felt old among the fake IDs and wet
dreams. You've gotta feel old when the undercover cops arrive,
when they start to haul up and bust all these kids whose mamas
are waiting up reading the *Times*.

Kids don't have a chance to grow up in New York. The minute
they're born, they're tossed into this high-tech scene; they go to

clubs instead of cookouts in someone's backyard. They drink vodka instead of Bud. They wear designer jobs instead of jeans and Reeboks. I remember when Mint and I first went to Studio 54, both fifteen and looking thirty. We approached the bouncers at the door and the crowd seemed to part like the seas. The man at the door pointed to us, and the red carpet was unrolled, the bridge let down.

And I knew why. Mint was nothing they had ever witnessed before. He was beyond beautiful. Beyond exceptional. He oozed charisma like a Mister Softee machine and everybody loved it. And we'd figured it out. We were children with power. Well, it was Mint who really had all the power. I just kinda kept him company.

The minute you were inside a place like that, you lost your pacifier on the floor. Men's shotgun eyes drilling into yours. Mouths opening, bodies grinding, and overnight you crossed from PG to triple X. And the kids from out of town waited outside in the hail and they tried so bloody hard to make it through those doors to what we were feeling, but they never made it. In a way, I really envied them. I envied their failure because it kept them young. It's no fun to feel lust when you don't know what lust is.

So anyhow, there I was at O'Riley's. In a cloud of smoke, in a blaze of boredom, I sat awaiting Minty's return to the table. My eyes fell dreaming on this prince of mine as he swept across the pulsing room. But my eyes, they weren't alone. Every girl there was watching him. God, sometimes I wished he was a monster. If he was a real monster then these girls wouldn't have cared about him. If he wasn't beautiful on the outside, they would have simply dismissed him. And then there would be nothing to fear. My darling beast would come to me and I would take his frightful face into my hands and kiss his crooked lips and stroke his thinning hair. This is what I dreamed sometimes. Only it would never be that way, so I could just forget about it. Mint would never be that beast. He'd always be a treasure to the eyes.

I was sitting in the back near the fireplace, staring at a guy who was trying to break a beer bottle on his head. All his buddies were rooting him on, hooting and hollering like primates. Jesus, was O'Riley's a nightmare. It was always filled with these crazy imbeciles who spit and pinched. A bunch of Neanderthals is what they were. About a minute later Mint came over to the table with this giggling blonde who couldn't have been more than fifteen and started to do all that mating bullshit. She, of course, was spellbound. She kept right on giggling and beaming. She was one of the rich kids. Most of the kids at O'Riley's were private-school kids, Upper East Side kids. The ones who hailed their first cab at thirteen. The ones who bought their school shoes at Bergdorf's and their bookbags at Hermes. I grew up with them. They'd gush into O'Riley's in their furs, glittering with gold earrings, spewing phony French accents. They went to debutante balls at the Waldorf and the Plaza, and would plow into O'Riley's afterward, all the girls wearing these puffy white gowns that rustled and dragged on the filthy wood floor. The guys would be half plastered, stumbling around in tuxedos, waving AmEx cards. A lot of girls asked Mint to escort them when they came out, but he only did it once, for this girl named Bunny. Bunny went to Spence and her father owned American Airlines or something. Something to do with airplanes. Mint and I weren't as rich as a lot of these kids. We were well enough off to go to private school, but we didn't have smoked salmon in our lunchboxes or anything. I didn't get an invitation to a debutante ball, and if I had I probably would have flushed it down the toilet. What a load of crap it was. Besides, I would never wear a ball gown. I'd look lousy. Honestly. Because I'd probably just stomp around in it with some high-tops on and a cigarette hanging out of my mouth.

Anyhow, as I was saying, Mint brought one of these rich kids over to the table. She was wearing this incredibly chic suede out-fit with big, hideous hexagon earrings. Boy, was she a regular mo-ron, this chick. She kept sucking in her rouge-smothered cheeks and making these asinine comments. When she wasn't giggling, she'd twist the gold cord of her Chanel handbag and let loose with the stupidest remarks I'd ever heard. At one point she said, "No, really? You paint stuff? That's like so cool. I like don't know that much about art. Who's that guy who chopped off his thing and sent it to his girlfriend? Van Goat?" That killed me. Van Goat, for christsakes. And the part about him chopping off his thing, that just took the cake.

Minty just smiled and corrected her: "You mean van Gogh, don't you? He chopped off his ear, not his penis." The girl started to giggle like mad when Mint said the word "penis." Honest to God, she just couldn't handle it. What the fuck kind of girl was this anyway? Mint didn't seem to care that much. He only wanted to screw her, after all.

I couldn't stand much more of this scene and started to chew my cigarette. It's this habit of mine. I chew on the filter. I suppose that's pretty lousy, but everybody has some kind of fucked-up habit. Like flushing things down the toilet. That's another one of mine. I'm one of those guys who flush anything down the god-damn toilet. When I find a stale bag of pistachio nuts from circa 1945 in the cupboard, I flush it. Just flush it, that's all you gotta do. Minty couldn't stand that. He'd get as mad as hell and tell me it was going to overflow and then the superintendent would come banging on the door, telling us all the goddamn pipes were clogged up with nuts.

When I'd finished chewing up my cigarette, I glanced back over at Mint and the whiz kid and knew he had it in the bag. He was already kissing her pouted lips. Only, as much as it hurt me to sit there and watch that stuff, I knew he didn't care about her. He

didn't care about any of them. He was always going off to sleep
with some tramp. He never had any deep discussion with them.
He never told them his fears or desires or took them out to a ball
game or a couple of Broadway shows. He'd just bang them, have a
smoke, and then get the hell out.

⁀

That year when Mint turned twenty-three was the year he finally
opened the Marzipan Pigeon. He didn't open it alone. He opened
it with this guy he knew named Anthony Morrison. Anthony
had been a chef at Elio's for years, and he and Mint used to hang
together sometimes. Mint knew him because he used to date Anthony's younger sister. Anyhow, Mint asked Tony if he'd like to
open up a restaurant with him. Tony was thrilled by the idea, and
he and Mint became partners.

You're probably wondering about how Mint got all the dough
to open a restaurant. He had quite a lot of money for a twenty-
three-year-old. Mint, you see, had made all his money when he
was a kid. He'd been one of those commercial kids. From age one
until he was around nine, Mint was all over the joint. You'd see
him on television in some pajamas brushing his teeth like a bastard. You'd see him on a cereal box holding up a spoon, his lumi-
nous green eyes leaping out at you. Jesus, was he ever a gorgeous
kid. Even if he'd been rolling around the park and was covered in
mud or something, he still looked gorgeous.

So anyhow, Mint and Tony went to work. They split up re-
sponsibilities. Tony was in charge of hiring a manager and book-
keeper and all the waiters and stuff. He was also going to be head
chef of the joint. Since it was originally Minty's idea to open up
the restaurant, he got to name it and decorate it. He named it the
Marzipan Pigeon so he could make pigeons the theme. He went
around with a ladder and painted these huge fabulous murals of

his crazy marzipan pigeons all over the ceiling and the walls. He hung fantastic white iron birdcages all over the joint and dressed the waiters up in these madman outfits with big silver wings coming off the shoulder blades. And before you knew it, the doors were bursting open and the phone was ringing and herds of people were clamoring to get inside. Practically overnight, news of the Marzipan Pigeon had swept through the city like a hurricane, and the flashbulbs burned in Minty's diaphanous eyes as he stood at the door. Champagne was shooting from bottles, squab was sizzling on the stove, and ribbons of smoke were swirling into the warped, feverish murals on the ceiling. The *New York Times* called it "the most remarkable dining experience in Manhattan."

Minty hired Brassy Griffith to play some cool jazz in this birdbath kind of setup. Brassy played tenor sax. It was like ice on ice, like crème de menthe. So smooth. So good. And by God, was she beautiful! It was really lousy the way she was so beautiful, a Pollock didn't have as many colors. She had stained-glass eyes and wicker hair; sometimes her skin was like tinsel, mica, something superbeautiful. Illegal. Everyone was mad for her, stretching out their hands to touch her; like the bubonic plague, she swept over each and every one of them. I was the only survivor.

I'd see Minty looking at her, sipping her up through his pupils, swallowing her whole like a fantastic white cobra, and, shit, I knew it would happen. This wasn't going to be some crazy hit-and-run. This collision was going to leave scars. I knew she'd pour herself into his bong and let him soar. She'd take him on a long journey, blow-dry his sweat, fluff him up, snort him down. She'd be his sex slave, his racy, spicy whore. As hot as Tabasco, as sharp as thorns.

I knew from the moment Mint hired Brassy that he was bananas over the bitch. He'd stand in the back of the restaurant watching her while she arched her back and breathed hot air into her golden gizmo. As soon as she finished a set, he'd race over to help her out of the goddamn birdbath. And then you know what he'd do? He'd set up the glittery bitch at a table and stuff her full of squab and wine and crème brûlée. When she was done she'd always pull out a cigarette, and Mint would scramble all over the joint for a match. It was really pathetic, the way he scrambled. Sometimes when she was smoking, he'd lean over and play with the nacreous beads dribbling down her chest. She never moved a muscle. She'd just sit there, ablaze in sequins, smoke stammering between her zinc-pink lips, her marbled eyes focused on something across the room—an exotic patron or a frenzy of roses.

My God, I despised her! That must sound terribly rotten, since she'd never really done anything to me, but you know how it is. I'm sure you've been in love at one point or another, and then one day you ran into your beloved with somebody else and you just wanted to stick that somebody into the microwave. You can't deny it. I know you've felt that way. The sick part is that that somebody, well, they could be a real saint, only you'd never see it. All you'd see is that they had their lousy hands down your beloved's pants and you'd want to strangle them. I wish it had been Minty I wanted to destroy. Only no matter how hard I tried, I'd never be able to inflict pain on him. He was my other half bound in a fleece of light. I was never gilded. Not like that. I suppose I could have been beautiful in an abstract sort of way. I had this mocha-colored hair and these ebony eyes. I think I had some South American ancestors—I think I would have looked real normal dragging a donkey along the back roads of Bolivia. But Brassy, she'd never have been able to get away with it. She was too classy, you know. She was really a very classy-looking bird. I couldn't picture her in Bolivia in a million years. I wasn't so ritzy. I was always wearing fedoras and ties, like Annie Hall, for christsakes. I liked baseball. I liked to get down and dirty in the dugout. I liked those radio stations at the end of the dial, the ones nobody's ever heard of, the ones with the manic-depressive

DJs who are always playing Simon & Garfunkel. I liked bars after four when the lights were beginning to dim and all the imbeciles were clearing out. I liked the way that felt. The way somebody'd left a beer bottle or a wool glove on a table. I liked to know somebody'd been there—I just didn't want to see 'em. I guess I just liked what they left behind. But what's funny is, I knew Mint liked it, too. We both had a whole lot of insomnia, and we would always sit up talking about all the stuff we liked.

But all that time, he never wanted me. He never made one goddamn pass at me. The closest he ever came was when he patted my head as if I were some drooling bloodhound. And that's no goddamn pass. I can recognize a pass when I see it, and that wasn't it. Boy, I just wanted him to grab my boobs or something. Only he probably didn't want to because they weren't awfully big. They weren't invisible or anything like that; they just weren't the type of boobs a construction worker would quit drilling for.

Brassy, of course, had the biggest knockers around. She also had this way of walking, like a leopard about to make a kill, real slow and sensuous. She must have been the wildest lay in town. God, I hated it when Mint touched her. It was like being trapped in some Turkish cell. Busted and busted some more, with a loaded gun pointed into your skull but never going off, and you sweating bullets, screaming like a maniac because you know your head's going to get blown off any second.

The first time I saw him kiss her, I was cleaning up in the restaurant (I helped out sometimes) and the whole place was empty except for Mint and Brassy and a few busboys washing dishes and ashtrays. Mint was watching her lock up her sax, and he walked over and grabbed her wrists. She was all shook up by the whole goddamn thing and had this really stupid expression on her face. He pushed her back against the wall and then he kissed her. For about twenty goddamn minutes he kissed her, and, Jesus, was I horrified.

So from that day forward, they were inseparable. His hand was always on her plump little ass; her eyes were always zipped up in his. She started sleeping over and used all my goddamn makeup. She blew fuses and ate all my yogurt. Minty never stopped treating me the way he always had, yet I was determined to hate him for bringing her into our lives. Sometimes at about two in the morning, they would go up to the roof and she'd play her goddamn sax, wake up everybody in the neighborhood. That really pissed me off. I'd just lie downstairs on the floor and smoke a couple hundred cigarettes. When I closed my eyes, Brassy was all I saw in the black: spouting breath into her horn, such a big new supersonic star; why did she have to get him? Why? It was so unfair.

One night they had gone up to the roof as usual, and I was on my twenty-eighth cig, when I just couldn't stand it. I got up and went into the bathroom and dropped my sizzling smoke into the john, and then I went over to the sink. I couldn't believe it. The fucking trollop had left her empty diaphragm container and that jelly and insertion gizmo right there on the sink. That nearly killed me. I rummaged around in the cabinet for a while until I found some old Valiums. I took one, but it didn't go right down. It got stuck on the back of my tongue and I shivered at its bitterness. Then I started to get paranoid. I had this feeling it was laced, like Minty was trying to knock me off. My heart was busting out of my chest and my head was spinning with the fan. I was so worked up I decided to do something really terrible. I decided to go up to the roof and spy on the two of them. I knew it was a pretty rotten thing to do, but Mint was trying to kill me, so he deserved it.

I started climbing up the fire escape. I hadn't even put any goddamn shoes on and my feet were freezing. Every step up made me sicker. That stupid horn got louder and louder. Once I reached the roof, I hid behind this jutting concrete partition and then I stuck my head out until Mint and Brassy came rushing into view. She was in his robe, and I wanted to shoot her. Her hair was blowing all over the damn place and Mint was just sitting there next to her with his hand on her thigh. She played and played and you could tell she was trying to be so sexy and all. Tossing her head around and hitting all those real deep notes like in *Casablanca*. Then it started getting real sick. Real X-rated, with Minty sliding off the robe and lathering his hands all over her. And then he threw her down on the tar and the sax fell out of her hands and rocked for a second before coming to a full glinting halt. I could tell the bitch was loving it. Loving every minute of it. She kept mumbling, "Oh, Minty. Oh, Minty." And I was burning up like a fire poker deep in the coals.

I was furious. I turned around and sped down the fire escape. Tears were streaming down my face and I couldn't stand it. I hated being human. I hated having to feel all this damned stuff. You have to be hot and cold and conscious. Self-actualizing before your time explodes and everybody's mourning over you with some goddamn black gauze over their faces. And you have to use your brain with all its stupid hemispheres and lobes. Even if you're the Great Goddamn Gatsby, you have to be a fascist or a Republican or a homo or a psychedelic rocker, and you wander all over the damn joint making up your mind. I wish I could have stayed two forever. Real little kids have it easy that way. They don't have anything to worry about. But then again, they do shit in their pants, and that's no bed of roses either. I swear, all life is one big Catch-22. You either use your brain or shit in your pants.

Chapter 3

Minty and I went to the park the day after I'd been spying on him. We brought some fried chicken and a bottle of Soave Bolla, and sat under this mammoth tree. It was fall again. Indian-colored leaves marbled with gold and cinnamon quilted the soil. Minty's hair was harnessed by the wind, his reflection abstracted in the boat pond.

He was chewing on a chicken leg and staring at me. I pretended I didn't notice. There was this really little kid falling into the boat pond, and I tried to keep my focus on him.

"Salty?"

"What?" I turned to meet his gaze and brushed some hair out of my eyes.

"What's wrong with you? You've been acting really strange lately."

I felt cold all of a sudden and turned back to the boat pond. The kid was looking really pathetic now, floating around with all the crap in the filthy pond. "I don't know what's wrong."

"Is it me? Did I do something?"

"No. No, you didn't do anything," I lied. The kid was screaming now, and I felt sorry as hell for him. I was about to jump in to rescue him when some blond woman (his mother probably) flung herself in and waded out to him.

"If I did something to upset you, you'd tell me, right?"

"Sure," I responded weakly, my eyes still on the kid. The mother was dragging him up on the grass, and then she started to smack him. The poor kid had almost drowned in the lake and she was smacking the shit out of him, for godsakes.

"Salty, you're pissing me off because I know I did something and you're not telling me."

I looked back over at him. His ravishing face was flooded with concern. Concern over *me*. Well, at least it was something. I tugged a handful of damp brown grass out of the ground and began to shred it hopelessly. God, I wanted to be mad at him, but I just couldn't. No matter how hard I willed it, my love for him just resurfaced like something terrifying and indestructible.

"Do you want to play some ball tomorrow?" I offered.

His face brightened. "Yeah. I've got to get a new glove, though." He was as excited as hell all of a sudden, just like when we were in the fifth grade. But then his expression crumpled again. "Oh, wait. Brassy's taking me to a matinee tomorrow. The Kool Jazz Festival."

"Fine, we'll do it next week," I spat out. The mention of her name nauseated me.

"Brassy's so damn popular. It's something, the way she knows all these really famous people. You know she knows Kashoggi? She spent a month last summer on his boat with him and Nebila."

"Who the hell is Nebila?" I asked. I don't know why I asked. I really didn't give a shit.

"Kashoggi's daughter, Salt. God, those Kashoggis are the richest bastards around. Brassy was telling me all about their homes in—"

"Look, Mint, I've gotta go—I have to meet Damon at the Whitney. I'll see you later." I couldn't stand it. Brassy this, Brassy that. So the fucking slut rode on a boat with some Arab. Who the hell cared? I got up and left really quickly so he wouldn't be able to stop me. He knew damn well I wasn't meeting Damon. Damon was out of town all week on some acting gig.

When I was out of sight, I started running like Marathon Man. I was really running. I hoped my lungs would explode and I'd die if I ran hard enough. Only all that happened was I tripped over this rock and fell flat on my face. Nobody was around, so I didn't have to act all cool about it. You know how it is when you fall down or trip or something when there's a whole wad of people watching you, you're always as embarrassed as hell, so you have to act as cool as possible. You have to get up and brush yourself off and pretend like you enjoyed breaking your ass on the pavement. Only, this time no one was around, so I didn't have to pretend anything. I just sat there in the dirt moaning, rubbing my foot.

❧

That night, Mint asked me to come to O'Riley's with him and Brassy. He didn't ask me why I took off in the park that afternoon, he just told me I should cheer the hell up and come out. The only thing I wanted to do was lie around the apartment in my old sweatpants, the ones with the hole in the ass, and write depressing suicidal love poems in my Mint Journal. I had this great collection of Mint Journals that I hid under my bed. I started them when I was fifteen, so I had a ton of them. What I'd do was date all my entries and write stuff like: "March 21, 1988. Watched Mint cooking spaghetti tonight. I was stirring the sauce when he brushed past me to reach for the strainer. The most transient touch, and delirium devours me. Oh, my love, my darling, if you would only understand . . . if you would only look into my eyes, lift me into your arms. . . ." Second verse, same as the first, etc. . . .

I didn't tell Mint, of course. I just told him I wasn't in the mood to go out, that I was tired and had to memorize some sides for an audition. He didn't badger me about it, just said he'd see me later then. As soon as he left, I yanked my current Mint Journal out from under my bed and turned on a Barbra Streisand tape. Boy, does that Streisand know how to sing a suicidal song. She was the perfect accompaniment to my journal writing. Always belting out about painful, watercolor memories or somebody not giving her flowers anymore or somebody coming along and raining on her damned parade.

After the tape got rolling, I sat down on my bed and started writing. "September 24, 1990. Mint just left for O'Riley's with that stupid, goddamned bimbo. I hate that bimbo. I hate her! I hate her! I hate her!" I guess that's not exactly poetic, but it's what I wrote. I kept on writing about how much I hated her until I got fed up with it and slammed the journal shut and started to honk my nose into a tissue.

I bet you're thinking I was asking for it. That I should have stopped dwelling on Mint and tried to meet someone else. Well, you don't know, but I tried. I really tried. I went out on quite a few dates, but I could never fall for anybody. I even went out with this guy I met in an acting class for three months. His name was Tommy and he was really a very chivalrous guy. Always lighting my cigarettes and opening doors for me. He had a good sense of humor and he was even good-looking. Anyhow, the point is, I just couldn't fall for him. Not in *that* way. I wanted to, but I just couldn't. I can never get sexy with someone unless it feels right, and when Tommy tried to grab my boobs it didn't feel right at all. I just can't let somebody do that stuff. Put their hands all over my boobs when it doesn't feel right. So consequently, I was what you might call a very sexually frustrated broad. I hate to admit it, but I only had sex once when I was eighteen and that was a goddamned mistake. I don't even want to think about it. Depresses the hell out of me.

After the tape ended and I finished honking my nose, I realized I was out of cigs. Pissed me off. It meant I had to go out in the pouring rain. It was really raining like mad. I threw on my black trench, left the apartment, and scuttled over to the deli on the corner of my block. It was awful out, raining so hard I could barely see a foot in front of me. I bought my cigarettes and ran back down the street.

Just as I came up to my building, I spotted old Mr. Gooter out walking his pooch. Mr. Gooter lived in the apartment over ours. He was really old. I don't know exactly how old he was, but from the look of him you'd think he belonged in a prehistoric diorama in the Museum of Natural History. Well, anyhow, there he was, soaking wet and shuffling around in his raggedy-looking cardigan. His old dog was moving slower than he was. I walked over to him and said hello. He didn't recognize me at first. He just sort of stood there with this bewildered expression on his glistening, rain-splattered face. Those old guys never seem to know who the hell it is. They're always shocked out of their mind when somebody says hello to them.

"It's Salty, Mr. Gooter. From downstairs."

Gooter raised his eyebrows and stared off into space for a minute. Finally he looked over at me. "Salty? Oh, my goodness . . . you live downstairs."

"Yes, that's right. Mr. Gooter, you're soaking wet—listen, why don't you come up to my apartment and I'll make you a cup of tea?"

Gooter's eyes brightened. He was an awfully lonely old geezer, and being invited somewhere was a helluva big deal to him. As for me, I really felt like I needed some company. Sometimes you just don't want to be alone.

The only problem with Gooter was his habit of telling you the same story over and over again. A lot of really old guys do that. And it kills me, because they really don't remember ever telling it before. I always had to let him tell the stories over again, though, 'cause he got such a kick out of it. It made his whole goddamn day. Gooter's favorite story was the one about his wife, Rugela. How he courted her for twenty years before she accepted his proposal. Then on the day of the wedding, when the ceremony was over and they were coming out of the church, Rugela, giddy with joy, blinded by rice, tripped on the hem of her gown, missed the first of the fifteen steps and plunged headfirst to the bottom, and broke her neck and died.

It's a wretched story, isn't it? The first time Gooter told me, I used up an entire goddamn box of Kleenex. But after about twelve times it became a little monotonous, and I started to wonder if it was true, because about the fourth time he told me, Rugela didn't fall down the steps, she was hit by a bolt of lightning. And the next time, he told me Rugela suffered a coronary in the middle of the wedding march. I really think the poor old guy had gone a little gaga, if you know what I mean.

Anyhow, I helped Gooter back to our building. The poor goddamn dog, who was almost older than Gooter, decided to collapse as soon as we got into the lobby. It wasn't dead or anything. For a moment there I thought it was, but then suddenly its mouth opened and it yawned. It was pretty sick-looking when it yawned because it didn't have any more goddamn teeth. It had like one tooth left or something. Gooter began to tell me it always did this. That it liked to be carried the rest of the way. So I leaned down to pick it up. I got a real good whiff of it, too. Anyhow, we started toward the elevator; Gooter's big clunky brown loafers were squish-squashing, and his face was still dripping wet.

On the way up, Gooter asked me if I would mind going to his apartment. He said that Zelda (who I assumed to be the exhausted doggy) got very nervous in strange apartments. I told him it was no problem. I'd only been up there a few times before. Most of my encounters with the guy had been in the elevator or down in the basement doing laundry. His apartment was filled with nostalgia. He had a big-ass radio with a gramophone and a couple dozen warped records by Louis Armstrong and Bing Crosby. He had a lot of laxatives lying around and a big framed photo of Tallulah Bankhead on the coffee table. When I leaned down to look at it, he said, "Wasn't she a beauty? My Rugela."

My Rugela? It was then I knew the guy had lost it bad. I put down the picture and asked him where he kept his tea. He told me he didn't know, but to try the kitchen.

The kitchen was minuscule. The cabinets were all as empty as hell except for a few stale boxes of graham crackers and oatmeal. What killed me was when I opened the refrigerator. The guy must have gotten mixed up, because he didn't have anything but a bunch of socks and shoes in there. It was awfully depressing. I began to wonder how he didn't starve to death.

"Mr. Gooter, you know, you hardly have anything to eat in here," I said on my way into the living room. He was collapsed in one of the crumbling chairs, Zelda sprawled at his feet chewing on a laxative.

"Oh, that's okay. I don't eat here much. I eat at Barney's coffee shop. After the little woman passed," he announced drearily, staring at Tallulah, "I never cooked. She cooked for me. Now I just eat at Barney's. Did I ever tell you about Rugela? She died, you know. Was gunned down by a bunch of Nazis at our wedding . . . wasn't even a goddamned Jew. The Lord's got her now. He has her now." Sighing, he reached down and took the laxative away from Zelda with his bony fingers. "She's always chewing up all my medicine, this dog. Then she gets the runs all the time."

I sat down and decided just to forget about the tea. Gooter didn't seem to want it anyway. He kept rambling about Rugela. And as he did, I had this terrible thought. This really lousy thought about the future. About me in sixty-five years sitting in a beat-up chair with a dog named Madonna at my feet and a photo of Mel Gibson on the coffee table. And every once in a while, some charitable young kid would come up to keep me company and I'd be going on about my husband Minty, pointing to Gibson and all. Telling the kid about how he got kidnapped by some homeboys. How he was struck by lightning or set on fire. And it was at that moment, sitting in that old geezer's apartment, that I realized what I had to do. It had never been so clear to me. I had to make my move *now*. I had to make Minty mine. Make him want me.

So as it turned out, I was damn glad I'd come up to Gooter's. The guy had really given me the courage to do what I had to do about all the I-should-haves. At about two o'clock, Gooter passed out. He was in the middle of telling me his war stories, how he'd gotten past all those damn Chinamen in the Battle of Waterloo, when his head tipped over and his jaw fell open and he began to wheeze with Zelda. Poor goddamn geezer had gone completely senile. I covered him with a blanket I found in his bathtub, and then tiptoed toward the door.

Chapter 4

When I got up to the apartment, I crept inside carefully, listening for that stupid sax. I figured Brassy would be sleeping over. But Mint wasn't home yet. The apartment was dark, sloshed with shadows. Occasionally the dizzy headlights from a passing car would ripple and dart across the ceiling in quicksilver flashes. I walked into my room and went and stood by the window. I didn't turn on any lights. I took my coat off, taking the cigarettes out of the pocket before flinging the coat over a chair. God, I was nervous. Because I knew I was going to do it. That if Mint came home without that blond bag of trash, I was going to make my move. I wasn't going to attack him or anything. I mean, I wasn't just going to go up to him and drop my pants, for godsakes. I figured I'd be real smooth about it. When he got into bed, I'd come in and tell him I couldn't sleep, and then he'd move over and make room for me. I think I told you that we're both insomniacs.

Mint wouldn't find it bizarre that I was awake and wanted to crawl into his bed for a while. All our goddamn lives we'd been crawling into each other's beds. I remember when we were little, about seven, Mint's mom would put us to bed. We slept in the same room, but we had those crazy bunk beds. Those army jobs. I slept on the bottom because I was too much of a chicken to sleep on the top. I always thought I'd roll off and kill myself. So Mint's mom would tuck us in and kiss us good-night, and as soon as she'd shut the door I'd see Mint's flashlight flare on the ceiling. Kids have always got a flashlight somewhere. I'll bet you had a flashlight. And as soon as your parents said, "Good-night, sweet-ums," you'd be yanking it out to play some moronic game.

Anyhow, I'd see the light go on and then Mint's head would come around the side of his bunk, tipped way the hell upside down so his hair was hanging all over the place. Then he'd come on down to my bed. He never used the goddamn ladder; he just came down like Indiana Jones. He'd grab onto the steel frame and then he'd be dangling by his fingers, swinging like a monkey, until he let go and landed on my bed. And as soon as he got down, he'd crawl under the covers with me. His mom had this very strict rule about us staying in our own beds, so we'd start giggling like mad the minute he got into mine. The minute kids do something illegal, they start to giggle like mad. Not that Mint and I understood in the first place why we couldn't sleep in the same bed. I mean, we were only seven, for christsakes. It wasn't as if we had some big sex drive going on.

Well, we'd stay up for hours making tents out of the covers, pretending we were a couple of crazy Indians in Arizona. Every time we thought we heard Mint's mom, we'd crouch down with our make-believe arrows and hold our breath. Sometimes Mint braided my hair. Beats me how he'd learned to do it, but he could. And then I'd be his woman, I'd be Pocahontas.

There was only one time he kissed me. Only once. It was when we were about eight, and we were still making our tents and do-ing all that crazy phony stuff, when he said, "Pocahontas, you wanna kiss?" And I was dying inside because Mint was going to kiss me. And kids, well, they don't know the first thing about it—kissing, that is—because they've only seen it on television, you know? As a matter of fact, I used to sit around watching those lousy shows like "The Love Boat" and the old movies just to see everybody kissing each other. It was a terribly big deal to me. I was always scared that when somebody tried to kiss me someday I wouldn't be able to do it, that I'd do it wrong and make a real ass out of myself. Honest to God, I was just terrified. But that night as Minty got closer to me and kind of looked at me funny, I felt pretty sure I'd be able to kiss him okay, that maybe there was no big trick to it after all. And just as he was leaning over to do it, he stopped and said, "Hey, Salty, you wanna do it? Honest?" I think he was a little scared about it, too.

"I dunno. You wanna?"

"Yeah, okay, but it's kinda gross."

"Well, do it fast, okay? Like don't make it long or anything, okay?"

"Yeah, just for a second. How about when I count to three?"

And then he was counting and I was so darn excited. Whether they admit it or not, everybody's as excited as hell during their first kiss. And on three he moved his little freckled face into mine, and God, I remember it so vividly. . . . At first I just felt our noses bash together, but then I felt his lips on mine and it was like we were a couple of robots or something. Our lips were as stiff as a wall and our eyes were wide open the whole time. I guess it did only last for a couple of seconds, but it felt like much more. When we pulled away from each other, we just sat there for a while, not saying anything. Mint was probably waiting for my reaction. I was waiting for his.

Eventually we both laughed and he said, "That was no big deal, huh?"

"Nah, no big deal," I echoed.

Well, that was the only time he'd ever kissed me. I doubted if he even remembered it.

Just as I was thinking about it, I heard the front door and Mint's keys jingling around. I listened like a hawk for the bimbo, but I didn't hear the clip-clonk of her stiletto heels on the wood floor. And then I thought, "You can never be sure, he might be carrying the bitch across the floor." So I got up and crept to my bedroom door and poked my head out. It was a miracle! Minty was alone! He was going into the kitchen. If Brassy had been around, he'd be heading straight for the bed.

I knew I'd have to wait around awhile, until he'd finished scrounging in the fridge and got into his room. The first thing I did was change out of my sweatpants into this *Dangerous Liaisons* nightgown I hardly ever wore. It was pure white with a bunch of ruffles on the bottom. It wasn't really sexy or anything. Nothing like the bitch would wear. I know, because one morning I spotted her gliding into the kitchen in this foxy black silk number with feathers and bullshit hanging off of it. The sad part was that she looked good in it. If I wore a job like that, I'd just look like a chicken or something. So, like I said, I changed into this nightgown. It was either that or my pajamas, and my pj's were about as sexy as "Sesame Street." Then I fixed up my hair. I took it out of its ponytail and brushed it so it flooded down over my shoulders. After that, I reached for my perfume. I was so nervous, though, that when I went to put a drop down my cleavage, I tipped the bottle too much and spilled about four ounces of it all over me. I tried to wash some of it off with a wet towel, but I don't think it did much good. Meanwhile, it had started to thunder and lightning outside and I figured it was some lousy omen.

I knew I couldn't wait any longer because Mint would be out cold. So I left the john and started to creep through the apartment toward his room. When I got to his door, which he'd left slightly ajar, I peeked in and made him out lying on the bed. All his lights were off, but when the lightning flashed I could see him pretty well. So I went into his room and crawled up onto his bed. He rolled over onto his back immediately.

"Mint, I can't sleep."

"Me either."

"Where's Brassy?"

"Oh, she saw some old girlfriend and decided to go to Nell's with her. I just couldn't go way the hell downtown tonight. Not tonight, for christsakes. Not in a storm."

"She's not coming back here, is she?"

"No." He turned his face to me. Then he started to sniff like crazy, and he said, "Salt, what's that smell?"

"What smell?" I asked, trying to sound as nonchalant as hell.

"That smell. Are you wearing perfume?"

"Perfume? No. No, it's probably my shampoo. I'm using this new shampoo."

Minty looked at me kind of awkwardly. His eyes were suddenly splashed with lightning, and man, was that something! It was goddamn gorgeous.

"Minty?"

"Hm," he said, yanking a cigarette out of the pack on the table next to him. Tonight he was smoking one of those real macho-man brands. The kind without any filters, the kind that are willing to give you a money-back guarantee if they don't kill you before all the others do. Minty never smoked the same brand. He was always experimenting all over the joint.

"Do you remember a long time ago, when we were kids . . . we used to play that game making a tent out of the covers?"

"The tent game? That was a helluva long time ago, Salt."

"Yeah, I know. Do you remember it?"

He rolled over to face me, resting on an elbow. He didn't answer me for a minute or so; he just kinda kept taking drags on his cigarette. It was very sexy, the way he was taking those drags. It was awfully sexy. He was holding the cig at the base between his thumb and forefinger, and every time he went to take a drag those two fingers would brush up against his lips, and then he'd never blow the smoke straight out. He'd hold it for about fifteen seconds and then he'd start letting it go. He'd let it go nice and easy so that it came out in a couple dozen pieces.

"Let's see. We'd wait until the coast was clear and then we'd set up the tent and pretend to be a couple of Indians, right?"

"Yeah, that's it. Do you remember the time you . . . well, you were Captain John Smith and you . . . kissed me?"

Minty got the biggest damn smile on his face. And then he said, "Pocahontas, you wanna kiss?" Then he started to laugh. I didn't think it was all that funny, but he was laughing. "We were such crazy kids. What made you think of that, anyway?" he said, still laughing.

Oh, God, I was going to have to tell him. Tell him the whole damn thing. That I'd wanted him ever since I'd first laid eyes on him. That he was all I could see in a blizzard of dreams, that—oh, Christ, I just couldn't do it. How could I say that stuff when he was laughing like that? He'd probably just keep right on laughing. He'd probably just tell me I was a real gas. I was as mad as hell. I really was. He wasn't supposed to laugh when I asked him if he remembered kissing me. I'd envisioned the whole thing back in my room. I was going to ask him, and then he was going to get all sultry and serious and lean over me and tell me it was the best kiss he'd ever known. And then he was going to rip off my *Dangerous Liaisons* nightgown and make love to me until the sun started to rise. But nothing ever works out the way you think it will. Life is like a fucking racetrack. You can make as many predictions and bets as you want, but you're never really going to know if the fix is in, if Bad-Ass Charlie is going to come in first. For all you know, Bad-Ass Charlie could have eaten too much goddamn hay that morning. Bad-Ass might have some real lousy indigestion and end up running like old Gooter or something.

I couldn't stand the fact that Mint was laughing, so I decided to get the hell out of his room. I told him I didn't know what made me think of that episode when we were kids, and then I told him I was going to bed.

"Wait a minute, Salt, what's the rush? You can't sleep any more than I can," he said as I got up and walked toward the door.

All I did was turn for a second to look at him. Christ, there was so much I wanted to say, but I just couldn't. My mouth was partially open, but the words wouldn't come. I could feel them all stacked up at the base of my throat, but no matter how hard I tried to release them, they kept resisting and resisting until I had no other choice but to swallow them and say, "I just don't feel like talking, I guess." And then I left, shutting the door behind me.

I'd blown it again, and you'll never know how embittered I was as I trucked back to my room. I tumbled down onto my bed and buried my face in my pillow. Then after a couple seconds, genius that I am, I realized I couldn't breathe so well with my face mashed up in the pillow, so I rolled over onto my side. A zigzag of lightning burst and swelled into my room, my eyes. I wondered if Mint's eyes were still open. I knew why I couldn't do it, couldn't tell him. It was because I was afraid he would think it was wrong. Sinful or something. Even though I wasn't his real sister, he'd always treated me like one, and maybe he'd think it was immoral or disgusting. I pounded my fist into the pillow. For one brief moment I wished I'd never grown up with him, that we had no past to obstruct the future. If we didn't, then it could happen. Our eyes could clash for the very first time in some dark, sexy bar and I'd light a cigarette, but I wouldn't chew it. I'd just smoke it very sensuously like that bimbo Brassy. And then he'd move toward me, like he moves toward her, and he'd lean over and ask me what a dame like me was doing in a joint like this. But no, I couldn't give up my past with Minty. It was my only salvation.

God, I felt so alone. I groped for my floppy bear, leaning over the side of the bed to yank him up from the floor and cuddle him next to me. I tried to pretend he was Mint. I stroked the old matted fuzz on the side of his stuffed head. "Oh, Minty, I love you . . ." I said. Then I spoke for the bear: "I love you, too, Salty. I've always loved you. . . ." And then I puckered up my lips and kissed the bear.

All the bear fuzz stuck to my lips. What a nightmare that was. I shot up to a sitting position and wiped my mouth with the back of my hand. I was muttering "Blech" and "Dammit" when lightning flashed into my room again and I practically had a coronary. Mint was standing at the end of my bed! Jesus! How long had he been there? Oh, God . . . he'd probably heard me . . . seen me try to make out with the bear. I was so humiliated. I sat utterly motionless, staring at him in the diluted gray-blue darkness. He didn't budge. I could see his eyes, wet, glistening, pinned on me.

"Minty . . . how long have you been . . ."

"Long enough," he said bluntly.

I squashed the bear in my hands, my trembling hands. He knew. Oh, God . . . he thought I was disgusting.

Why didn't he say something? The silence was horrible.

But when the lightning lit his face again, I saw that he wasn't disgusted with me. He was looking at me in a way I'd never seen him look at me before . . . his eyes bristling with a sort of arrogant intensity, a dark, astounding hunger. Just as I realized that, he crawled up onto my bed. He crawled like a predator, blazing white, devouring darkness. And suddenly my wrists were in his hands and the weight of him was over me, crushing me back into the mattress. I don't think I breathed. I swear, I think my heart simply stopped. I wasn't dreaming. None of it was a dream. My eyes dissolved into tears as he pressed his lips over mine. The power of his kiss was indescribable. It wasn't like when we were kids. It wasn't goofy or lopsided. It was the best damn kiss around. It was like one of those train-station kisses, you know? The kind where the two bastards are standing right next to a rush of train tracks, drowning in each other's arms. It's all black and white and old rain is dripping off the guy's fedora and the woman's got one leg bent up in the air; steam is rising and purling and the choo-choo's honking its horn, but neither of them moves a muscle.

Minty pulled his head back a little and looked at me. He gently pushed back a strand of hair that had tumbled into my face. Silent tears kept gushing down my face.

"Salty . . . I never knew . . ." he whispered.

"I know." I could hardly see him through my tears.

"I've always wanted you, Salt. But . . . I just, I thought you'd feel uncomfortable if I made a pass at you, you know? And you never made a pass at me, so I didn't."

"Minty, that's what *I* thought. I thought you'd be . . . oh, I don't know, you'd be offended or think it was wrong. Oh, God." I started to laugh. I couldn't help it. It was so crazy, both of us feeling the same way but thinking the other would feel differently. Mint started laughing, too. He was shaking his head, laughter just gushing from him.

When we calmed down, Mint smiled and gently tugged on the sleeve of my nightgown. "You aren't wearing this because your pj's are in the wash, are you?"

"No."

"And that isn't your shampoo, is it?"

I smiled with embarrassment and told him no again. He didn't ask me anything else. He leaned down and kissed me and I closed my eyes and wound my arms around him. Oh, God, he was so tangible . . . so hopelessly tangible. I felt his lips glide down, the white fire of his breath graze my neck. Slowly, he began to unbutton my nightgown, and when his palms covered my breasts my stomach cringed with the sensation.

"My God, Salty, your heart's beating like mad," he whispered. I knew it was. I could feel it pounding through every inch of me. I gripped the headboard of my bed; my room was reeling, tilting like a ship seized by wind and raging waves. Minty's lips were parting, droning down between my breasts, his hands straying up my thighs. As he pulled the nightgown from my body, a spasm of lightning shuddered, electrified him like something bloodless, born from burning sun and raw white sky. He knelt over me and drew me up into his arms. I felt as weak as an infant, melting into his smooth bare chest like liquid. My lips pressed against his neck, his shoulders. I thought I'd drown in the bittersweet musk of his skin.

Gently he pressed me back into the sheets. He removed his shorts and lay over me until my body disappeared against his. He looked deeply into my eyes . . . but there was no uncertainty or apprehension. My legs parted and tightened around him. As he thrust into me, his mouth covered mine, muffling my scream. In one moment, a lifetime of pain and emptiness had suddenly dissolved. I was finally a part of him, entangled with him in a storm of motion. I didn't care if he tore me apart inside. I didn't care, I just arched my back to bring him deeper, to fill myself with his blinding white brilliance. Suddenly I was every carnival balloon ever released into the sky, and all the jelly beans melting in a small child's hand. When it ended, Minty collapsed over me. I trembled like fire beneath him, my eyes still choking on tears.

A few moments later, Mint lifted his head. His forehead was slick with perspiration. He leaned down and kissed my forehead, my nose, my lips. When he pulled back, he smiled at me and reached behind my head. I didn't know what he was reaching for and then I saw my stuffed bear in his hand.

"It's not a very good likeness," he said, holding up the bear.

"Stop that!" I told him, laughing.

He chucked the bear over his shoulder and leaned down over me again. "I don't think you'll be needing that bear anymore, Salt."

"What about . . . Brassy?" I asked tentatively. I'd completely forgotten the bimbo until now, what with all the excitement.

"I'm going to break it off with her," he said evenly.

My God, I can't tell you the happiness I felt at that moment. He did love me! And he was going to get rid of that stupid bimbo. He was going to drown her sax in the birdbath and tell her to scram and shoo and all. *Ha!*

For the next couple hours Mint and I lay awake in each other's arms. We drank wine and shared cigarettes and caressed each other with an endless curiosity.

At around four o'clock, Mint fell asleep. He fell asleep in my arms and I couldn't move or breathe, but it didn't matter. He was finally in my arms and I'd never known such rapture. I just lay silently, listening to his deep breaths, to the thunder drift away and the rain subside. I couldn't sleep at all. I felt like you do on the night before your birthday when you're a kid, so wound up thinking about all the loot you'll be getting, all the cake and ice cream. I treasured every second of that rainy night. There are some things you are always going to remember as if they'd just happened yesterday, and this night was one of those things. I think when I'm very old and as senile as hell, I'll still remember it as if it had just occurred. I might not be able to recall one other thing, my brain might have turned to porridge and all that jazz, but I'd never forget it. It would be as fresh as milk straight from the udder. It would be as strong and severe as pain the moment you feel it—not before or after, but just when it's begun to climax and lock its ruthless jaws. I would always remember it like that. Always.

Mint didn't waste any time. The next day he called the bimbo right up and told her he wanted to break it off. I couldn't believe it! He made me dinner that night and told me about it: How he met her at the Pigeon and said he was sorry but he was seeing me! I asked him how she took it, and he said she grabbed her sax, told him to fuck off, and stormed out of the joint. That really blew me away. I could never picture Brassy using foul language like that. There are some guys you can't ever picture using it. Like nuns, for instance. It's very hard to picture a whole bunch of nuns running around telling everybody to fuck off.

Anyhow, Mint didn't seem to be bothered over it. He dropped the subject and started to serve the meal he'd made. I could barely eat. I felt the change occurring. I didn't feel it from our conversation because we basically talked about the same stuff we always did. But I felt it in his eyes. He wasn't looking at me like a child anymore. He wasn't looking at me on the surface anymore. He was looking deep inside me.

We'd barely been at the table for fifteen minutes when I just couldn't stand it anymore. I pounced on him. He was in the middle of telling me about this group of Arabs who'd come into the Pigeon the other day in their nightgowns and all, when I dropped my fork and just leapt right on top of him. I must have a libido the size of the Macy's Thanksgiving Day Parade, for christsakes.

So we fell down on the floor. I'd leapt on him too hard, you see, and his chair tipped over backward. I swear, I couldn't be sexy if my life depended on it. The minute I try to be sexy I start knocking over chairs and stuff. Only Mint didn't think it was so serious because he started to laugh. He pushed the chair away like an animal and grabbed me and rolled on top of me.

"Salty, what am I going to do with you? Is this how it's going to be from now on? You're going to jump on me and knock me to the floor at dinner every night?" he said, laughing.

"Yup," I replied, as giddy as anything.

"Oh, you are, are you?"

"Yup." I was chuckling my head off.

"You think this is humorous, huh?" He raised an eyebrow cunningly.

"Yup." I giggled some more and looked up at him very innocently. I thought he was going to say something, but he didn't. He got this very ardent look on his face, his green eyes locked in mine, squinting and shimmering. Then he kissed me. His kiss was stained with wine, so deep and powerful and intoxicating I felt like I'd keel over. I couldn't, of course, since I was already on the floor, but if I'd been standing up I know I would have keeled over. God, my whole body was burning up from that kiss. It was like a drug invading my bloodstream, devouring my strength, scrambling my mind. I felt him shove up my skirt and press himself hard against me. I gasped and ground my hips into his, my hands drenched in the thick, soft gold of his hair. When he pushed himself into me I felt his warmth spread through me like a current. I was made for him. My hands knew his flesh before they even reached out to touch it, and my eyes burned with recognition. And it was finally me, not Brassy, in his arms. Maybe there was a God after all. A great, merciful God who remembered what he'd done to me . . . and was finally remorseful.

Chapter 5

Minty and I had been lovers for about two weeks when I ran into Brassy. I was coming out of the Gulf & Western Building, where I'd just finished an audition for a commercial, when I spotted her coming toward me. I didn't even recognize her face; what I recognized was that case she carried her sax in. The minute I saw that case, I knew it was her. She looked very snappy, too. She had on this bright red dress and bright red lipstick. Her hair was glinting with fresh new highlights and her body looked just as perfect as ever. I wondered why she looked so good. Normally, when a woman gets dumped, she doesn't look so hot. But apparently this wasn't so with Brassy. Brassy looked so confident you would have thought she'd just been awarded Woman of the Year.

So, as she was crossing the street with her slim, sassy legs, I started to get very nervous. I started to get nervous because women are pretty touchy about things like another gal stealing their guy. They really are. But she came up to me and acted like I was some old college roomie she hadn't seen in a couple of years. Shocked the daylights out of me.

"Salty! How are you?" she said, as pleasant as could be.

"I'm fine, and you?" I was pretty damn cordial myself. I was waiting for her to clonk me with that lethal gizmo in her hand, I guess.

"Listen, I'd really like to talk to you. Can we go somewhere, get a cup of coffee?"

Aha! I knew it. All this sugar and spice was a con. She was going to drag me off somewhere and beat the shit out of me. I stuttered out some incredibly bad excuse, something about having to rent a video.

"It'll only take a few minutes. I just want to talk for a minute. It's rather important," she said. She was very sincere about it, too. I don't know why, but I decided to take the risk. I guess I was pretty curious about what she wanted to tell me.

So we ended up going to this smoky-looking hamburger joint. It was about noon, so the place was really congested. We had to wait a couple of minutes to get a table. I was standing next to her, trying to look casual. I was scratching my arm. Whenever I'm nervous and want to look casual, I scratch my arm like a madman. She didn't scratch anything. She could've looked casual on a tightrope, for christsakes. When we finally got a table, we ordered some coffee and the waiter got all huffy about it. He said we couldn't just sit at the goddamn table and drink coffee, that for the honor of sitting at the table, we had to order a whole goddamned meal. So I ordered a piece of pie. Brassy ordered the special. The special turned out to be a hamburger. A hamburger in a hamburger joint didn't seem so special to me. But joints like that, they never know what the hell they're doing.

So Brassy, she looked at me very seriously, like somebody we knew had kicked the bucket or something. And then she lit up one of her cigs and said she heard I was going with Mint.

"Yes. We, um . . . well, yes," I said like a moron. I was very uncomfortable talking to her about it.

"Listen, Salty, I know we don't know each other that well, but women have got to band together in certain situations."

Jesus, band together? I pictured a whole group of broads parading down Broadway playing a bunch of horns and drums. Brassy's lingo, it always had to be a metaphor of her life.

"What do you mean, band together?"

"Well, the male species can be ruthless sometimes, and women need to stick together. Help each other."

"What male of the species are we talking about, if you don't mind me asking?" I was scratching my arm like crazy.

"Mint."

"Mint?"

"Mint."

"What about Mint?" My arm was starting to burn.

"Salty, what has he told you about us?" She blew a smoke ring into my face.

"Not much. I mean, I really don't know anything about what happened between you two."

"So you don't know that he wanted me to move in?"

"Move in? Where?"

"Your apartment. He told me he was going to ask you to move out."

My arm was definitely on fire. "That's impossible. Mint would never ask me to move out."

"Well, that's what he said. Besides that, he promised me all sorts of things. Things he never came through with. He told me he loved me, Salty."

I was about to sock her. How dare she tell me all this shit!

"Look, Brassy, I don't know what your point is in telling me all this. What happened between you and Mint is your business, not mine." I felt another smoke ring coming.

"Oh, but you're wrong. It *is* your business, Salty. It's your business because you're involved with him now. You should know that things may not be the way they seem. Minty's a very charis-

matic man, a great charmer, Salty. He's devastatingly good-looking and very good in bed, but when it comes to important things
like honesty and sensitivity, he doesn't know the first thing about
them. And I'm not telling you this to distress you. I'm really not.
I'm telling you because I want to save you from being hurt by
him."

I was getting as mad as hell. "Brassy, I don't know if you know
this, but I've known Minty since I was five years old. Five. I've
practically lived my whole life with him, and believe me, I know
him a lot better than you do, and none of what you've said is accurate."

"It is. It's extremely accurate. I know you don't want to hear it,
but it's all true. He cheated on me, Salty. He cheated on me, lied
to me, and he'll do the same to you," she remarked stoically.

"How dare you!" I barked. "He'd *never* cheat on me. Christ,
you don't know the first thing about us!" The people at the tables
near us had all turned around to stare at me now, and I realized I
was being a little loud. I leaned forward and lowered my voice.
"You're just saying these things because you're hurt and angry.
But personally, I think it's . . . I think . . ." I forgot what the hell I
wanted to say to her. What a pain in the ass that is, when you're
in the middle of making a point and you forget what you wanted
to say.

Brassy just stared at me for a second with smoke curling out of
her mouth. Then she started to yack again. "I'm not saying this
out of vindictiveness. Honestly. Minty wasn't that important to
me that I would waste my time trying to hurt you for being involved with him." She stubbed out her cigarette and raised her
crisp blond eyebrows. She was so goddamn calm I wanted to sock
her in the nose.

"Look, if all you're going to do is sit here and rag on him, I'm
not going to stay. I'm sorry if he hurt you, but it really doesn't
have anything to do with me," I said coolly, and then I dropped

five dollars on the table for my pie. Of course, the exact moment I stood up to leave the waiter arrived with the food. What a nightmare it was. I'd wanted to make this smooth, dramatic exit, but no, I had to bump right into the waiter. He almost dropped Brassy's hamburger and then he started to yell at me, calling me a *hootspa* or *yutzpa* or something. God only knows what he was saying. He was Greek or maybe Turkish, but anyhow everybody started to stare at me again. I finally got past him and walked out of the joint, as mad as hell. I don't know why I was so stupid as to have gone with Brassy. I should have known she'd pull something like that.

When I got outside I was so aggravated that I ended up going to a pay phone. I needed to talk to Mint. But once I was on the phone I remembered Mint was hosting at the Pigeon. So I ended up trying a few other guys, but nobody was in. That's the way it is. Nobody's ever around when you want them to be. When you want them like a hole in the head, they're always around.

Just as I was hanging up the phone, I noticed a movie theater up the block and thought that would be a great way to change my mood. I didn't recognize the name of the film, but I really didn't care what the hell it was so long as it took my mind off that stupid bitch. So I went and bought my ticket and it was very good timing because it was almost time for the next show, which practically never happens. There was quite a line outside the door. But then, when I got on line I kind of wished it wasn't showtime. Because whenever you go to the movies by yourself, people always start flashing those pathetic looks at you. They figure you've gotta be some lonely loser because you came by yourself. Because everybody else has a date or something. So I pretended I was waiting for somebody, kept checking my watch and peering up and down the block. But then I realized that if you make like you're waiting for somebody, everybody's going to think you've been stood up. And being stood up is almost worse than being some lonely loser who can't get a date in the first place.

I was one of the last on line, so by the time I made my way into the theater they'd already turned out all the goddamn lights. That just drives me crazy, because I always end up sitting on somebody's Coke or squashing some old bag with sciatica or something. It took me about five minutes to find a seat, way the hell off in the boondocks.

Then the picture started. What a disaster it was. The chick who starred in it looked just like Brassy. Besides that, the entire film was about musicians. I thought the film was going to be about a couple of pastry chefs or something, since it was called *The Fabulous Baker Boys*, but no, it had to be about musicians. I was annoyed at first, but eventually I calmed down. I realized I had nothing to be upset over. Minty cared about *me*, and Brassy was just jealous. Once I relaxed about the whole thing, the picture wasn't half bad.

Have you ever met an actor? They're all a bunch of lunatics. I was in the profession of lunatics. Sitting in a casting office waiting to read for some VIP who's determined to hate you before you even walk through the door, who's manhandling your resume like some kind of grocery list and studying your photograph with that "she needs a nose job" look.

I was reading for "Today Is Tomorrow." I'd never even seen the stupid show, not once. I'm not too big on soaps. They bore the daylights out of me. So I was sitting around in the waiting room. And boy, is it murder in that waiting room. It's murder because there are always a bunch of other guys waiting with you. And those other guys are about as pleasant as pit bulls. They're always looking you over, not surreptitiously either, they're very blatant about it. Maybe you're not an actor and you've never been in that situation, but I bet you've been on the bus at one point or another. And you know how it is when you're on the bus and the guy opposite you starts giving you the hairy eyeball? Well, that's exactly what it feels like in that waiting room. But what's worse is that they don't look away when you catch them. Normally when you catch people staring at you, they look away very quickly. They pretend they were looking at the potted plant to your left or something. But not these lunatics in the waiting room. If you catch them looking at you, they just stay right the hell where they are and stare the shit out of you.

So that's what everybody was doing. Staring the shit out of everybody else. When they weren't staring, they were fixing up their faces or rustling their scripts around. Finally I got called to read, and this very good-looking chick with a lot of hair who was sitting next to me—I mean, this chick had hair like Lady goddamn Godiva—she got up and started to yack about how she was there before me and how she should read first. The fact was, I'd gone up in the elevator with her and she got out before I did. She was about two bloody seconds ahead of me, for christsakes. Anyhow, the woman who was calling us to read said it didn't matter who got in before whom. She said she only went by the order on the list. So the hairy chick was forced to shut up and sit down.

The woman with the list led me to Janice Grey's office. Old Grouchy Grey. I'd read for her a whole bunch of times. The woman was like a drill sergeant. I'd never once seen her smile. She was always very curt about everything. "Hello, sit down . . . turn to page ten, begin . . . thank you, good-bye." That's about all the woman ever said to you. The worst part about reading for Grouchy Grey was that she had all this clutter on her desk. She had a regular landfill of rubbish all over it, and she always started fussing around with it while you were trying to read. It's a helluva thing to have somebody start winding up a plastic duck when you're trying to make a goddamn living.

So I went into her office, and as usual she was sitting in her big leather chair with all the funky paraphernalia strewn in front of her. I immediately had to start the bullshit. That's the other thing about being an actor. You've gotta be very good at bullshit. You've gotta make like you think the casting director is the swellest guy on the whole damn planet. So that's what I did. I told her how bloody nice she looked and admired all the crummy ducks and rabbits' feet and Hot Wheels cars and all the rest of the garbage. Typically, she hardly said a thing. She told me to sit down and begin on page two.

So I was reading, and all of a sudden her phone started to ring and she stopped me. She picked up the phone and, I'm not kidding, she spent about twenty minutes talking with some guy in Italy. I know because she kept saying, "How's Rome, baby? Are you staying at the Excelsior? Remember our room last year?" I couldn't believe it. Here I was in the middle of my reading, and she was stopping me to talk to some guy she'd obviously screwed in the Excelsior. I mean, I could understand if it was something professional, if she had to talk to some NBC big shot on the coast or something, but this conversation was strictly for the boudoir. So I just sat there, waiting, looking at all the junk. When she finally hung up, I was as mad as hell, but being the king of bullshit I smiled and pretended I was having the time of my life waiting around for her.

When I finished reading, she asked me about my last job, a walk-on gig on "Ryan's Hope." I told her about it, being as saucy as ever, and she wrote something down on the back of my resume and ended our little rendezvous with "Thank you. Please have a Polaroid taken before you leave."

Even though I should have been thinking about the audition and Grouchy Grey, leaving the building all I could think about was Minty, that I'd bet a million dollars Grouchy Grey didn't have it so good, that the guy on the phone was probably some gigolo who only called her when the monsoon broke in Africa.

I walked uptown to meet this great friend of mine, Damon, another actor. We had both been booked for a Sprite commercial about two years before, and the minute we met we hit it off.

In the commercial I had to squirt the hell out of him with a garden hose. We were supposed to be cleaning a car and I had to let him have it with the hose. Then he had to squeeze out a big soapy sponge over my head. It was a pretty stupid commercial but we had a helluva lot of fun doing it.

When I got to the cafe, Damon was already there. It was very easy to spot him—he always wore a baseball cap. He was a real baseball fanatic. He was sitting outside and I could only see his back.

"Dame!" I hollered at him as I came down the street.

"Hey, Salt. Where were you? We were supposed to meet half an hour ago," he said as I sat down across from him.

"I had a reading with Grouchy Grey, and she made me wait forever while she talked to some loverboy in Rome."

"Old Grey, huh? The last time I read for her, she started to give herself a manicure." Damon smiled and folded up his newspaper. He was always reading the sports section. "Whadda you want, babe?" he asked as the waiter came over.

"Oh, I'll have a . . . a toasted bagel with cream cheese, and a coffee."

Damon ordered a double cheeseburger, french fries, a hero, and a Coke. Damon ate like a madman. The funny thing was, he was as skinny as anything.

"Why do you look so happy?" he asked when the waiter was gone. "Wait a minute, lemme guess . . . it has to do with Minty, right?" Damon was the only person I'd ever confided in about my feelings for Mint. I trusted Dame. He was a great guy. A real lunatic sometimes, but a helluva nice guy. I wouldn't confide in just anybody. He wasn't at all like those rich, pretentious bastards I grew up with. Plus he never tried to stick his hand down my pants or anything. He knew I was in love with Mint and he never made a pass at me.

"Damon, it's finally happened! He told me he's always wanted to be more than friends! I've moved into his room now, and he

dumped that bimbo. I swear, I still can't believe it. I've been waiting for this for so long that I think I'm in shock or something."

Dame leaned back and put his feet up on the seat between us.
I really adored the guy, but he was a helluva slob. Always putting
his dirty sneakers all over chairs and stuff.

"That's great, Salt. Really . . . but . . ."

"But what?" I asked.

"Oh look, nothing, I just, I just think you oughta be careful,
that's all. I mean, from all you've told me about your golden man,
I get the feeling he's not too crazy about long-term relationships.
I don't want to bring you down or anything, I just think you
oughta be careful."

"Oh, this is different. He doesn't see me the way he sees all the
others. I mean, I'm not just another lay to him."

Damon was pretty quiet for a few seconds. He was sucking on
an ice cube and watching me like a hawk. "Look, Salt, just be
careful, okay?" he said at last. "Because guys like Mint, well, to
tell you the truth, they don't change all that much. I know you've
known him for ages, and I'm sure he thinks you're much more
than a lay. But if he used to screw around like you said, he's not
going to change overnight."

"I know you're trying to look out for me and it's really nice of
you, Dame, but I swear I know what I'm doing."

Damon shrugged and took his feet off the chair. "All right, I
won't hassle you about it. I shouldn't even talk, really, because
I've barely even met the guy. If you say you know what you're doing, then you probably do."

Our food came, and he grabbed a fistful of french fries before
the waiter even set the goddamn plate down in front of him. As
we ate, we got off the Mint topic. He started to tell me about this
new part-time job he had. Damon always had a new job, and it
never lasted more than a month. It was kind of his own version of
"musical jobs"—he could never stay put for a second. He'd been a

waiter, a chauffeur, a salesguy, you name it and he'd been it. This time he'd become a dog walker.

" . . . so I spent an hour looking for the mutt's leash. I told the woman to leave the leash in the foyer, but it wasn't there. I ended up going into the pantry. I went through all the drawers until I found a piece of rope and used that as a leash for Bunky. That was the mutt's name—Bunky, for godsakes. So now I had all twelve of 'em and I took 'em to the park. It was like a shit festival. Every two seconds one of 'em would take a dump and I had to keep scooping it all up and then, this is the clincher . . ." He stopped for a second with one hand in the air, the finger pointed up, while he took a gigantic bite out of his burger. I just sat there waiting for him to go on, but his mouth was too full of the goddamn burger and he kept chewing like crazy. Finally he swallowed it. "Okay, so what happened was, the mutt on the rope, Bunky, well, it just took off. I guess I didn't tie the noose tight enough, and the mutt got loose and started to run like a demon. All the other dogs were yapping and trying to follow it. I was being dragged along by eleven dogs. And eleven dogs, that's some horsepower. . . ." Another bite. Chew . . . chew . . . chew. "So that's how I lost the job."

"What? You never found Bunky?"

"Hell, no. The dog was like a bullet. It took a nasty turn into a bunch of bushes, and that was it. I spent two whole hours combing the park. I figured the other dogs would lead me to him, you know? But Bunky was long gone. Shit, he must be in Spain by now."

"How did you break it to the woman?"

"Oh, yeah, that. Boy was that a pain in the rear. I told the woman, and she's this very high-strung dame already, a lawyer or something. When I talked to her on the phone about the job, she sounded very high-strung. Kept asking me dozens of questions, like if I had a criminal record and all this stuff. Then she spent a half hour going into how Bunky was her poopsy-pie and how he was her life and that he needed special attention. So you can imagine how I felt having to tell her that her poopsy-pie was missing in action. . . ." He stopped to grab the waiter and order another plate of fries. The waiter looked revolted. "Where was I?"

"You were telling the woman that her poopsy-pie was gone."

"Right. Oh, Salt, are you going to finish that?" He pointed at my half-eaten bagel, and I rolled my eyes and shoved it over to him. He was a goddamn garbage disposal. "Okay, so I go over to the woman's house later on because she told me she worked until five-thirty. So I go over there about six and she opens up the door, and I'm not kidding, she grabs me by the jacket and screams, 'Where the hell is my dog?!!' I thought she was going to kill me. But I had to tell her, so I told her all about how I couldn't find the leash and used the rope I found in the pantry, and I think she was catching on because her face was going haywire. When I got to the part about Bunky taking off, she lost it. She started to scream like I was an ax murderer or something. . . ." He paused to finish my bagel. He ate the entire half bagel in about two seconds. "And then she came after me."

"What?"

"She came after me, chased me down the hall like a psychopath. She kept screaming stuff like 'I'll see that you never walk another dog as long as you live, you little creep. I'll sue you.' I felt sorry for her, but what the hell could I do? It was an accident, after all." His french fries came and he started to slop ketchup all over them.

"So she called the service and told them what happened?"

"Oh yeah, right away. I was out on my ass in a minute. But you know what I'm going to do?" He was waving his ketchupy finger around again. "I'm going to get her a new dog."

"Are you kidding?"

"Oh, no, not at all. I'm going to go out and get her another poopsy-pie. It was one of those miniature poodles and they're all over the place. I'll get her a white one, just like old Bunky."

"Why, Damon, that's a very nice gesture."

"Ah, yeah, cut it out. I'm just doing it because she's so suicidal about the whole affair."

I knew he was lying. I knew he was doing it because he felt awful about losing her dog. Damon always tried to be as macho as ever, but underneath he was quite a sensitive guy.

We stayed at the cafe for another hour or so. Damon ordered two desserts and we talked about acting for a while.

After we paid our check, Dame hailed me a cab and I hugged his sloppy, bony body and told him to stop reading the help-wanted ads. He laughed and told me to get lost. As my cab drove off I turned around to wave to him, but I couldn't see him anywhere. I figured he probably went into the David's Cookies next door to the cafe.

❧

That night Mint took me to Nell's. This friend of his, a regular customer from the restaurant, Johnny Vane, was throwing a private bash there. I'd only met Vane a couple of times at the Pigeon, but I was pretty sure I didn't care for him. He was always making some goddamn grand entrance with a couple of fashion models on his arms. He was some hotshot designer. At first I thought he was gay, but then I figured he was bi since he was always sticking his hand down some model's blouse. He seemed like a terrible chauvinist, but since I'd only met him a couple of times I couldn't stamp any label on him.

So Mint and I went to his freak show at Nell's. The place was just loaded with photographers and models. All the models were wearing numbers from Vane's new line. And, wow, was that line hideous. Everything was purple, for christsakes. Besides that, the dresses could barely cover anything—the skimpiest, sheerest shit I'd ever seen. Minty and I wandered around for a while. Everybody was staring at him. The minute my Sundance Kid walked into a place, everybody started to stare at him. It distressed me to death sometimes.

"Minty, I'm so *pleased* that you came." Johnny Vane swung around and gripped Minty's hand. He was wearing a murky purple vest with a red cape. Designer, my foot.

"It's some bash. Love the new collection," Minty said, running his hand up my spine. Whenever he touched me, even if it was absently, fleetingly, his touch controlled every inch of me. It sharpened every nerve and crossed out every face, and for those wavering split seconds there was nothing but the pounding of my chest and the alabaster sweep of his palm on my back.

"Yes, well, this year I opted for violet. Violet's such a *sensual* hue. Although one must be careful one uses the right fabrics when using violet. Personally, I think a woman should look quite *naked* even when she's dressed. Just *washed* in color." Vane paused for a moment and looked at me. "For instance, that, what do you call that you're wearing, Salty?"

I looked up at him and frowned. "It's a dress."

"Well, don't be silly, my darling, I *know* it's a dress. It's just rather *boring*. Much too long and full. And black is so dismal with your coloring, you need something bolder, brighter. Why don't you come up to the showroom, darling, and let me try out a few things? I have the most sensational strapless silver lace body dress that would look *divine* on you. It looks best with nothing underneath, but you wouldn't mind that, would you?"

The pervert was getting on my nerves. "Thank you, but that's really not my style. I prefer to preserve a little mystery." Mint flashed me a languid smile.

"Hm, pity," Vane said.

He dropped it after that. Asked us to come over and sit at his table. He led us through the crowds and it took about half an hour to get there because he kept stopping every five seconds to greet some Ford beauty. He'd say, "My darling, you're fabulous!" And then he'd kiss 'em on both cheeks, French-style. I'd never seen such a synthetic bastard in my life. When we got to his table, he introduced us to everybody and told us to sit down. Then he said he had to go talk to some other people, but he'd be back in a while. "Have to mingle, darlings . . ." is how he put it. That darling stuff was driving me crazy.

I ended up sitting between two Swedish twins. "Hi, I'm Salty," I said to the one on my right.

"Ya," she said.

"Are you a model?"

"Ya," she said, fiddling with an earring.

"What agency?"

"Ya," she said.

My conversation with that one ended pretty fast. The one on my left was even more of an idiot.

"Hi, I'm Salty."

"Saulty," she said.

"You're Swedish, right?"

"Svedish," she said.

"Is she your twin?" I pointed at dopey on my right.

"Tvin," she said.

A fucking parrot. I stopped talking after that. I poured myself a glass of champagne and looked over at Mint. He was sitting across from me between two of the most gorgeous women I'd ever seen. So I was watching them, and all of a sudden the one on Mint's right, this russet-haired masterpiece who'd been talking and flirting with him like nuts, well all of a sudden one of her breasts fell right out of her dress. I couldn't believe my eyes. She was lifting her arms up over her head, probably to describe the zenith of her popularity or something, when this breast came tumbling right out of her dress. The dress, of course, was a Vane original. The thing was, she wasn't even embarrassed about it. She just looked down at herself and started to laugh like mad. Plus she didn't even put it back in her dress right away. She just let it sit there for a while as if that were a perfectly customary thing to do. Unbelievable. Fucking unbelievable. Minty was trying not to laugh, but he wasn't doing such a good job. He looked at her face, and then he looked down at her breast, and then he looked back up at her face, and then he started cracking up. Finally, the chick stuck her boob back into the revolting garment and began to quiet down.

About two seconds later, Vane reappeared. He strode right up to Mint and said very flamboyantly, "Minty, how is everything? Is Raquel *amusing* you?" He leaned down and gave the russet slut a big smooch on the cheek.

"Oh, yes, she's marvelous."

Oh, please. Marvelous, my ass.

"She is, isn't she? *Aren't* you, my darling?" He put a finger under her chin and tilted her face up.

"Stop, Vaney, you're embarrassing me," she trilled.

Embarrassing her? She wouldn't be embarrassed if you draped Christmas tree lights all over her and hung her naked from the chandelier.

"Minty, there's someone I'd like you to meet," Vane said. Then he leaned down and whispered something in Mint's ear, and Mint started to nod and burst up out of his seat. What the hell was this all about? I watched Mint and Vane wind off through the crowd, the russet slut sulking over Mint's vacated chair. I started chewing my cigarette. I figured Vane was leading Mint off to meet some other half-naked bombshell. I must have eaten about ten cigarettes by the time Mint returned to the table. I wanted to ask him what had happened, but I decided to hold off until we were alone.

"Who did Vane want you to meet?" I asked him the moment we stepped outside of that madhouse. It was almost three-thirty and I was exhausted.

"Who?" Mint said absently, raising his arm to hail a cab.

"Vane came over to you and whispered something and you went—"

"Oh, right. He introduced me to Alessandro Jori. He's one of the hottest art dealers in Manhattan. Vane had told him about me, about my paintings, and Jori wants to take a look at them." A cab stopped in front of us. After we got in, Mint rolled down the window, lit a cigarette, and continued, "I'm going to show him some of my paintings at the Thanksgiving bash."

"What Thanksgiving bash?"

"I'm throwing a big Thanksgiving party at the Pigeon." He took a long drag from his cigarette and raked the frost of bangs back from his forehead.

"When? On Thanksgiving?" I took the cig from his fingers.

"No, on Christmas. Of course on Thanksgiving."

I frowned and started to chew up his damned cigarette. "But Mint, I thought we could spend Thanksgiving together. Just the two of us. I was planning to cook a turkey and . . ." I quit talking because Mint was laughing. He was doing one of those laughs where no sound comes out. Just heaving all over the joint with his mouth open.

"Salt, you can barely boil an egg."

"I know, but I'll practice with the turkey. I really wanted—"

"Look, Salt, we can spend next Thanksgiving together. It's just that I already started making arrangements for this party," Mint said gently, reaching for my hand.

"Okay, okay."

"I want you to pick out something fantastic to wear."

"What do you mean? What's wrong with my green dress?"

"That archaic thing? Salt, you've been wearing that dress for the past five years. It's not sophisticated enough. I want you to dazzle everybody. Is there anything wrong with me wanting to show you off?" He smiled sensually, his eyes burning with assurance, chunks of pearl-white hair swept over his forehead.

I dropped my cigarette in the ashtray and gripped the lapels of his coat, drawing him toward me. I felt his breath graze mine, the scrawled lace of his palms on my cheeks. "I'll find a dress for you," I whispered. "I'll do anything for you. . . ."

Chapter 4

When I woke up the next morning I was hanging halfway off the goddamned bed. Well, not exactly. One of my legs was hanging off the bed. I don't know what the hell I do when I sleep. I'm always strewn all over the place when I wake up. I have a feeling I don't look especially attractive when I'm sleeping. Besides my limbs tossed everywhere and my hair splattered all over my face, I'm pretty sure my mouth hangs open. I hated to think about Mint waking up and seeing me like that. I always wanted to be one of those graceful dames who sleep with their hair perfectly fanned out on the pillow and one arm dreamily draped overhead. Of course, things could have been worse. I could have been one of those sleep-eaters or whatever they're called. I saw them once on the "Donahue" show. They're these poor fat bastards who eat while they're asleep. Then they wake up the next morning with barbecue sauce all over their pajamas and a bed full of chicken bones, for christsakes.

I slowly sat up and looked over at Mint. He barely moved a muscle when he slept and his mouth didn't hang open either. He always slept curled up on his side, even when we were kids. I lit up a cigarette and sat there for a while, staring at him. All the smoke started to slither around in the sunlight over his head. I was going to pounce on him, but I knew he'd get annoyed if I woke him up so early, so I decided to go out for a jog. Not that I was one of those crazy bastards who get up every day and run a couple hundred miles. I just did it when I was in the mood.

I got up and put on some sweats and sneakers and had about three cups of coffee. Before I left, I wrote Mint a note and told him where I was going, and then I grabbed his hand weights and hauled myself out the door. They were three-pounders, and I thought they'd make me look like a real professional bastard. In fact, they seemed to have the reverse effect and made me look like I had some kind of severe scoliosis or something. This new age deserves to be kicked in the ass. All this granola and aerobics is about as fun as a hole in the head. It's all advertising, too. Billboards, magazines, television—if they'd just shut up and sit down for a second, people might not be so crazy. Everybody's being brainwashed. That's why I jogged. Because I'd been brainwashed with everybody else. I'd open up some magazine like *Vogue* and see an airbrushed anorexic doll in a swimsuit, and think, "That's the ticket. If I'm a heap of bones like that, then life will be a piece of cake." Images, they depress the hell out of me sometimes.

When I got to the park, I decided to go to the reservoir, which was a pretty stupid decision. The reservoir is always loaded with hotshots. White Carl Lewis look-alikes are always zooming past you left and right and you end up looking like a contestant in the Special Olympics. When I started out, I always looked like a superstar because I'd run as fast as I could for about two minutes until I started to heave and trip all over my feet. I had terrible endurance. Cigarettes and jogging aren't the most spectacular combination.

As usual, I started out running like a cougar until the sting set in and I got as sloppy as ever. I kept thinking, "Just one more mile and you could have a rock-hard ass. You can do it . . ." You try to psyche yourself up like that and it gets worse. Think about sex or something, and it goes a little faster. By the time I'd gotten to the halfway mark, I was pretty fed up. There was all this slimy mud all over the track and I kept slipping on it. Besides that, my arms were killing me from the bloody hand weights. So I leaned up against the wire fence that surrounds the reservoir and hung out there for a while watching all the hotshots go by.

When I got back, Minty had left a note on the bed saying he was up on the roof. I decided to take a shower. The first thing I did when I got into that shower was reach down and feel if my butt was any harder—the damn thing was about as hard as a rotten avocado. I was pissing myself off by feeling my butt, so I started to wash my hair. Then, as I was washing it, I kind of wanted a cigarette, which is pretty depressing when you think about it. I mean, what a place to have a cigarette, for christsakes. But I'm a lunatic. Honestly. I bet you if I was underwater, snorkeling, I'd still want a cigarette.

Just as I was stepping out of the shower trying to remember where I threw my last pack of cigs, the phone started to ring. I kept waiting for the answering machine to pick it up and then I remembered I'd turned it off. I charged into the bedroom in a towel and snatched up the receiver. It was my agent.

"Salty, honey, it's Jackie."

"Oh, hi," I said. Aha—I found my cigs! They were on the floor, under a pair of jeans.

"Guess what?" Jackie asked.

"I've run out of resumes," I muttered, lighting a match. She was always ringing me up to tell me to bring her more head shots or resumes. Her office was way the hell down on Eighth Street in one of those office buildings where everybody looks furious. Whenever I went down there she was on the phone. She had one of those phones with fifty lines on them, and she'd have about five people on the phone at once. She'd say the same thing to everybody: "Oh, baby, I'm dying to talk to you, you wanta hold for a sec . . ." Then she'd click over to another line and tell that guy she was dying to talk to him and to hold on. Everybody was either honey or baby or sweetie. I was usually honey. When she got off the phone she'd squint at me from behind her desk and tell me how gorgeous I looked and all this crap. She was about as sincere as a hole in the head.

Anyhow, this time she wasn't calling about resumes.

"You've got a screen test, honey!"

"What?! Oh, my God . . . for—"

"Oh, you wanta hold a sec . . ." She clicked onto another line.

I sat down on the bed and started to chew the hell out of my cigarette. When she came back on the line, I asked her what the screen test was for. I couldn't imagine what, except maybe this stupid beer commercial where I'd auditioned for a bar wench.

"It's for 'Today Is Tomorrow.' I just got a call from Janice Grey. She was very impressed with your reading."

No! Grouchy Grey was impressed with me? I didn't even think she was listening to me! I was really stunned.

Jackie went on to tell me that the test was in two weeks. She told me I'd be testing with the audition scene and that I had to memorize it upside down and backward. For the whole rest of our conversation I was bouncing up and down with excitement. I couldn't wait to tell Mint.

The moment I hung up, I threw on my clothes and dashed up the fire escape to the roof.

"Mint! Jackie just called and told me I got a screen test for 'Today Is Tomorrow'!" I cried, running over to him. He had a cigarette hanging out of his mouth and was mixing up some paint on his palette.

"That's great," he said, looking up at me. His eyes were squinted and splattered with sun. "Oh, Salt . . . could you come around here, you're scaring the pigeons." I moved away from the cluster of distressed-looking pigeons and went up to him. "When's the test?" he asked.

"Two weeks from now."

Mint nodded and dropped his cig onto the tar, squashing it under his Timberland boot. "Don't forget about Thanksgiving. The party's next Thursday."

"I know. I know it's next Thursday."

He dipped his paintbrush into a jar of muddy water and knocked it around. "You need to get a dress," he said, lifting the brush to peer at it.

"I know. I'll go get it today so I won't forget."

Mint looked up at me and smiled. "Thanks, baby. And it's really great about the screen test. I knew you'd get one sooner or later. C'mere . . ." He set down his brush on the folding table behind him and reached for me. He hugged me against his thick wool sweater and I felt his hot mouth press to mine, his hands slither into my wet hair. The cold surrounding me fused with the heat of his kiss was spectacular. I clung to him, I felt his mouth devouring mine, the stubble on his jaw grazing my face like sand. He pulled back slowly and I opened my eyes to his sun-swept brilliance.

"You'd better go dry your hair or you'll catch pneumonia, Salt," he told me, snatching up his palette.

"Yeah. You're right. I'll see you later, Picasso."

I went over to Bloomingdale's that afternoon. God, do I hate that Bloomingdale's. Just the thought of it gives me a migraine. That day, Bloomie's was worse than ever because it was loaded with tourists. All of Long Island and Japan and New Jersey were there that day, and I hate to be rude about it, but all those guys do is

create chaos. They just don't know where the hell they're going.
They stand like dopey statues in the center of the floor, twisting
their heads around and squinting at directories. If there's one
thing an authentic New Yorker knows, it's that you don't quit
moving. You move like a funky madman even if you don't have
the faintest clue as to where you're going. If you don't move like
that, you'll either cause gridlock or you'll be knocked unconscious by a stampede of authentic New Yorkers.

I was in that stupid store for about four hours. I think I tried on
almost every dress in the designer-evening-wear section before I
found this plain black silk job that looked all right on me. Normally I didn't feel comfortable in dresses. I suppose I just wasn't
feminine enough. I had one of those skinny bodies with hardly
any chest and long, restless legs. I looked very nice in Minty's oxford shirts and tight, low-waisted black jeans. The kind Jim Morrison wore.

When I came out of Bloomie's I was exhausted. I stopped off in
a coffee shop, Bolts of Nuts or Chock Full of Bolts or something,
and had a cup of coffee and a cigarette. It was almost six when I
got home. Mint was in the bedroom getting dressed to go to the
Pigeon when I trudged in with my shopping bag.

"You got it. Great. Let me see," he said the minute he spotted
me. I handed over the shopping bag and slouched down on the
bed. My feet were killing me.

"Salt, this isn't a black-tie dress. It's not formal enough." I
looked up at him wearily. He was mauling the dress, pulling at
the tag. "Who's this designer, anyway? Never heard of him. You
should have gotten an Alaïa or a Vane." He tossed the dress on
the bed.

"Are you kidding? I wouldn't wear one of Vane's sleazy outfits
for anything. What do you mean, it's not black-tie, I should have
gotten an Alaïa?"

"I mean just what I said." He moved in front of the mirror and started to button up his shirt.

"When did you become such an expert on fashion?" I asked coolly.

He swung around and stared at me. "Salt, I'm not an idiot. I can recognize a dinner dress when I see one. I just think you should have gotten something a little more . . . nonconformist, interesting. Every woman in Manhattan wears that dress. I see that dress ten times a night at the Pigeon." He turned back to the mirror. "Oh, forget it. If you really like it, wear it. I guess I should be lucky you didn't go to Banana Republic."

I gazed up at him. He'd grabbed the tie laid out on the dresser and hooked it around his neck. I couldn't understand why he was getting so upset; this party must really mean a lot to him. I hated the thought of going back to Bloomingdale's, but I didn't want him to be annoyed. I got up and walked over to him and tugged him sideways to face me. He stopped fussing with his tie and his eyes drove down into mine.

"I'll take the dress back, Minty. I'll get something more suitable. You're right, I suppose it is a dinner dress."

Mint's eyes softened, his brow unfurled, and he pulled me into his arms. I tilted my head back and looked into his eyes. I felt so safe there, so unafraid. I was like an innocent child, with hardly any words to play with, with no knowledge of despair or death or madness. Mint ran his fingertips down the side of my face and, suddenly, before I could stop them, all my thoughts tilted into my throat.

"Minty . . . Minty, I love you. I love you so desperately." His fingers paused, and I was startled by the intensity of his gaze.

"I love you, too, Salt," he said.

I could hardly stand. I'd waited all my life to get here, to this one breathtaking moment. For the first time he'd said he loved me, and my heart simply overflowed. It was finally real. I slid my arms around his neck, drenched in his transparent eyes. His hands curled around my neck and he drew my face to his, kissing me deeply. Waves of goosebumps tore up my arms, and all my muscles were melted and rippling.

"Make love to me. Please . . ." I begged. I thought he'd tell me he had to leave for the restaurant, but he didn't. He didn't tell me anything. He just kissed me again, more furiously than before. His tongue slipped inside my mouth, his breathing hastened, and I could feel him swelling hard against me. He picked me up in his arms and carried me to the bed. I locked my hands in his and watched his eyes turn vermilion in the melting dusk. When he moved inside me his mouth swept mine and I drank his disheveled breath, I kissed his precious lips and hands and smoldered in the ashes of his words.

Chapter 8

The night of Mint's bash I showed up an hour early to help out with some last-minute details. Mint had really gone all-out for this one. He'd hired this very hot singer, Shana Whitman, to do her thing in the birdbath. Since Brassy had split, he'd gotten a couple different musicians to come play in the birdbath, but he hadn't decided to hire anybody permanently yet. He would have loved to hire Shana, but she was too much of a hotshot. She would never have agreed to hang around in a birdbath. She was already on the charts and she was only doing this one-night gig as a favor. When I showed up she was there, nibbling on some hors d'oeuvres at the buffet.

The buffet table was extraordinary, bursting with these mad beautiful flowers in yellow and orange. Dried stalks of corn and gourds and squash were strewn all over it. Gilded candlesticks that held six candles apiece were blazing on a zigzag down the table, their stems partially hidden beneath a coppered sprinkle of leaves. Tremendous silver platters lay bare, awaiting the obese turkeys browning in the kitchen. Besides the turkeys, there was about every kind of vegetable on the planet. Normally I'm not too crazy about vegetables, but these were really good-looking. And the desserts looked great, especially this gigantic Black Forest cake in the shape of a pigeon.

Mint had dressed up all the waiters as Pilgrims and Indians. Now, wait a minute. I know exactly what you're thinking: that it sounds like some kind of grammar-school play or something. Well, it wasn't. It wasn't the least bit corny. These were some incredibly authentic-looking costumes, the kind you might find in some Broadway production. Plus the makeup on the Indians was right on target. I hardly recognized anybody who was made up as an Indian. Mint had even given Shana an Indian costume, a skimpy suede outfit full of beads and feathers and a pair of terrific moccasins. She also wore a black wig with two thick braids coming down, and her face was full of bronzing powder.

By eight-thirty, about half the guests had arrived. Most of them were devoted patrons of the Pigeon. A fair number were members of Nouvelle Society and all that bullshit. I was glad Mint had made me return the plain black dress I'd bought. I'd exchanged it for this taffeta and velvet affair. It wasn't really my style, but I knew Mint would be pleased with it so I went ahead and bought it. At least it didn't look stupid. You should have seen how many stupid outfits the dames at this party were wearing. There was this one woman who looked like she wanted to be a mermaid or something. She had on a full-length gold and silver dress that flared out at the bottom like a fan. Besides that, the dress was so tight she couldn't even walk across the floor. It squashed her all the way down to her ankles and she had to do this funky shuffle to get anywhere. Unfortunately, at one point she managed to shuffle over to me. Started to tell me about how she was the chairman of some la-di-da committee to raise money for a t'ai chi school for private-school youngsters, about how marvelous it was for the little children to find inner peace and equilibrium and all this nonsense. I could tell she was just waiting for me to rip out my checkbook and hand over a big fatso donation. As if I'd throw out all my dough to help a bunch of spoiled Park Avenue brats learn some kind of ritzy kung fu. Tons of children in the world were homeless and starving, and this woman wanted to suck up dough like a Dustbuster so Rockefeller, Jr., could learn how to balance on one foot in his fancy pajamas, for christsakes.

Right in the middle of this heartfelt monologue, I spied Johnny Vane blasting through the door. He blasted in with that russet slut, the one whose boob fell out of her dress, and this very tanned guy with a long black ponytail, who I assumed was the art dealer Mint had made such a fuss over.

The mermaid stopped dead in her tracks when she noticed Vane. Started to squawk, "Oh, oh look! It's Johnny Vane with Alessandro Jori!" So much for the poor little children. She started to fix her hair, patting it down all over the place. Why she needed to pat it I have no idea, since it was already packed into this fermented meatball. If the roof fell in, the stupid broad would probably shuffle out of the rubble without a scratch, saved by her goddamn hairdo.

She didn't say another word to me. She just took off in Vane and Jori's direction. She wasn't the only one. About half the guests were migrating toward Vane and his entourage like a bunch of starstruck groupies. It was pathetic. I turned around and went over to the buffet. A Pilgrim sliced me some turkey, and an Indian gave me some corn soufflé and chestnuts and brussels sprouts. Then I moved over near the birdbath, where Shana was doing her rendition of some Cole Porter classic. She had her eyes closed and all the drippy beads on her outfit were swishing around her thighs. When I glanced back over at Vane, I saw the crowds had cleared and Mint was over there shaking hands with the dude with the ponytail. Some woman with firecracker red hair was snapping photos of them.

After a couple of minutes, Mint started to lead Vane's clan to the royal table up by the birdbath. Miss Firecracker wouldn't knock it off with the camera. She kept right on after them, the flash going off every two goddamned seconds. When Mint had arranged Vane and his friends at the table, I realized I should go say hello. I didn't feel like going over there at all, but it was kind of rude to just stand around, stuff myself with turkey, and ignore them. So I put my plate down on a nearby table and went over to Mint, who was hovering over the guy with the ponytail.

Mint turned when I put my hand on his arm, smiled, and immediately said, "Mr. Jori, I'd like you to meet my girlfriend, Salty."

Jori looked at me clinically, voiced a curt "How do you do." I told him it was a pleasure and all that jazz.

At a distance you might really think Jori'd been to the tropics or something, but up close you knew his version of the tropics was mixing up a tequila sunrise and lying around in an electric coffin. Those sunlamps are straight from hell. I know, because I've read a dozen articles about them saying they should have a skull and crossbones plastered all over the place. But I can't rag on anybody, because I smoke like an inferno and those cigarettes are no goddamn good for you either.

Besides his tan Jori wasn't exactly unattractive. He was probably in his late forties and he had that bored, worldly look about him. You could tell he was a real cocky bastard just by the way he lounged back in his chair and idly glanced around at everybody. He had very dark, European looks: black eyebrows arched above slitted brown eyes, spewing wrinkles. Then he had his black hair slicked back over his skull in the wet look, pulled taut into the ponytail. His charcoal gray suit was impeccable. Probably Armani or something.

After he introduced me, Mint had me sit down at the table with him. He put me right next to that damned Vane, who barely spoke to me except to disparage my outfit again. He said something about taffeta being passé and how my neckline was absurdly puerile, and then he summed up his whole commentary with, "Hope I haven't offended you, darling, but I am the Master, you know." I am the Master—what a bunch of pompous crap. He didn't say a word to me after that; he started to chew on the russet slut's earlobe.

When I glanced back over at Mint, I saw that he and Jori had left the table and were standing in front of the back wall where Minty's largest mural was. I couldn't see them that well, though. Guests were slopped all over the joint.

I didn't know what the hell to do with myself. After a couple of minutes of staring into space, I got up. I merged into a couple of clusters and tried to be social and all that. I remember talking to this spindly idiot and his ball and chain for a while. Boy, were they a couple of imbeciles. All they did was ramble on about what good friends they were of Donald Trump. About how he'd invited them on his private jet to Saint Moritz and how he'd thrown a huge party for them at the Plaza. As if I cared. I don't know what the hell people think sometimes. I must have spent a whole half hour listening to this pair yack about the Donald, and it was giving me a pain in the ass. At one point, I just quit listening. I kept staring at them and nodding and every so often I'd say, "Uh-huh . . . oh . . . yes?" Meanwhile I was thinking about the name Donald. I was thinking about what a dopey name it was. Donald. Donald Duck is all it reminds me of. It's amazing how you can con somebody into thinking you're listening to them when you're really thinking about some dumb cartoon. I really think it's amazing the way everybody's got a mind and it's theirs and nobody can get in there. Sometimes when I'm walking down the street I think about it. I watch all the guys passing me, and God only knows what the hell they're thinking about. One could be thinking about something kind of trivial, like what he had for dinner last night. The guy right next to him might have a brain tumor. He might be worrying about dying while the guy walking past him is thinking about some shredded beef Szechuan-style, for christsakes.

So I was standing there, making like I was listening to this couple, when Mint came and rescued me. He told them he had to speak to me privately for a moment and then he grabbed my hand and led me through the mobs and down to the wine cellar. I was just bursting with excitement. I figured he was bored out of his skull too and wanted to do the wild thing in the cellar. I swear, that's what I thought. I was all ready to pull down my panty hose when I realized the wild thing wasn't on his mind. I realized it when he grabbed me by the shoulders and sputtered, "You're never going to believe this, Salt! Jori wants to meet for dinner tomorrow night to discuss the prospect of a show!" His eyes were blazing, scintillating.

"Mint, that's wonderful."

"Alessandro Jori is the hottest dealer in Manhattan. Even on the coast. He's got a gallery in L.A., and he's got one in France, too." Mint released me. He started to pace around in front of the wine racks like a lunatic.

"What did he say, exactly?" I asked.

"What do you mean? He said he wanted to meet for dinner—"

"I know. I mean, what did he say about your work?"

"He didn't say anything. After I showed him the murals and the paintings in the back, he just turned to me and said, 'I'd like to talk to you about a show.' Then he asked me to dinner tomorrow. God, this is incredible!"

I just stood there, watching Mint pace back and forth. He had this look in his eyes I'd never seen before. It was this very dramatic, transfixed look that had no entrance. Wherever he was, he was somewhere I couldn't find or see, or possibly imagine.

Chapter 9

I went to dinner with Jori and Mint the next night. Mint didn't want me to come at first. He said it was strictly business and that I'd probably get bored and start eating my cigarettes or something. I told him that anything concerning him concerned me. That I wouldn't doze off and embarrass him. That if the waiter turned out to be some old acting buddy I used to take classes with, I wouldn't slap him on the back and ask him to join us for a slice of pie. That I wouldn't wear a fedora or combat boots or anything. I summed up the whole thing with a heartfelt, "I swear, Mint, I won't say a word."

He finally gave in. "Okay. You can come. But not a word."

Yup. Yessirree. You got it. So we went to Le Comptoir. Jori was a regular there and had his own special table and all that crap. He was already seated when we arrived, reading *Arts* magazine and smoking a cigar. The headwaiter ushered us to his table.

"Mr. Jori . . ." Mint said as we reached him.

Jori looked up abruptly and set down his magazine. "Minty, so glad you could come."

"You remember Salty?" Mint said.

Jori's eyes flicked to mine for maybe a split second. He said some baloney about it being delightful to see me again, and then looked back over at Mint. "Please, sit down. Let me order you a drink."

We sat down in the two chairs across from him, and Mint said he'd have a pink lady. I asked for a Perrier. (Yes, I spoke. But I was allowed to speak when spoken to. That was part of the arrangement.)

After the drinks came, Jori started to babble like crazy. I'm not going to bore you by recounting everything he blabbed about, but I can sum it up for you in one word: himself. In a way, it didn't shock my pants off. He looked exactly like the type of guy who never shut up about himself. He practically told us his life story, from how he rose up out of the gutter in Sicily where he'd been a shoeshine guy to his immigrating to the melting pot on some squalid cargo vessel to his supersonic rise to fame and fortune. To give you an idea of about how long this sordid autobiography took, we were already halfway through our entrées when he got to the part about the squalid cargo vessel. Just before we ordered dessert was when he hit the jackpot and began to list all his material possessions: the palazzo in Rome, the priceless Beckmanns, the Porsche. . . . Ah, shut up and sit down, is all I wanted to say to him. But I didn't. Respecting Mint's and my agreement, I remained mute. I have to tell you, though, it wasn't easy, especially when Jori started on the topic of hunting. If there's one thing that really steams me, it's hunting. Anybody who gets a thrill out of watching things die is a real son of a bitch, in my opinion. I can't stand to think of all the poor goddamn animals who get gunned down for no reason, as if their lives weren't worth anything. Jori couldn't have been more adamant about his passion for hunting, and, man, did I ever want to say something. I kept stuffing cigarettes into my mouth to keep from blurting out some expletive. I must have had about ten cigarettes in the ten minutes when Jori was going on about his bloody game trophies.

So finally the guy brought up Mint's painting. It certainly took him long enough to get around to it. The dessert had just arrived, and as Jori was digging into his crème caramel, he looked up at Mint and said, "You know what it feels like to make the big kill, Minty?"

"I suppose so," Mint said.

"You think you've made it with your restaurant, don't you?" Jori slurred out, his mouth full of crème caramel.

"Well, it is quite a success." Mint responded with casual confidence.

Jori put down his spoon, wiped his mouth with his napkin, and leaned forward. "Success? Minty, you haven't even grazed success." He leaned back again and licked his lips. "But you could. I'll tell you right now, you can make it. And I don't dish out compliments very often. When Vane mentioned you, I'll admit I was skeptical. I have to be skeptical. Somebody's always calling me over to check out some potential superstar's work, and normally it's just a waste of my time. But your painting," he paused, "it's extraordinary. It has this childlike, almost primitive quality. A lot of quirky color, detail . . . but it works. It works in the adult world because it's got an inner logic." He paused again to light up a cigar. He took it out of this carved ivory case, which immediately made me think of the poor goddamn elephant. I'll bet he gunned down some poor goddamn elephant just for a stupid cigar case. "The thing is, Minty, I have an eye. Instinct, intuition, whatever you want to call it, I have it. I can tell in less than ten seconds if somebody's going to make it or not."

"You really think my painting is that good?" Mint asked.

"I wouldn't be offering you a show if I didn't. But there's one thing. I've got to have your answer now."

Mint put his fork down and slid his plate forward. "What do you mean, now? Tonight?"

"That's right."

"But I thought shows were scheduled months in advance."

"They are, only there's something you don't know. . . ." Jori lit a cigar and leaned forward a little. "I had Daniel Ward scheduled for December fifteenth. Just before your party, I got a call telling me that the cross-eyed fuck who was transporting his paintings crashed his truck into a Toyota Corolla and all the paintings were destroyed."

"Jesus," Mint muttered.

"Yeah, Jesus is right. Here I've got Daniel down for a three-week segment, I've got all the catalogs printed, all the paintings ready, and this fuck goes and crashes the truck." Jori was getting very emotional all of a sudden. He was waving his cigar around like a conductor's baton. "So as you can imagine, I'm out of my mind. But the minute I saw your work, I said to myself, This guy's damned good. I've been thinking about this all night, Minty. There wouldn't be time to print up catalogs, but I was thinking of sending out mailgrams to about two hundred of my best clients inviting them to the opening. It would be unusual, but I'm sure we'd get a good response."

"December fifteenth is less than three weeks away. . . ."

"Look, Minty, what I'm offering you is a once-in-a-lifetime opportunity. You haven't got a thing to worry about. You've got the goods. You've got, what, close to sixty paintings stashed away? Isn't that what you said?"

"Yeah."

"Okay, so you won't have to lift a finger. You'll get fifty percent and I'll do all the work." Jori took a couple puffs off his cigar. Between his damned cigar and Mint's and my cigarettes, the whole bleeding table was disappearing in something comparable to a gigantic cumulus cloud. "So what's it gonna be?"

"You've got a deal, Mr. Jori," Mint said suddenly.

"Fabulous." Jori's arm reached out, the gold Rolex glinting

brightly on his wrist as his bronzed hairy hand solidly gripped Minty's.

I was watching the goddamn handshake with slitted eyes, crunching on an ice cube. I wasn't too sure I liked this Jori character. Not just because of the hunting. I had a feeling he wasn't the most trustworthy guy I'd ever laid eyes on. I kept thinking he'd make a very nice pimp if you dressed him up in a leather jacket or something.

After they shook hands, Jori ordered sambuca and made this grand-slam toast to December 15. He told Mint he had a gold mine in his hands, and then he lit up his cigar again and smiled at him, the smoke seeping from between his teeth in gaunt gray threads.

When Mint and I got home that evening, I didn't tell him anything about my feelings about Jori being a dirty rat. He was in such a good mood, for christsakes, how could I tell him? Besides, I wasn't one hundred percent certain Jori was a dirty rat, so I kept my trap shut and simply told Mint I was happy for him.

Mint fell asleep before I did that night. I sat up in bed, munching Corn Pops and memorizing the sides for the screen test. What a lousy scene it was. The character I was playing was Laura Smith, this ruthless, scheming, conniving bimbo who decides to take advantage of some rich ex-boyfriend with a trust fund and shows up on his doorstep with her suitcases. The old boyfriend, who's named Andrew Bregman, is some preppy jerk who's excited as hell to see her. He invites her in, and about two seconds later she clutches onto him and bursts into tears. She tells him her father's been abusing her and her mother won't believe her and she has nowhere to go. This is all a crock of shit, but Andrew is apparently still in love with her and he pulls her into his arms and invites her to stay for a while. In the end, he delivers this mawkish speech about how much he's longed to be with her again, and then they have this big dramatic kiss.

It was really an awful scene. I was having a very hard time with the crying part. I wasn't one of those actresses who can just burst into tears at the drop of a hat. Sometimes I'd try so hard to cry that I'd give myself a headache. I could only cry if I was really into character. Right after I graduated from high school I took a bunch of classes at this very famous acting school near Columbus Circle. They have this big, fancy technique. They teach you to rely on personal experiences to cry. They make you pick out an actual experience you had, like the time you were hit over the head with a flowerpot or something. That memory is supposed to evoke the emotion you need for a scene. Well, it never worked for me. I'd be too wound up in the scene to start recalling some goddamn experience. I always had to fake it. The teacher would stop me in the middle of a scene to ask me what memory I was using, and I'd have to make up something right there on the spot. I'd blurt out, "Oh, the time Uncle Fred gave me gerbils." God only knows what the hell I said.

I don't know why I stayed at that school as long as I did because I hardly got anything out of it. I remember in the morning they'd make you sit in a metal folding chair for three hours. This was another big secret technique. They claimed the only way to relax the body effectively was to sit in a metal folding chair for three hours. You couldn't even open your eyes. If you did, the teacher would come over and hit you with a stick. If you want my honest opinion, quite a few of those teachers were flying over the cuckoo's nest. What annoyed me the most, though, was the actors who took it so goddamn seriously. Once, during a break, I was outside having a cigarette with a couple of classmates, when

I happened to make some disparaging comment about the whole metal chair relaxation technique—knowing me, I probably called it a pain in the ass or a load of crap or something. And this big, tall bastard in a beret went completely berserk. He threw down his cigarette and started to rant and rave, saying how dare I malign one of the great master's techniques and all this crap, and finally stormed off into the building like a regular psychopath. I should have seen it coming, though, because I knew something was up with that guy from the moment he walked into the first class in his crazy beret, humming the overture to *Les Misérables*.

That next day I had a lunch date with Dame at this sushi bar on the West Side. I decided to walk through the park since it had snowed the night before. It was the first snow of the year and it was the nice powdery kind. All these kids were out in the park, all smacking each other with snowballs, slipping and sliding around, their nannies chasing after 'em screaming that nanny bullshit like, "Don't you get near the pond, Billy! Lordy, Lordy, child, God help me!" or "Put your pants back on, Greg! Jesus, Mary, and Joseph!"

When I came out of the park, I headed downtown for a while on Central Park West and then cut over to Broadway. The only problem with Broadway is all the sleazy construction workers who are always popping out of manholes, barking, "Hey, baby! Legs! Legs!" or "I'd screw chu, chiquita!" There's nothing like a toothless guy with a Whitesnake tattoo and a soiled undershirt trying to pinch your ass. In summertime it's worse, though. Because you're always in something short and airy and if the breeze starts up you've gotta hold the bottom of your skirt down like mad. It's an awful nuisance. I used to be very paranoid and kept a pair of scissors in my purse for a while, just in case somebody tried to rape me. They were comforting to have with me, but the thing was, I knew I'd never be able to stab anybody with them. I'd probably just stand there, shaking all over the joint looking like a hairdresser.

When I got to the sushi place, Damon was already at the bar. As usual he was wearing his baseball cap backward, a big baggy Mets sweatshirt, faded jeans, and a new pair of sneakers with Teenage Mutant Ninja Turtles all over them. Mutant Ninja Turtles, for christsakes. I felt like his mother.

"Hey, babe! Congratulations!" he said as I sat down beside him. He raised his hand and I gave him the high-five.

"Thanks, but I haven't got the part yet."

"You got a screen test, Salt! And from Grouchy Grey. You're gonna do great. I know it." Damon smiled at me and I punched him in the arm. Then I lit a cigarette and we started to discuss the menu. Dame was pointing to the special when he took a drag off my cig.

"Still chewing the filter, huh?" He grinned and handed it back to me. "Mint not satisfying you?"

"What?"

"They say chewing on things is a sign of sexual frustration."

"Who's they?"

"I don't know. They, them, the guys who say things that guys like me believe and quote."

I laughed and told him I was thoroughly satisfied. The waiter came over. Dame ordered half the goddamn menu. And then he asked for this big bowl of rice on the side. He kept repeating to the waiter to make it a very big bowl. After the waiter took off, I asked him what had happened with the dog.

"Oh, I got this great dog for the woman at the ASPCA. They were just about to annihilate it. Looked just like the other one, but it needed a good soak in the tub. So I scrubbed it and buffed it and brought it over to the woman and told her, 'Peace.' "

"Did she accept it?"

"Yup. Didn't invite me in for tea and gingersnaps, but she took the dog. I'd put this bow on its head, too, which looked pretty stupid, but I thought it kind of needed the bow. It would've looked better around the dog's neck, but I tried that and the mutt was furious about it. Kept trying to eat the bow. So I got one of those bows with the sticky stuff on 'em and stuck it on his head."

The waiter came along and set down our California rolls. Just before he disappeared, Dame mentioned the big bowl of rice again. I think he was very worried the guy would forget about it.

"I got a new job, Salt," Dame announced, trying to pick up a roll with his chopsticks. It kept slipping out of them before he got it up to his mouth. "Damn sticks. How the hell do these people eat with these things? When Franklin discovered electricity, nobody kept on lighting candles when they could have a lamp—except for the Amish, but those guys are crazy."

"Damon, what are you talking about?"

"I'm talking about forks. Some guy, Mr. Fork probably, invented the fork and it was a very good idea. Made everything easier. Everybody caught on to it"—he lowered his voice and leaned toward me—"except the Asians. They're retrograde countries, Salt. They could have a perfectly good fork, but no, they wanta eat with a couple of twigs." He shook his head, then grabbed a roll with his fingers and popped it into his mouth.

"Damon, you're nuts. Asians are probably the most sophisticated guys on the planet. They're taking over technology. They only eat with chopsticks because it's part of the culture."

Dame smiled at me. "I know that. I'm just kidding around with you, babe. You're so gullible sometimes, Salt."

"I am not gullible. You're just a better actor than you think you are. What were you saying about this new job?"

"Oh . . . well, it's kind of embarrassing. You'll laugh if I tell you."

"I won't. I won't laugh. What is it?"

"Every weeknight from four to eight, I pass out pamphlets for Chuckles Chicken."

"So? There's nothing wrong with that."

"Salt . . ." Dame leaned in closer. "I have to wear a chicken suit."

"What's a chicken suit?"

"Shhhhh, not so loud. . . . I've gotta dress up like a chicken. I have to wear this yellow chicken suit with feathers all over it."

I burst out laughing. I know it was rotten, but I couldn't help it. I'd never seen anybody who had worse luck with jobs than Damon.

"You see! I told you you'd laugh."

"Oh, Damon, I'm sorry."

"I'm really getting paid for this, you know. Helluva lot more than the dog-walking."

The poor bastard was desperate. Let me give you a hint: Don't ever be an actor. Not unless you've got some dough stashed away. If you don't have that dough, you'll probably wind up in a chicken suit. Of course, if you're some kind of genius, some kind of Hoffman or Streep or something, forget what I just said.

For the rest of lunch Damon asked me questions about the character I was testing for and all that. When his big bowl of rice came along, he squirted soy sauce all over it and wolfed it down in about sixty seconds. He had to rush off before I did. Told me he was late for his commercial class. He wasn't rude or anything. He hugged me and told me to let him know how the screen test went and wished me luck and all that. After he split, I lingered at the bar for a while. I had a smoke and watched the sushi chef hack up some salmon. When I got up to go I asked the waiter for the check, and he told me guy in hat already pay. The sneak.

He'd told me he was going to the can, but he was really paying the check. Man, he was a real class act, Damon. I couldn't believe him. Here he was, barely getting by, making chicken feed, for petesakes, and he still went ahead and paid for me. Ha. Ha, ha. That's kind of funny. Making chicken feed, because, you know, he was a chicken . . . oh, forget it.

Chapter 10

The night before my screen test was murder. I went to bed at ten and was still wide awake at two. I was incredibly nervous. I tried that good old sheep routine after a while. I got about a dozen sheep in my head and I conjured up a fence. The thing was, I made the fence too high, and every time I wanted a sheep to jump over it, it would bash into it. It got pretty annoying after a while, so I decided I'd go into the living room and watch some television. I grabbed my cigarettes and tiptoed out of the bedroom so as not to wake Mint. He was one of those very light sleepers. You just had to sniff or scratch your head or something, and Mint would wake up and tell you to keep it down.

I made myself comfortable on the couch and turned on the TV with the remote. Television was a stupid idea, though. It was after 2 A.M., and after 2 A.M. television only caters to cretins. On one channel there was this show called "The Matchmaker." It starred this dirty old man who came out with a couple of fifteen-year-old bimbos on his arms. He was supposed to be the matchmaker. He had to ask questions of all these dumb-looking teenagers behind him and match them up by their answers. The whole show was a regular catastrophe. On channel nine there was this irritating woman called Anushka. Anushka was wearing a radioactive pink leotard and telling everybody about her marvelous behind. Then she announced her magical cellulite cream and started showing all these before and after photographs of women's rear ends. On the next station there was the stop-smoking show. That annoyed the daylights out of me because I had a cigarette hanging out of my mouth when I turned to it. The host of the show was looking right at me and saying, "My friend, put out your cigarette and breathe . . ." Like hell, I'll put out my cigarette. How can I enjoy my smoke when some guy is making me feel guilty about it? I changed the channel. Off the air. . . . Off the air. . . . "The Home Shopping Show." Swell. There was this hand with a big ugly ring on it. The ring was the size of a golf ball, and this Southern woman's voice was saying, "Now, will ya look at this. Have you ever seeeen anythang so lovely in yur liaf? The cubic zirconia—" I changed the channel. Off the air. . . . Some nude guy with a microphone talking to some nude chick who obviously needed to speak with Anushka.

"How do you feel about Gorbachev?" the nude guy asked, holding the microphone up to one of the bimbo's droopy breasts.

"He's okay. I betcha he'd be a wild man in the sack."

"So, you'd like to make it with a Russian leader?"

"Right on, Daddy-o. I make it with everybody."

That was it. I'd had it. I'd smoked about fifteen cigarettes and it was three-thirty in the morning and I'd had it. I went back to bed and rounded up the sheep.

❧

When my alarm went off at six, I was absolutely exhausted. To make matters worse, as soon as I left the apartment you should have seen the wacko I got as a cabdriver. He was this Chinaman named Hong something or other, and I was probably the first guy he had ever picked up. After I gave him the address, he cut over to Fifth, and since it was the beginning of rush hour the traffic was a nightmare, so I leaned forward and told him he should go through the park. You'll never believe what he said to me then. He cranked his head around and said, "Wah pak?" Wah pak, for christsakes. We've been going down Fifth Avenue for ten minutes right next to the park, and the guy doesn't even know it's there. I couldn't believe it. So I said, "You don't know about Central Park?" And then Hong turned around and snapped, "How you tink I know?! I Chinese! How I know?"

I leaned back and sighed. Then Hong started to talk to himself. I've noticed a helluva lot of cabdrivers do that. They either talk to themselves or they start to sing or whistle or something. The traffic didn't get any better and I was getting pretty nervous. I scrounged through my bulky handbag for my cigarettes. I lit one up, and I hadn't even taken a goddamn puff when Hong started to throw another fit. "No! No smock!! No smock!!" So I had to put out my cigarette, and I sat there and looked around. I looked at the photograph of the plump Chinese woman dangling from the rearview mirror. I looked at the black spiky hair on the back of Hong's head. I looked at the "FUCK YOU ACEHOLE" carved into the vinyl on the back of the front seat. Finally, after a whole half hour, Hong pulled up in front of the NBC building.

After the security guy checked my name off a list, I went up to Grouchy Grey's office. Of course, I didn't think of her as a grouch anymore. Now that she'd chosen me for a screen test, she was sensational. When I met with her she read the scene with me one last time, and then she told me two other girls were testing for the part and that I'd be sharing a dressing room with them. Grey's assistant led me to the dressing room. The two other girls were already there, sitting on the sofa eating donuts when I came in.

One of them seemed pretty nice; the other one was possibly the offspring of my cabdriver.

"Hi, I'm Sarah," the nice one said.

"I'm Salty. Nice to meet you." I shook her hand and then went to shake the other one's. She didn't shake it. She just grunted, "Hi," and kept right on eating her donut.

"Can I just dump my stuff here?" I asked the nice one, pointing to the other couch.

"Oh, sure. Make yourself at home. You want a donut?"

"No, thanks, I'll have a smoke if it doesn't bother either of you."

"Go ahead," the nice one said. The other one didn't say anything.

As I was smoking, I realized they'd both been to Makeup already since they were caked with heavy base and smeared with eye shadow. Unfortunately, they were both pretty good-looking, though. I had a rather low self-image. I knew I wasn't a monster, but I also knew I wasn't a knockout. Jesus, I always had this fantasy I'd wake up one morning and be a real drop-dead knockout, with great big cheekbones and blue eyes. But I wasn't about to get suicidal over it. It would have been nice and all that, but I wasn't going to kill myself over it.

"Lemme have one of those," the girl who wouldn't shake hands suddenly blurted out.

"You'd like a cigarette?" I asked her.

"Yeah."

What a cordial way she had about her. She didn't even move. She wanted me to get up and bring it to her as if she were the Queen of Sheba, for petesakes. But I went over and gave her a cigarette anyway. What I really wanted to do was sock her in the nose, but I have a problem with being assertive around arrogant people; I always tend to act very submissive around them. It's a wonder I didn't compliment the bitch on her lovely outfit as I gave her the cigarette. I'm a lunatic sometimes.

About ten minutes later there was an announcement over the horn for me to go into Makeup. Makeup was pretty boring, so I'm not going to waste time telling you about it. After I was fixed up, I was called into the studio with the other two girls to block the scene. Then we were ordered back to the dressing room and called down one at a time to test. I found out I was going last, which kind of bothered me because the more I waited around, the more nervous I got. I just sat there in that dressing room, and there wasn't a whole helluva lot to do in there. I kept wishing I'd brought along a book or something.

When I was finally called down to test, I was as jittery as hell. The minute I walked onto the set and saw all the blinding lights and cameras and technicians and prop guys and guys who weren't doing anything but standing around, I started to shake all over the joint. I tried to do some deep breathing to calm myself down. When you breathe from your diaphragm, it's supposed to calm you down. I was exhaling when I recognized the guy who played Andrew on the show. When Jackie told me I had the screen test, I'd turned on "Today Is Tomorrow" to get a look at the guy who played Andrew. He was a very attractive, wholesome-looking blond with dark, brooding eyes. Anyhow, he wandered toward me, cleaning his eyeglasses on his pale yellow polo shirt, and then he smiled and put the glasses on.

"Hi. I'm Lucas Freeman," he said warmly, extending his hand. I really didn't want to shake hands because mine was all sweaty and trembling, but I didn't have much choice.

"Salty Spencer. Nice to meet you." I shook his hand as fast as possible.

"Nervous?" he asked.

"Well, yeah. I'm kind of nervous." I started to scratch my arm like crazy.

"Don't worry. It's not so bad. Once the scene starts you'll forget about everybody." He yawned and leaned back against a prop rack. Jesus, was he calm. He looked like he'd keel over about any damn second. Of course, he didn't really have a reason to be nervous since he already had a part on the show.

When everybody was ready, Lucas and I were told to take our places on the set. The set was supposed to be Andrew's living room. It was painted sky blue and had a lot of scrubbed pine furniture and a big rust-colored couch. There was also a window with some fake ivy and branches behind it. Right before we started, a makeup woman came over and brushed my hair and touched up the powder on my nose. Man, was I broiling, though. Those big lights they have, they could kill a guy, I swear. I'll bet if you left a guy underneath them for a couple of days, they'd broil the poor bastard like a goddamn halibut. When the makeup woman left, Lucas leaned over and wished me luck. I was glad he was such a pleasant guy instead of some cavalier bastard or something. Half the actors in the world are cavalier bastards.

Finally the broad with the board came along and snapped it in front of my face. She said, "Salty Spencer, reading for Laura Smith, Take One . . ." Then we were rolling and I started to bang on the door. When Lucas opened it I was really in character. I don't think I've ever been so in character in my life. I had enough adrenaline to power the Concorde, for christsakes. The best part was when I had to cry. You remember I was having a hard time with that part? Well, I cried right on cue. I didn't even have to strain.

When the test ended I was very pleased. Lucas said I did a really good job, but he probably said that to the other two, also. But when I was walking off the set, one of the technicians, this older black guy in a baseball cap, came over to me and said, "You're a heck of an actress, Miss." I'll never forget it. It made my whole damn day.

After I washed all the crap off my face, I went back to the

dressing room to take a last look at it. I wanted that part so badly I just stood there and stared at that dressing room for a whole ten minutes. I was picturing myself in there Monday through Friday, getting changed for scenes, and all that. I pictured the shelves covered with all my goddamn loot, all my personal effects. A framed picture of Mint and one of my mom and all my cigarettes and books and stuff.

When I finally left the building, I decided to walk uptown a little before catching a cab. It was quite chilly out, but it didn't really bother me. I started to pray as I was walking. I started saying, "Please, please, please, let me get it." But then I realized God might not know what the hell I was referring to. He might think I wanted a toaster oven or a bowling ball or something. So I made sure I wasn't so ambiguous. I said, "Please, please, please, let me get the role of Laura Smith on the soap opera 'Today Is Tomorrow.' "

So I was walking along, praying and all that, when I happened to walk by a church. Normally I stay the hell away from churches, but this time I really wanted to go inside. I thought I'd ask for the role in the church. I figured God would hear me better in a church, him being such a religious guy and all. It wasn't a very sensational church, though. I mean, it certainly didn't bring to mind visions of the Vatican or anything. It was muddy brown and splattered all over the place with graffiti. Plus there were about six bums strewn across the front steps, but I decided to go in anyway.

I started up the stairs, winding around all the bums. I'd almost reached the top when one of them latched onto my leg and offered me a swig out of a bottle he had in a paper bag. I shook my leg loose and told him, "No, thank you . . . really . . . thanks, but no." I'm such a polite son of a gun. I swear, I'm always as polite as hell, even when I'm talking to a bum.

When I finally got up to the ratty-looking door, I got a little nervous. I hadn't been in a church since I was five, and I didn't even know the rules—I mean, if you could just barge into one like you do Bloomingdale's. It's stupid, but I thought I might need a membership. I thought there might be some kind of bouncer at the door who'd want proof I wasn't a Jew or a Hare Krishna or something. I finally just decided to go inside. There wasn't any bouncer. The place was deserted, actually. Some old geezer was sweeping under some benches, but that was it.

I took a seat in the first row. There was Jesus on the cross in front of me. I figured I was supposed to talk to him. So I pressed my palms together and asked Jesus if he would be kind enough to ask his dad to give me that role on the soap opera. I thanked him about a thousand times and then I said amen. I wasn't sure if you were supposed to say amen or not, but I threw it in anyway. I was going to get up then, but I remembered I wanted to thank God for Minty. I wanted to tell him how grateful I was that he'd given me Minty.

I was right in the middle of thanking him when it happened. It all came back to me, and I just couldn't stop it. . . . I'm sitting between Minty and his mother. We're both five years old. My hands are the size of small leaves. My feet are dangling in patent-leather shoes. When I look up at Minty's mother, black is melting around her eyes. She keeps bringing one hand up to her mouth, pressing two fingertips over her lips. Her other hand is wrapped around mine. It feels huge and cold. Minty is sitting on my right. He's wearing his special navy blue suit. He keeps looking around and squirming on the smooth wood. He's holding my other hand. It feels like mine. I can't tell where my hand ends and his begins. I want to go home. I ask Minty's mother if we can go home.

"In a little while, sweetheart," she whispers.

Minty's father gets up and goes over to the place where the man in black was. His father doesn't look as tall as usual. When he starts to talk to everybody, his voice is strange though I'm really not listening to what he's saying. Minty's mother is crying.

She doesn't make any noise, but when I look up at her I can see silver-black tears running down her cheek. She keeps squeezing my hand.

When Minty's father sits back down, the man in black comes back. I hear my name, and I look at him. I want him to go away. I want Mommy, but she isn't there.

"I want my mommy," I say to Mint's mother.

She doesn't answer. She looks down at me with her shiny eyes and then pulls me toward her, presses my head against her chest. Her heart is very loud. I close my eyes and listen to her heart. I want to go home now. I'm scared. I'm scared of the man in black and the big white flowers and the candles and the unhappy man with the blood on his hands and the patchwork windows and all the strangers and I want to go home . . . I want home . . .

" 'Scuse me, Miss, are you all right?"

"What?" I looked up; there was a man, a janitor I think, but he was blurred. I was choking.

"Are you all right?"

I rubbed my eyes. They felt like puddles. I was trying to answer him, but I kept gasping. Finally I managed.

"Yes . . . thank you . . ." My eyes began to focus and the man's face became clearer. He patted my shoulder and moved away. I wiped my face, and after about a minute I got up and left.

❧

When I got home it was around five-thirty. Mint was in the living room studying some of his paintings. He had them lined up against the wall and was pacing in front of them with a pink lady in his hand. I was so weak that when I saw him I didn't say anything. I just walked in and stood there in my coat, staring at him.

"Hey, baby, I didn't hear you come in. How'd your screen test go?" he asked without really looking up. I was so distressed I had forgotten about it. He must have looked up and seen how upset I was, though, because he put his drink down on the coffee table and came over to me. I didn't say anything. I guess I didn't say anything because I knew I was going to cry. I could feel it happening all over again. The burning in my eyes.

"Salt? Salt, baby, what is it? What's wrong?" Mint took my face in his hands. His hands were so warm against my red, cold cheeks. It felt like my skin was suddenly melting.

"I went into a church today, Minty. For the first time since . . . and, Minty, it was . . . it all came back to me and . . ." I couldn't say any more. I really couldn't. My voice was smothered. There was this pain and it was everywhere, like fire, it was spreading into every inch of me. I felt his arms tighten around me and I collapsed against him. The thick, soft wool of his sweater blurred against the side of my face and the pain began to smolder into orange, into gray.

I don't know how long he held me like that, but it seemed a very long time. Then he led me to the couch and made me sit down with him, and I felt calmer. He brushed a strand of hair from my face and kissed my forehead.

"I . . . I didn't think after all this time it would be like that. . . . I just try never to think about it, you know? But today, when I was sitting there and it was so vivid. . . ."

Minty pulled me into his arms and kissed me so heatedly, so tenderly that my memories began to shudder and recede. When he touched me, it all seemed to go away. That day of my parents' funeral was torn from my life. My mother was still alive when I was in his arms. Her love was tangled with his, and I was desperate for it. Minty was my only way to her. She was the only serenity I'd ever known.

Chapter 11

I guess I never told you very much about Mint and me. I mean, how we met and grew up and all that stuff. I can't really tell you very much about my mom and dad, because I don't remember them all that well. I lived with them until I was five in this big building on Central Park West. It was one of those lovely old buildings with all the intricate moldings. It's still there, too. Normally they knock all the beauties down and replace them with modern-looking catastrophes, but this one's still around.

I don't remember my dad very well. He wasn't around much. I saw him in the mornings sometimes. He wore big eyeglasses and ate a lot of eggs. I would sit at the breakfast table with him, and Gloria, this day maid, would serve him eggs while I had my oatmeal. He never paid much attention to me. He was always reading the paper. Sometimes he'd take me to the park on Sundays and read the paper while I climbed on the jungle gym or fooled around in the sandbox. But he never looked up. You know how it was when you were a kid, you always wanted somebody to watch you do something. You always wanted them to compliment you on your somersault or your sand castle. Well, my dad never did that. And you know, I wanted him to say something so much that every time he took me out, I'd try like a freak to impress him. I figured that maybe if I built a really smashing castle, a really tremendous castle, he would say something. But he never did. Shit, I could have built Versailles and he just would have kept on reading his blasted paper.

My mother was different. She always said something. She called me her "little lambie." She'd say, "What a nice castle my lambie's made." I think I loved her very much. I wish I could remember her better, though. When I look at pictures, I don't see her the way I did as a kid. It's hard to remember her. I can't remember her eyes. Mostly I remember her legs. She had these very long, clever legs that could walk up stairs very easily, and I always hoped that someday I'd have long, clever legs, too.

It's funny, because even though my mind is full of static when I try to remember my parents, the day I met Minty is impeccably preserved in my brain. It's like an old film that I've watched a thousand times, like *The Wizard of Oz*. I can always remember what happens. My mother came into my room one afternoon and told me that my godmother, Mrs. Bishop, had moved into an apartment in our building with her husband and little son, Minturn. I found out all the details when I was older. Christa Bishop was my mother's closest college friend. After they graduated, Christa married her college sweetheart and moved to California, where he'd landed some important job. My mother moved to New York, where she eventually met and married my dad. Christa and my mother swore they'd never lose touch. They wrote letters constantly, and when they found out they were pregnant at the same time, they were so excited that they decided to pronounce each other godmothers of their babies. When I was five, Christa's husband landed an even hotter job in Manhattan. My mother suggested they buy an apartment in our building, and Christa and her family ended up moving into an apartment three floors below us.

So my mother was telling me that afternoon about my god-mother and how she wanted me to meet her and her little boy. I didn't know the first thing about godmothers. I figured they wore ball gowns and had magic wands. The part about the little boy I didn't like at all. First of all, I wasn't too impressed with little boys. The only one I'd ever played with before had been this red-haired kid named Spider who ate my only two goldfish. The little bastard was a menace, and since I didn't know any better, I fig-ured all boys were just like him. But since I was only five, I didn't have any goddamn choice. I had to go along to meet my god-mother and this little boy.

After my mom dressed me up, we took the elevator down to the fourth floor. When we got down to the Bishops's apartment, the door was opened by the prettiest lady I'd ever seen. She was very pale, like alabaster, with long flaxen hair and garnet red lips. She looked like a movie star. The lady hugged my mother, and then she bent down and hugged me. When she pulled away, she said, "Look at you! What a darling girl you are, Sally! Your mother sent me so many photographs of you, but you're even prettier in person."

Then Mrs. Bishop told me that Minty was very eager to meet me. I walked behind my mother. I was clutching the back of her skirt, hiding behind her. The first thing I noticed was the smell of paint. There were tons of cardboard boxes lying around and white sheets on the floor with dripping buckets and ladders on them. We entered a big room with a couple pieces of furniture and these big windows. Through the big windows I could see the tips of buildings on the east side of the park, just like I could see them from our living room windows. Then, poking my head out farther from behind my mother, I noticed someone sitting on the floor.

Mrs. Bishop went over to him and said, "Minturn, sweetheart, come meet your godmother and her daughter."

The kid had had his back turned to us, and when he started to get up I shot back behind my mother with visions of Spider dancing through my head. I heard my mother say hello to the kid, and then she bent down and hugged him. I was still hiding behind her.

"Sally, what are you doing? Come on, say hello to Minty," my mother said, pulling me out.

Standing in front of me was a boy whose drunken little legs were wobbling slightly in a pair of blue knickers, whose right hand was fondling a yellow Lego, whose gold hair was swimming out like a sunlit wave over his wondrous speckled eyes. That's when it happened. I was suddenly gripped by a feeling I'd never had before, like a cup of hot cocoa rushing warm and smooth into my belly, only better. This wasn't Spider. Never in my few years had I seen a boy like that. He was the prince in my fairy tales. The one on the white stallion scrambled in light, the mist rolling down his spine and the stars clustering in his eyes.

We were very silent in an odd, almost charmed sort of way. We spoke through our eyes. Eyes that seemed to be created from the very same genes. Our chromosomes swarmed together like a pack of minnows in shallow water, and when he took my hand and led me to his pile of toys, I felt I'd known that hand forever.

❧

From that day forward, we were inseparable. I was always at his apartment, he was always at mine. You know how it is when you first meet somebody, you usually start off at a distance from each other. You usually take time gaining each other's trust, understanding each other. It wasn't like that with Minty and me. The first moment our eyes met, we understood, we trusted. There was never a distance we had to run through, a place we had to get to;

we'd just stumbled over a treasure without even searching.

Minty even gave me my name. Officially, my name was Sally, but the first time we met he pronounced it wrong. He called me Salty. I hated my name, so I didn't tell Mint he said it wrong. From then on I wanted everyone to call me Salty. Especially since Mint was the one who made it up.

Our mothers began to take us to the park together. We'd ride our bicycles over dusty trails and swing from the branches of trees until our five-year-old hands began to sting. That fall we were enrolled in the same school. In the white mornings, our mothers would walk us. We'd all meet in the lobby of our building, and Mint and I would dart ahead of them, swinging our lunch buckets and playing hopscotch on the squares of sidewalk. In school, we always begged to sit together, to be partners at game time, to be teammates in gym. Christ, we were like peaches and cream, like Batman and Robin, like cookies and milk . . . we were the sweetest, freshest combination around.

That winter my parents decided to go to Jamaica for a two-week vacation. Mrs. Bishop told my mother she'd love to have me while they were away. I vaguely remember my mother packing my clothes and taking me down to Minty's apartment. I was very upset she was leaving and she tried to calm me down. Mint was there, fooling around with a model airplane, and she looked over at him and said, "Minty, honey, you're going to take care of Sally for me, aren't you?"

Mint looked up at her and smiled. "Yes, ma'am. I'll take care of Salty." It was the last time I saw my mother. Eight hours later their plane crashed. No survivors.

I survived. Somehow. I really don't know what I would have done if Minty hadn't been around. Sometimes I'd wake up in the middle of the night, I'd start to cry and call for Mama, over and over again. Mint would crawl down from his bunk and sit with me. He would hold my hand and tell me not to cry. I can still remember his face, glowing in the fragile light of the night lamp beside my bed. He looked like something from the Renaissance, a disheveled seraph with his rumpled gold hair and hot, sleepy hands. And he would gaze down at me, his eyes hazy with exhaustion, and wait so patiently for the storm of tears to subside.

All my toys and clothes were brought to Christa's. She told me my apartment was being sold. She said I'd never have to worry, that my mommy and daddy had left me a trust fund. I didn't understand what a trust fund was until later. Honestly, it's not something I really think about much.

By the time I was seven, I'd adjusted quite nicely. I still cried sometimes, but I wasn't a wreck. I'd gotten used to Aunt Christa and Uncle Edward. Minty's parents had me call them aunt and uncle. They treated me just like Mint. Uncle Edward would tell us these incredible stories sometimes before bed and Aunt Christa would tuck us both in. She'd give us warm milk and kiss us good-night.

Minty's career was booming, by the way. I think I told you about Minty's Gerber baby-food jars and all that. He was always being taken out of class to go do a commercial or something. I was never allowed to go with him, but he always told me about it. He'd tell me about how they made him wear icky stuff all over his face and how he had to spit out the food he was supposed to be eating over and over. I knew he enjoyed it, though. He would always make me wait around with him to see his commercials on TV.

Minty's commercial success made him very popular in school. Kids would hang around him and call him a big star all the time. Some of the nerdier ones asked him to autograph their notebooks and bookbags. Sometimes they offered him their dessert at lunch and asked him to do a line from one of his commercials.

Minty always did it for them. He'd stop eating and stand up, and everybody would start shushing each other. He'd say, "I'm always hungry for Mom's Beef Zoonies. Beef Zoonies are the best!" His Beef Zoonies commercial was his all-time favorite.

When Minty was nine, things started to change. He wasn't getting taken out of class as much and he wasn't on the tube as often. It was kind of strange the way it happened so suddenly. I mean, one minute he was all over every can of Beef Zoonies and every box of Corn Flakes, and the next minute he wasn't. It upset him for a while. I remember Uncle Edward kept telling him it was for the best. Uncle Edward was the vice president of this electronics company, and he was always telling Mint to study harder. He wanted Mint to go into the business.

"I won't ever do something boring like that," Mint would tell me. "Not ever."

By that time Aunt Christa had moved me out of Mint's room. She said we were too old to be sharing the same room, so she turned the guest bedroom into my room. I was very upset at first. I remember pleading with Aunt Christa to let me stay with Minty, but she insisted that I have my own room, and eventually I got used to it.

By the time we were thirteen, Mint's career was over. I think it was pretty hard on him for a while. He was so used to everybody making a fuss over him, and now nobody even remembered his Beef Zoonies or his Crackle Snaps. But then something happened. Something horrible. Puberty. That's what happened, dammit.

By the time Mint hit fifteen, he was right back in the spotlight. He was already five-nine and gushing with masculinity. I don't know how it happened. It just happened. Suddenly all these bitches in school were following him around, squealing with laughter when he cracked a joke, bumping into him with their ripening breasts, and I was in hell. Where had these bimbos come from? They couldn't have been the same ugly rodents I used to play jacks with in the fifth and sixth grades. They were so glamorous now. They just rammed into puberty, and all of a sudden they were glamorous-looking rodents. Jesus, I'd never want to be fifteen again.

I remember Minty's first girlfriend, Renee. She'd just transferred from Trinity, and all the guys were just dropping their pants every time she walked by. She'd screw anything. No kidding. It was like her mission in life—to fuck. A walking sex machine on automatic pilot. So she took a liking to Mint. She'd sit next to him in class and yank up her sleazy skirt so he could catch a good glimpse of her thighs. You'd see her chasing him down the hallways, her spiked heels clip-clonking, her big blazing red lips open and whining, "Minty! Ohhh, Minty, wait up! Like, where are you going?" God, what a tramp. I was completely stunned when Minty started dating her. He actually carried her books around and walked her home after school. I think it was mostly because of the guys. All that locker-room macho stuff.

Anyhow, he went out with her for about a month and then lost his virginity to her in the bathroom at this club, Danceteria, where we'd all go with our fake IDs. The night after it happened, he told me about it. His parents were out to dinner and we were watching a movie in the living room when all of a sudden he got this tremendous smile on his face. I was wondering what it was he was smiling about, since the movie was a real tearjerker. Then he told me. It damn near killed me.

"I lost it last night, Salt."

"What did you lose?" I asked like a moron. I really didn't have the faintest idea what he was referring to.

"I had sex with Renee."

You should have seen my goddamn face. I was horrified. "Why?"

"Why? 'Cause we're going out, I guess." He put his feet up on the coffee table and lit up a cigarette. He always lit up when his parents weren't around. He'd started smoking when he was thirteen.

"Well, how was it?" I asked, trying to sound undisturbed by the whole thing. I was pretty curious about how it was, though. Kids always want to know about it. It's a helluva big deal when you're a kid.

"Well, it was great. I really didn't know what I was doing, but it was fun."

Fun? It's supposed to be romantic and beautiful. Shit. "How long did it last?"

"Oh, come on, Salt, I don't know." He took a long drag on his cigarette and let out a couple of smoke rings.

"What do you mean, you don't know?"

"I didn't time it, Salt. I didn't have a stopwatch with me. I don't know. I suppose about five minutes."

"Five minutes!" I gasped. I didn't know anything about sex. I thought sex took a couple of hours or something. I didn't want him to think I was so naive, so I ended up saying, "Oh. Well, that's about right."

Minty smiled at me. He could read me inside and out.

"Do you love her?"

"No."

"Does she love you?" I pried.

"Oh, for christsakes, Salt, I don't know." Man, was he ever clear about the whole thing.

I didn't feel like talking to him anymore, so we just sat there watching this maudlin film and I started to lose all control. I was biting my lip and I knocked over my soda, and Mint, Mint was just sprawled all over the couch with this beastly smile on his face. He was so bloody calm. He kept taking these slow, sensuous drags on his cigarette, and I couldn't stand it. Now that he'd drilled this chick, he thought he was Robert Redford or some-

113

thing. It just takes one piece of ass and the guy is a damn professional. I hung around until about twelve-thirty, and then I told him I was going to hit the hay. He looked over at me and asked if I was okay.

"I'm fine, why shouldn't I be okay?"

"Because you never crash this early on Saturday."

"Oh, well, I'm beat, that's all. I want to get up early and read *The Importance of Being Earnest.*"

"You going to try out for that?"

"Yeah, the tryouts are Monday and I haven't even looked at the play." I started down the hall toward my room.

"Hey, Salt . . ." he called out.

"What?"

"Are you sure you're okay?"

"I told you, I'm fine. I'm tired. 'Night, Mint."

When I was in my room, I closed the door and went and looked in the mirror over my dresser. Tears were inflaming my eyes and I just wanted to stick my foot in a socket and let myself explode. Ha! How would you like that, Minty? You know that song by the Police, "and you'll be sorry when I'm dead, 'cause all this guilt will be on your head"? Well, that's what I wanted. I could picture it all so perfectly: the procession of shiny black deathmobiles, the church bells a-gonging, and Minty sobbing great fluorescent tears into a white handkerchief, the priest's voice, the crowds disguising their moist eyes behind mirrored shades. God, what a scene. The sadness—the despair. A white band of light strikes my coffin as I am slowly lowered into the earth. Minty is devastated. He drops bushels and bushels of roses into the ground. And wait! He is about to make an announcement! I am bleeding with anticipation. "Dear friends, how guilty I feel about this tragic incident. Only do not dwell on the past— proceed with your lives! For this is what I am going to do. On the fourth of next month, I am wedding my lovely Renee. My first lay! I invite you all." The crowds go wild! Holy shit! Here I am lying in the gutter in a blasted box, and all these maniacs are celebrating. I slaughtered the vision. Suicide wasn't the answer.

It was at that moment, standing in front of the mirror, that I realized how much I loved him. I'd always loved him, but I felt something different now. When he touched me, I didn't want his touch to end. When he hugged me, my stomach plummeted like an anchor, my heart beat like a demon. And all I knew was that I wanted him. I wanted to look into his eyes and stay there. I wanted to kiss him on the lips and run my hands through his burning white hair. My reflection was blurring and smearing because of all the tears in my eyes, and I kept thinking what an ugly bastard I was. My body was like a bumbling vertical line; I was always stuffing socks in my bra and waiting for my hips to show up. Why did Renee have hips and breasts? Where were mine, for petesakes? I wanted my mother. I wanted her so much then. I wanted her to sit with me on my bed and tell me it was okay. Tell me about what it was like for her at fifteen. Sometimes Aunt Christa would have talks with me. When I complained about my ugly boyish body, she would say, "Salty, darling, you're only fifteen. Some people develop faster than others, but you will." But it wasn't the same as having my mother. I couldn't tell Aunt Christa that I was in love with her son. I could have told my mother. I hated the fact that I could have told my mother.

Aunt Christa was right, though. In the following year my marvelous bones began to swell, my hips got a little fuller and I actually got some breasts. What a sumptuous thing—to emerge from a gray cocoon and discover you are beautiful after all, only temporarily disguised in adolescence. I can't sit here and bullshit you that I was any Raquel Welch, because I wasn't. But I finally had a few curves. My hooters weren't all that big really, but it wasn't the end of the world. I had a nice pair of cheekbones where all that baby fat had been. Guys in my class who'd never looked twice at me where beginning to notice me all of a sudden. One especially: the captain of the baseball team, Jason Ross. Shit, did I think I was clever to have Jason Ross leaving me notes in my locker and saving me seats in English. The guy was brain-dead, but it didn't matter. It wasn't his brain I was interested in. It was his reputation. God, what gorgeous bait! What perfect propaganda. Basically what I'm telling you is, I was using the big oaf to make Mint jealous. Unfortunately, I wasn't aware there were certain flaws in my brilliant plan—that this hoax wasn't going to be as easy as I had imagined. I couldn't just pretend to be his girl, I had to make it look good. You know what I'm talking about.

So I lost my virginity to him. God, it was a nightmare. We were in his red Corvette. His loaded dad had given him this Corvette for his birthday. It was the most idiotic thing in the world. I can understand giving a kid a car if he lives in the suburbs, but to give him a car when he lives in the city is just plain retarded. You can't even park in the city without getting a pain in the ass. Jason couldn't have cared less. He was always driving around because he thought the car made him look like a hotshot. He'd hang out the window and crank up the stereo. The worst part was his obsession with the horn. The guy was always honking the goddamn horn. Even if there was no traffic and he was the only guy on the road, he'd still honk the horn like a maniac. He gave me a first-class migraine.

Anyhow, like I said, we were in his stupid car and he'd just beaten Trinity on the final game of the season so he was even more in love with himself than usual. He drove into the parking lot of Area, this club where we were meeting everybody. So I started to get out of the car, but he had something else in mind. He latched onto my blouse and yanked me back in, and then he started to let loose with all this terrific bullshit about how much I meant to him and how I was the only girl he'd ever loved. The most terrific bullshit I'd ever heard in my life. I knew what he wanted, of course, and I was going to tell him to forget it, when something happened. I'd seen Mint earlier that evening at a bar we'd all gone to after the game and he'd been making out with his current flame and, God, did it piss me off. I still had the image of it in my head and I was really furious about it. I guess that's why I ended up doing it with Jason—because I was so pissed at Minty and all his damn girlfriends.

God, what a stupid mistake it was, though. It was one of those really big mistakes that come back to haunt you a thousand times. I remember, I was just sitting there watching Jason fumble with his pants. As soon as I told him okay, he didn't waste a second. He didn't even try to warm me up with some foreplay or anything. He just tore off his pants. God, what a romantic bastard he was. Then, after he got his pants off, he climbed into the backseat and said, "Gimme a rubber, Salt. They're in the glove compartment." When I opened up the glove compartment, it was like a prophylactic avalanche. He must have had about a hundred rubbers in there. I'd never even seen a rubber before. I'd seen the square packets lying around on Mint's dresser a couple times, but I'd never seen the rubber itself. I wasn't exactly dying of curiosity either.

When I got into the backseat I handed Jason the damn packet and watched him tear it open with his teeth. He was a goddamn animal. Then, as he was putting the condom on, he kept telling me to take off my jeans. I hadn't even thought about that. The second I took them off, he crawled on top of me. He hadn't taken a shower after his ball game and he really smelled like a landfill. So he kept trying to stab himself into me but it wasn't working. He got very annoyed that it wasn't working. He told me to relax. I think I was hoping he'd give up, but then he finally pushed himself inside me. I remember there was this godawful pain, but I think it was more mental than physical. The pain was in my heart, and it's funny, but the whole time he was thrusting into me I wasn't even underneath him. It was as if I were just watching the whole thing. Watching myself as if I were some other girl with tears running down her face.

When it was over, Jason sat up and tossed the rubber out the window and told me I was a real natural and all this crap. Then he pulled his pants back on and crawled into the front seat. He started to fix himself up in the rearview mirror. He started to comb his sweaty hair and smile at himself in the mirror while I was just lying there in the backseat bleeding all over the place. When I told him I was bleeding, he couldn't have cared less. He kept fixing himself up. And when I asked him if he had any Kleenex, he told me to chill out and that the club had a can. That's when I pulled my jeans on and got out of his car. I started to walk as fast as I could to the street. I remember Jason yelling at me. He kept screaming "Where the hell do you think you're going?" and "What's your problem?" I didn't stop for a second. As soon as I got to the curb, I hailed a cab.

When I got home, I had to walk past the doorman with a big bloodstain on my jeans, I didn't even have a sweater to wrap around my waist or anything. When I got upstairs, I cleaned myself up and then I fell down on my bed. I was crying like crazy. Mint came home about half an hour later and knocked on my door.

"What?" I said. I knew it was Mint. He always knocked on my door the same way. He'd knock three times. When he came in, he sat on the side of my bed. I was lying on my stomach with my face leaning on my crossed arms. Mint started to stroke my hair.

"Salt, I heard about what happened."

Oh, Christ. Jason had already blasted it all over the place.

"Mint, please, I don't want to talk about it." How desperate the sound of my very own voice. Sometimes when you speak you don't even notice how you sound. But this time I noticed. I sat up slowly and looked at him.

"You know, Salt, I'm here for you. If you need me or some-thing, I'll always be here for you."

He was spinning in my eyes, and you'll never know how much I wanted to say, "Minty, I love you." Tell him it was all a stupid scheme. That I was only dating Jason to have him. Only I could-n't do it. I couldn't tell him. So all I said was, "I just wish it hadn't happened. I don't love Jason . . . I . . . I'm so stupid."

"Salt, we all make mistakes. You went out with him for a long time, you enjoyed being together. I mean, I saw the way you used to look at him. You may not have wanted to lose your virginity to him, but those things happen."

If he only knew, God, if he only knew how synthetic those looks were! How wooden below the surface.

"It wasn't like . . . like you were raped or anything, was it?"

"No. No." Only yes. I was raped. Only hours ago there had been a child inside me, and now she was gone. I let him take her, crying, in his frightful arms. I wish to God I could have given her to Minty. Because I knew she would have been all right with Minty.

❧

When Mint and I graduated from high school, we decided to get an apartment together. His parents weren't too jolly well pleased with the fact that we didn't want to scoot off to college, but they didn't force us. They listened to our explanations over coffee in the living room. They sighed, stirring sugar into their porcelain cups, as Minty announced his dream of opening a restaurant with

Anthony. "I'll use my own money, of course," he said, referring to the bounty he'd made from his childhood career. They sighed equally as much when I expressed my wish to be an actress. Ever since I had won the role of Cecily in *The Importance of Being Earnest*, I'd fallen head over heels in love with acting. Acting let me disappear for a while. It let me be someone else. When I was on the stage I was able to forget about whatever was hurting me, I could immerse myself in a character and forget the way Minty looked at some bimbo. Besides being a terrific distraction, acting was something I found I was good at. I'd never been a genius at school, so it was very reassuring to find something I excelled in. I remember I used to get very depressed on the closing night of a play. It always felt like an old friend was going away. I'd go backstage after everyone went home and take something from the set as a souvenir. Not a goddamned chair or anything. I'd take a matchbook or the fake cartridge from a gun or the feather that fell off my hat. I still have all that stuff in my scrapbook, too. Anyhow, I told Aunt Christa and Uncle Edward that I wanted to take acting classes and find an agent. Like Minty, I had the money, money from my trust fund. I just had to convince Aunt Christa to let me use it for this.

After many hours, many sighs, and many cups of coffee, Aunt Christa and Uncle Edward reluctantly decided to let us do what we wanted. I figured they would anyway, because they'd never been a couple of Spartans about discipline. Uncle Edward had given up on his dream of Minty going into his business a while back. By eleventh grade it was clear through many a report card that Mint would not be attending Yale, as Uncle Edward had. It wasn't that Mint was an idiot; he was really rather bright. He was just more creative than academic. Anyhow, his parents helped us find an apartment on the East Side.

When Mint and I were twenty, Uncle Edward's company opened another branch in London, and he and Christa moved there. They came back to visit us every so often, but we didn't really see them all that much. We talked quite a bit on the phone, though. At times I really missed Aunt Christa. But I had Minty. I had the angel child who had stitched my wounded heart, and whose mere presence kept those stitches from unraveling.

Chapter 12

About three days after my screen test, I got a call from my hysterical agent. She told me I got the part, and did she ever kiss my ass all of a sudden. All of a sudden I was her most treasured client. It's amazing how the minute you start making money for somebody, they're in love with you. Anyhow, after about ten minutes of praising the holy almighty out of me, she went on to tell me about the part. She told me I had a helluva lot to do since I aired right after Christmas. She said I had to sign all the contracts and meet with the head honchos at the studio and get a wardrobe fitted.

I wanted to call up Mint at the Pigeon and tell him the news right away, but then I decided to wait until he got home. I was so wired with excitement over the whole thing I couldn't even sit my ass down in a chair. I paced around like a shooting-gallery duck, with a cigarette hanging out of my mouth. For hours I was circling around like a maniac.

When Mint came home, as soon as he walked through the door, I ambushed the poor bastard. He hadn't even set his keys down when I flung myself on top of him. He was staggering around, trying to keep his balance, asking me what the hell I was doing. Then, when I told him, he got this big smile on his face and he said we had to celebrate. He went off and got a bottle of Dom Pérignon from the liquor cabinet. He always kept two bottles of good champagne in the apartment for special occasions. In the living room, Mint made a fire and we sat on the rug in front of it. He poured the champagne and held his glass up to mine.

"To my baby, the soap star!" he said ebulliently.

"Oh, come on, Minty, I haven't even aired yet."

"Yeah, I know. But you're going to be sensational."

After we'd had a few glasses of champagne, Mint lit a cigarette and lay sideways on the rug facing me. Firelight trembled across his face and trickled down the side of his neck. I swallowed hard, seized by torrents of emotion. My hand reached into his hair and he leaned over me, kissing me with his hot, smoky mouth. I melted beneath him, my mind thrashing with memories. When he pulled back, I gazed into his eyes.

"Do you know how long I dreamed of this? Of us together? When we were in school, I was so jealous of all the girls you went out with. I always used to imagine us like this. Sometimes I still can't believe it's real," I said quietly.

Mint brushed a strand of hair from my eyes and smiled. "It's real, Salt. It's real."

The night of Mint's opening, we arrived at the gallery at about seven-fifteen. Nobody was there yet except the bartenders and a few regular employees. I'd never been down to the gallery before, but it was just as I'd expected. It had your characteristic white walls and wood floors and track lighting and all that. But what made you know it wasn't just any old joint was that it was so huge. It had these incredibly high ceilings and large spaces that flowed into each other. Plus it was in this very impressive lime-stone-fronted building.

"Where's Jori?" I asked Mint.

"He must be in his office. Come on."

He grabbed my hand and led me to the back of the gallery, where we came to a closed door. Mint rapped on it nervously a couple of times before it was opened by Jori, who was barking into a wireless telephone. When he saw us, he motioned for us to come in with his free hand, shut the door, and began to stomp around the room like a Nazi storm trooper.

"What do you mean, the fuck hasn't got it? I'm running low, Jack. . . . What? . . . Oh yeah, well, I'll tell you what, you tell the fuck to get his ass in gear or I'm taking my business elsewhere, you got that? . . ." Jori moved behind his desk and stood with his back to us, looking out the window.

Mint and I ended up sitting down in the two horrible-looking double-jointed chairs across from Jori's desk. Jesus, was it an ugly office. About as warm and inviting as liquid nitrogen. Everything was black. And I mean everything—Jori's desk, the walls, the chairs, the phone.

". . . You just tell the son of a bitch that! I've got to go, Jack." Jori swerved around suddenly, his left hand compressing the phone antenna into obscurity. "Sorry I made you wait. Some urgent business I had to take care of," he said, replacing the phone in its cradle and slicking back his raven black hair. It wasn't in a ponytail this time, which revealed its true Rapunzelesque length. All the way down to his armpits. The thing is, hair like that looks okay on some puberty-stricken kid whose hormones are doing the cha-cha but on Jori, well, he just needed some god-damn scissors.

"Well, Minty, this is it. How do you feel?"

"I feel great. Nervous, but great."

"No need to be nervous. Why don't you try to relax . . . have a drink."

"Yeah. Yeah, that's a good idea."

As Mint stood up, Jori walked over and put an arm around him. "Cheer up, my man! This is just the beginning." Mint smiled, and Jori removed his arm and turned to me. "Salty, you take our man out there and make sure he has a good strong one. I've got to finish up something, but I'll be with you momentarily."

Our man? What was Mint, a commercial property? I stood up and took Minty's hand, and we left the office.

By seven-forty-five, the place was a mob scene. It's amazing how a place can be so barren and silent one minute, and then so cram-packed the next. Shit, there was some pandemonium going on. There were a lot of women in tight, black dresses with brick red lipstick and powdery white skin. Some of them had these exotic chunky earrings on and some of them had very fancy hair twisted up on top of their heads like modern sculptures. Practically all of them were smoking and they were all very chic and French-looking. To tell you the truth they all looked as phony as hell. Like they really stood naturally with a hip jutted out, head thrown back, an arm bent up against one side with the cigarette jutting out between their fingers. Then there were a couple of real weirdos. There was some fortyish-looking dame in a pea green dress with a live lizard on her shoulder. She had a pin on her shoulder and it had this gold chain attached to it, and at the end of the chain there was a collar for the lizard. There was a lanky black woman with this African stuff on. She had about fifty silver bangles on her arms and all these beaded necklaces and a silver hoop hanging out of her right nostril. It wasn't a small hoop, either. No, this was like a goddamn onion ring, for christsakes. How does somebody live like that, is what I'd like to know. It's gotta be pretty damned annoying to have a hoop the size of an onion ring stuck through your nose.

The men weren't as diverse as the women. The majority of them were in their forties and fifties. They were all very tailored-looking, very spiffy in dark suits with fancy watches and shiny shoes. A lot of them were smoking pipes or cigars.

At around eight o'clock, the press arrived. They plowed through the crowds to get to Mint. And suddenly flashes were going off like fireworks and Minty was deluged in the madness, his eyes squinting at the frantic gale of light. He was the new sensation. Minty baby; the press was wild for him. Wild for the blond boy, the so-blond-on-blond boy. The crowds kept closing in on him from every side and I felt myself being shoved backward. Lit cigarettes were waving near my flammable outfit and the fat broad with the lizard practically ran me over, and I thought, Fuck this shit. I wasn't going to hang around and get a concussion or something.

So I maneuvered out of the chaos and made my way over to the bar, which wasn't nearly as crowded. I asked one of the bartenders for a glass of champagne, and then I leaned back against the bar and watched Mint from a distance. Jori was standing next to him now. He had his arm around Minty and this huge smile on his face. Everybody was still leaning in toward Minty and the photographers were still swarming around and Jori kept sticking his tanned mug into every photograph.

I took a sip of champagne and dug my fingers into the bowl of nuts on the bar. I'd just popped a couple nuts in my mouth when I noticed Johnny Vane arriving. He made one of his usual dramatic entrances. He swept into the gallery in this long black cape and dark sunglasses with a supermodel looming on his arm. He thought he was Zorro or something. He was an absolute imbecile. He tore right through the crowds to get to Mint, dragging this amazon along behind him. Then, of course, he had to get himself into the photographs. As soon as he reached Mint and Jori he scrambled in between them and started to pose all over the place.

I decided not to watch it anymore and went over and looked out the gallery window. The streetlights were splashing down all over the cobblestones and there was some guy in a tweed overcoat walking one of those funny-looking pug dogs. The dog was wearing an outfit, a red sweater with some goddamn booties or galoshes or something and it looked retarded. And you could see the dog didn't like it one bit, either. It kept pausing every three seconds and then it would lift up a foot and shake it like a bastard. As if the poor dog needed galoshes in the first place. It wasn't even snowing or raining, for christsakes.

I kept staring out the window. I didn't feel right in that gallery. I felt like running out of there. I felt like crying or punching someone in the nose. It reminded me of the time I lost my mother in the Museum of Modern Art. I let go of her hand for a second, and suddenly she was gone and all these gigantic grownups were swarming around me and I was terrified. I thought I'd never find her again and that I'd be forced to spend the whole rest of my life in goddamn MoMA. That's how I felt that night at the gallery. It felt like I was a lost little kid and that Minty was being swept away and I'd never find him again.

I was still staring out the window when I realized I had to use the john. Someone was in the one and only ladies' room, but while I was waiting, the bartender told me that since I was Minty's girlfriend I could use the one in Jori's office.

I started to press through the mobs, since Jori's office was on the other side of the joint. It must have taken me half an hour to get to it—I would have been better off waiting. When I found the door to the john, I yanked it open without knocking and, God, it was awful. Jori was in there. He didn't have his pants down or anything, but he was hunched over the sink with a straw up his nose. He jerked his head up, and at first I thought he was going to start screaming at me or something, but he didn't. All he did was say, "Why, Salty, what a pleasant surprise." His voice had this terrible creepy sweetness and it scared the hell out of me.

I was so nervous all of a sudden that I didn't know what to say. I muttered, "I'm sorry . . ." and then I was about to take off when he moved forward and grabbed my arm.

"Care to join me in a line?" he asked, as tranquil as hell.

"No . . . no, I don't feel like it." I don't know why I said something so stupid. No, I don't feel like it. As if I felt like it on other occasions. I'd never done a goddamn drug in my life. I'd never even taken a puff off a joint or anything. I should have told him I didn't do drugs, period. I guess I said I didn't feel like it because I was nervous.

"You seem nervous. Anything the matter?" His black, overgrown eyebrows arched up and a subtle smile formed on his lips. His face was so close to mine I could see all the damage in his bronzed skin, the deep creases in his forehead and the crisscross of spidery lines under his bloodshot eyes.

"No . . . I'm fine." I was trying to act all cool and tough, but it wasn't working so well. He hadn't released his grip on my arm and I was really getting frightened.

"But you're trembling." He said it practically in a whisper, with that irritating smile on his face. I couldn't stand it anymore. I yanked my arm away.

"I'm fine."

"I see. Well, then, go ahead." He stepped out of the doorframe into his office and gestured to the bathroom. I looked at him warily. "It is the bathroom you want, isn't it?"

I nodded.

"Please, be my guest." God, you should have heard the sticky, syrupy tone in his voice. When I first met him, I wasn't sure, but I thought there was something wrong with him. Now I knew—he was a lunatic.

I moved into the bathroom really fast, shut the door, and locked it behind me. I was so anxious now I didn't even have to go to the john anymore. But there I was in his john with his stupid cocaine all over the place. Well, it wasn't exactly all over the place. There was one line left on the black marble counter of the sink. I didn't even want to look at it. I ended up looking at this framed photograph on the wall above the toilet. It was a picture of Jori and Vane and Andy Warhol. They must have been at some nightclub, because the background was stuffed full of spastic beams and choppy silhouettes. Jori was between the other two. His inky black hair was loose, pouring limply down on either side of his face, and his grinning mouth was gaping wide open. Vane, who was on Jori's right, looked about ready to pass out. He was waving a glass at the camera, and his eyes were half shut and melting. Warhol was Warhol. His hair was like a blob of whipped cream and he was staring at Vane with this absolutely vapid look on his face. All I could think when I looked at that picture was what a disaster it was. Instead of seeing three successful guys at the height of their glory, all I saw was three narcissists who needed a good kick in the ass.

When I turned around I saw that the wall opposite the toilet was jam-packed with nude studies. They were done in pencil and, boy, were they perverted. I'd never seen such pornographic drawings in my life. A bunch of bimbos all straddling each other and having an orgy. Then I noticed the artist's flashy signature. It was Jori. Jori drew all this garbage.

I had to get out of that bathroom. I was getting very claustrophobic all of a sudden. When I opened the door, I saw that Jori was pacing around behind his desk. He was on the cordless phone again, yacking in Italian. I left the bathroom and darted through his office as quickly as possible.

By nine-thirty the crowds had pretty much simmered down. The voices were trailing off, crackling down the elevators, into the street. The bartenders had started to clean up, stacking glasses stained with lipstick, fogged with fingerprints. I went up to Mint and kissed him. He tasted like gin and lemons.

"I sold six paintings, Salt," he announced, grinning from ear to ear.

"That's wonderful! I'm so proud of—"

"Hey, Minty, come on!" Jori trumpeted out. He was grabbing a long black overcoat from the coatrack.

"What's going on?" I whispered to Mint.

"Oh, Jori's invited us and a couple others to Canal Bar for dinner."

"Now?"

"Yeah."

Before I could say anything, Mint grabbed my hand and started to lead me over to the coatrack. Ah, shit. I wanted to hang out with Jori and his clan like a hole in the head. Especially after witnessing that business in the john. I couldn't do anything about it, though. Mint was all revved up and raring to go.

So we ended up piling into Jori's limo. It was one of those Mafia jobs with the Scarface chauffeur and tinted windows. It had these tiny yet potent lights on the ceiling, plus a complete array of gizmos and gadgets, electronics, and rattling bar. There were six of us altogether: Jori and some dame who looked vaguely familiar from the nude studies on the wall in his bathroom, and Vane and his six-foot-two raven-haired skeleton, who spent the whole ride staring at her warped reflection in the silver champagne bucket.

The trip downtown went something like this. Vane would occasionally look over at my outfit and wrinkle his forehead. The dame with Jori, the one who looked familiar, had obviously been sniffing around his sink since she was about as calm and composed as a mechanical bull. She was perched on Jori's lap and kept squirming and bouncing and snorting and giggling. Jori had put on a pair of mirrored shades the moment he left the gallery so I couldn't even tell what he was looking at. All I remember about the conversation in the limo was that Jori and Mint had a discussion about how collectors can be manipulated. Jori yacked the most, though. I remember he went into this very impassioned speech about how the simply different and merely clever can be promoted as truly inventive and genuine by unscrupulous dealers.

I just stared out the window and watched all the blokes with spiked blueberry hair and nose rings go by.

At one point, God, this killed me, the limo came to an abrupt halt at a red light and the chortling creature on Jori's lap lost its balance and toppled to the floor with a terrific thud. Mint paused in the middle of another prophecy to ask it if it was okay, but Jori told him to forget about her. The chick, by the way, didn't move. It just sat there on the floor with legs splayed and electric red dress hiked up to pelvic region. It was when I saw her in this lurid position that I knew for certain that I'd seen her on Jori's bathroom wall.

When the limo finally stopped in front of Canal Bar, the chick was still on the floor. She started to scream then because she saw something she liked outside the window. She stumbled up with about as much grace as a gorilla and tore open the car door and shrieked, "No way! Ronnie Darling! God, you're wicked. I love you! You know, I've always loved you!"

Indeed, it was Ron Darling. He was standing in front of the place with three thugs, who I assumed were bodyguards, and did not even look in her direction. But seeing as how she was not the type to throw in the towel so easily, she continued to scream at Darling. And I've gotta tell you, she was really looking stupid doing that. Finally Jori stepped out of the car and grabbed her arm, shook her, and began to drag her inside the bar, saying, "Come on, baby, he's just a motherfucking pitcher."

Canal Bar was a pretty small joint. It had a stripper painted on the wall beside the bar, a mirrored dining area, and cowhide on the covers of the menus. We got a table in the back, where I had the good fortune to sit across from Jori. Mint was to my right, and Vane, thank you God, was way the hell down on the other end, his raven-haired date choosing a seat near him that allowed her a perfect view of herself in the mirrors. I really don't want to yack about the whole dinner because there's no real reason to torture you with it. But there were a couple of things, like Jori never taking off his sunglasses, that stick out in my mind. I knew why he was wearing them, of course, since I'd seen his gorgeous red eyeballs when I encountered him in the john, but, Jesus, did he ever look stupid wearing a pair of shades at dinner.

Then there was that creature of Jori's, which didn't seem to be familiar with the art of eating with utensils. When its prosciutto and melon arrived, it giggled in glee (yet another thing it found sidesplitting—a plate of ham and melon; it was easily amused, this creature), and dug in with its hands. It was, I'm afraid, rather unpleasant to watch.

Mint was more talkative than ever. He and Jori kept getting into one discussion after another. They hardly glanced at anyone else at the table. Plus, you should have seen the way Mint was kissing Jori's ass. Every time Jori told a joke or story or something, Mint would start to laugh like a goddamned madman over it, or he'd say, "Oh, that's brilliant." Brilliant, for christsakes. I'd never heard Mint refer to anything as brilliant in his life, except perhaps some oncoming headlights.

Everybody was about halfway through their main course when Vane shot up out of his seat and uttered a poignant "Shit!" He was wiping the crotch of his pants with his napkin. Apparently he'd spilled pesto sauce all over them. He stormed off to the bathroom, the greasy napkin still fluttering in his hand. His departure was accompanied by a series of "shits," which turned the head of many a patron.

Later, when it came time to order dessert, Jori ordered the chocolate mousse cake all around. He insisted that it was fabulous and everyone must have a piece. After he announced this, Vane's skeleton raised her bones and told the waiter she would not be having a slice. Jori interrupted her and told the waiter she *would* be having a slice. "*Non, non, vraiment* . . . reeely . . ." she protested, and Jori said, "You must have a slice, Gazelle." Gazelle? Jesus, her name was Gazelle? The waiter stood there unsure of what to do, since Jori kept saying, "Bring her a piece," and Gazelle kept saying, "*Non, non,* reeely." All the rest of us at the table just sat there in complete silence watching this, our heads sloshing back and forth to Jori, to Gazelle, to Jori, to Gazelle, until the waiter, who'd been holding a pen suspended in front of his pad, finally scribbled something and ended the quarrel with a curt, "I will bring her a piece."

What occurred after that was really unbelievable. Gazelle started to sob and, rising up out of her chair to her glorifying six foot two inches, sped off. At first I thought she'd left the place, but then I spotted her making a sharp turn toward the ladies' room. The poor woman was hysterical. Why? Over a piece of goddamn chocolate cake. You would have thought Jori was trying to get her to gobble up a plate full of arsenic or something. The truth is, I felt pretty bad for her. I assumed she'd been brainwashed by her agency or by all those anorexic advertisements, and subsisted solely on diet pills, ice cubes, and toothpaste. Shit, did I hate it sometimes. Manhattan, that is. Sometimes I just wanted to live way the hell out in the boondocks where I wouldn't have to bump into any coked-up art dealers or starving models or baseball players. That's the problem with Manhattan. You never get a moment's peace. You're surrounded by lousy big shots

and preppy killers and jackass suits. By wannabes and the ones
on the guest list and all the air-kiss bastards and Eurotrash and
aspiring debutantes, and nobody gives a shit if you drop dead in
the middle of dinner because everybody's too busy gossiping or
applying lipstick or rejecting wine or blowing smoke through
their nostrils. And outside, some poor bastard is staggering
around in the steam and slush, rattling a tin can full of pennies
and gum balls and pro-choice buttons. Everywhere you look
there's some poor bastard half frozen or half plastered or half conscious. The pavement is erupting with drills, the subways are clat-
tering and rumbling so nobody hears the screaming as the guys in
the masks open fire. The blood just blends in with the graffiti
anyway. In the morning all the bastards come back for more.
They swarm onto the streets like larvae, dripping with sweat,
throbbing with rage. Bicycle messengers with callused palms and
surgical masks swerve through gridlock like schools of fish. Over
a static-filled CB, a cabby converses with the Middle East while
the boss lady boils, "Why the hell are you going up Madison!
Park is much faster!" But nobody hears her. Her voice is drowned
out by a passing siren, by the static, by the cabby's radio, which
pulses out something rebellious in Mexican now. I could go on,
but I'll shut up.

Anyhow, I ended up going into the ladies' room after Gazelle.
I found the human toothpick hunched over the sink making dismal noises, her spinal cord jutting out like a chain saw.

"Hey, it's okay, Gazelle," I said, walking up to her.

She took her face out of her hands for a second and looked at
me with mascara-smeared eyes. "*Non . . . non*, you don't underztand. Zee agency, she don't want me if I put on zee kilos."

Put on the kilos?

"But you're incredibly skinny. You shouldn't worry."

"*Non.* One cake, and I am zrough. Jori underztand nozhing."
She sobbed on.

I put my hand on her hunched-over shoulder. If she'd been standing up straight, the highest I could have reached would have been her hipbone. Her shoulder wasn't so pleasant, anyway. Go to Kentucky Fried Chicken, buy yourself a chicken leg, and eat all the meat off of it—there you have Gazelle's shoulder.

"Why don't you come back to the table? You don't have to eat it."

"*Non.* I will stay here, reeely. You come tell me when cake is not zhere, yes?"

I told her I'd come tell her when cake is not there. So I went back to the table and sat through dessert. Mint asked me what was up with Gazelle, and I told him I'd tell him later. Jori and Vane didn't ask anything. About as sympathetic as two scorpions, those two. At one point Vane asked if anybody would like Gazelle's slice of cake, and Jori's creature seemed extremely interested. It stretched an arm out in Vane's direction and said, "Ohhhh, I want it. I want it. Gimme." It belonged in a playpen, for christsakes. When the dessert was cleared away, I went back into the can to fetch Gazelle.

By now it was twelve-thirty, and Jori, after paying the tab, suggested we all hit Au Bar. I couldn't stand the idea, but everybody else was thrilled, including Mint, who I knew despised Au Bar as much as I did. So we all piled back into the limo. The Creature once again perched on Jori's lap, bits of chocolate cake still lodged in the corners of her mouth (no, she was not familiar with napkins, either).

Mint was beside me, rambling about the club scene with Jori. Jori kept mentioning all these new clubs and Mint kept making comments about them. I'd never seen Minty act so phony in my life. He kept saying stuff like, "Oh, that club won't last. Trust me. It's not trendy enough." Or "The place is outrageous. I hang there all the time." I wished he'd shut up and sit down because he was giving me a pain in the ass.

About five minutes before the limo arrived at Au Bar, the Creature discovered something: the sun roof. It had been playing around with all the mechanical buttons, flips, switches, and so on when suddenly it hit the sunroof, and presto, the damn thing opened. To be frank, I am not particularly fond of sunroofs in the middle of December at fifty miles an hour. But the Creature was just delighted. It spent the whole rest of the ride to Au Bar standing up on the seat with its goddamn body stuck through the sunroof. Every two seconds it would scream "Wooooooo! Wooooooo!" I kept hoping it would fall out of the car or something, but it never did.

Anyhow, welcome to Au Bar. If you've never had the pleasure, let me give you a quick description. Au Bar is a very ritzy midtown club. You need to be in one of these three categories to gain admittance: Category One: Rich and famous. Category Two: Sleazy and European. Category Three: Breathtaking and brain-dead. Since I was in a party that had at least one person from each of these categories, I was able to move smoothly inside without being knocked unconscious or twisted into a pretzel by the two possible relatives of Mike Tyson who guarded the joint. Jori seemed to be a devout patron of Au Bar; upon seeing him, the maitre d' raced over, and I do mean raced, and announced that he would "have a table ready momentarily, Mr. Jori." Au Bar, you see, is not only a club but a restaurant. On one end there is the dance floor, surrounded by flowing *Arabian Nights* curtains looped at the waist with thick ropes of gold sparked with tassels. Behind the curtains are small linked rooms decorated with plush red velvet couches, gleaming sconces, and foxhunt paintings. These rooms are occupied primarily by dirty old European men from Category Two, who, after scanning the dance floor, would abduct something from Category Three (breathtaking and brain-dead) and drag her off to one of the rooms. On the other side of the place was the dining area and bar. The dining area catered mostly to those in Category One (rich and famous). This was where we ended up.

"A magnum of Roderer Cristal!" Jori blurted out to the waiter right after we were seated. I could have sworn the waiter bowed to Jori before he went off to retrieve the bubbly.

"Tonight was one of the best nights of my life, Alessandro," Mint said to the imbecile, who was seated on his right. He'd already told him that at dinner.

Jori leaned back, smiling guilefully. "You're young. You've got plenty ahead of you."

Mint lit a cigarette and ran a hand through his hair. "Do you think it will last, though? Maybe it's just a transient—"

Jori put his broad, tanned hand on Mint's shoulder and cut him off. "Hey, hey, hey, of course it's going to last! Warhol wasn't talking about you when he said famous for fifteen minutes. You're a hit and you're going to stay at the top. Hey, put out that cigarette and have a cigar, my man. It's time you started getting used to the good life." Jori pulled out his cigar case and handed Mint a cigar. Mint stubbed out his cigarette and held the cigar out in front of him. He was looking at it like a little kid looks at a gigantic cookie. "Well, go on. It's Cuba's finest," Jori added, passing him a gold lighter.

After Mint lit it, the champagne arrived and Jori decided to make a toast. He seemed to live for that shit, making toasts. The thing is, when you make a toast you're normally supposed to be commending somebody other than yourself. Am I going a little nuts, or is that not the standard procedure? When Jori stood up, he let out all this rubbish about his keen eye and his magnifico discovery and how he knew straight from the start Mint would make a killing, etc. He used Mint's name, but basically what he was doing was honking his own goddamn horn.

About five minutes later, a song came on that Vane seemed deeply fond of. The song, not to my astonishment, was "I Want Your Sex" by George Michael. Vane insisted that the group dance to this number. He rose from his chair and clapped his hands in an effort to gain our complete and utter attention, and we all ended up following him out onto the dance floor. The dance floor was probably registering 7.8 on the Richter scale. I'd never seen anything so crammed and vibrating. Vane didn't seem to mind, though. He rudely cleared us a path by bumping and shoving people out of the way as Jori shouted out encouraging comments such as "Atta boy, Johnny! Charge!"

When Vane reached the middle of the floor, he halted and peered around for his troops. When we were all gathered, he began a series of movements suitable to a porn star, bumping and grinding his hips toward Gazelle, who had commenced some kind of aerobics. She had the dental floss of both arms straight against her sides, her fists clamped, and she would raise her forearms as if lifting barbells while running in place. Jori and the Creature were just as nauseating. He was about as lewd as Vane, while the Creature just looked like she was having an epileptic fit. She'd jerk, twist, bounce, throw her head to the side, and swing her arms, and all this was accompanied by that irritating "Wooooo! Wooooo!" that seemed to be the only remark she deemed suitable to describe an experience she found amusing.

I'm not such a gorgeous dancer, but dancing around these guys made me feel like Baryshnikov. Mint, now, he was a sensational dancer. And I'm not just saying that because I'm biased and thought everything he did deserved a couple of medals and a round of applause.

Anyhow, our group danced, and then the rest of the evening went something like this: Group returned to table. . . . Creature passed out around 2 A.M. . . . . Gazelle amused those of us remaining and conscious with a story about a friend of hers who had all the fat sucked out of her butt. Liposuction, you know. But apparently her friend had too much sucked out and she ended up with no butt. She had a butt in a jar. A goddamn Smucker's butt. . . . At around two-thirty, something from Category Three approached Vane at the table; Vane knew this bird, called her "darling." . . . Two-forty, Vane left with bird and Gazelle burst into tears and jogged off to the bathroom. Two down, three to go. . . . Three o'clock, Mint finished fifth glass of champagne and didn't look so good. I told him we should go, and he gave me a wobbly nod. . . . The last thing I remember is Jori splashing a glass of ice water on the Creature.

2

When Mint and I got home that night, I was pretty goddamn distressed. Not because Minty had been a hit. I wasn't distressed about that. What bothered me was the scene surrounding him. Jori's scene. It was the most arrogant, destructive scene I'd ever laid eyes on, and I'd seen plenty of New York scenes in my short lifetime. And Jori, well, I'd never liked that bastard to begin with. I probably shouldn't have said anything, but I couldn't stand it. After Mint and I got into bed, I was so upset I couldn't knock off or anything. I just kept rolling around and thinking about it until I had to wake Mint up.

"Mint? Minty?" I moved over and shook him a little.

"Oh, come on, Salt . . . not now . . . I'm too tired . . ." he grumbled. I think he thought I wanted to do the wild thing or something.

"I don't want to have sex, Mint. I need to talk to you." I kept shaking him.

"What is it? Can't you tell me tomorrow?" He opened his eyes and I quit shaking him.

"No, Minty, I'm really upset about something and I can't sleep."

"Okay. What? What is it?" He sat up a little and looked at me. I didn't say anything for a moment. "Well, what is it?"

"Minty, I was going to the bathroom tonight in the gallery and . . . I barged in on Jori. He was snorting coke. Then he grabbed my arm and asked me if I wanted a line."

Minty raked his bangs back and sighed. "So?"

"What do you mean 'So?' He does cocaine."

"So, he does a little blow. What's the big deal? Tons of people do it."

"You've always been against drugs."

"Look, what's your point, Salt?"

"I'm worried, that's all. It scares me. You being involved with him."

"That's ridiculous. What do you want me to say, Salt? You want me to say I'm gonna break off this deal with Alessandro because he does some coke? Because that's not gonna happen. He's giving me the opportunity of a lifetime."

"But, Mint—"

"No. This is ridiculous," Mint said harshly. "You really piss me off. I've just had the best night of my life, and you have to lay all this crap on me—"

"Minty, I didn't mean to. I was just worried about you."

"Well, you can stop worrying 'cause it's idiotic. Alessandro's a good guy. He's doing everything he can for me, and I don't give a shit if he does cocaine. Now go to sleep, will you?"

He didn't say anything else. He rolled over with his back to me and this horrible silence surrounded me like dark, cold water. I felt so frightened.

I slid up against him. "I'm sorry, Mint. Please don't be angry with me. I never want to hurt you . . ." I whispered, pressing my cheek against him.

He didn't say anything, he just rolled over and pulled me into his arms. And all my fear was ravaged. He was like something mythological. Something bloodless and shimmering, a merciful angel who had come to drive away my tempests and devour my despair.

Chapter 13

My debut on the soap was right before Christmas. Had to wake up at four-thirty in the morning. What a nightmare that was. A rooster doesn't even get up that early.

Part of the reason I had such an early call was that wardrobe wanted to fit me some more. I'd been going in that whole past week for fittings for Laura's wardrobe. Laura's parents had fortunately been fairly well off, so she was able to afford a rather nice wardrobe which consisted primarily of chic, sexy-looking blouses and skirts. She wore a lot of tailored jackets in black and yellow, and almost always these ridiculously high-heeled shoes that were so high I had to practice walking in them for a week 'cause I was afraid I was going to fall flat on my ass.

When I arrived at the studio at five-thirty, the place was already buzzing. The hallway lights were blaring, and announcements were spilling out over the horn. Actors were milling around, smoking cigarettes, and gulping coffee. Through open dressing-room doors you'd see some guy rehearsing, screaming "You bastard!" to a chair or a lamp or something. By seven-thirty I was assigned to my dressing room. I was sharing with Lola Walters, a regular on the show, who played Jenny Bregman, the psychotic daughter of Edward Bregman, who was the wealthy CEO of Bregman Enterprises and also the father of Andrew, the preppy jerk who was in love with my character. (Have I lost you yet?) Anyhow, Lola's character was supposed to have one of those multiple-personality disorders, and Edward was so embarrassed by it that he stuck her in this chichi loony bin. It was a hell of an acting challenge to play Jenny, since Lola had to assume a different personality every two days.

When I first met Lola, she greeted me at the door of our dressing room with a beehive of curlers on her head and offered me a vitamin pill. I was soon to discover that Lola was a vitamin guru, a health nut. Lola, you see, originated in L.A., where she'd begun her career in a series of sloppy flicks that never made it to the big time. Before she got her big break on this soap, she'd spent a sufficient amount of time on the "Coast" to adopt that "Tofu, anyone?" mentality. I mean, the woman ate rice curd and beeswax and birdseed and green things I wouldn't go near with a ten-foot pole. I'd rather live in a place where everybody is killing themselves than live in a place where everybody is trying to break a record and live to two hundred. God, do I love the suicidal atmosphere of New York. Nobody cares. Nobody gives a flying fuck. They smoke, they drink, they slurp up saturated fat, and when a big bus chugs by, they all breathe in deep to get a good riveting whiff of that exhaust. But out on the Coast, well, those guys are always doing the right thing. You even think about lighting up around one of them, and they'll club you over the head with a surfboard. They're all lifting weights, popping vitamins, eating foliage, hanging upside down like a bunch of bats. Is all that stuff really necessary for a few extra years? Well, maybe it is; I don't know. I don't want to tell anybody what the hell to do, if you want to hang upside down like a bat, it's your own damn business.

At about eight, Lola and I and a couple other actors were ordered to go to Rehearsal Studio B. When we got there, the director, this tubby guy in a baseball cap, started to block scenes. He wasn't the only director, but he was the one we got that day. Lola whispered to me to beware because he had this real Jekyll-and-Hyde personality. She wasn't kidding, either. One minute he was very calm and good-humored, kidding around with a couple of actors, passively eating a Danish, and then the next minute—*Wham!*—the Danish was flying through the air, the guy's face was bright red, and he was shaking his fists and ranting and raving "I told you to move down left! Left! Do you know what left is? And you! You're not even in this scene! What are you doing here? Where's Sam! Somebody find Sam. This isn't a junior-high play, where you can traipse in two hours late! This is television, dammit!"

Lola ran her scene before me. After she went off to Makeup, I sat down on the floor and leaned back against the wall with a couple other actors who were waiting around. Out of the corner of my eye, I spotted Lucas slipping into the rehearsal hall in a long black overcoat. He darted over to the wall where everybody was sitting and slid down next to me.

"Hey, it's Salty, right?" he said. His hair was damp and kind of spilling over his forehead and he looked very cute.

"Yeah. Hi." I lowered my script and smiled at him.

"He hasn't called our scene yet, has he?" Lucas gestured to the director, who was in the middle of another tantrum. He'd whipped off his baseball cap and was smacking some actor over the head with it.

"No."

"Oh, good." His face relaxed a little and he started to unbutton his coat. "I knew you'd get it, you know. You were definitely the best."

I was stunned that he said that. "Really? The others weren't so good?" I asked.

"Not as good as you." He smiled at me and took a crumpled-looking script out of the pocket of his overcoat.

"Thanks," I said.

"Hey, what dressing room are you in?"

"I'm sharing with Lola Walters."

"Oh, cool. Lola's great. Don't be freaked out by all her herbs and holistic stuff, though. You'll get used to it. She's always trying to cure the cast. Last week Mick came in with a sore throat and she chased him around the whole day, trying to get him to eat this green crud in a jar."

Right then the director called our scene. We were doing the same one I'd done for the screen test. I was kind of afraid I'd do something wrong and the director would start yelling at me, but he didn't. He was actually very nice to me. He shook my hand and welcomed me to the goddamn show. Then he turned to Lucas and said he'd seen him sneak in, and that if he came in late again he'd murder him.

After we blocked the scene, I went to Makeup, came back down to the set for a fast walk-through, and had about an hour break, in which I studied my lines.

At around one-thirty I was called down to the set for a dress rehearsal, and then we taped the scene. I was kind of disappointed with the way it went, though, because I didn't cry. Well, I cried, but only one tear fell out of my right eye. I kept trying to squint so more tears would fall but it just wasn't working. I figured Lucas was going to think I was nearsighted or something, and ask me if I needed glasses.

He didn't though. When the scene was over I guess he could see I was kind of upset about it. He was really nice and told me it happens to a lot of actresses, especially when they're nervous. Lucas had another scene to shoot directly after ours, so I told him I'd see him later and went off to the actors' lounge for some chow.

The actors' lounge was a medium-sized room with a lot of couches and a gigantic TV where you could watch the scenes that were in the process of being shot. It had a table full of all that suicidal East Coast chow: donuts, Danishes, cookies, bagels buried under heaps of cream cheese—just looking at this table must have given Lola a coronary.

That first day, I saw most of the stars of the show in the lounge. They all seemed pretty nice, actually. There was this one guy, though, who couldn't sit down and shut up for a second. Some actors need a helluva lot of attention, so they tend to perform around the clock. This guy, for example, he got up to get a donut at one point, and turned it into a three-part drama. Part One: He leapt off the couch and imitated that Dunkin' Donuts guy (the pudgy one with the mustache), waddling over to the snack table and saying, "Gotta make the donuts. . . . Gotta make the donuts. . . ." Then, when he was sure all eyes were on him, Part Two began: He grabbed three donuts off the snack table and started to juggle them like a circus clown. Hoots and clapping from various lounge members ensued. On a roll, he began Part Three, which I didn't understand: He held two donuts in front of his eyes as if they were glasses and said, "No, no, Mitchum, I'm looking for despair. Give me anguish . . . more anguish! I want absolute misery! Dig deep, Mitch—that's it! Yes! Use your instrument. . . . I want pain! Pain!" Much laughter and more applause. (On my third day on the soap, I got an inkling as to what was going on when I got a director with huge eyeglasses who thought every scene, even if it wasn't a tragedy, should end up looking like the last act of *Romeo and Juliet*.)

When I finally got home at about seven, Mint was off at the Pigeon. I decided to take a hot bath and study my lines for a while. I got into the tub with a cigarette hanging out of my mouth and started to look over my script. What a nightmare. I mean, if Tennessee Williams or some very good writer had been

around to read this, he probably would have committed suicide
or something. Andrew, the preppy jerk who's in love with me,
gets hit by a speeding laundry truck on his campus, and I get a
phone call at his apartment from the hospital, saying Andrew
wanted them to notify me. So I go over to the hospital, and when
I get there the nurse informs me that I can't see Andrew because
he's slipped into a coma, for christsakes. (It's right about here
that Tennessee would have thrown himself out the window.) Just
then Edward Bregman rushes up and asks the nurse where the
hell his son is. When she tells him about the coma, he clutches
his head and reels backward against the wall. While Edward's
staggering, I get a close-up while my character suddenly realizes
this would be an opportune moment to seduce Andrew's incredibly wealthy, widowed, grief-stricken father. (Tennessee is long
gone by now.) So I slink up to him and tell him I'm a good friend
of Andrew's at college and that I'd just left him outside the library when the accident happened. Then I pretend to be over-
wrought with despair, and Edward begins to tell me what a gentle
boy his son is and all this crap. The scene ends with the doc coming out and informing us that Andrew has suffered a depressed
skull fracture and that the degree of damage is difficult to assess,
but the prognosis isn't too promising. At this, Edward gasps, "Oh,
God . . . no . . ." and I reach out and tenderly squeeze his hand.
Oh God is right. At that point I tossed the script on the floor—I
couldn't read this crap anymore. I slid underneath the water and
counted how long I could hold my breath.

Chapter 14

Holidays. They annoy the shit out of me. I hate to be so depressing, but they really do. Maybe I'm just being pessimistic about it because Mint forced me to go to Jori's Christmas party. Well, he didn't hold a gun to my head or anything, but either I went with him or I stayed home, ate a pot pie, and watched *Miracle on 34th Street.* As much as I hated the idea of Jori's, I couldn't stand the thought of sitting through *Miracle on 34th Street.* Not that it wasn't a nice movie. I'd just seen it fifty times already.

So when Christmas Eve rolled around, off we went to Jori's apartment, which was located on Fifth Avenue right across from the Met. We got there a little after eight, since we had trouble finding a cab. Outside his building, the street was cluttered with limousines, double-parked and gleaming. A few of the drivers in their crisp navy blue uniforms were leaning up against their masters' mobiles, gabbing with one another to pass the time, exchanging tidbits of dirt about their employers. What a merry Christmas those guys have. Waiting around forever in the freezing cold for the big cheese to swagger down and tell you what a blast he had.

Anyhow, Mint and I went into the building. The doorman was
this very spiffy-looking chap with white gloves. From the mechanical way he moved and gestured, you would have thought
he'd just graduated from West Point or something. The lobby was
one of those dim, creepy-looking affairs with a lot of red lacquer
and sconces, and the elevator was one of the old-fashioned gizmos with the brass gate and steering wheel. At last we made it to
the penthouse. The gates rattled open. Marble and mirrors was
the theme. Jesus, do I hate mirrors. I guess it's because I'm always
doing stupid things and I'd rather not have to watch myself do
them. That's one thing about mirrors, they don't bullshit. They
show you exactly what you're doing and they don't fast-forward
the lousy stuff.

Mint rang the doorbell and started checking himself out in the
mirror. He looked like a million bucks: shiny black shoes, long
black cashmere coat hanging open, tux beneath, blond locks
slicked back. A goddamn work of art. Me, well, I looked okay.
Not worthy of any frame, mind you, but I wasn't half bad. I was
wearing that taffeta dress I wore on Thanksgiving. Dangling from
my earlobes was a pair of my mother's diamond earrings that I'd
worn maybe once before.

My hair was hanging loose, blending into my black wool cape.

The door finally opened. Drumroll, please. . . . Before us was a
maid in a black outfit with a white apron. Good evening. May
she take our coats? Yes, thank you. Please, follow me. We followed the maid into the enormous marble-floored entrance
gallery. You should have seen what was hanging on the goddamn
wall. You know those Warhol silk-screen portraits? Well, Jori had
this huge four-panel painting of himself. Right there in the goddamn entrance. The maid led us into the living room then, and
you've never seen such a pretentious display of wealth in your
life. Beneath our feet was an Aubusson; surrounding us were
gilded Louis XIV armchairs; way, way in the distance on the west

side of the room were windows draped with weeping silk brocades. Afloat on every richly ornamented table were vases filled with exotic melanges of flowers. And, of course, art. Beckmann, Hockney, Braque . . . extraordinary pieces. Oh, and the Christmas tree. Talk about a Christmas tree. How they got it in the elevator is something I'd like to know. This was the fattest, tallest tree I've ever seen indoors. It was slopped over with tinsel, twinkling with ornaments, scintillating with lights.

Shit, was it crowded in this room. All the guests were yacking in clusters while brigades of servants offered caviar and champagne. Mint dragged me across the room. He'd spotted Jori by the window.

"Alessandro," Mint said when he reached him.

"Minty, Salty, how wonderful you could make it." He smiled mildly and whispered something to the *Playboy* centerfold standing beside him, who quickly departed.

"This is just incredible," Mint said, glancing out the window at the Met.

"Yes . . . it is." Such a modest guy, that Jori. Jesus, was he ever a modest guy. "Just you wait, Minty, someday you'll be able to afford a place like this."

Minty didn't say anything, he just stood there looking out the window. Jori was watching Mint looking out the window. I was watching Jori look at Mint look out the window.

Finally Jori broke the silence. "I have some news for you. This morning, a good friend of mine, Alec Stone, came down to the gallery and bought *Iced Motion*."

Mint looked at Jori, wide-eyed. "You're kidding! I didn't think anyone would touch it. *Iced Motion* is the largest canvas I've done."

"With the largest price tag, too." Jori winked at Mint and took a sip of champagne. "Listen, Alec's here tonight. He's dying to meet you. Let's go find him. Salty, would you excuse us for a moment."

"Oh . . . sure," I said cheerily. I leaned back against the windowsill and watched Jori put his arm around Mint and lead him off. I turned to look out the window, and saw my frowning expression in the glass. I was mad. Why couldn't I go along and meet this Alec? I almost felt that Jori was jealous of me and wanted to present Mint as his date or something.

I stayed by the window for about five minutes, and then I decided to wander around, braving the mobs: "Excuse me, pardon me, excuse me." I dipped a triangular piece of toast into a bowl of caviar. Damn good fish eggs. I went over and paid my respects to the Christmas tree; I stood in front of a painting of a nude recumbent bimbo eating grapes; moved away; sat in a gilded armchair and smoked cigarettes and dropped ashes into a marble ashtray. When . . . oh, no, it couldn't be. Oh, shit. It was. Jori's creature was coming right toward me, wearing a red catsuit with courtesan cleavage and high-heeled boots.

"Hey, didn't I meet you last week at Regine's?" she asked me, scratching the blob of red hair on her head.

"No, I don't think so."

"Well, I know I've met you. Wait, let me think. . . ." Silence, please, the Creature is thinking . . . using all three brain cells. You might want to go get a cup of coffee or something, since this may take a while.

"Oh, I know! I know! I met you at Jacob Spitzer's party."

She was as sad as hell, but she really thought she'd placed me. I decided to tell her she was right. I figured that way I'd get rid of her faster.

"Ohhh, wasn't that party wicked? Jacob's such a . . . such a . . . such a . . ." Go on, work those brain cells; we're looking for a descriptive word now. ". . . ultra-stud. Don't you think he's an ultra-stud?" She sat down in the empty chair next to mine and stared at me.

"Oh, yes. A regular ultra-stud, that Jake."

"You mean Jacob."

"Oh, right, I mean Jacob."

"Hey, you think maybe I could have one of those?" She pointed to my cigarette. I took one out of my bag and handed it to her.

"Listen, would you excuse me? I have to use the bathroom," I said, stubbing out my cigarette.

"Oh, yeah, sure."

I got up and moved like a bat out of hell. I didn't really have to use the can; I just wanted to get out of that room. I wanted to sneak around for a while. Check out the rest of the apartment.

The first room I came upon was what I assumed to be the library. It was, I have to admit, incredibly beautiful. Two walls of it had built-in paneled bookshelves. There was a marble fireplace and a gigantic desk with legs carved into claws. There was also this huge glass case of African stuff, masks and spears and all that. They must have been worth a fortune, because they were extremely decayed and crumbling—which means the suckers were from B.C. or something. I snooped around the bookshelves for a while. Jori's taste in literature was rather disturbing. He seemed to have a passion for violence. Books like *Helter Skelter*, *A Clockwork Orange*, *Mein Kampf*, *In Cold Blood*, *The Execution-er's Song*. On the opposite bookshelf, he had all his art books. There must have been three hundred of them. Everything from the Lascaux cave to the birth of cubism, surrealism, realism, pop—you name it, he had it.

After the library, I came into a mirrored room full of weight machines, barbells, and other bullshit. It was a gymnasium, for petesakes. I'll bet you anything Jori had never laid a finger on any

of it, either. He was about as muscular as Cinderella. I kept on
going.

The bedroom was a bloodbath. He had a fur bedspread and a
water buffalo head over the fireplace. Right over his bed he had
this huge Max Beckmann. Jesus, do I loathe that Beckmann. All
he ever seemed to paint was a bunch of people with chopped-off
arms and blood gushing out all over. Who the hell wants to sleep
with something like that over his head? Jori, that's who.

I went over to a closed door at the end of the bedroom and
opened it. Stupid, *stupid* thing to do. I was greeted by a growling
Doberman pinscher the size of a moose. Well, not really the size
of a moose, but the fangs seemed to magnify its bodily dimen-
sions. Anyhow, I wanted to shut the door but the dog was
halfway through it, so I just kind of backed up, v-e-r-y s-l-o-w-l-y,
saying all that futile stuff you say to a dog when he's about to eat
you. Stuff like, "Nice, sweet puppy . . . friendly vegetarian
puppy . . . oh, yes, what a good boy . . ." And you know, it
worked. The dog stopped growling and tilted its head sideways
and shoved an ear forward. Poor dog. It was probably starved for
attention. Jori probably yelled at it and kept it locked up all the
time. I reached out my hand carefully and the dog moved forward
and sniffed it. After I dared to pat it on the head, well, let me tell
you, I had the pooch wrapped around my finger. It folded up its
hind legs and sat very nicely, its stubby tail twitching.

After I'd scratched the dog for a while, I went into the bathroom, where it had been. It moved in right along with me, was
just crazy about me, this dog. The bathroom was monstrous. It
had a tub that could hold about six people. I went over to the
sink and opened up the medicine cabinet. Nobody should ever
let me into their house, because I always end up going through
their medicine cabinet. Jori's was like a pharmacy. A pill fiesta.
I'd never seen so many bottles of pills. Along with the pills there

were a couple of bottles of cologne and hair mousse. I'd just reached in and grabbed a bottle of pills to examine the prescription when Jori appeared in the doorframe. Scared the shit out of me.

"We always seem to encounter each other in the bathroom, don't we?" he said.

Lord, was I embarrassed. There's nothing like being caught snooping around in somebody's medicine cabinet. You can't make up an excuse, either, because nobody's going to buy the story that you had a migraine and were looking for some aspirin. They know damn well what you're up to.

"I'm . . . I'm sorry, I had a headache and was looking for some aspirin," I said. Well, it was worth a try. I fumbled with the pills in my hand and stuck them back in the cabinet.

Jori's lips twisted up into a maniacal smile. He didn't say anything, though. He didn't buy the headache.

"You have a gorgeous dog," I blurted out.

He still didn't say anything. He just kept smiling and staring at me. I couldn't think of anything else to say, so I decided to just walk by him. I'd almost reached the door when he stuck out an arm and pressed his hand against the doorframe, blocking me. His face was right up in mine, the nicotine brown skin matted by pores, the nostrils raw and wincing pink.

"You don't like me, do you, Salty?"

I was really shocked that he said that. I folded my arms across my chest and glanced away from his searing black gaze. "No . . . I like you," I mumbled. What the hell was I supposed to say?

"No. No, I don't think you do." He was so goddamned serene. From the tone of his voice, you'd think he'd just asked me to pass the mashed potatoes or something. "It's too bad, you know . . ." He dropped his arm and pushed himself against me. "Because I'm really quite fond of you," he whispered in my ear. I'd backed up against the glass door of the shower, and he reached out his arm and idly ran a forefinger down the side of my face. I jerked my head away. I was completely disgusted. Who the hell did he think he was to stick his stupid finger on my face? Boy, did I want to tell him to go jump in the lake. But I couldn't. Minty would have been furious. So all I did was say, "Excuse me," and stormed past him.

I zigzagged through the maze of rooms till I got back to the party. Things hadn't changed much since my departure. Everybody was still babbling in clusters, except for one guy who'd lost his mind and was pounding out a drunken interpretation of "Santa Claus Is Coming to Town" on Jori's Steinway.

God, *Miracle on 34th Street* would have been a thousand times better than this. All I wanted to do was go home. I was just standing there, thinking about it, when I spotted Jori strutting into the living room, so I ducked into a cluster. I didn't even look to see what cluster I'd ducked into, since all I wanted to do was hide from that sleazebag. Of course, out of all the clusters in the joint, I had to end up in the one with the Creature. But it was worse than that. It was the Creature's cluster. What I mean is, the whole damn thing was made up of the Creature and her followers. It's hard to imagine that the Creature had followers, but apparently she did. A group of four women all trying to impersonate the Creature. All dressed in similarly lewd outfits, all seeming to have undergone lobotomies. Good-looking? Yes. Very good-looking, but looks are immaterial when the mouth opens and words like "Bummer!" and "Potty" chirp out.

Upon my arrival in this cluster, the Creature took me under her wing and introduced me to the other creatures as a close friend of Jacob. This Jacob must have been quite a popular fellow, since all the creatures began to ooh and ahh in unison. One of the creatures actually waved at me. Think about that for a minute. I can understand waving to someone if you're on a cruise ship pulling away from the dock; I can even understand waving to someone if you see them coming down the street. But to wave at somebody when they're standing four inches away from you is just plain idiotic. Another one did something even more peculiar: She gave me the thumbs-up sign. You know, the kind the Fonz gave. I didn't know if she expected me to give her one back or what.

I couldn't bear it anymore. I told the whole mess of creatures to pardon me, and slipped off to find Mint. I must have scanned the entire room for fifteen minutes before I spotted him in a cluster by the Christmas tree. I went over and tapped him on the shoulder.

"Mint."

"Hey, babe." He smiled down at me. I leaned over and whispered that I wanted to go home.

"Salt"—he raised an arm and squinted at his watch—"we've only been here for an hour."

"I know, but I really want to leave."

Minty sighed and took a sip of champagne. "If you really want to leave, then go. I'll see you back at home," Mint said evenly.

"You're not going to come with me?"

Mint looked down at me, and then he gently gripped my arm and led me away from the cluster to the windows.

"Look, Salty . . . Jori is a very important person, and he was nice enough to invite us, and I'm not just going to waltz in and out of here. It's rude. I'm having a good time. I don't know why you can't loosen up and enjoy yourself for once."

"It's just not my kind of crowd, Minty."

Mint regarded me wearily. All the voices in the room were crackling and smearing.

"Okay. Go home. I'll see you later," he said listlessly. He walked past me and went back over to the Christmas tree and rejoined his group.

I just stood there and watched him for a moment. Watched

him roar with laughter over something. God, I didn't understand. What could he like about this? The most interesting part of my evening had been my encounter with Fido in the john. Minty kept laughing. I didn't want to watch him anymore. I turned away and went to get my wrap.

When I came out of Jori's building, I decided to walk a couple of blocks. It had begun to snow, that powdery kind of snow that melts the instant it touches something. It was around nine-thirty, and Fifth Avenue was pretty much deserted. All the lights were on in the windows, all the Christmas trees shimmering. I ended up walking all the way home, thinking about what I was going to do with the rest of the night. All of a sudden something occurred to me when I was about five blocks away from my building. I thought of old Gooter. I don't know why he just popped into my head like that, but I thought of him and figured he was all alone. Some old guys, they have a couple of geriatric friends who hang around with them and play gin rummy, yack about their ailments, but Gooter didn't seem to have any. At least, I'd never seen him with anybody, and I ran into him a decent amount. So anyhow, I decided to go up and have a little Christmas celebration with him.

At the dinky-looking deli about a block away from home I picked up some groceries. I got a loaf of French bread, some cheese, a chocolate cake, and a bottle of wine. Yes, the deli sold wine. A five-dollar Mexican wine called Fine Dry Gonzales, "from the Gonzales vineyards." Nothing like a Fine Dry Gonzales. The grocery guy, he knew me, because I always bought cigarettes in there. He was a short, bald Italian guy who always tried to get you to buy more stuff.

"Ah, you like-a the Fine-a Dry Gonzales? I have-a some pastrami that would go perfect with the Gonzales," he announced as I dumped everything on the counter.

"No, no thanks, this is fine."

He tried with the shrimp salad after that, and finally gave up and came back to the cash register. Whenever I went in there to buy cigarettes, he'd try to get me to buy more cigarettes. "I gotta some nice Camels here. You like-a Camels? Or what abouta the menthols? I gotta Virginia Slims one hundreds in the menthols. She's a good cigarette." I always had to explain to him over and over that I only smoked one brand. He wasn't a bad guy or anything. He just made an extra effort because he didn't get a helluva lot of customers.

When I got home, I went straight up to Gooter's. I rapped on the door about ten times before he opened it.

"Mr. Gooter? Hi. Are you busy?"

Gooter squinted at me. He was standing pigeon-toed in a pair of ancient slippers, brown polyester pants, and a red cardigan that was buttoned wrong.

"Who?" he mumbled.

"It's Salty, Mr. Gooter."

He had glasses on one of those chains around his neck, and he groped for them and put them on. "Salty . . . oh, my. What are you doing out in the hallway?"

I held up the groceries and told him I thought we could have a little Christmas party.

"Well, that's fine. A girl of your age should go to parties. You have a nice time, now. Thanks for dropping by. . . . " He was about to close the door, for godsakes.

I held out my hand and stopped him. "No! I want to come in! Celebrate with you!" I shouted. I had a feeling his hearing had dramatically deteriorated since the last time I saw him.

"With me?"

"Yes! May I come in?!"

"Oh . . . oh, sure. Sure, you can." He shuffled aside, and I walked into his apartment.

I'd been right. He was alone. And you know, it was just the

saddest thing, because you could see he'd tried to make a little Christmas for himself. He had this miserable-looking two-foot Christmas tree on the coffee table, with one dilapidated ornament hanging off of it. Beside the tree there was a can of yams with a plastic spoon in it, and on the windowsill stood this five-and-dime plastic Santa Claus, the kind teachers use to decorate kindergarten classrooms before Christmas vacation. The worst part was the TV. He had the TV going, and it was some telecast from St. Patrick's Cathedral or something. And you know how sometimes the image is screwed up? From what I could figure out there were a bunch of kids singing carols because on the top of the screen you could see all these hands holding out open books, and on the bottom was a row of heads. It was just awful. I could picture exactly what Gooter had been doing before I showed up. He'd been sitting in that beat-up armchair that had the imprint of his rear end in the plushy used-up seat, eating yams out of the can, watching a bunch of hair and books sing "O Come All Ye Faithful." His dog, by the way, was passed out cold under the coffee table.

"I was just watching the Christmas show," he said, returning to his chair. He groaned and slumped down into it. You could see it was quite a big ordeal for him to sit down.

I set down the groceries on the floor and walked over to the telly. "This isn't a very good picture, Mr. Gooter." I fiddled with the vertical hold for a few minutes. It still was horrendous reception, but at least now you could see what was going on. All the kids in white robes were singing in front of Jesus on the cross.

"Well, I'll be . . . will you look at that. When I was a youngster, I used to sing in the church choir like that. Yup. As a matter of fact, I used to play the trumpet, just like Neil Armstrong." I think he meant Louis Armstrong. I'm pretty sure he didn't mean the astronaut.

"You played the trumpet? Well, that's great." I went over to the bag of groceries and started to unload them on the coffee table. "Mr. Gooter, I have some wine and cheese and bread—"

"Can't drink wine. Gives me gas," Gooter said suddenly, his eyes still glued to the set.

"What about some cheese and bread?"

"Who? Who's dead?" Gooter turned to look at me.

"No. No, I said bread! Bread!" I held up the bread for visual stimulation. Gooter didn't seem too interested in it. "What about some cake? Some chocolate cake?" Bingo. I hit the jackpot with the cake.

"Cake. Like cake. My wife, Rugela"—he pointed to the picture of Tallulah Bankhead next to the Christmas tree—"she used to bake me cake sometimes. She died, you know? Died on our wedding day. She ate a bad fig at the reception and got poisoned. Happened in a matter of seconds." He snapped his fingers and shook his head back and forth. "I won't go near figs. You get a bad fig and it can kill you in seconds."

Gooter turned back to the TV, and I went into the kitchen. After I found two plates, a knife, a couple of forks, and a glass, I went back into the living room. I cut Gooter a slice of cake and handed it to him.

He scrutinized it for a second, then stabbed his fork into it. "That's good. Good cake," he said, chewing. Zelda, the dog, must have smelled the food, because she was suddenly coming to life; she lumbered out from under the coffee table, wet black nose pulsing, the shiny new bell on her collar ding-a-ling-a-linging. She went straight over to Gooter and sat in front of him, her front paws with the yellowish nails pressing into Gooter's slippers. "Well, what do you want? You want some cake, don't you, old girl?" Gooter leaned down and set his plate on the floor. Zelda went over and wolfed down the cake, licked her chops, and returned to Gooter's slippers, where she collapsed, panting. Getting up to eat a piece of cake was like running a goddamn marathon to this dog.

"Say, how's that beau of yours?" Gooter asked me. I handed him a second slice of cake and sat down in the chair next to the coffee table.

"Minty? He's fine."

"Good-looking fellow, that Miffy. Yup. Very good-looking. Reminds me of that actor, the drunkard . . . " Gooter looked off into space for a second. "The one in *Lawrence of Arabia*, you know?"

"Peter O'Toole?" I volunteered.

"Yup. That's it. That's who I'm thinking of." Gooter looked back over at the TV. Minty did look a lot like a young Peter O'-Toole, come to think of it. "Your Miffy, he's got a job?"

"He owns a restaurant," I said, pouring myself a glass of Fine Dry Gonzales.

"Oh, yes . . . the Marzipan Parrot."

"Pigeon."

"Penguin?"

"The Marzipan Pigeon!"

Gooter started to bring his fork up to his mouth, the wavering chunk of cake that he was lifting falling onto his cardigan mid-route. "Dirty birds, pigeons. City is full of pigeon poop," he commented, trying to pluck the piece of cake off his cardigan. It broke apart into a zillion crumbs. Gooter looked back up at the TV screen. The kids in the white robes had stopped singing, and some high priest was standing up front, going on about the Virgin Mary and the miracle birth of Jesus in the barn.

"You going to have any children?" Gooter asked me.

"Someday. I hope so."

"Miffy want children?"

"I . . . I think so."

"You got all your eggs?"

Did I have all my eggs? I had a feeling this was a reproductive question.

"Do you mean, am I fertile?" I asked him.

"Well, you see, a woman, she's got to have eggs to have a child. Yup. Gotta have eggs." Gooter nodded thoughtfully. "Miffy ask for your hand yet?"

"Has he proposed? No. Oh, no." I took a sip of the Fine Dry Gonzales. Big mistake.

"Well, I don't see why not. A fine young lady like you. . . . You remind me of my Rugela. Choked to death on a fig at our wedding reception, God rest her soul." Gooter gazed over at the picture of Tallulah Bankhead and sighed.

"It must have been awful for you to lose her. I . . . my parents died when I was very young, and . . . I know it's very hard. . . ." I stopped talking and looked down at Zelda. When I looked back up at Gooter, he was staring at me.

"You never told me about that," he said.

"Oh, I don't think about it very much. I mean, I don't discuss it with people. . . . It was a long time ago." I felt my eyes watering, and Gooter stretched out his bony hand in my direction. When I took it, he squeezed my hand in his.

"It might have been a long time ago, but it still hurts. You ever want to talk about it, you come to me, Salty. I know how it is. The pain comes back. It just comes back." It's funny, but for that instant, Gooter didn't seem senile at all. I wiped away a tear that was beginning to roll down my cheek and smiled. "You promise me you'll come to me if you need to, okay?"

"Yeah . . . yeah, sure. Thanks, Mr. Gooter."

He reached out his other hand and placed it on top of my head. I think he wanted to stroke my hair or something but forgot that's what he had in mind, so he just left his hand there on top of my head. I didn't mind, though. It was really kind of nice.

A few seconds later he passed out. His hand slipped off my

head and his chin slumped down onto his chest. I got up and put the rest of the groceries in his fridge, except for the Fine Dry Gonzales, which I poured down the sink. I decided to leave the TV on. I thought it was probably comforting to him to have the TV going. Right before I split, I leaned down and kissed his cheek.

"Merry Christmas, Mr. Gooter. . . . Merry Christmas."

Chapter
15

"I just feel so helpless," he muttered, lowering his gaze.

"I know. But try to remember that there's always hope. You can't give up hoping, Ed," I said gently, gazing at him across the hospital bed where Andrew lay unconscious, hooked to four different machines. He was swathed in bandages and there was some sort of snorkel taped to his mouth.

"You're right. I'm just . . . this is so difficult, Laura. I went through this only three years ago when my wife was crushed by that . . ." Edward's eyes glazed over, and I walked toward him and placed a hand on his shoulder. He gripped it fiercely and looked at me. "Oh, Laura, you've been so helpful to me this past week. I can't thank you enough for all the time you've—"

"Ed, please. I want to be here with you. You shouldn't be alone."

"Would it be an imposition if I asked you to have dinner with me again tonight?"

"Of course not." I paused, staring deeply into his eyes. "I'm here for you, Ed." The camera held on us for a moment, then zoomed in on Andrew, whose right eyelid was faintly twitching.

"Cut!" the director cried. "Good work, people!"

"Thank God . . ." I mumbled. We'd taken the scene three times because the heart monitor kept going berserk. I took off Laura's silver earrings and looked up at Mick Kelsey, who played Edward. He was smiling at me.

"What?" I asked him.

"Lucas and I are going to grab some dinner. You want to join us?" he asked.

"Yeah, sure. I'd love to," I said.

Mick was around forty, and he was one of those suave, distinguished-looking bastards. He had dark, wavy hair that was graying a bit at the temples, and a long elegant nose. Mick wasn't anything like his character, though. Mick was a goddamn madman. But I don't mean that in a bad way. What I mean is, he was just kind of reckless and eccentric at times. He was the type of guy who'd set his finger on fire just for the hell of it. When I first met him, I noticed that his left forefinger was all scarred and screwed up. When I asked him what happened to it, he told me he'd set it on fire back in '72. I didn't know what the hell to say, or what you're supposed to say to something like that. "Oh, that's nice"? I thought he was pulling my leg, but then I asked Lucas about it, and Lucas told me he wasn't kidding. The funny thing was, you'd see Mick come riding up to the studio on his goddamn Harley with his busted finger and a red bandana tied around his head, and then an hour later he'd come down the hall and you'd never recognize him. He'd be Mr. Edward Bregman in a stylish three-piece suit, with his hair all coiffed and his scarred finger disguised with makeup.

Anyhow, after we all changed we went over to Cosa Mia, this Italian joint about three blocks from the studio. I was walking in between them, and Mick offered me one of his cigarettes. Mick smoked like crazy. He smoked Marlboros, and he smoked them the way those French bastards do, always keeping one in the corner of his mouth. It would stick to his lips after a while and he'd talk with it bobbing up and down. He didn't even take it out to tap off the ashes, just kept smoking until they fell off by themselves and spilled all over his leg or his shoe or something.

Cosa Mia wasn't a fancy joint, but it wasn't a dump. It was very rustic, with a brick oven and big bunches of dried flowers in straw baskets. We got a corner table by the oven. I sat next to Lucas, and Mick sprawled out in the booth seat. Our waiter was named Luigi, and he was as excited as hell to see us. He was also a little plastered, you could tell. He kept wavering around, and forgetting which specials he'd already mentioned and even what they were, and making up his own damn specials on the spur of the moment.

"Tonight we gotta the Fusili Gennaro with the jumbo shrimp, and then we gotta the Penne Gorgonzola with shallots and, um, ah . . . the Fettucine Paesano with, uh . . . chopped tomato, and the Penne Gorgonzola with . . . jumbo shrimp and the Fusili Gennaro with chopped garlic and shallots . . ." Finally, Luigi stopped talking and right out of the blue told Mick he was crazy about Mick's jacket. Mick was wearing his big bruised biker's jacket, and you could see Luigi was nuts about it. He told Luigi thanks. I'd noticed that both Lucas and Mick were very polite and said "thank you" and "please" when somebody was taking their order or something. Not all the actors on the show did that. There was this one bitch named Sherylin Jefferys who'd been on the show since the very first episode, and she thought she was a goddamn treasure. She was always clomping into the actors' lounge in her high-heeled mules with a big towel turban on her head, and she'd order everybody around like mad. She'd tell someone to go fetch her cellular phone, and some other guy to get her some coffee, and she never said "please" or "thank you" to anyone. Then she'd practically walk all over the day players. Sometimes they sat on the floor in the actors' lounge if there weren't enough seats, and she'd just trample them, barking "Move it!" She had the personality of a barbed-wire fence.

Lucas and Mick didn't hang out with Sherylin at all. It was funny, but the cast was kind of split up into these little cliques like you had in high school. For instance, Sherylin only hung out with this arrogant bastard named Peter and another bitchy actress named Rita. Mick and Lucas and Lola were another clique. Even though I hadn't been on the show that long, I was pretty sure I was part of their group. They were always asking me to come along to lunch or dinner or if I wanted to run lines or if I needed help with a scene. Especially Lucas. Lucas was constantly explaining things to me and giving me pointers.

When our food came, Mick started to talk about how much he missed hang gliding. Mick had been on a soap out in L.A. before he moved to this one, and he used to go out to the mountains with his buddies and hang glide. They'd take a backpack full of beef jerky, and leap off cliffs and soar. You could see Mick lived for that type of thing. As he was telling us about it, he could hardly contain his excitement. Then Lucas made Mick roll up his sleeve and show me his tattoo. He had a tattoo of a boa constrictor on his bicep.

"That's Lu," Mick said.

"Who?" I asked.

"Lu. My snake."

"He's got a boa constrictor at home," Lucas explained. "It's huge."

"Where do you keep it?" I asked.

Mick rolled down his sleeve. "Oh, he just hangs around. He likes it under the radiator."

"Aha." I took a bite of my pizza and made a mental note to stay away from Mick's apartment.

About halfway through dinner, Mick started to tell a story about a ski weekend he and Lucas had gone on. I was listening, watching him pause to gulp down some beer, when, it just hit me over the goddamn head that I was going to have to make out with him. I completely lost track of the ski story and started to wonder what the hell it would be like, him being such a madman and everything. I'd already had to kiss Lucas in the first scene we'd done, but it wasn't that big a deal. We'd only kissed for a couple of seconds. But this scene I had coming up with Mick was a real, full-blown love scene. I jiggled my foot under the table. It made me a little nervous to think about it.

When we came out of the restaurant, you should have seen it outside. The whole damn street was beaming and glistening, and sheets of rain were slashing sideways in the wind. Neither Lucas nor Mick had an umbrella. I had one of those miniature jobs you can stick in your handbag, but it was useless. Who makes these goddamn umbrellas? I couldn't even get it open.

I was fussing with it, and Lucas was looking for a cab, but there wasn't one in sight, so he said he'd walk over to Sixth to get me one. And all of a sudden, Mick went completely bananas. He ran right out into the middle of the street and stood under a streetlight with his head thrown back and his arms stretched out. Then he grabbed the lamppost and swirled around it and started to sing, for christsakes. He started to sing "Singin' in the Rain," and I was stunned. He had the most beautiful voice I'd ever heard. Lucas and I just stood there watching him with our mouths hanging open as he kicked up the shimmering water in the gutters and stomped around in the puddles. I'd never seen anything like it in my whole life. The thing is, actors are basically lunatics. They can go completely bananas at any given second. It's that whole lack of inhibition thing—they aren't afraid to look like morons. Mick was having a ball, though. Man, was he talented. Lucas told me later that Mick used to do a lot of Off Broadway musicals before he started doing television.

Mick was about halfway through the song, when he danced

over to me, grabbed my hand, and yanked me out into the street with him. It was pretty cold and we were both drenched at this point, but he couldn't have cared less. I didn't care either. I don't know why, but suddenly it was really thrilling, the way he was singing to me in that wonderful voice and making me dance around with him, as if I were really in the movie. Lucas finally joined in, and all three of us capered around in the rain for a while, laughing and hamming it up. We finally knocked it off when we saw a group of people come out of the Italian joint.

When I got home that night, Minty was doing paperwork on the couch in the living room. When he saw me, he lowered his little reading glasses and raised his eyebrows.

"Jesus. What happened?" he asked.

I glanced into the mirror over the bookshelf. My cheeks and nose were scarlet and my hair was completely soaked and matted, big clumps of bangs were pasted to my forehead. I started to tell Mint what had happened as I took off my dripping coat.

"He what?"

"He started to sing 'Singin' in the Rain.' "

"In the middle of the street?" Mint asked incredulously.

"Yeah, but no one was around really." I took off my wet shoes and socks. "He has an incredible voice. I couldn't—"

"You just stood there and watched him in the rain?" Mint interrupted.

"Lucas and I danced a little, too. It was really fun." I scraped my bangs off my forehead and walked into the bedroom. I was shivering a little, and as soon as I got all my wet clothes off I got into the shower and turned the water on hot.

A couple of minutes later, Mint got in with me. He didn't say anything. He pressed his chest against my back and kissed the nape of my neck. As we were enfolded by a sheer white blanket of steam, I closed my eyes, and the world crumbled.

New Year's Eve came along. It was spent at a club called the Tunnel. What a place to spend it. Underground on a bunch of railroad tracks. Jori was throwing another bash in the VIP room there, and Mint said he just couldn't refuse his invitation. Those were his exact words, by the way. I didn't want to go out at all, but I owed it to Minty. When he'd come home from Jori's Christmas party at about 3 A.M., I'd told him I was sorry I'd left early and that I should have stayed and all this stuff. I hated to upset him. I really did. So when Mint told me about the party at the Tunnel, I made a real effort to be pleasant about it.

Jori's party was just what I'd expected, full of the same imbeciles who'd been at his Christmas bash. Mint and I hadn't been there for even two minutes before a whole mob of people came charging at him. I swear, the way they booted me out of the way to get to him it was like a fucking game of kick-the-can. I couldn't understand how Mint had become so popular with Jori's crowd all of a sudden. Everybody seemed to know him.

Stranded, I wandered through the mobs and went over to the bar. I ordered a gin and tonic. I didn't even want the stupid drink.

I'd just heard some guy next to me order it and I was too lazy to
come up with a drink of my own. So I sat there on this bar stool
and watched. Everybody was all jazzed up, and the room was full
of mirrors and balloons and all this silvery stringy bullshit was
hanging from the ceiling. I finally spotted Mint over by this pillar
with Jori and Vane and a couple of other people. I didn't go over,
I just looked at him. He was something. He was like a painting, a
really incredible painting that you just have to keep going back
to. No matter how many times you've seen it, it's always like the
first time. There's always something new to see. Christ, he was
electrifying.

I don't know how long I sat on that bar stool; I figure about an
hour. At one point the Creature came up to order a drink, and I
tried to cover my face with my hands, pretending I had something in my eye. Didn't do any damn good. She spotted me anyway, said, "Hey! I know you!" and hugged me. Liked me to death,
this creature. Tonight she was sporting a sequined halter top, velvet short shorts, and a top hat and battery-operated bow tie that
flashed in your face about every two seconds. I also happened to
notice that her lips were huge. What I mean by that is, the chick
had some real Zulu lips. I didn't remember her having those big
lips at Jori's Christmas party.

The lip enigma was solved the moment she sat down on the
stool next to me. "Howdja like my lips?" she blurted out. "Aren't
they groovy?"

Groovy, for godsakes. She was in a fucking time warp.

"They're, um . . . they're very nice."

"I got the silicone lip."

"Really?"

"Yeah. You should get it. I'm gonna get the silicone cheekbones next."

I raised my eyebrows. What a disaster. As if she needed all this.
She was really very good-looking, the Creature.

"You know, you really have very nice cheekbones . . ." I was going to say her name, but then I realized I didn't know her name. I was so used to thinking of her as the Creature that that's all I knew her as. "You really don't need silicone cheekbones."

"Yeah, I do. Alessandro told me I should get 'em."

I should have known Jori would have something to do with it. He'd probably forced her to get the Zulu lips.

"Do you do everything he says?" I asked.

"Well, yeah. Alessandro gets stuff for me, so I owe him." She paused to chug some of her drink.

"What . . . what do you mean by stuff? What kind of stuff?" I inquired.

This devious smile flashed on her jumbo lips and I realized what kind of stuff. I sighed and shifted my ass on the stool.

"The cheekbones are gonna be real good for my career, though," she blurted out.

"Oh? What do you do?" I was honestly very curious. I had a pretty good idea it wasn't brain surgery.

"I'm in music videos. You know Zowie Slick? 'Suck It'? You've heard their new single, 'Suck It,' right?"

"Oh, sure. I have all their albums." I smiled slightly. I'd never heard of Zowie Slick in my life, but it was kind of fun to bullshit.

"I was in their video. Near the end, you know. I'm the girl in the fishnet outfit who gets hosed down and stuff." What a nightmare. She was serious. I mean, you could tell she was proud of this. That it got hosed down in a fishnet outfit.

About two seconds after she told me this, the countdown began. What a disaster. The only reason I'd come to this affair, besides to make Mint happy, was to kiss him when the gong went off, and now the gong was going off and all I had to kiss was the Creature.

But Mint found me. The countdown was on five when he grabbed me from behind and yanked me into his crystal arms. I was beaming, of course. I couldn't even wait for the three-two-one; I just mashed my lips against his. Everything around me was suddenly fading . . . receding. When midnight hit, I could hear people shouting "Happy New Year!" I could hear them singing that song about forgetting some old acquaintance, but their voices seemed miles away. It felt like the moments right before you fall asleep.

But then he released me, and I was horribly awake again. The voices soaring in volume. . . . People were tossing confetti, popping balloons. The Creature came back into view; it was hopping up and down, screeching, "Woooooo! Woooooo!" . . . Some French fruitcake in one of those dopey party hats was doing a striptease over on the dance floor.

I was just standing there beside Mint, blinking at it all, when I spotted Jori strutting over with a whole herd of broads behind him. He came right up to Minty, slapped him on the back, and told him, "Some of my friends here are dying to dance with you, my man!" And then the herd of broads, they all surrounded Mint, and I wanted to upchuck. There must have been about five of them all wiggling and giggling around like a bunch of morons. All whining, "Come on, Minty!" and tugging on his arms.

Mint stuttered, "Hey . . . hey, wait . . . come on . . . no . . ." But he was smiling and laughing and I could see damn well it wasn't killing him.

"Go on, Mint!" Jori belted out. Then he looked over at me and said, "Salty doesn't mind. Do you?"

"No. No, I don't mind. Go ahead, Mint," I said dryly.

So then the five gorgeous broads all started to drag him off to the dance floor. I just stood there for a moment and watched him like I was in a trance.

"He's quite a rising star." Jori's voice startled me. I turned my head to find him staring at me. Studying me.

"What?"

"Minty. He's remarkable. It won't be long now."

"What do you mean, it won't be long now?"

Jori's eyes shifted back to mine. They were degrading, almost frightening in their intensity. "I mean, you'd better get used to this." He smiled subtly and ran a hand back through his loose mane of hair.

A second later a pair of white hands slid over his eyes and the Creature's voice, severely warped with alcohol, demanded, "*Guess who?*" Jori gripped one of her arms and yanked her up against him. Her top hat fell off then and Jori reached down and lewdly grabbed her crotch. I'd never seen anything so vulgar in my life.

I moved away from them as fast as I could and went back over to sit at the bar. I felt so goddamn out of place. All these crazy sons of bitches were making me sick to my stomach. I glanced back over at Mint on the dance floor. The broads were gyrating all around him and these beams of light were coursing back and forth like in *Star Wars*, and I thought, Mint doesn't belong here. I didn't belong here. We should have been in a quiet cafe somewhere. One of those auburn joints with ceiling fans and washed wooden floorboards. We'd sit at a table drinking wine in a haze of candlelight. The air would be smudged with long tendrils of smoke, and slow, smoldering jazz would trickle from a black man's horn. And when you looked out the window, you would see the moon like a giant jewel, framed in mist. But no. I had to be in this stinking joint where there was no moon. Of course there was no moon. I was in a goddamn tunnel, for christsakes.

Mint was attempting to leave the dance floor now, but all the broads had latched on to him and were trying to stop him. What a bunch of barbarians they were. All yanking and tugging on his jacket. Finally Mint freed himself and went over to this couch where Jori and Vane and a couple of other guys were sitting. I didn't feel like going over there, so I just looked up at the ceiling and let my thoughts drift back to a real New Year's Eve. The one when Mint got me to watch the fireworks with him. We were about seven, and I was terrified of fireworks. It's kind of stupid, but they reminded me of bombs, and I always thought they'd smash through the windows and kill everyone. I don't remember the whole thing, but I remember that Mint was wearing his Spider-Man pj's and that he dragged me to the window in the living room and I was really having a fit. I was screaming and crying and covering my ears and Aunt Christa was telling Mint to let me go. But Mint didn't let go. He held right on to me and looked me right in the face and said, "Salt, quit cryin' now, will ya? You just hold on . . . like this . . . you just hold on to my hand, okay, and I won't let nothing bad happen to you. Okay?" And then all I remember is that I let Mint take me over to the window. I was holding on to his hand like a bastard, but I wasn't crying or screaming or anything. I guess I just trusted him. I trusted him more than anyone else in the world. And I was safe with him. In a way, he was what I imagined an angel to be, if angels existed. If when you died one came to meet you in the darkness, you would follow him. You would lie down in his arms and let him take you. There would be no need to ask questions or wonder or worry . . . you would just lie down like a defenseless infant in his arms and let him take you.

I glanced back over at Mint on the couch. He was still talking to somebody, but I knew he'd come get me when he was ready. I could see his profile, the white rush of his neck, the frost of his hands, the fingers spread out and blazing against the black of the couch. I didn't see anything, anyone but Minty. Just my angel, suspended in darkness.

Around *the end of January,* big things started happening for Mint. For one thing, his show had cleaned out. No kidding. Every painting was sold by January 17. The Marzipan Pigeon became the hottest joint in town. It had always been popular, but nothing like it was after Mint's phenomenal art debut. Even if you were a real hotshot, a celebrity or something, you'd still have to wait around for a table. Word was really spreading about Mint. He'd gotten these sensational reviews for his show, and people were suddenly curious about the "Marzipan Prodigy," as he was labeled in the *Times.* Then, on January 22, Mint got a call from GQ. They wanted him to grace the cover of their May issue. Mint decided to do it. He said it would be good publicity since they were also running a long article on him.

The photo was taken on February 5 on the roof of our building, only I wasn't there. I really wanted to be there, but I had to pay a visit to the doctor that day since it was the only day of the week I had off. I wasn't feeling so sensational. For the last three days I'd had this awful migraine and I was nauseated all the time.

I kept hoping I'd just feel better so I wouldn't have to go to the doctor. I'm one of those crazy bastards who always think they have the plague or something. I always think the doctor's going to find something wrong with me and then I'll end up in a grave that people walk by and shake their heads at: "Oh, Walter, will you look at this. This one named Salty died so young. Poor dear."

I was so damned nervous the day I went to the doctor. I sat there in the waiting room pretending to read a *New Yorker* magazine. I was really just looking at the cartoons, but I didn't want the rest of the guys in the waiting room to think I was a moron. I could barely even concentrate on the cartoons, though. I kept glancing up at the wall across from me. There was this big horrendous "NO SMOKING" sign, and it made me as mad as hell, because when I'm nervous, I've just gotta have a smoke. Oh, it's lousy, I know it.

I stopped looking at the "NO SMOKING" sign and started to go through my handbag. I wasn't looking for anything special, I was just going through it for the hell of it because I was bored. The thing is, it's not really very entertaining to go through your handbag since you already know what's in there. I already knew I had my date book in there and my lipstick and my wallet with the picture of my mother in it. I also had my cigarettes, some Tic Tacs, and a book of matches that said "970-SLUT" on them. What a nightmare. You can't even get a decent book of matches nowadays. Everything's covered with "970-SLUT" or "BUTT" or something.

Finally the nurse came out and called my name and told me I could go into Doc Morris's office. I'd been going to Doc Morris since I was eighteen. He was a very nice guy, but, Jesus, was he goofy-looking. He was about five foot three with this Tweedle-dum mustache. I don't particularly like mustaches. The only guy I ever liked with a mustache was Clark Gable, but he's dead, so that doesn't really count. Anyhow, I walked into Morris's office, and he told me to have a seat and tell him what the problem was. After I told him, he said it was most likely the flu. Then he told me to go into the examining room and he'd be with me in a minute.

Minute, my foot. Doctors are never with you in a minute. They tell you to go into some exam room and then they probably leave for a ball game or something. So, just as I expected, I had to sit around forever. I got pretty restless after about ten minutes and decided to pace around in that comfy construction paper gown they give you. Then I poked around in some cabinets and drawers for a while. You'd think they could leave you some kind of entertainment. Not a goddamn lounge singer or anything, but they could at least put a couple of magazines in there. I eventually did find something to read. There was a framed article up on the wall over by the EKG machine. It was titled "What's Up, Doc?" and it was an interview with Morris about the benefits of carotene.

I was still looking at it when the door burst open and Morris plodded in. He told me to have a seat on the table, and then he started to take my blood pressure and listen to my goddamn heartbeat. As he was listening, he leaned over and started to sniff me. I was wondering what the hell he was up to when he jerked his head up, grimaced, and said, "You're still smoking. I smell smoke." A regular bloodhound, that Morris. He started up on his no-smoking speech then. He always gave me the same speech, and I always nodded and told him I'd knock it off.

When he finished examining me and taking my blood and all that, he told me to leave him some urine and that he'd have the results of my tests back tomorrow. What a way to bid adieu to somebody—by asking them to leave you some urine, for god-sakes.

So it turned out I had some kind of virus. I was very relieved it wasn't malaria, but it wasn't exactly fun to go back to work with a virus. I had to go to work, too, because soap opera guys don't get to call in sick or anything. If you call in sick, you're liable to come in to work the next day to find that your character was electro-cuted or something.

So I trudged into the studio the next morning at 6 A.M. When I opened the door to my dressing room, I found Lola standing on her goddamn head in the center of the room. I muttered good morning, and then I went over and slumped down on the couch. I started to rub my temples to ease the pressure of my migraine. Lola tipped over backward and leapt up. She was in her deep pur-ple leotard with the matching tights, and her freckled face was all red and flushed. She came over and squatted down in front of me, staring at me.

"God, you look really awful," she exclaimed.

"I know. I have a migraine and a virus," I mumbled weakly.

"Oh, I have something super for cranial tension." She bounced up and sprang over to the makeup table, where she started to scrounge through this enormous Indian-looking handbag. She returned about ten seconds later with a handful of reddish-brown bark.

"What's that?" I asked suspiciously.

"It's black haw. It's really amazing."

"Black haw? What . . . what do I . . . I just eat it?" I asked.

"No, you mix it with water. You put two teaspoons of it per cup of water, and then you boil it for ten minutes. You should drink three cups of it a day." She dumped the stuff into a plastic bag and handed it to me. "You should take some honey with it, though— it's really bitter," she added merrily.

I thanked her and stuffed the black haw in my duffel bag. She went over and sat at the makeup table, and started to yack about her boyfriend, Chad, while she rolled up her butterscotch blond hair in curlers. I just sat there on the couch and watched her reflection in the mirror.

". . . So I told him this fantasy I have about the two of us stranded on this beautiful island. All we do is make love and swim and eat fresh fruit and lie in the sun. I was describing this to him and he kept saying, 'Uh-huh. Uh-huh,' and then when I asked him to tell me his fantasy, you know what he said?" Lola swiveled around and looked at me. "He said he wanted to be swimming in a sea of boobs." I cracked a smile, and Lola shook her head, grimacing. "Can you believe that? I mean, I wasn't even in his fantasy. He just wanted to be completely smothered with boobs. What a schmuck." She was still rambling about what a perverted schmuck he was when my name was called over the horn to go to Makeup.

My makeup artist was Jerome that day. I liked Jerome the best. He was always laughing and kidding around with you. He was one of those gay guys who die over everything. He'd yack a mile a minute about how he'd died over a pair of white leather pants or how he could have died for the sumptuous man at some party or how he was going to die if he didn't get tickets to see Elton John. He was madly in love with Liza Minnelli. He was gay and everything, but he was still in love with her. That type of thing baffles the hell out of me.

Anyhow, that day as he was doing my makeup, he asked me how it felt to be on television, and I told him I hadn't really thought about it. The thing is, it's not such a big deal to be on television. What kills me is when I'm watching the news and they start to interview some woman whose son was tied to an explosive device and is now strewn all over the tristate area. They'll be interviewing this poor broad, when all of a sudden you'll see half a dozen cretins making retarded faces and waving in the background. That type of thing irritates the shit out of me.

Whenever there's a television camera, people always want to stick their mugs in it.

Personally, I can't stand watching myself on the tube. In the beginning Minty and I taped a few episodes, but I quit doing it because watching them just gave me a pain in the ass. First, I hated the way the camera made me look. It made my nose look too wide. Even though I was always asking Jerome to put some dark shading on either side of my nose, it didn't help much. My chin looked pretty goddamn bizarre, too, if you ask me. I have a square chin and the camera accentuated it too much. Plus, I hated listening to my voice. I thought it sounded horrible. I was always judging my goddamn performance every two seconds. Every time I said something, I'd tell myself I didn't say it coldly enough, or maybe I should have looked away as I spoke. The worst was when I watched myself laugh. When I heard myself laugh on the tube, I didn't believe it for a second. Mint said he believed it, but he was probably just being nice.

The other reason I didn't like to watch myself on the show was that I couldn't get used to all my dramatic facial expressions. I'm sure you've seen a soap once or twice in your lifetime, and you know how they zoom in on a character's face at the end of a scene? Well, whenever they zoomed in on my face, it would always be twisted up in anguish or snarled up in rage, and I couldn't stand the way I looked, because you normally don't see yourself when you're arguing or sobbing. Sometime when you're really hysterical over something, really upset or furious, go stand in front of a mirror and you'll see what I mean.

Later that day after my second scene, I ran into Lola in the hallway. She told me I'd gotten some mail and that it was on my couch. I didn't know what the hell she was talking about. No one except Aunt Christa ever wrote me letters. It didn't even occur to me it was fan mail until I was walking into the dressing room.

Jesus, was I excited. I rushed over and snatched up the letters. There were only three, but I didn't care. I tore open the goddamn envelopes and started to read them.

The first one was from this woman in Tulsa, Oklahoma, and she'd addressed the letter to Laura. She told me she knew I was after Edward and that I had no business sticking my nose where it didn't belong. That killed me. Then she went on to say how cruel I was to take advantage of dear, sweet Andrew. (I hadn't kissed Edward or had my big love scene with him yet, but I guess it was pretty obvious to the viewers I was going to.) At the end she said I never should have come to the town of Clairmont, and that she hoped for my sake I found faith in Jesus. I couldn't believe it. She actually thought Laura was real. It made me happy, though, because it meant I was doing my job. If she hated my ass so much, it was really quite a compliment.

The next letter was addressed to Salty, and it was from a teenage kid. I could tell because of the pink stationery with the little balloons on it and the handwriting, which was pretty lousy. Anyway, the girl's name was Carolyn, and she said she really hoped my character would get together with Andrew. She thought we'd be a neat couple. Then she wanted to know if I was the girl who used to play so-and-so on "One Life to Live," and she asked me to send her an autographed picture. I practically keeled over. I couldn't believe she wanted my autograph.

The last letter was from Rachel in Ohio. She said she thought I was a really good actress and that she wanted to be an actress herself. She told me quite a bit about herself and requested an autographed picture like Carolyn had. Then she added, "P.S. I hope Andrew comes out of the coma." Poor goddamn Andrew was still in the coma, still breathing with the goddamn snorkel, while I went out on the town with his dad.

Chapter
18

That Thursday night Mint dragged me to a fashion show and dinner at the Plaza to benefit AIDS research. I didn't really want to go. It wasn't because I was sick, though. Amazingly enough, Lola's black haw had really gotten rid of my headache and my nausea was gone. I just wasn't in the mood to go out. But Mint was insistent. He said Johnny and Alessandro were expecting us.

I didn't get out of work until six, so I had to rush home and change. I put on this old green velvet dress and the diamond earrings I'd worn to Jori's party. I didn't have to do my hair or makeup since they'd already been done on the set. I only had to wipe off some of the blush, since they put on about six layers of it. Mint and I were just about to leave when I noticed a run in my goddamn stockings. As I was changing them, Mint kept telling me to hurry up. As soon as I'd put on the new pair, he grabbed me and yanked me out the door.

In the cab, Mint was all agitated. He kept muttering that we were late.

"Oh, we're only ten minutes late," I said, pulling on my gloves.

"I told Alessandro we'd be there at quarter of seven and it's almost seven now. The fashion show starts at seven." Jesus, was he worked up over this. So we were going to miss five minutes of some stupid fashion show. Mint lit a cigarette and started to take these quick, heated drags off it. Headlights from passing cars were streaking his profile, illuminating his sullen expression.

I didn't say anything. I turned around and looked out the window. We were coming up to the Plaza and all the poor goddamn carriage horses were standing around in the freezing cold. When the cab pulled up in front of the hotel, Mint thrust a ten-dollar bill at the driver and told him to keep the change. I looked at Mint, astounded. The meter only said four fifty. I started to ask him what he was thinking, but he just shouted for me to come on and then shot out of the cab and raced up the carpeted front steps of the joint like a lunatic. I could barely keep up with him. When we got to the area the fashion show was being held in, we checked our coats and Mint held out his invitation and gave our names to one of the women with the guest lists, sitting behind a long table.

So we finally walked into the fashion show. The damn thing had already started. As Mint started to lead me down an aisle, I looked from side to side. The lights were dimmed but you could see all right. There were rows and rows of seated guests sitting in a kind of semicircular formation around a long spotlit runway. Mint kept tugging me down the aisle until we got right up near the runway. He paused, peered around for a second, and then led me into the second row. The seats Vane had reserved for us were right next to Jori and that charming creature of his. At least I didn't have to sit next to the creature. It was sitting on Jori's right. Mint was to Jori's left, and I was between Mint and some trendy old broad in a pair of gigantic Jackie O. sunglasses.

So the moment we sat down, Jori leaned in to Mint and started to have a powwow with him. I tried to hear what they were saying, but the music was too loud. I think it was INXS. Some song about a guy needing a bimbo tonight because he can't sleep and he's sweating like a pig. Up on the runway this giant, slinky-looking model was coming along and there was this guy up on the side of the stage behind a podium commenting on what she was wearing. He was going on about this fabulous Christian Lacroix dress with an Andy Warhol print and the sensational "branch" hat, also by this Lacroix guy. Sensational branch hat, my ass. The woman was wearing a goddamn tree on top of her head. A tree, I tell you. You could have chopped the mother down and made firewood out of it. All the photographers crouched below were taking pictures of it, too. What a waste of film. After that, a European-looking model began to sashay down the catwalk. She had her black hair molded up into a torpedo on top of her head and a big triangular honker that reminded me of the ones in Picasso paintings. So she came out and the commentator started to yack about her leggings. She was wearing these beaded Versace harlequin-patterned leggings and I'd never seen anything so ugly in my life. A couple more models came out in what the commentator referred to as Gianni Versace haute couture.

Then this blond model came out in a Johnny Vane swimsuit and she was probably the most gorgeous woman I'd ever seen. I wanted to sock her in the nose. She was like six feet tall with hair just like honey pouring out of the jar—rippling, gleaming gold hair that ignited in the lights like a goddamn cherry bomb. I couldn't see the color of her eyes, but they were catlike and framed in smoky gray and charcoal black. Her mouth was apathetic, swollen, shining Moulin Rouge red. She had an absolutely perfect figure. She wasn't reed thin with no chest or anything. She was all toned and curvy with these voluptuous va-va-voom kind of breasts. Jesus, was she a work of art.

I turned to look at Minty. He wasn't drooling or anything, but you could see that he was knocked out by her. He kept fooling around with his bow tie, readjusting it left and right. He also had his ankle crossed over his knee and he'd started to jiggle his foot like a bastard. When I looked back over at the model, she was standing at the end of the runway in that skimpy metallic swimsuit. All around her, flashes were spurting out like big electric white flowers, and she just ignored them and gazed off into the darkness. I started to chew on the side of my thumbnail.

Finally the model turned around and started to stroll back up the runway in her flashy sling-back sandals and, boy, did I wish she would slip and fall flat on her ass. That probably sounds just awful, but I couldn't help it. I can get extremely jealous sometimes. I remember once, I was watching one of those Miss America or Miss Universe pageants on television, and all I did for the whole show was wait for one of the contestants to slip and fall on her ass. It was a live broadcast so I thought there was a chance I'd see it. But of course none of them fell down and I was very disappointed 'cause I'd sat through the whole stupid show for nothing.

The fashion show went on until a quarter to eight. When the applause dissolved and the lights came up, everybody headed into a connecting room for drinks. It was a fancy pink room with a lot of gilded mirrors all over the walls. After Mint and Jori and the creature and I got drinks at the bar, we stood around for a while. Jori started to yack as usual. He was yacking about how he'd purchased this spectacular Eskimo mask from Baffin Island at Christie's on Monday.

"I had to have it. Those masks are extremely rare and valuable. Guess how much I paid for it?" he asked Mint crudely.

Minty shrugged. The creature blurted out, "Three zillion dollars!"

Jori didn't even acknowledge her. "One hundred and fifty grand," he announced, smiling.

Mint's eyes gaped open. He started to ask Jori something about the auction, but I couldn't hear it because the creature was suddenly squawking in my ear.

"Oh, my God . . . look in back of you. It's Michael Douglas! Do you see him? God, he's so hot. You know, a friend of mine's girlfriend used to make it with him and I hear he has a really big schlong."

I drew my head back and stared at her wearily. This was going to be another of those endless evenings, I could feel it. I started to scrounge through my evening bag for my Tylenol. Then all of a sudden I heard Jori's voice cry out, "Johnny! Over here!" And I looked up and it was my worst nightmare. Johnny Vane was coming right toward us with that gorgeous model on his arm. All the guests were turning around to stare at her as she glided across the room in this fluid black silk evening gown.

"Alessandro! Minty! How fabulous you could come! I'm so sorry I couldn't come out sooner, but I was held up backstage," Vane gushed in that histrionic way of his. "Oh, and this breathtaking vision is Sabina. Isn't she fabulous? She's Elite's newest superstar. She's just signed a three-year contract with Revlon." Vane gazed at her like she was the Mona Lisa or something. "Normally she doesn't do runway, but she wanted to model my collection tonight as a special favor."

What a disaster. The woman was even more beautiful up close. She'd taken off all that heavy stage makeup and dark eyeliner and she looked like a goddamn goddess. Her skin was eggshell white and her wildcat eyes were an electrifying indigo blue flecked with violet. Her sexy mouth was painted pastel pink and her hair was wound up in some kind of elegant twist. I kept scrutinizing her. I wanted to find just one thing about her that wasn't flawless. I wasn't that picky, either. I'd settle for anything. Like some lopsided ears or something. But even her goddamn ears were perfect. They were so perfect they didn't even look like ears. I wanted to strangle her.

You should have seen Mint when Vane introduced her. All of a sudden he was Don Juan. He stuck a cigarette in the corner of his mouth and flicked open his sleek new silver lighter. Then, after he lit his smoke, he looked her dead in the eyes, as debonair as hell, and told her what a pleasure it was and all that crap. She just stood there passively and skimmed all our eyes with hers like she had something a helluva lot better to do.

A couple minutes after Vane introduced her, the paparazzi started to circle us like vultures and Vane became very excited and started to order everybody around. "Alessandro, come stand on the other side of Sabina. That's it. Marvelous!" I stood there beside Minty and watched Vane and Jori get their picture taken with Sabina. Next, Vane swung around and placed Sabina next to Minty with Jori on the other side of her, and then he glanced down at me and said, "Oh, Salty, darling, you don't mind stepping out of the way, do you?" And then he actually had the nerve to shoo me along like some farm animal. Minty didn't even say anything. He just started posing for all the lousy photographers. I was furious! I couldn't stand it anymore. I started to wind my way around all the guests and when I got out of that room I wandered off to find the can.

In the bathroom, I dumped my purse on the long marble counter and looked into the mirror. I didn't look so bad, but I certainly wasn't any Sabina. I frowned and went into one of the stalls and started to pile toilet paper all over the seat. So I was sitting there on the john, and normally I wouldn't go into it with you—I mean, it's not exactly enchanting to hear about somebody sitting on the john—but I have to mention it since something happened while I was sitting there. All of a sudden I heard some women come into the can. I could hear their high heels clicking on the tiled floor. Then they started to yack. One of them went on about how the house in Southampton was being redone and then another asked if so-and-so had had a face-lift. I kind of tuned them out until all at once they started talking about Minty, yacking about what a *stunning*-looking man he was.

"Well, I just hope Minty's at my table tonight. Maybe I'll sneak in and rearrange the place cards," one said as they all trooped out the door again.

"Careful, Katherine, haven't you got a son his age?" another one said, and they all chuckled like a bunch of dingbats.

When the door banged closed, I came out of the damn john and got a cigarette out of my purse. I stomped around that fancy pink can, taking infuriated drags off my smoke. I had to stay in that bathroom for a whole five minutes until I was calm enough to go back to the stupid affair.

When I got back, everybody had drifted into the grand ballroom right next door, which was huge and creamy with tons of round tables all glowing with candles and decorated with magnificent floral centerpieces. Some of the guests were seated already, others were still milling around. I stretched my head up and looked for Minty. I eventually spotted him by a table in the center of the room and headed over there.

"Minty."

Mint turned around and looked at me. "Oh, Salt . . . good, you're here. We're just sitting down. You're over there between Biblos and Jack." Mint pointed to the other side of the table. I never got to sit next to Mint. Everybody was always seated a thousand miles away from their escort at these stupid parties. I went over to where Mint had pointed and everybody sat down and, of course, I was seated next to a pair of lunatics. But I'll tell you, it didn't surprise me in the least. Jack, the guy on my right, was a bald, middle-aged man with stormy black eyebrows and big, dry, callused-looking hands. When I asked him what he did, he said he was an erotic artist.

"Oh? What kind of art? Do you paint?" I asked.

"No!" he snapped. Jesus, was he touchy. "I do nude sculpture." He paused to slurp some of his soup.

"What sort of material do you work in?"

"I use my own *matière*."

"What's that?"

He turned his head and looked at me. "Women's undergarments."

"You mean—"

"That's right. Bras. Panties. Garter belts. Stockings. Compacted, shaped, and bonded with a special epoxy glue."

"Oh."

"Women's sexuality is being molded and repressed by our hypocritical, puritanical society!"

The guy was a raving lunatic. I nodded at him and turned back to my appetizer.

"I also do mobiles."

I looked up to find him staring at me again. "Oh? Mobiles?"

"Big ones," he snapped. "They're very big."

"Yes?"

"Big and phallic." He looked back down at his soup and took another slurp.

"Well . . . that sounds very . . . interesting."

"What?!" He turned and stared at me with this furious expression on his face, his lips all shiny with soup.

"I just said that sounded interesting." I attempted a smile.

"How do you know? It might be garbage," he snarled. Jesus, was he something. A real charmer.

"I don't know, but it sound—"

"Yeah. Sure. So what do you do?" He was staring at me again and I wished he'd knock it off because it was very unnerving.

"I'm an actress."

"In the movies?" he demanded.

"No. On television." He didn't say anything. "I'm on a soap opera." He still didn't say anything. He stared at me for a couple more seconds and then he turned around and started to work on his soup again. He didn't say another word to me for the whole rest of the evening.

On my left was a French guy named Biblos, and Biblos just needed a muzzle. He was one of those guys who use social events as psychotherapy. I'd just met him and here he was telling me about how his father had abused his mother and his mother had been in a loony bin for the past twelve years drawing pictures on black paper with a black marker. Then he went on about his prostate, his divorce, and his manic depression. He made me want to jump out the window, for christsakes. I looked over at Minty across the table. He was seated right next to Sabina. She was telling some story and he was absolutely spellbound. He hardly even looked down to cut up his goddamn food.

". . . but my urologist says they have a new drug that shrinks it now . . ."

God, I wanted to kill her. She was holding her long-stemmed glass up near her face, taking these tiny, dainty sips of champagne, and her big, feral, long-lashed eyes were gazing down, as coy as hell.

". . . have to talk to my lawyer. I mean, why should I pay when she's living with a lesbian and she still has my VCR . . ."

And then, right there in the middle of the main course she started to take her goddamn hair down. She plucked the gold combs out of her hair and shook her head so that her sexy mane spilled down, devouring her shoulders and chest. The bitch was a menace.

". . . then he tried Prozac. I'd heard it didn't have the side effects other antidepressants had. I mean, with Norpramin you gain twenty . . ."

Minty couldn't take his eyes off her. He didn't even say one word to the broad on his left. I kept squirming around in my seat.

". . . don't know. Have you ever heard of it?" Biblos's voice paused.

"Oh, that sounds nice," I told him.

"What?"

"What?"

"What sounds nice?" he asked.

Ah, shit. What the hell was he talking about? "Um . . . I . . . what did you just say?" I stammered.

"I asked if you'd ever heard of Zoloft."

"No, I don't think I've heard of him."

"Zoloft is an antidepressant."

"Oh. Oh, yes . . . right. I meant, yes. I mean, no. No, I haven't heard of it."

Biblos took a sip of wine and looked at me dubiously.

Ah, Jesus. I hated this stuff. I hated listening to lunatics and pretending I was so goddamn fascinated by all their goddamn mobiles or something. I hated being so artificial. I hated the wealth in that room because it made everything as cold as ice. Even though it was a benefit, it felt like hardly anybody knew or cared about the cause. It felt like everyone was there because they were bored and needed someplace to wear their fancy getups. And me, why was I there? Minty.

❧

Dinner ended around eleven-thirty, and man, was I exhausted. After everybody got up from the table, I went over to Mint and he told me Alessandro was heading over to Au Bar. I didn't have the faintest idea why he was telling me this. As if I was so goddamn curious about where that imbecile was heading off to. I was about to ask him how we could get back to the coat check when he blurted out, "So we're going to go on over there."

"What?"

"We're going over to Au Bar for a while with Alessandro and Johnny and—"

"Minty, I have to work tomorrow. I have to get up at four-thirty in the morning. Besides, I'm still getting over—"

"Salt, we're not going to stay for hours."

"I can't," I said firmly.

"Okay. Fine. I'll—"

"Hey, Mint . . . are you coming or what?" Jori called out. He was leaving the ballroom with the creature.

"Yeah! I'm coming," Mint shouted back.

"Meet us out front. We're taking my limo," Jori instructed.

Mint looked back down at me. His face was marbled with candlelight and I just wanted to fall into his arms like a sleepy child.

"Minty . . ."

"What?" His eyes searched mine impatiently.

"Nothing."

"Come on. I'll put you in a cab."

It was bitterly cold when we stepped outside the Plaza. As windy as hell, too. The canopy was slapping around all over and everybody's coats were rippling and thrashing. Mint ran out into the street and flagged me a cab. When I got into the backseat, he leaned in for a moment and kissed me deeply on the mouth.

"I won't be home late," he said.

"Okay."

"I love you," he said, looking directly into my eyes.

"Me, too," I said.

He slammed the door and I watched him dart over to Jori's blazing black limousine. The goddamn car was longer than a fire engine. Only an arrogant son of a bitch like Jori would want a limo longer than a fire engine.

During the cab ride home, I was kind of depressed. There's something about Manhattan in the middle of the night, when you're all alone in a cab . . . it can depress the hell out of you. You look out the windows and, I swear, there's not a thing around. Well, maybe sometimes you'll see some poor bastard wandering around in the freezing cold, but not very often. My cab went up Park Avenue and stopped at a red light, and not one guy crossed the street. Mohammed and I just sat there like the last two guys on the whole goddamned planet. Up ahead all this diaphanous white steam was erupting out of a pothole, and it looked very spectacular with the wind dragging it sideways, tearing it to shreds. Then the "DON'T WALK" sign started to flash and I could see Mohammed was getting a little restless. He was drumming his fingers on the steering wheel. When he started driving again, all the buildings began to fuse and blur together. He went right over that pothole and the steam engulfed the cab for a second. Jesus, was it depressing. You couldn't hear a damn thing except the cab's motor. If he'd had the radio on, it probably wouldn't have been so depressing.

I leaned up against the window and part of it was kind of fogged up. I took off one of my gloves and wrote "Minty" on the freezing glass. I wished he were sitting right next to me, kissing my neck or something. He was very good at that stuff. God, was he good at it. It always made me recall how much goddamn practice he'd had at it. He was very slow and sensuous about it. Then he'd stop for a second and look into my eyes like a wolf and a madman and an angel all swirled together, and I'd forget to breathe.

I heard Mint come in around three. When he got into bed, I rolled over to face him. He was lying on his back and a streak of moonlight was illuminating his profile.

"Mint?"

"Go back to sleep, Salt," he said quietly.

"How was Au Bar?"

"The same as always."

"Did Sabina go?"

"Who?"

"Sabina . . . the model you sat next to at dinner."

Mint stuck a cigarette between his lips and the darkness was suddenly punctured by a fluorescent blue flame. "She came with Johnny." He clicked his lighter closed. I watched a plume of smoke jet up from his mouth and stretch out above our heads like mist.

"What's she like?" I asked.

Mint rolled over to face me. The moonlight slanted into his emerald eyes. "She's arrogant."

"Really? Did she—"

"Salt."

"Huh?"

He reached around and put out his smoke. When he rolled back around, he slid on top of me, and I felt myself dissolve with the pressure of his body.

"Let's not talk about her. . . ." He kissed my mouth so slowly and gently that every thought I had drowned in his touch. "Let's not talk. . . ." he whispered. I didn't talk. I wound my arms around him and fed my tortured heart.

Chapter

19

The night before my first big love scene with Mick, I just lay there
with my eyes wide open and blinking. I was very anxious about it.
I got up at four-thirty and took a shower and shaved under my
arms around five times. After I got out of the shower, I studied
my face close up in the mirror to make sure I didn't have a goddamn blemish or something.

When I got to the studio, wardrobe gave me my outfit for the
day, a sexy little black dress with a black lace teddy and black
pumps. I practically fainted when I saw the teddy—it was about
the size of a Kleenex. Back in my dressing room, I started to have
a nervous breakdown, while Lola tried to get me to relax.

"Don't worry. You'll be fine," she assured me.

"Were you this nervous before your first love scene?" I asked.

"Are you kidding? I was petrified. But it's not so bad." She massaged some goopy gel into her hair. "Besides, you're lucky you're
doing it with Mick and not Peter. I'd do a love scene with Mick
any day." Lola tilted back in her chair and smiled devilishly at
me.

On my way to run-through, I stopped in the actors' lounge to get a cup of coffee, and, wouldn't you know it, Mick was in there. It never fails. Whenever you don't want to run into somebody you always end up running into them. He was snatching a green apple from a bowl of fruit when he turned around and spotted me.

"Hey, Salty," he said brightly.

I mumbled, "Hi," barely looking at him, and brushed past to go to the coffee machine. I grabbed a Styrofoam cup and began to fill it.

"Caffeine. Now, that's a good idea. I went to hear this friend playing in a band in SoHo last night, and I didn't get home till about an hour ago. Lu was pissed. He kept hissing at me," he said jokingly.

"Oh. Um . . ." I stood in front of him, glancing all over the place like a moron. "I . . . I have to, um . . . I've gotta go to my dressing room," I stuttered like an imbecile. I couldn't believe I'd said that. I didn't have to go to the dressing room, I had to go to the blocking rehearsal. And I couldn't even look him in the eye. Completely flustered, I hurried out of the lounge and headed toward the dressing rooms. Halfway there, I turned around and went to the rehearsal studio instead. Mick was there, leaning up against the wall in his biker's jacket, looking down at his script and chomping voraciously on his apple. I sat as far away from him as I could. This went on all day. I barely said a word through all the rehearsals. I just stared down at my script and scratched my arm a lot.

When it came time to tape our love scene, I ran out into the stairwell and had about four cigarettes one right after another. Then they called me over the horn to get to the set, and I was about to go when I realized that my breath would stink from the cigarettes. I had to run all the way up to the dressing room to get my goddamn toothbrush. I was running like a madman in my high heels, bumping into extras and prop racks. They kept calling me over the loudspeaker, but I couldn't go without brushing my teeth. I scrabbled frantically through my tote bag, flinging crap all over the dressing room until I found my toothbrush and toothpaste, then rushed out to the water fountain in the hall. Jesus, were they paging me, though! They must have thought I'd flown the coop or something.

When I finally got down to the set, Hal, the director, didn't say anything, but he looked a little annoyed. I glanced over at Mick. He was standing beside the king-size bed in a dark three-piece suit while Indera, one of the makeup artists, sprayed his slicked-back hair. The director called for places. I took a deep breath and teetered over to Mick. Indera touched up my hair and powder as the crew got ready to shoot, and then she left.

Mick grabbed my hand and whispered, "Don't be nervous, Salty."

"What? No. I'm not . . . I'm . . ." I looked up at him. He was smiling warmly, knowingly, and I glanced down in embarrassment.

The director called for quiet. Mick and I stood at the end of the bed, facing each other, and they cued us to begin.

"I think I'm falling in love with you. . . ." Mick said, gazing into my eyes.

"Oh, Eddie . . ." I took a step toward him, and he drew me into his arms. I tilted my head back and his mouth pressed over mine. He kissed me forcefully but he didn't really open his lips. His scent engulfed me. He smelled like cigarettes, apples, and wind. I forgot to run my fingers through his hair like I was supposed to, but the director didn't cut us off. We held the kiss for a helluva long time. I didn't want to move my mouth too much, though, because I was afraid I'd end up looking like a fish or something. Mick moved his mouth. He slid his hand up my back and unzipped my dress. He was pretty damned smooth. He'd probably unzipped a good number of dresses in his time.

When we pulled back from each other, he looked deeply into my eyes and slid the dress from my body. I kept fading in and out of the scene. First it would be Edward, then it would be Mick, then Edward again. I sucked in my stomach like a bastard as the dress collapsed like a black puddle on the floor. Now I had to take his jacket off. Jesus, you should have seen how I was trying to be sultry. I was trying to act like Kim Basinger in *9 1/2 Weeks*, only I don't think it was working. I got stuck with his goddamn tie. I started to tug at it, and Mick's mouth twinged helplessly with a smile.

"Cut!" Hal shouted.

"I can't get his tie off," I announced despairingly.

"Yes, we can see that," Hal remarked. The crew started to crack up a little then, and suddenly I found myself chuckling with them.

Stephanie, the director's assistant, came over and showed me how to take off the tie. I felt a little stupid. But at least we didn't have to take the scene from the beginning.

This time I got his tie off okay, and Mick led me around the side of the bed. I lay back on the sheets under the blinding lights and slid the shirt from his body. He had a very broad, hairless chest. As I ran my hand over it I kept thinking about how different it felt compared to Minty's chest. Minty's chest was so much flatter then Mick's. Mick's was all swollen with muscles. He lifted my right arm and started to kiss the living daylights out of it. Then, when he got to my shoulder, he gazed at me and muttered, "Laura, oh, Laura . . ." I almost cracked up when he did that, but luckily I didn't. He lay down over me and started kissing my mouth again. Sometimes during the scene, I'd literally go out of character for a second to instruct myself to do something. For instance, I'd tell myself, "Okay, you're going to look at him after this kiss ends, but don't open your eyes too fast and don't close your lips all the way, and when you do open your eyes don't look at him too fiercely because it'll look fake. Just look at him softly with your eyes half open." I had this whole running monologue in my head. But then there were times the monologue would just evaporate and I'd really fall into the moment. I'd get this kind of queasy feeling in the pit of my stomach during the kiss. He was so goddamn sensuous it was making me disoriented.

Anyhow, we kept kissing for a while. He was just running a hand up my leg when the bedroom door was flung open.

"Daddy!" Lola cried in horror. Mick and I turned and stared at her.

"Jenny! What . . . how . . . how'd you get out of the asylum?" Mick demanded, hastily scrounging for his shirt on the bed. I slid under the sheet, holding it up to my chest.

Lola glared at me, maniacally twisting the wool hat she held in her hands. Her blond hair was matted and tangled, and her large eyes were ringed with dark circles. "Who is this?! How dare you cheat on Mother!" she screamed.

Mick got off the bed and tentatively approached her. "Mother's dead, Jenny," he said gently.

"No! No!" Lola dropped her hat and covered her ears with her hands.

Mick extended a hand toward her. "Jenny, darling, don't become—"

"Jenny? Who's Jenny?" Lola asked abruptly in a haughty, aristocratic voice.

"Who . . . who are you?" Mick asked warily.

"Who am I?" Lola repeated. "Who are you?"

"It's Daddy, darling."

"Daddy?" Lola threw back her head and unleashed a shrill, disdainful laugh. "My daddy is the ambassador to the Court of St. James! What's going on here? Who are you people?"

"I'm your father's friend. He's gone away for a while. Why don't you come and sit—"

"Don't come near me!" Lola shrieked. "I've got a knife." She brandished a long kitchen knife in front of her, her eyes burning on Mick.

"Oh, God! Eddie! She has a knife!" I wailed.

"It's okay. Just relax . . ." Mick said softly, taking a couple of steps toward her.

"Don't come any closer!" Lola exclaimed frantically. Mick lunged for her then, and grabbed her wrists.

"No! Eddie! Look out!" I cried.

The cameras closed in around Mick and Lola as they fell to the floor, struggling over the knife. Lola freed herself for a moment and raised her arm, ready to stab Mick, who was cringing beneath her.

"Cut!" Hal yelled. "That take's good."

"No! Lola . . . stop!" gasped Mick, laughing. Lola had dropped the knife and was tickling him half to death.

"Here, Salty." Indera tossed me a robe.

"Thanks," I said, getting out of the bed and slipping it on. Mick and Lola came over and we started walking off the set together.

"You were great!" Lola declared enthusiastically, putting her arm around me.

"Yeah. And it wasn't so bad, was it?" Mick stuck a cigarette in the corner of his mouth and flashed me a smile.

"No. It wasn't so bad," I responded, smiling back.

Chapter
20

One day near the end of February Mint came home early from the Pigeon and, Jesus, was he excited. He came charging into the kitchen with the biggest damn smile on his face.

"Salt, you'll never . . ." He couldn't finish his sentence, he was so goddamn out of breath. He leaned up against the wall for a second and heaved some air in. I turned off the kettle and walked over to him.

"What is it?"

"Alessandro's arranged for . . . he's giving me a show." He beamed. His cheeks were flushed frantic pink and his eyes were glinting like jewels.

"But you just had a show," I said.

"No . . . not here. In California." He grabbed me by the shoulders and pulled me up against him. My face sank deep into the damp cashmere of his coat. "Oh, baby . . . baby, this is unbelievable. He told me he's got tons of clients on the West Coast who are dying to see my work! Salt, people are asking about me."

"That's wonderful, Mint. I always knew you'd be a hit." I drew my head back and looked up at him. "When is the show scheduled for?"

"The end of June. Oh, Salt . . ." Mint looked down at his watch. "I've gotta go downtown in about half an hour."

"Why?"

"Helmut Huldheinz is having a party at his loft and I'm supposed to meet Alessandro there."

"Who's Helmut Huldheinz?"

"You met Helmut. He's with Alessandro's gallery. He's that big German guy." Mint walked past me and went over to the fridge.

"I don't remember. Mint . . . could I go with you?"

Minty was drinking some milk out of the carton; he stopped and looked at me. "I thought you had to work tomorrow."

"I do, but I don't have to be in until nine. They're doing a location shot. But if you don't want me to go—"

"No. No, I'd love you to go. I just didn't think about it 'cause you normally can't go out late on weekdays. But you're going to have to rush, Salt, 'cause it's already ten-forty and we've gotta—"

"I know. I'll rush. What should I wear?" I asked.

"Wear anything. You can wear jeans if you want." He started to drink the milk again and I bolted into the bedroom to get dressed.

Helmut's place was down in the West Village. He had a huge loft and everybody was mashed together in the front of it where the living space was. I hate parties where it is so crowded that people are always coughing all over you and God only knows what kinds of contagious diseases they've got. I always hold my breath like mad because I figure I'll snort up all their goddamn germs and die. Of course, I'm always a little overly dramatic about those things.

Finally, Mint and I got to the middle of the loft, which was a lot less mobbed. There were a couple of people standing around a sculpture of a high-heeled shoe the size of a helicopter. Minty spotted Helmut down by the heel and we went over there.

"Minty! How vondervul!" Helmut exclaimed. Man, you should have seen Helmut. Remember that guy Jaws from the 007 films? The big crazed-looking bastard with the bulging eyes and metal teeth? Well, Helmut looked exactly like him but without the metal choppers. I swear to God, he was the most monstrous guy I'd ever laid eyes on. He must have been six foot eight with fingers the size of knockwurst.

Minty started to compliment him on his giant shoe and then Helmut told Mint he wanted to show him a couple of his recent paintings. So we followed the guy down to the working area of his loft, where some finished paintings were lit by track lights. The first painting he showed us was of a urinal with a high-heeled shoe lying in it.

"Zis is zomezing new. Zis is called *Shoe* und it vant reprezent vomen becoming men. Vomen invading men's vorld zo zat men have nozzing left." Helmut took a gulp of his drink and looked down at Minty for his reaction.

"That's just incredible, Helmut. Just spectacular," Minty commented.

Helmut led us to the next painting, which was of a high-heeled shoe halfway submerged in a plate of pasta.

"Zis is called *Shoe 2* und it vant reprezent vomen's insatiable hunger to devour men's vorld." Helmut gripped his bronze belt buckle and gazed at the painting adoringly.

The last one he showed us was of a high-heeled shoe with a grenade in it. Helmut just stood in front of it and squinted at it.

"Oh, this is great," Mint said. "What's this one called?"

"*Muzzer!*" Helmut barked. Then he swung around and told Minty to come along. What a nightmare. The guy was obviously in need of about twenty years of therapy.

Just as we got back to the giant shoe sculpture, Jori came charging out of a cluster in this sleek Hugo Boss suit with his mirrored sunglasses on.

"Minty! I was looking all over for you," he exclaimed.

"Oh, we were in the back. Helmut was just showing us a couple of paintings." Mint lit a cigarette and glanced over at Helmut, who was hugging some man near the bar.

"Did he show you *Shoe?*" Jori asked.

"Yeah. He showed us all three."

"The guy's a fucking genius. I just sold a piece he did for fifty thousand." Jori took a sip of his drink and looked over at me. "How are you, Salty?"

I couldn't believe it. He actually said hello to me. Most of the time he just nodded at me. "I'm fine, thanks," I told him.

"Listen, Mint . . . um . . . what do you want me to tell Sam?" Jori's eyes darted back to Minty.

"What? Sam who?" Mint asked.

"Sam. You know, the guy you were going to meet with. . . ."

"Oh, oh. . . . Just tell him I can show him the painting some other time. Hey, I wanted to ask you about the painting for the cover of the catalogue. . . ." Minty started to talk business with Jori and I kind of stopped paying attention and leaned up against the giant shoe. It was freezing cold, that shoe. So I was standing there, sipping my drink, when I spotted the Creature bounding toward me. She was in a pair of skintight white jeans with a sparkling halter top and stiletto heels that Helmut would probably have found inspiring.

Anyhow, she gave me a big air kiss and started to yack. I hardly remember what she was yacking about because I wasn't really listening. I was just standing there, nodding, making like I was listening to her, when I happened to notice her fly was undone. I mean, it was really undone. The whole damned zipper was down and her pink underwear was completely displayed. I felt so embarrassed for her. I kept trying to interrupt her to tell her about it. Finally she stopped yacking for a second.

"Your fly's undone," I whispered. She looked at me strangely for a moment, like she didn't know what I meant. "Your zipper is—"

"Oh, sure! I know. It's supposed to be that way," she exclaimed dizzily.

I couldn't believe it. I'd never seen anything so idiotic in my life. I was about to tell her to excuse me when one of her giggling girlfriends skipped over and, wouldn't you know it, this bimbo had her fly down, too.

"Oh, my God! You'll never guess who just walked in!" she blurted out.

"Who?! Who?!" the Creature asked breathlessly.

"Keith Richards!"

"No way! No way! Where is he?" The Creature grabbed onto the girlfriend's arm and took off like a goddamn bullet. Keith Richards? I thought that guy was dead. The last time I saw the Rolling Stones, they all looked about eighty. I swear to God, I was watching MTV and they all came on to play a goddamn song and they could hardly lift up their instruments. Mick Jagger looked just like Mr. Gooter, and Richards, well, he was just a disaster. He was all hunched and wrinkled up with the cigarette still hanging out of his mouth. What made the whole thing so depressing was that you could see they still thought they were young and gorgeous. Jagger was still trying to do those aerobic kicks he was so crazy about, but he could hardly raise his goddamn leg, and Richards still had the same fucked-up hair and tight leather pants. All I can say is, once you hit eighty or however old those guys are, you should just take up golf or something.

After the Creature departed I went over to Mint. I stood around listening to him and Helmut and Jori discuss art for awhile. Helmut kept yacking about his idol, some German expressionist who painted everything upside down. He said, his favorite painting was called *The Forest on Its Head*, for christsakes. At about one o'clock the DJ started to play David Bowie and Helmut, with smoke shooting out of his walnut-size nostrils, commanded everyone to dance. Jori tore off his jacket and began to do this sleazy looking mambo. Then the Creature popped out of the crowd. "Woooo! Woooo! Sandro baby!" she erupted. Jori stared at her lasciviously and began to loosen his tie as she shimmied over to him on her wobbly stiletto heels.

"Her fly's undone," Mint whispered to me.

"It's supposed to be that way," I told him.

When the Creature reached Jori, he mashed her against him and they started to do this convulsive cucaracha. Then someone dimmed the lights and all hell broke loose. People were suddenly thrusting and jerking and bouncing on the wood floor. Glasses and bottles were rattling on the bar and the joint was a goddamn madhouse.

"Come on, Salt. Let's dance!" Mint said.

"No . . . Mint, it's after one already. I'm going to head home," I told him sleepily. He looked down at me and I brushed a piece of hair out of his eyes. God, I loved him. I wanted him to leave with me, to make love to me, but I knew he'd want to stay longer. I couldn't stay. I was fed up with it.

"Okay, baby. I'll see you later." He kissed me firmly on the mouth, and I started to make my way through the mobs. What a disaster.

When I came out of Helmut's building, I spotted an Optimo up the block and headed over there to buy some cigarettes. There was an old friendly-looking Indian guy behind the counter who nodded at me when I walked in. I said hi to him and looked over the magazines for a while. On the cover of *Vogue* was that Sabina bitch, and I couldn't stand it. She was looking sideways into the camera with her hair blowing behind her and she had this big toothy smile on her face. I frowned and moved over to the counter. After I bought my cigs, I stood outside the Optimo for a while and waited for a cab. I must have stood there for fifteen minutes freezing my butt off and not one cab came along. I finally decided to go over to the next avenue. I didn't want to because it was a very dark and creepy-looking area, but I knew I'd never get a cab otherwise. So I started up this side street, and I was right in the middle of the block when this big, scruffy-looking guy in torn jeans and a ratty leather jacket leapt out in front of me from a doorway. Scared the shit out of me. My heart was slamming into my ears like I was listening to it through a stethoscope. He was twenty-something with long greasy hair and huge, wild eyes. He kept clenching his fists and I could see he was as jittery as hell.

"Gimme some Valium!" he demanded hoarsely.

"I . . . I don't . . . I don't have any Valium," I stammered. Jesus, was I terrified.

"Whaddaya mean, you don't have any Valium? Everybody's got a Valium!" he bellowed. "Gimme your fuckin' handbag!" I was shaking so badly I could barely hand it to him. He tore it out of my hand, knelt down, and started to fling all the goddamn contents of my handbag out on the pavement. When I tried to take a step back, he snarled, "Don't fuckin' move!" I didn't.

"What about a Xanax!? You gotta fuckin' Xanax?" What the hell did I look like to this guy, the local pharmacy? He kept tossing stuff out of my bag, muttering, "Fuck . . . fuck . . . fuck . . ." until he came across something. He held whatever it was up to his ear and shook it with this possessed expression on his face. "*Aha!*" he cried. "*Aha!* What's this! Huh?! What's this!?" He held it up in his trembling hand and rattled it.

"Those are Tic Tacs," I told him.

"*What?!*" he barked, staring furiously at the small box.

"They're . . . they're breath mints."

"Ahhh, *fuck*! FUCK!" He started to slam the Tic Tac container into his forehead. Then he whirled around and tore off up the sidewalk. I stood there in shock for a second, and then I got ahold of myself and snatched up my keys and lipstick and wallet and everything and stuffed them back into my handbag. Then I ran back to Helmut's building to get Minty to come out to get a cab with me.

When I entered the loft, everybody was still dancing like maniacs. They were all swishing their hips and tossing their heads around. Long hair was thrashing and cigarettes were burning into a silver-white labyrinth of smoke. I kept winding around people and they kept bumping into me. Up ahead I could see the giant shoe looming. I scanned face after face after face. Where the hell was Minty? Just as I escaped the dance area, I bumped into Helmut.

"Oh, Helmut, have you seen Minty?" I asked.

"Ja," he said. Then he just brushed past me. What a nightmare. I kept wandering around. I'd just moved around a cluster of people when I saw a flash of gold hair up ahead and I knew it was Mint. When some more people cleared away I saw him sitting, kind of hunched over, on Helmut's enormous wooden bed. Jori was hunched over next to him and I caught a glimpse of the Creature behind him. I remember walking toward Minty, people kept weaving in front of me and I kept getting flashes of him and Jori, and then I stopped moving. Suddenly, I saw the mirror and I saw the cocaine and Minty jerked his head up and looked straight into my eyes. He didn't even look away. He just stared at me, and there was this indifference, this coldness in his eyes that I'd never seen before. Jori sat up, slicked back his loose hair, and pinched the end of his nose. His tie was completely undone and the Creature's bangled arms were slipping around his chest from behind. Jori said something to Mint, but Mint just continued to stare at me.

I felt sick. Without even thinking, I turned around and started to push my way through the mobs. I brushed someone's cigarette and the orange embers sprayed onto my coat. I didn't stop. The gleam of that mirror was still in my eyes and everyone's face was obscured by it, everyone's . . . except Minty's.

❧

I heard Mint come in at three-thirty. I hadn't slept. I was too shocked to sleep. When he came into the bedroom, I sat up and turned on the lamp beside the bed. He leaned back against the door with his head tilted down.

"Minty—"

"I hardly did any, okay?" He lifted his head and looked at me. "I did one line."

"Oh, come on. You're always going out with Jori. You've probably been doing—"

"Salt, I haven't been doing it. I did it maybe once before and that's it." He walked across the room and opened the bedroom window. He leaned forward, resting his hands on the sill, and his black jacket swept behind him in the wind.

"This is all Jori's fault. He wants to corrupt you. To turn—"

"Don't you dare start with him!" Mint swung around and stared at me fiercely. "You've been against Alessandro from day one and I'm getting really sick of it! He's giving me something I've wanted all my life, and you know that better than anybody." He turned to face the window again, and I got out of bed and walked over to him.

"Minty . . ." I put a hand on his shoulder. "Mint . . ."

He gazed at me. His eyes looked red and exhausted. "What?" he asked bitterly.

"I'm sorry," I said, delicately. "I don't mean to . . . I know how much this means to you and I want more than anything for you to be successful. I just . . . I got so frightened when I saw you tonight." I looked down for a second. I felt my eyes welling with tears. "You're all I have in the world, Minty, and . . . I'd die if anything happened to you."

He tilted my chin up and the tears streamed from my eyes. "Salt, nothing's going to happen to me. I'm not going to do it anymore." He wiped a tear from my face and I pressed my head against his chest. "You don't have to worry, baby," he whispered.

Chapter 21

About two weeks after Helmut's party, I went ice-skating with Dame at Mitsubishi Center. Mitsubishi Center, for christsakes. Those Japanese guys are going to take over the whole damn planet. Dame and I went skating over there once every year. It was kind of a ritual, I guess. We went on a Sunday and it was a very pleasant afternoon. It was cold but the sun was out and the wind wasn't so nasty. When I got to the rink, Dame was waiting for me at the top of the big stairs, and you'll never believe what he was wearing. He was wearing a pair of long johns. The son of a gun was leaning up against the wall in broad daylight in a pair of long underwear, for crying out loud. Besides that, he had on those hip-hop sneakers and a Lakers sweatshirt and an oversize red plaid lumberjack jacket. Plus, he was eating one of those big pretzels and he was eating it like a maniac, as usual. He was tearing off these huge chunks of it with his teeth and then he'd chomp like a big dog does when he's tossed a cracker or something. I was mortified. As soon as I reached him, I asked him where the hell his pants were.

"Whaddaya mean, where the hell are my pants? Whaddaya think these are?"

"Long underwear, Dame. You're wearing a pair of long underwear," I pointed out.

He glanced down at his legs. "Yeah, well, they aren't obscene or anything. Want some pretzel?" He held up his pretzel and I started to laugh. He was a hundred percent hopeless sometimes.

We walked down the stairs and went inside to put on our skates. When we found a bench, Dame stuck his pretzel in his mouth, unzipped his knapsack, and pulled out his banged-up hockey skates. I had my old white ones. They were a little tight, but they didn't kill me.

"Hey, you know, I saw this thing on Mint in *Rolling Stone*. It was about how he's this new up-and-coming artist, and there was a picture of him with some guy with mirrored shades on," Dame said as he was lacing up his skates.

"That was probably Jori," I said sourly.

"Yeah, that's right."

"He's Mint's dealer. I can't stand him. I'm really worried about what he's doing to Minty."

"Whaddaya mean? What's he doing?" Dame looked over at me.

"He's just . . . well, he's a real sleazy guy and he does cocaine and I'm worried that he's influencing Mint. I went to a party a couple weeks ago with Mint, and I saw him and Jori doing coke." I finished lacing up my skates and sat up on the bench.

"Mint's doing coke?" Dame asked.

"No. I mean, he said he's only done it twice and that he won't do it anymore. I just . . . I'm afraid Jori's going to try to pressure him into it or something."

"Mint's not a kid, Salt. I mean, I doubt he's gonna do coke just 'cause his art dealer does it."

"I don't know. I mean, he's really obsessed with Jori. He's always going out with him to after-hours parties, and he talks about him like he's the greatest guy on the face of the earth. And he's such a bastard, Damon."

"I think you've just gotta relax about him. You're always worrying about him, babe. It's probably no big deal." Dame flashed me a warm smile and I smiled back at him.

"Maybe you're right," I said.

When he was finished lacing up his skates, we clomped out on the black rubber carpet. The moment we got out onto the ice, Damon started his typical antics. He started to skate like one of those guys in the Olympics—the speeders who bend forward and swing their arms from side to side. I thought he was going to kill somebody. Eventually he calmed down and we skated side by side. It started to get a little cold after a while, and we decided to knock it off. When we were back inside taking off our skates Dame told me he left his agency.

"What? Why?"

"Because that imbecile sent me out for a porno flick."

"No!"

"He sent me out for this movie called *Island Boy*." Dame took off one of his skates and used the bottom of his sweatshirt to wipe the wet blade. "When I went to audition, they asked me to stand in front of the camera and say, 'Gimme a dozen bananas.' "

"What?"

"Then the guy in charge told me to read the line again, but this time he wanted me to make it more *sensual*. Then he said, 'Oh, and would you mind taking off your pants?' " Damon reached into his knapsack and pulled out a Snickers bar.

"Jesus! What did you do?"

"Whaddaya think I did? I got the hell outta there." He took a big bite of the candy bar and started to chomp like that dog again.

"But didn't your agent tell you anything about the audition?" I asked.

"He told me it was for a major motion picture and that it was going to be filmed in the Caribbean."

"God, I can't believe that." I dumped my skates in my duffel bag and massaged my feet a little.

"Yeah, well, that was it. I went over to his office and told him he was a fat, lazy bastard, and then I told him where he could stick his porno film and asked for all my head shots back. Then he threw his ashtray at me and told me I was a little punk who wasn't gonna get anywhere in the business."

"Jesus, that's terrible," I said. Dame stuffed the remainder of the candy bar into his mouth and dropped the wrapper on the wet rubber carpet. I leaned over and picked it up. I felt like Felix Unger, for petesakes.

"You know, in a way . . ." He chewed for a second. "In a way it's not so bad, 'cause I've wanted new representation for a while now, and I've already got an appointment with William Morris."

"Are you still doing the chicken gig?"

"Oh, yeah. But I'm not the chicken. I mean, I'm still working for Chuckles but I'm wearing the frank suit now," he explained, looking in his knapsack. He pulled out a yellow bag of peanut M&M's.

"Frank suit?" I asked.

He tilted back his head and popped some M&M's into his mouth. Two of them hit him on the nose and fell on the floor. "Yeah, Chuckles serves franks, too—hot dogs—and Ed the manager, he told me I could be the hot dog instead of the chicken. I was pretty glad 'cause that chicken suit itched like a bastard."

"Damon, you're not! You're a hot dog now?"

"Hey, don't knock it, Salt. It's not so bad. This older woman, about thirty-five and a real looker, came up to me the other day and told me I had nice buns. . . . Ya get it, Salt? Nice buns?"

Dame started to laugh all over the joint. He was slapping his knee and the M&M's were spilling out of the bag and I'd never seen such a happy-go-lucky bastard in my life.

In March, Mint did a lot of work on new paintings for his show in June. He'd turned my old bedroom into a studio so he could continue painting when he came down from the roof. He spread all this newspaper on the floor and covered my bed and bureau in plastic. He laid all his brushes and crunched-up tubes of paint and big pots of ivory black and titanium white out on a folding table. He took down my pictures and used the wall space to hang his canvases. Sometimes when I got home from work I'd go in there and watch him. I'd stand in the doorway with a glass of wine, as he serenely blended his acrylics and squinted at his canvas. Then he'd lean forward and with the precision of a surgeon he'd touch the tip of his brush to an embryonic wing. His big white work shirt would be all dented and creased and there'd be a cigarette dangling from the corner of his mouth. He'd look like a fantastic madman with smoke weaving around his head and slashes of alizarin crimson and burnt sienna all over his hands.

One Friday in the beginning of April, I came home and went in there. He didn't notice me. He was touching up a magnificent painting. It was a very large canvas, and he'd painted all his pigeons so they looked like they were coming straight at you. They were flying in a V formation, like geese, and the one in the front was huge and fabulous with iron-colored wings and piercing, liquid black eyes. The background was streaked with an orgy of seething red, high-beam gold, and smoldering orange. Sometimes when I looked at his paintings, I wished I could just trade places with him for a minute, so I could see through his eyes.

Minty saw things no one would even notice. He saw brilliance in a bird no one even cared about.

As I stood, silently watching him, I began to remember one winter, right after my first Christmas with Minty. I'd woken up very early and he wasn't in his bed. I wandered around the apartment in my bare feet, looking for him, until I found him seated on the wide windowsill in the living room. I remember the sky was deep slate blue, like the ocean when it rains, and Minty was kind of hunched over, wrapped in the wool blanket Aunt Christa kept by the fireplace.

"Whatcha doin'?" I asked him.

He looked down at me, startled. "I'm drawing the pigeon."

"Where's the pigeon?"

"He's here on the outside part of the window." I tried to climb up on the windowsill, but I had a helluva time. I kept slipping back down. Finally, I made it up and sat down across from him. I looked outside and saw a puffy, pale gray pigeon sleeping on the wet windowsill.

"He's a pretty one," I commented. "Pretty" was my word when I was six. I was always pointing out how goddamn pretty everything was. I'd say, "What a pretty hamburger." Or "Look at the pretty toothpaste." I would go on like that for days.

"Uh-huh." Mint started to erase something on the sketch pad in his lap. "I made his nose too long. I mean, his whatchamacallit. What's his nose called?"

"His beak," I said proudly.

"Yeah. That's right."

"Can I see?" I leaned over to look at his drawing. He tilted it in his lap so I could see it better.

"This is the pigeon and then these, down here, are the trees and this is the pigeons coming out of the trees," he explained.

"Wow. You made a really good pigeon."

"Yeah. I like doing pigeons. Someday I'm gonna do a humongous drawing with zillions and zillions of pigeons and I'm gonna make 'em stand out so everybody stops and looks at them. I'm gonna do it so good everybody is gonna look at them. . . ."

My vision blurred and the pigeons raced toward me. I blinked rapidly. It was all so clear to me. I could still see Minty sitting there, deluged in that creamy wool blanket. I could still see the smudged drawing in his hand and hear him explaining it in his lovely choirboy voice. I walked up to him and wrapped my arms around him from behind.

"Oh, baby. I didn't hear you come in," he said, running one of his hands over mine. I pressed my cheek into the back of his shirt and breathed him in like a poison.

"Your painting looks incredible," I said.

"Thanks. I want to darken the skyline a little, though." I let go of him and stood next to him, studying the painting. "Oh, Salt, let's stay in tonight. Rent movies or something."

I looked at him, astounded. This was the first Friday in months he hadn't wanted to go out. I was very excited that he didn't want to go out because I wasn't exactly what you'd call a party machine. Besides, I hadn't rented a movie since I'd gotten the job on the soap, and I kind of missed it.

So Mint and I decided to go over to the Couch Potato Video place and rent something. It was drizzling when we walked over but it wasn't so bad. When we got to Couch Potato, Mint stood in front of the window for a minute.

"Salt . . ."

"What?" I let go of the door handle and walked over to him.

"Why do we belong to this video store?" he asked, stroking his chin. He hadn't shaved in a day or so and it was dark with stubble.

"Because they're the closest and they're friendly."

He looked down at me skeptically. "Salt, this store is pathetic. They've got about three films, and just look at this. Look at this display." Mint gestured to the window, and I'll have to admit, the display was a little ridiculous. It had a dilapidated garage-sale couch with two big saggy stuffed brown sacks on it. One of the sacks was wearing a lopsided blond wig and it had those round paper eyes glued to it. The other sack was wearing a dopey-looking cowboy hat and it only had one eye. Its other eye was lying on top of the bucket of popcorn in front of it. I could just see the manager of the store screaming at one of the employees, "Hey, kid, we need somethin' to put on this potato! Gimme your cowboy hat. And cut out some eyes for it! It needs some eyes."

"All right. The display is a little pathetic, but that doesn't mean the store is," I countered.

"Salt, there's a Blockbuster two blocks up on Third."

"Yeah, and it's cold and impersonal and they don't give you the Potato discount coupons."

"Oh, God forbid we don't get the Potato discount coupons!" Mint cried, waving an arm over his head.

"Oh, cut that out." I smacked him on the shoulder and he started to laugh.

When we walked into the store, there was only one other customer, in the X-rated section. Some new guy I'd never seen before was working behind the counter. He waved at us and told us to feel free to browse. I don't know what the hell else we'd do in a video store. I followed Mint into the foreign-film aisle. I hated the foreign-film aisle. All the boxes were covered with bosomy women shaking their fists, and men in dark sunglasses smoking cigarettes. I moved over to the comedy aisle and scanned the titles. I picked up *Manhattan* and brought the box over to Mint.

"All right, maybe. Let's see what else there is." Mint strolled over into the drama section. "Look at this. Look at this. They've got nothing," he complained. He picked up a box, read it, and stuck it back on the shelf. "The whole drama section's as long as my arm."

I wandered away from him into the next aisle, which turned out to be the Western section. What a nightmare. I swear, every box has some tough bastard (usually the Duke) in a cowboy hat. Of course, that's because Westerns are all alike. All you ever see in a Western is a bunch of guys in cowboy hats, riding around, shooting each other. Only sometimes the plot will vary a little and they'll get off their horses before they shoot each other. And if they haven't started shooting each other, they're in one of two places. They're either down by a stream, chewing tobacco and rinsing out their smelly pants, or busting into the local saloon for a whiskey and a piece of ass. They bore the hell out of me.

I started to look at some classics just as Mint came around the corner holding up a box. "How about *Network?*" he asked.

"Oh, okay. But let's rent *Manhattan*, too."

"All right."

When we got home, we got into our robes and brought a big tray stacked with cheese, crackers, nuts, fruit, and wine into the bedroom. Mint slipped *Manhattan* into the VCR and we sat up in bed and munched on the food as we watched. Mint didn't eat as much as I did. He started to smoke these super-duper strong cigarettes, these *Apocalypse Now* kind of cigarettes. Lucky Strike is what they were. I just kept stuffing crackers into my mouth until the box was empty. I should never eat when I'm watching a movie 'cause I'll turn into Damon. I'll just keep eating until I don't have anything left to eat anymore. When the movie ended, I curled up next to Minty.

Mint started to flip through the channels then. He stopped on channel four. Carson was ending and Johnny was shaking hands with all his guests.

"Oh," Mint said, looking down at his watch, "Letterman's on."

He sat up a little, and I looked over at him.

"You want to watch Letterman?" I asked. "I thought you wanted to see *Network*. I'll put it in." I started to get up.

"No. I don't feel like it, Salt. I guess the Woody Allen just changed my mood. I feel like watching something light. Let's just watch Letterman."

I shrugged and lay back down, resting my head on Mint's stomach and gazing at the television. The Energizer bunny was going by and I wanted to sock it in the nose. Every time you turned on the TV, that goddamn bunny would bang through the picture. I know they're trying to be witty and all that, but eventually you lose your sense of humor and want to sock the bunny in the nose. Minty was turning the channels while the commercial was on and paused at some slut in a sausage dress who asked me if I was lonely. She asked me if I wanted to be alone with her to tell her my wildest fantasies. Then she licked her glossy red lips and told me to call now, that she was waiting for me, that it would only cost five dollars a minute to talk to her. What a nightmare. This whole damn country was going down the toilet.

Mint changed back and finally Letterman came on. He walked out briskly in a black sports jacket, flashing his gap-toothed smile. He started to tell some jokes and I dozed off for a while. When I opened my eyes, he was introducing Marcie from North Carolina and her pit bull, Elvis. Elvis was a huge, lumbering dog with a lot of drool dripping out of his mouth.

"Oh, my, my, my, my, my, my, my . . . will you look at Elvis." Dave's eyes gaped open and he whistled in appreciation. "Now this . . . this is no poodle." Marcie had Elvis sit down near Dave, and the dog looked up at him with a vigilant expression. "Why . . . why's he looking at me like that?" Dave asked nervously. "You have fed him, haven't you?"

I closed my eyes as Marcie began to yack with Dave. I was half asleep when I thought I heard Dave say, "And now, our next guest, leggy supermodel Sabina!" Then my eyes fluttered open and wouldn't you know it, the bitch was really on Letterman. I thought was having a nightmare but she was really on the goddamn program. She oozed out from backstage in a blazing coral dress about the size of a pot holder, and Letterman was wiping his forehead with his tie and all the males in the audience were hollering "Yahoo!" "Hallelujah!" and "Mama mia!"

"Isn't that the model from the benefit?" Mint asked.

"I don't know. Why don't we see if something else is on," I suggested casually.

"Why? You love Letterman."

"I know. It's just . . . oh, forget it." I decided to drop it. Of all the goddamn guests, he had to have Sabina on. I rested my head back on Mint and glowered at the screen. Sabina was lounging like some kind of royalty in the chair beside Dave's desk. Her sparkling blond hair was draped down over one shoulder and her long bronzed calves were stretched out like skis.

"Well, well, well . . . it is the greatest of pleasures to have you here on our little show. . . ." Dave kissed Sabina's hand, and she glanced around like she couldn't care less. "I was talking to one of our producers earlier . . . he saw you in the hallway and walked into a wall. He was just so gosh-darned overwhelmed by the sight of you that he walked straight into a wall. But then I suppose you're used to that."

"About three weeks ago, I was hailing a cab and this guy saw me and fell into an open manhole," she remarked nonchalantly. What a nightmare she was. All of a sudden I was hungry again. I grabbed a chunk of cheddar and stuck it in my mouth.

"My lord! That's amazing. Did you hear that, Paul?" Dave called to the bandleader. "Some guy saw her and fell into a manhole!"

"Oh, well . . . I can believe it," Paul commented into his mike.

"But you just started modeling recently and you're this *hot, hot* supermodel now," Dave said.

"I started modeling about a year and a half ago." Sabina tilted her head to look at Dave, and you could see she was being so goddamn coquettish. Playing with her goddamned earring. She had on these drippy chandelier-like earrings and she started to twist one around in her fingers.

"I'll bet you have a great story about being discovered," Dave said.

"Sort of. It's funny. I'd just graduated from high school and I was in New York with a girlfriend for the summer. One night we went to eat at Le Relais, and John Casablancas came over to the table and told me I should be a model. But I didn't know who he was, and since men were always telling me, 'Oh, you're so beautiful, you should be a model,' I thought he was just another creep who was trying to get near me, so I . . ." She giggled and covered her face with her hand for a moment. "I told him to piss off." She started to laugh, so of course Dave started to laugh, and then the whole goddamn audience started to laugh. Oh, boy, that was some knee-slapper.

"Oh, my, heh, heh, heh . . . ha, ha, ha . . . so you just thought he was another creep, then?" Dave asked.

"Yeah. And when I found out he was the head of Elite, I couldn't believe I'd said that." She shifted a little in her chair and one of the spaghetti straps of her dress slipped off her shoulder.

"Oh, well, naturally." Dave leaned forward and smiled at her. "So you began modeling then."

"Well, I'd planned to study interior design, but then I thought, if you look the way I look, why shouldn't you take advantage of it?" She shrugged and the other spaghetti strap started to slip. "Oops." She noticed it and pulled it back up. "I don't want my dress to fall off." The audience went bananas. All hooting and whistling like a bunch of cretins.

"Ah, now, you can't tease them like that, Sabina. They're all in misery now." Dave gestured to the audience. Then he leaned his elbow on the desk, rested his head on his hand, and stared at her. "My, but you're a lovely lady." He sighed loudly, and Sabina began to play with her stupid earring again. "Isn't she lovely, Paul?" he called over to the bandleader.

Paul rubbed his palm over his chest and leaned into his mike. "Oh, she's just stunning, Dave. Just breathtaking . . . words can't even express . . ."

I stuffed another big piece of cheese into my mouth and chomped furiously.

"Oh, my, I almost forgot. Do you know what I have?" Dave smiled wickedly.

"No. What?" Sabina asked.

Dave reached under his desk and pulled out something square and held it up for the camera. Ah, Jesus. It was a Sabina calendar, for christsakes. There was a photo of a glistening, golden-brown Sabina arching her back all over the sand in a white string bikini.

"Oh, God, you have my calendar," she remarked, tossing her hair back. Of course, the audience was going bananas again.

"Now, now, calm down or you'll force me to come up there and smack you all around," Dave shouted. The audience quieted down and he turned back to Sabina. "These photos are just magnificent," he commented, flipping through the calendar in his lap.

"They came out well," Sabina said. She had her legs crossed now and one of her sexy pink shoes was half off her foot. She was dangling it on her toes.

"Where were the photos taken?"

"All the shots were taken in Bali. God, it's such a long way. It's like twenty hours by plane and when we got there they'd had this storm on the island, I guess it was right before we arrived, and the beach was full of mosquitoes. I must have been bitten twenty times on my legs." Oh, the poor broad. What a trauma.

"I've said it before and I'll say it again, some insects just get all the luck," Dave remarked with a goofy grin. "Say, how would you like to break into my house sometime?"

Sabina smiled and tossed her hair again.

What a nightmare.

Chapter

22

"*Oh, please, don't get upset*," I said.

"Don't get upset?! You seduced my father! You slept with my father while I was lying in the hospital in a coma! God, you're sick!" he wailed, turning his back on me.

"Please . . . please don't say that." I touched him, and he swung around and glared at me.

"Get out of here! Get out!" he cried. "I never want to see you again!"

"Well, that's just too bad, because you're going to have to see me again." I smirked mercilessly and narrowed my eyes at him.

"Why the hell should I?!"

"Because I'm going to be your stepmother."

"God, no! No!" He covered his face with his hands and backed into the lacquered commode.

"Cut!" shouted Mark, the director. "That's it. We're going to use that one."

I rubbed my temples and squinted at the blinding lights. Lucas staggered over to me, clutching his chest dramatically. "I can't believe you're doing this to me! Laura! You slut!" he bellowed. I smiled at him and punched him in the arm. "Hey, how long till your next scene?" he asked me.

"About two hours."

"I've gotta go make a phone call, but you wanta meet up in the lounge in about ten minutes for some chow?"

"Absolutely. I'm famished," I said. I hadn't eaten all day and it was already two something in the afternoon.

"Great." Lucas dashed off toward his dressing room.

I clumped off the set in those irritating spike heels my character wore. Everybody was darting back and forth with ladders and fake trees, and cables were slithering across the floor like snakes. You could kill yourself in a joint like that.

When I reached the heavy door that led into the stairwell, I took the goddamn shoes off and went up the back stairs to the actors' lounge.

There were only a couple of other actors in there. I got a bagel and coffee and sat down on the couch in front of the large television. Peter Garrett said hi to me and I said hi back. He was sitting on the couch next to some day player. Peter was the show's gigolo. He played Dirk Wilder, and in every scene he had he was half naked. He was always coming out of the shower or rolling out of bed or chopping wood or something. In real life, he wasn't much better. He always wore these supertight black jeans and muscle T-shirts. Even if the studio was freezing cold, he'd walk around in those T-shirts so he could show off all his damned muscles. Then he had all his sleazy jewelry. He wore these two thin gold chains that would sink into his matted chest hair and this chunky gold-link bracelet on his wrist. His dressing room was enough to kill you. He'd plastered the whole thing with publicity posters of himself. Every poster was exactly the same, too. He was always topless in a pair of tight jeans, flexing his muscles and cocking his head. He'd have his nostrils flared and these big shaded hollows under his jutting cheekbones. At the bottom of the posters it said, "Dirk Wilder of 'Today Is Tomorrow.' " Whenever there were extras or day players in the studio, they'd all sneak around after him like a bunch of imbeciles. The worst were the poor bastards outside, waiting for him to come out of the studio. I know they were waiting for him, because whenever I walked out, they'd ask me if Dirk was coming out. They called him by his character's name, for christsakes. They were only kids, though, mostly around fifteen and they'd have all those *Teen Idol* magazines with Pete's picture all over them. If they knew what he was really like, I doubt they would have wasted their time. He was about as charismatic as a can opener.

So I was sitting there next to him on the couch, sipping my coffee, when he turned to me and asked if I'd mind running some lines with him. I wanted to run lines with Pete like a hole in the head, but I'm very lousy at saying no to people. Whenever I say no to somebody, I'm afraid they'll think I'm a snob or a bitch or something.

"Sure. I don't mind." He handed me his script and I put down my bagel.

"It's page seven. The scene with Eve," he instructed.

I turned to page seven, and you should have seen the doodles all over it. All the margins were crammed with these deformed-looking profiles. He'd draw a forehead and then a big hill for the nose, and then there'd be another long line until you got these two tiny bumps right next to each other, which I assumed were lips. Then he'd place a gigantic eyeball right beside the nose. This was the work of a true nitwit.

Anyhow, I ignored all the profiles and looked at the scene. The script read:

> The Clairmont Health Club. Eve is relaxing in a hot tub when Dirk enters. He is glistening with sweat from a work-

out and wears a towel around his waist. Eve looks up at him, startled.

DIRK

You don't mind if I join you.

EVE

(*With obvious anger*) Do what you want. (*Dirk drops his towel and enters hot tub. He sits across from her, watching her.*)

DIRK

You look beautiful, Eve.

EVE

Oh, stop it. I know all about your little trip to St. Martin with Heather Holmes. You make me sick, Dirk. I don't ever want you to touch me again!

DIRK

But, Eve—

EVE

I believed you. I gave you that loan and you just took advantage of me. (*Her eyes begin to tear.*) I thought you cared.

DIRK

Oh, Eve, I do care. The whole time I was in St. Martin, I was thinking of you. (*Dirk looks at her longingly.*)

EVE

I don't believe you.

DIRK

It's true. Every night I dreamed of holding you in my arms again.

EVE

Oh, Dirk . . . (*Eve begins to sob.*)

DIRK

Oh, Eve, darling, don't cry. (*Dirk slides over and takes her in his arms.*)

EVE

No, Dirk . . . no . . . Dirk . . . no, no.

DIRK

Oh, Eve, I want you. (*Dirk kisses her passionately. She struggles for a moment, but then she stops protesting and wraps her arms around him.*)

EVE

Oh, Dirk . . . Dirk . . . (*They entwine in a heated embrace, when suddenly a door slams.*)

HEATHER

(An explosion) Dirk! How could you! (*Dirk looks up at Heather in horror and slides away from Eve.*)

DIRK

Heather! Wait! It's not what it looks like! (*Dirk leaps up and races after Heather, who has left the room. Eve sobs in hot tub.*)

I had to read this idiotic scene with him two times because he kept screwing up a line. I probably would have had to read it a third time if there hadn't been an announcement for him to get to the set.

Pete was just strutting off when Lucas arrived. You should have seen the look Lucas gave Pete's outfit.

"Is it my imagination, or are Pete's pants getting tighter?" Lucas said as he sat down next to me with his coffee and donut.

"You should have heard the scene I just read with him."

"It couldn't have been as bad as ours."

"It was worse." I took a bite of my bagel.

"I went on a double date with him a couple of weeks ago. He's so cheap it's unbelievable," Lucas whispered.

"What did he do?"

"Oh, his date was like sixteen and he hardly spoke to her the whole night. He kept talking to me about the Rangers game. Then he took us to this dive down in the West Village. It was called Guaco Ariba, Home of the Discount Enchilada."

"No! You're kidding," I said, laughing.

"No, I'm totally serious. It was like this Mexican fast food. All the tables were covered with plastic and half the customers looked like they'd just escaped from Sing Sing." Lucas took a big bite of his donut and got powdered sugar all over his face. I handed him a napkin. "Then when we left the restaurant, this really attractive girl recognized him on the street, and Pete got her number right in front of his date."

"Oh, my God," I muttered.

"He's so unbelievable. He's just like his handwriting."

"What do you mean?"

"Oh, I'm into handwriting analysis," Lucas said. "Well, I'm taking a course on it."

"Really? That's interesting. What's Pete's handwriting like?"

"It's really huge and thick and showy, full of loops and flamboyant capital letters. He—oh, look, he's on the monitor."

Lucas pointed at the TV, and I looked up to see Pete standing there in a towel with Luna, one of the makeup artists, misting his face with water.

"Oh, they must be shooting the hot tub scene I just read with him," I said. Lucas started to laugh like crazy, and we kept watching the monitor. Luna was misting Pete's chest now, and he was trying to swat her away. The camera angle altered, and Natalie James, the actress who played Eve, came into view. She was in a black bikini, standing beside the fake door Peter would come through. Another makeup artist was pressing pancake powder all over her forehead and nose. You could hear the crew yacking and feet stomping and things clanking in the background. Then the screen went blank for a couple seconds. When the picture came back on, Natalie was stepping into the hot tub.

"God! It's freezing!" she cried. "Can't they get it any warmer?"

Somebody off-camera told her they couldn't keep it heated. I could hear Mark screaming for Peter.

"Does anybody know where Peter went?" Mark's assistant yelled.

"He's changing his swimsuit!" Luna called out.

"What the hell is he changing his swimsuit for! Nobody's gonna see him below the waist!" Mark bellowed. Boy, was Mark in a testy mood. Mark was normally one of the calmer directors, but that day he'd been really pissed off.

Natalie got out of the hot tub and Luna came over and handed her a robe. When she got it on, she folded her arms across her chest and muttered, "This is so typical." She stood there bouncing up and down for about two minutes until someone shouted, "Here he is!"

"Goddamnit, Peter! We're already behind schedule!" Mark shouted. "All right. Quiet, everyone! We're shooting!"

Natalie gave Luna her robe and stepped back into the hot tub. After she immersed herself and the scene was slated, they began a take. Natalie leaned back and ran a hand through her tousled blond hair. She looked up suddenly, and they cut to Peter closing the fake door behind him.

"You don't mind if I join you?" he asked.

Natalie narrowed her eyes at him. "Do what you want," she said sharply. You saw a shot of Peter's bare feet then and the towel collapsing around them. He stuck his foot in the water.

"Jesus Christ! What is it, below zero?! We have to sit in this! Jesus Christ!" he yelled.

"Cut!" Mark yelled. "Peter, we have four more scenes to shoot today. I would appreciate it if you would grin and bear it."

Peter muttered something inaudible and then he said, "Yeah, okay."

They took the scene from the top again. This time Peter got in the water and everything went all right until Natalie started to sob and Peter said, "Stop it. I want you."

"Cut!" Mark repeated. "Peter, if you're going to make up your lines, could you at least try to make them remotely intelligent?"

Peter glared in Mark's direction. "What's the line?!" he demanded.

" 'Oh, Eve, darling, don't cry!' " said Carol, the script monitor.

"Okay, I've got it," Peter called. They took the scene from when Natalie started to sob again.

"Oh, Eve, baby, don't cry!" Peter lunged roughly toward her, and this wave of water rose up and sloshed all over her made-up face.

"Oh, God!" she wailed, blinking frantically.

"CUT!" Mark erupted. "Do you have any idea how much time we've wasted here?!"

"I didn't know that would happen!" Pete cried.

"Oh, God! I can't believe you did that." Natalie stood up, her face dripping, and Luna rushed over with a towel.

"How long is it gonna take to fix her makeup?" Mark asked.

"About five minutes. At least five," Luna said, surveying the damage.

"All right! Take five, people!" Mark ordered. Luna helped Natalie into her robe and they walked off the set. Peter was the only person left on screen. He stood up, looked down at his blue Speedo suit, and covered his groin.

"Could somebody bring me a goddamn towel!" he yelled. Somebody threw a towel at him and the screen went blank.

❦

One afternoon in April I got off work early because they cut me from a scene at the last moment. It was a scene where Mick and I were supposed to go to the loony bin because Jenny's case was being reviewed by the medical board and they wanted to ask Edward some questions. My character was originally going to accompany Edward, but they decided it wasn't necessary. Lola was back in the loony bin, though. Remember when she was going to stab Mick? Well, he ended up getting the knife away from her, and I clonked her on the head with Edward's nine iron.

Anyhow, I had most of the afternoon and decided to use the time to get Mint's birthday present. His birthday was about three weeks away and I wanted to get him this cashmere sweater I'd seen in a shop window on Madison Avenue. Normally, I never shop on Madison, since it's such a freakin' fortune, but I wanted to get him something really nice this year. So I went to the men's store, it was called Buffi or Biffi or something. I must have waited for twenty minutes for the sales guy because this fancy dame with her hair like a soufflé kept ordering him around. I finally got him to help me and I shelled out three hundred and fifty bucks for the sweater in the window. I knew Minty would adore it, so I splurged.

When I came out of the store, I decided to walk uptown on Madison for a while. I saw a ton of those dames with that same soufflé hair. Madison Avenue is loaded with them. They're always popping out of limousines in Chanel suits with alligator handbags. Sometimes they'll have these little cocktail parties on the street. You'll see two of 'em chatting up a storm and then another one will be going by in a limo and she'll call out the window, "Yoo-hoo! Catherine, darling! It's Bitsy!" And then Bitsy will pop out of her limo and join the other two and it'll turn into a goddamn cocktail party. I hate seeing them in the winter, though, because they're always enveloped in huge fur coats with fur hoods and fur bonnets and it's just so sad. All I can ever think about are the poor goddamn animals who lay dying with their feet in some steel-jaw trap so these dames could have a fancy hat. I can't stand it.

Anyhow, that day I was going along and right up ahead of me there was this fairly corpulent nanny in a white nurse's uniform with two little boys. You could see they'd all just come back from the park, and it was just terrible. It was terrible because one of the kids—he looked around five—he was on one of those plastic motorcycles with wheels. He was going along very peacefully, smiling and shuffling his little feet, while the other kid was on a leash, for christsakes. This kid was probably four and, man, was he furious. The nanny just kept yanking him along on the leash and he was shrieking and slobbering and the little behind of his red trousers was covered with dirt and it was just terrible. He kept stopping to point at his brother on the motorcycle, and I'll tell you, I didn't blame him in the least. You can't just let one kid ride on a motorcycle and drag the other one around on a leash. It's just not fair, for christsakes. The younger one did have a box of animal crackers, but still, that's not enough to make up for being on a leash and not having a motorcycle.

I was still looking at the poor bastard when I had this vision in my head of Minty and me with our little son. I know I was jumping the gun, but I couldn't help it. I could see all three of us coming back from the park together. Our son would be between us, but he wouldn't be on any leash. He'd be holding our hands and beaming up at us. He'd be a clone of Minty with cream in his blood and emeralds in his eyes and I'd dress him up in blue overalls and little red sneakers. I wouldn't put a leash on him in a million years. I'd buy him all the animal crackers he wanted, too.

Smiling at the thought of it, I was about to cross the street on Sixty-eighth when across the street I saw Minty getting out of a long black limousine with Jori and the Creature and Sabina. My mouth fell open and I ducked behind a pay phone and poked my head out. They all went into Billy Martin's, this snazzy Western boutique on the corner. I couldn't believe it. What was he doing with her? My heart was pounding like crazy. I had to see what was going on.

As soon as the traffic stopped, I darted across the street and snuck up to the shop window. The four of them were standing in front of a wall mirror trying on Stetson hats. They were all laughing and kidding around. Then Sabina, she put on this white one and started to strike all these glamour-girl poses. As if Scavullo was going to leap out with his camera from behind a belt rack, for christsakes. She was wearing a skimpy leather miniskirt and a black bodysuit top with a fuchsia shawl draped over her shoulders. Every couple of seconds she'd gaze over at Minty with this come-hither motherfucker look in her eyes. Oh, I knew exactly what the bitch was up to. She was flirting with him like Scarlett O'Hara at the Twelve Oaks picnic.

Then Jori grabbed Mint's arm and they went over to the counter together. The Creature wiggled over to Sabina in her skintight leopard-print pants and ten-foot-tall Stetson and said something, and from the perplexed look on Sabina's face I was sure she had just made another one of her inane comments. Sabina just ignored her and stared at herself in the mirror. She was smiling and puckering her lips and tilting her head around so she could worship every angle of her face. What an arrogant bitch she was. When I look in the mirror, the first thing I do is frown at the dark circles under my eyes or something. I certainly don't stand there and drool over myself like a happy-go-lucky bastard. After a few minutes Jori turned around from the counter in his chic black Italian trench and said something to the Creature, which caused her to bounce up and down like an idiot. Then suddenly, all four of them were heading toward the door, cowboy hats and all.

I ducked and scrambled around the corner as fast as I could. When I sneaked my head out, they were all getting into the limousine. When Sabina got into the car, Jori leaned over and whispered something to Mint. Mint started to laugh, and then Jori slapped him on the back and they both got into the car and slammed the door.

Once they got in the limo I couldn't see anything anymore, since it had those goddamn tinted windows. After it drove off, I just stood there, leaning up against the side of the building. I felt so cold. My hands were like ice and I was overwhelmed with confusion. When I watched Minty get into that limo, I barely knew him. All I saw was a beautiful stranger with his people. The one who flashes past you, and disappears forever.

❧

Minty didn't come home until around midnight. I was in bed pretending to read when he came into the bedroom.

"Hey, baby, how was your day?" he asked casually. He took off his black jacket and went over to the closet. I just sat there staring at him. After he hung up his jacket he glanced over at me, loosening his tie. "What?" he muttered, raising his eyebrows. "Why are you looking at me like that?"

"Minty . . . why did you lie to me?"

"What do you mean, lie to you? When did I lie to you?" he demanded brusquely.

"When I left this morning, you told me you were going to paint this afternoon."

"Yeah, so?"

"I saw you on Madison Avenue today with Jori and those women."

He sighed and started to unbutton his crisp white oxford. "Yeah. I went out with Alessandro this afternoon. He called and asked me to come out for a while. I wasn't getting any work done so I decided to hang with him." Mint took off his shirt and flung it onto the chair near the closet. His eyes swept back to mine. "It was no big deal, Salt."

I looked at him standing there. He looked so exquisite. So ethereal, so unbearably beautiful . . . but for some reason, his beauty only hurt my eyes. I closed them; tears seeped through my lashes and I pressed my fingertips to the sides of my forehead. "What is it? What's the matter?" I heard him say. I didn't want to make him mad. I didn't want to cry, but I couldn't help it.

"Minty, it was a big deal," I gasped. I opened my eyes and looked at him. "When I saw you on the street today, I was so hurt. I felt . . . I felt . . ." I couldn't get out what I wanted to say.

Mint came over and sat down on the bed beside me. He took me in his arms and pressed my head against his warm bare chest. "What? What did you feel, baby?" he asked gently.

"I felt . . . you didn't love me anymore. That you were having an affair."

Mint drew my head up and stared at me with an astounded expression. "Is that what you think? You think I'm having an affair?"

I sniffed and nodded.

"Salty, for godsakes, I just went around town for a couple hours with Alessandro. If you think I'm having some sort of affair with that redheaded slut with the big lips he—"

"No . . . not the Creature," I mumbled, and wiped my eyes.

"The what?"

"No, I meant Sabina."

"Oh, come on, Salty. That's ridiculous."

"Why was she with you?" I asked.

"She wasn't with me. She was with Alessandro. She's a friend of his and Johnny's. Look, Salt, I'm not having an affair with her."

"She's pretty . . ." I groaned.

"Well, of course she's pretty. She's a model."

"And she has big hooters," I added.

Minty started to laugh. When he quit laughing, he leaned over and got a Kleenex out of the bedside drawer and handed it to me. "Blow your nose, Salt." I blew my nose.

"Minty, I'm sorry. When you told me you were going to paint and then I saw you with Sabina, I thought you lied to me so you could be with her."

"You've got to stop being so paranoid, baby." Mint reached over and brushed a lock of hair out of my eyes. "I would never cheat on you, Salty."

I looked at him, and he seemed so powerful. So celestial. Just as he always had. I leaned over and clung to him. I was so afraid, because I needed him so desperately. He was like a drug to me, and I was no different from an addict whose shadow spills out of a downtown alley. Whose shifty eyes are darting over anything, everything. And then for a minute he thinks he sees . . . but no. It's just an old newspaper afloat in the wind or a homeless dog limping out of the night in search of a deity to fetch slippers for. That guy needs his goddamn fix so bad because it's the only thing in the world that makes it okay.

I know, I understand. I wait for mine. And it scares you, when you need it so bad. It scares you because, shit, how do you know you'll always be able to get it?

❧

That next week I went to lunch with Lola. Ever since she'd cured me with that goddamn black haw we'd become pretty good friends. Anyhow, we both had a break at the same time and she took me to this goddawful little joint called Organic Delight. This was not a delight at all.

Organic Nightmare is what they should have called it. The whole place was painted spinach green and it was mobbed with bushes and trees and hanging ferns and it was like a goddamn jungle. You could hardly find the tables, what with all the tendrils of ivy drooping in your face. They should have handed you a compass and a machete at the door, for christsakes.

When we finally got to a table for two right under a six-foot schefflera plant and looked at the menus, Lola warned me not to order the raw turnip salad. I was very disappointed, as you can imagine, since I'd had my heart set on a good heap of raw turnips. Lola ordered something called the Seaweed Plate. I didn't want anything, but since I needed to put something in my stomach I ordered the Chickpea Delight, which, of course, turned out to be a chickpea nightmare. It was a big wooden bowl loaded with chickpeas, alfalfa sprouts, and shredded carrots.

"How can you eat this stuff every day?" I asked, trying to stab some chickpeas with my fork.

"You'd like it if you ate it more often. I know you like your bagel and cream cheese and those things you bring in the Ziploc bags—"

"They're Yodels," I mumbled.

"Yodels. But they're awful for you, Salty. They're pure sugar and fat. And you shouldn't drink so much coffee because caffeine is terrible for your nervous system. And the cigarettes are, too. You should definitely take extra vitamin C if you're going to smoke, because nicotine depletes you of vitamin C. You have to care more. Your body is a temple, Salty."

"My body isn't a temple, it's a 7-Eleven," I muttered.

"Ha, ha," Lola said, digging into the clumps of slimy green seaweed on her plate. "Hey, Salty, what do you think of Lucas?"

"What do you mean? He's great."

"Do you think you could ever like him as more than a friend?"

I looked up at her, puzzled. "I'm living with Minty, Lola."

"Oh, I know. I was just curious."

"Why?"

She hesitated. "Well, I shouldn't tell you this, but he likes you."

"He does?"

"When you weren't around on Tuesday, he came in and asked me if you were happy with your boyfriend."

"What did you say?"

"I said, as far as I know she is. Then I asked Luke if he liked you and, Salty, he blushed and said he thought you were incredible."

I gaped at her in astonishment. "I don't believe it. He said that?"

"Uh-huh. But he made me swear I wouldn't tell you, so you can't say anything."

Jesus. I felt like I was in fourth grade all of a sudden.

"Do you want to try some of this?" Lola extended her fork toward me with a soggy tendril of seaweed dripping from it.

"No! Uh, thank you . . . but no, thanks. I'm fine, really," I stammered. "What happened in the elevator scene with—"

"Oh, my God! What time is it?" Lola gasped, dropping her fork.

I glanced down at my watch. "It's one-thirty-six."

"Oh, shit. I knew there was something I forgot. I have a one-thirty run-through with Mick."

"Just grab a taxi. You'll be okay."

"He's going to kill me. I'm so sorry, Salt," Lola said, dumping a ten-dollar bill on the table.

"Don't worry about it. I'll see you later."

Lola grabbed her bag, raced off, and vanished behind a ficus tree and a big potted fern. So I sat there, looking at all the god-damn foliage, and lit up a cigarette and started to think about what Lucas had said about me. Then, as I was thinking about it, this waitress came charging out of the bushes and ordered me to extinguish my cigarette. Man, was she a delight. She was one of those bohemian health nuts, I could see it right away. She had this rosy makeup-free complexion and superlong urine-colored hair that swung all over the place like goddamn drapery. Any-how, there wasn't an ashtray on the table so I had to put the ciga-rette out in the Chickpea Delight. Meanwhile, the waitress was staring at me like a hawk. From the look on her face, you would have thought I'd murdered her whole family or something. She finally took off with her hair swishing back and forth.

When she was gone I pulled my script out of my bag and started to look it over. I began to get distracted by the four broads sitting at the table next to mine, though. They were all about twenty-something and they were having one of those boyfriend-battering conversations. I kept trying to tune them out until all of a sudden something caught my attention.

". . . is that Marzipan Man."

I looked at the table out of the corner of my eye.

"Oh, isn't he the hottest thing you've ever seen?" said this blondish one with a lot of blue eyeshadow.

"Minty owns the Marzipan Pigeon. You know, we should go there one night and check him out," a brunette said.

"Oh, yeah, right. I hear it costs a fortune and it takes like two months to even get a reservation. He probably doesn't even go," the blondish one remarked.

Then, oh Jesus, was this a nightmare, this other brunette with her hair in a stupid-looking ponytail said, "Maybe he does. It might be worth it, Becca—he's not married, you know."

I wanted to hurl the bowl of chickpeas across the room. I dropped some money on the table and stormed out of the joint. I was absolutely furious. My Minty. Complete strangers were talking about him as if they'd met him. As if they knew him. I stalked down the street at top speed, abruptly brushing past everybody.

Then at the end of the block, I stopped dead in my tracks. The corner newsstand was flooded with him.

I rushed over and grabbed one. Mint was dressed up in a steel gray suit with a black trench and, shit, did he look smashing. He hadn't struck up some phony smile or anything. He was looking at the camera but he wasn't posing. He was smoking a cigarette and I guess he'd just taken a drag before they shot the picture because there was this hazy line of smoke scribbling up from the corner of his mouth. His chartreuse eyes were sort of squinted up and his trench was billowing open in a gust of wind. Behind him I recognized the view from our roof, the buildings receding into a stormy, metallic gray sky. And then there were the pigeons. A whole pack of them were sputtering, bursting into the air around Minty, their wings fantastically smeared. The headline read "The Marzipan Man Takes Manhattan." Minty's picture was blazing on every cover of GQ. Minty was everywhere.

Chapter 23

About two weeks before Mint left for L.A., Jori invited us to a party at his apartment. I put on my formal garb and tried to be pleasant about it. We arrived at Jori's at about eight-thirty. One of the doormen asked for our names when we entered and he told us he'd have to call up.

"He's expecting us," Mint said curtly.

"Yes, sir. But I'm afraid the building has been experiencing some security difficulties and we have been instructed to announce all guests," the doorman explained. When he got off the intercom, he gestured to the elevator with his white-gloved hand and told us we could go up now. When we got to Jori's mirrored foyer, Mint rang the doorbell, and we stood there for about a minute.

"Did you ring it hard enough?" I asked.

"Yeah." Mint pushed it again, and we finally heard shoes clomping and the door was opened by a Spanish maid who smiled politely and led us into the entrance gallery.

"Man, it's so quiet. Are we the first ones here or something?"

Mint asked the maid as we followed her toward the closed double door that led into the living room. She muttered something about not speaking English, and then she opened the doors and the living room was pitch black.

"What's going on? Where's Alessandro? It was tonight, wasn't it?" Mint asked. When all of a sudden the lights came on and about forty people leapt up in front of us and screamed, "Surprise!" Scared the daylights out of me. I jerked backward and practically knocked over the poor goddamn maid.

"Oh, my God . . ." Mint muttered, glancing around. You should have seen the living room. The entire ceiling was smothered with black and silver Mylar balloons and all these streamers were spiraling down. There were musicians: a guy playing a sax, another on drums, and another playing Jori's piano. Three gorgeous black women in fire-engine red dresses were positioned in front of the fireplace. They were standing around a microphone singing a soul rendition of "Happy Birthday." Jori was leaning up next to a giant birthday cake in the center of the room. He was wearing a slick black suit and raising a glass of champagne. What a fucking extravaganza it was. I could see Helmut Huldheinz towering over a bunch of people in the back and Johnny Vane standing up front next to Sabina. I saw a couple of the Creature's girlfriends giggling together like morons and a few rich-looking bastards scattered around.

The three women in red were almost done singing "Happy Birthday." They were simultaneously extending their arms toward Minty, coming to the "to you" part, when the Creature burst out of the giant cake in an electric red bikini and screeched, "Wooooo! Wooooo!" Then it started to bounce up and down and toss confetti, and its enormous, unnaturally round breasts didn't even move. It was just horrendous. All the guests started to clap and blow noisemakers, and Minty held his hands up to the sides of his face in shock. He walked over to Jori and playfully slugged him in the arm, and Jori started to laugh and slapped him on the back.

I couldn't stand it. I wondered how Jori knew it was Mint's birthday. Well, it wasn't his birthday yet; it was two days away, but Jori obviously knew about it. I figured that he had Mint's birth date in his files or something. Of course the sleazy bastard didn't even involve me in his plans. Ah, screw it, I thought. I was going to have my own celebration with Mint on his real birthday, and there would be none of these imbeciles at that celebration.

I wandered into the room and grabbed a glass of champagne from one of the servants' gleaming silver trays. All these people were crowding around Minty and I didn't want to get squashed, so I went and stood in the entrance to the dining room, where there was this long buffet set up. The singers started to sing that old Supremes song, the one about love being an itchin' in your heart and, baby, you can't scratch it. They were very talented, those singers. They sounded just like the Supremes. I lit a cigarette and watched everybody begin to diffuse into the rest of the living room when my eyes snagged on Sabina. I saw her slink over to Jori's Steinway, and then she sat on top of it in her shimmery silver slip-dress. As if she wasn't conspicuous enough, for crying out loud. The room was overflowing with chairs, but no, the bitch had to go perch herself on top of the goddamn piano. Of course, in less than five seconds she was completely surrounded by men. I shook my head and took a big gulp of champagne.

After a while I decided to mingle. Everybody was in their familiar stupid clusters again. I went over to one. What a cluster I chose. It was filled with these thirtyish-looking women in little black dresses with pearl necklaces and glinting diamond rings. They were having one of the most ridiculous conversations you've ever heard. It was all about spas and some trainer named

Ragu or something. Then one of them mentioned Sabina and asked if anybody thought she'd had implants. Nobody knew, but this one broad blurted out, "Did anybody hear about the model whose breasts exploded on the airplane?" Everybody gasped in horror. Then, after they finished gasping, they all wanted to know who it was and exactly how her hooters exploded. What a nightmare this cluster was. I slipped out of it, and they didn't even notice.

The next one I came upon was commanded by Johnny Vane. He was standing there like a fashion evangelist, yacking to a group of completely riveted women. ". . . that's why you can't use chiffon in that way. I refuse to use taffeta, and I abhor velvet. Silks and crepes are my preferred materials. Everything should be fluid. Simplicity. Sensuality. Just look at Sabina." Vane motioned to Sabina, over on the piano, and everybody turned around and gawked at her like a bunch of robots. "Isn't she fabulous? Look at how my slip-dress falls on her. Such clean lines. And the silver fabric. Silver is marvelous. Silver is fantasy."

Oh, please. I'd heard enough. I turned around and looked for Minty. I spotted him over by the giant cake and went over there.

". . . can brief you on that later. But the big news is, the curator of the Los Angeles County Museum is coming to your opening," Jori announced.

Mint's jaw dropped. "No! Sandro, that's fabulous!"

Sandro? When had he started calling him Sandro?

"He called me yesterday afternoon and told me he was very interested in your work." Jori took a long swig of bubbly and smiled.

"Oh, Minty! Darling! The painting is just exquisite! You have to come over and see how it's lit," this older dame with bleached soufflé hair and chunky gold necklaces burst in. Minty didn't notice me standing behind him. He started to talk with her, so I decided to go get some chow.

When I went into the dining room, there were about six people lined up in front of the buffet. I took a plate and got on line behind a bald guy. He turned around and looked at me, and guess who it was? The Erotic Sculptor, for christsakes. I'd been longing for another encounter with him, boy.

"I know you from somewhere," he said.

"I met you at the Plaza benefit."

His dense black eyebrows furrowed and he glared at me. "No. That's not it." He stared down at my legs.

"Yes, I was sitting next to—"

"You like mobiles?"

Ah, Jesus. Here we go again. "Yes. Sure," I responded.

"What kind of panty hose are you wearing? The kind that comes in the egg?" he demanded.

"What?"

"What are they? Control-top? Thigh-highs? Sheer Energy?"

"They're just regular sheer stockings," I said.

"How much do you want for them?" he asked.

What a lunatic. I didn't say anything. I put down my plate and walked back to the living room. I decided I'd go back to the buffet later. I'd just entered the living room, and was about to light a cigarette, when Jori came up to me.

"Salty, I'm so glad you could come tonight," he said pleasantly. Almost too pleasantly. I looked at him curiously.

"It's a nice party." I didn't know what to say to him. I didn't know why he was talking to me.

"I'm very worried about Hadrian," he said.

"I'm sorry. I don't know Hadrian."

"He's my Doberman."

"Oh. Why are you worried about him?"

"He's been limping for the past two days and I haven't had a chance to bring him to the vet." Jori's face tensed with concern,

and I was astonished. I didn't think Jori had sympathy for anything.

"Oh, the poor dog. Well, maybe he's got a sliver of glass in his
foot or something. Could I look at him?" I asked.

"Yes. Sure. He's down the right hall in my bedroom."

I couldn't believe Jori was concerned about his dog. I went back
into the dining room and took a piece of filet mignon off somebody's discarded plate, and then went off down the hall, through
the library and gym, until I came to Jori's closed bedroom door.
When I opened it the tiniest crack, the dog's long, black snout
popped out. I held out the piece of meat, and the dog snatched it
up and devoured it in two seconds. Then I opened the door a little
more and carefully scratched the dog's pointy ears. He tilted his
head and gazed up at me ardently. "Yes. . . . Good Hadrian. Good
puppy," I cooed. I slipped into the bedroom and closed the door
behind me. I walked around the king-size fur-covered bed, calling
the dog to come along, and I couldn't see a damn thing wrong
with it. He walked back and forth behind me and he didn't seem
to be limping in the least. I finally got him to sit and was going to
look at one of its paws, when I heard the bedroom door close and
turned around. Jori was standing there staring at me with this
frozen, ominous expression.

"You know, I don't think he's limping any—"

"There really isn't anything wrong with Hadrian," Jori said, ad-
vancing.

"But I thought you said—"

"Shut up, Salty," he hissed. He gripped my upper arms and
roughly shoved me back on his bed. I was absolutely stunned. I
tried to sit up, but he pressed himself over me and began to shove
up my dress. I kept twisting and squirming but I couldn't get out
from under him. I felt his hand groping for my breast and his hot,
moist mouth on my neck.

"Stop it! Stop! I'll scream!" I said.

"Go ahead and scream, Salty. Nobody's going to hear you," he whispered.

I strained and strained to push him off me, but he was just too heavy. My muscles were burning and my thoughts were horribly blurred and disheveled. I could smell his cologne and feel his hand slipping down between my legs. My whole body tightened and I thought I was going to throw up.

"No! Stop! Stop it! I'll tell Minty!" I cried.

His ecliptic black eyes seared into mine, and suddenly he stopped. He got up and stood calmly before his mirror. "Fine . . . tell Minty," he said idly, smoothing back his hair. "But I wouldn't expect your immaculate prince to rescue you, my dear." He turned slowly to look at me. "He's not as immaculate as he appears."

Tears rolled from my eyes and I drew in a jagged breath. I watched him as he tucked in his shirt and smoothed down his jacket. He didn't looked at me again. He just walked to the bedroom door, turned the lock, opened it, and left.

I couldn't breathe right. I kept gasping, and my stomach was clenched in hard knots. I looked down at Hadrian. He was peacefully folded up on the floor, sleeping. He was probably used to seeing Jori attack people. I went into the bathroom and splashed my face with water. I could still feel Jori's hands crawling all over me, and it made me shiver with disgust.

When I got back to the living room, I searched and searched for Minty until I found him talking to Vane by the piano.

"Mint—I have to talk to you," I interrupted.

"Salt, I'm in the middle of a con—"

"It's very important," I said harshly. He told Vane he'd be right back and I led him over to the windows where it wasn't so crowded.

"What is it?" Mint asked.

"Jori just . . ." I felt a lump rising in my throat and I swallowed. "He just attacked me."

Mint cocked his head to the side and smiled down at me. "How much have you had to drink tonight, Salt?"

"Goddamnit, Minty! I'm serious. He just attacked me in his bedroom. He told me his dog was limping and I went into his bedroom to see it, and he pushed me down on his bed and started to . . . to molest me."

"Salty, how could you say something so ridiculous? Alessandro would never do anything like that."

I looked up at him in disbelief. "How can you say that? You don't even know him. You've known him for seven months or something. He just attacked me," I repeated in exasperation.

"Salt, would you calm down."

"You don't believe me?"

"It's just not possible." Mint stared out the window for a moment. "Jesus, why are you doing this?" he asked quietly.

"What?"

"Why are you doing this? Do you want so badly to fuck things up for me? To destroy my relationship with Alessandro?"

His eyes drove down into mine and I cringed at their fierceness. I was so hurt I couldn't even speak. I just turned around and started to wind through all the guests. Just as I was leaving the living room, I spotted Jori. He was standing beside Sabina. He glanced over at me and smiled.

2⁄

Minty came home at two-thirty. I was curled on my side, pretending to be asleep, when he came into the bedroom. I listened to him quietly open the closet door. I heard hangers clanking together. I heard the water running in the bathroom. When he got into bed, he slid up behind me and put a hand on my shoulder.

"Salt? Salty? Are you awake?" he asked gently.

"I don't want to talk."

"Salt, please. Come on. I want to apologize. I shouldn't have spoken to you the way I did." He pulled me onto my back and leaned over me. He'd forgotten to turn off the hall light and it was dimly illuminating his face. "I just didn't know what to do, you know."

"So you believe me."

"Look, I . . . I don't know what happened. I can't ruin everything I've worked for because . . ." He looked away from me for a moment. His mouth was slightly open and his eyes were wet and glistening. "I just can't do it." He turned back to me. "I love you. I just need you to understand how important my career is. Please understand, Salt."

He hugged me tightly against him, and without even thinking my arms wrapped around him, my hands slid into his hair. Tears coursed down my cheeks, but I wasn't crying because of what had happened. I was crying because something was gone from his eyes. Something I would have died for was gone from his eyes.

The next day at work, I trudged into the dressing room with a cup of superstrong coffee, mumbled hello to Lola, and slumped down on the couch. She bounded over to me in her white leotard and pink, bare feet.

"Salty, what's wrong" she asked.

I didn't really want to talk about it, but I ended up telling her all about Jori attacking me and how Mint had reacted.

"That's awful! Minty should have beat up that asshole!" Lola exclaimed.

"It's difficult, though, because Jori's giving Mint this huge opportunity. I just . . . I'm stunned that he spoke to me the way he did. That he accused me of trying to . . ." I paused and looked down at the carpet. I still saw Mint's face in front of me, the fury in his eyes. "It's strange. I used to think Mint was perfect. Literally like a god." I looked up at Lola.

"Well, it's good that you're realizing he's not, because it's unhealthy to think of someone like that. It's really destructive. When I was in L.A. I went out with this guy who treated me like absolute shit, but I was so obsessed with him I didn't even care. I thought he was perfect and I just took his abuse. Don't let Mint abuse you, Salt."

"He doesn't. I mean, normally he's good to me. He's affectionate and he looks out for me. It's only when he's around Jori and all these jet-set socialites that he behaves so differently. . . . God, I just hope it's temporary. I think he's so overwhelmed by his success, he doesn't realize how he behaves." I stopped, feeling a little self-conscious. "Anyhow, you have to get to Makeup. I've been sitting here yacking—"

"No, it's okay. Anytime you want to talk, just tell me," Lola assured me, smiling.

"Thanks." I smiled back at her. I was glad she was there to talk to. She was really a very nice person.

2

When I woke up on the Thursday morning Mint was leaving for California, he was already in the shower. I decided to make him breakfast. I got out of bed and padded into the kitchen in my big floppy socks. When I peered into the fridge, I saw eggs, so I decided to make him French toast. Aunt Christa used to make French toast every Sunday morning for Uncle Edward and I used to help her, so French toast was one of the three things I really knew how to cook.

I was mixing the eggs and milk in a bowl when the kitchen door swung open, and Minty was standing there naked with a towel around his waist. His hair was wet and slicked back and he had a cigarette hanging out of his mouth.

"What are you doing?" he asked.

"I'm making you French toast."

Mint snatched the cigarette from between his lips and set it in the ashtray on the counter. He came up behind me and ran his hands up under my nightshirt. My blood went up in flames and I turned around and slipped my hands into his wet white hair. His mouth pressed against mine, but he wasn't gentle. His kiss was deep and strong and endless and when he exhaled I felt his breath as if it were mine. I didn't want to let go. I didn't want him to leave. When he pulled back from me, I looked out the window, squinting at the sun.

"What time is Jori meeting you at the airport?" I asked.

"He's going to be here at nine." Mint opened the fridge and took out a carton of orange juice.

"I thought you were going to meet him at—"

"I was, but when I spoke to him last night, he said he'd pick me up." Mint guzzled some orange juice from the carton. "Why should I take a cab when I can kick back in a limo?" he said hoarsely.

After Mint and I ate breakfast, he went into the bedroom to pack some last-minute stuff. I was scrubbing a charred pan in the kitchen when the doorbell rang. Mint went to get it, and I cringed when I heard Jori's voice in the living room.

"Hey, we've gotta be out of here in about five minutes," Jori said.

"I've just got to finish closing up my bags," Mint told him.

"I've got to make a call. Is there a phone I can use?" Jori asked.

"Oh, yeah, there's one in the kitchen. The door to your left."

What! Minty was going to let him come into the kitchen! Shit, shit, shit! I couldn't hide in the dishwasher or anything. I had to face him in my flimsy nightshirt and floppy socks, for christsakes. The door swished open and Jori burst in. He was wearing yet another tailored suit and his hair was yanked back. He looked over at me immediately, and his lips curved into a small, smug smile.

"Well, I was hoping I might run into you," he said softly.

I didn't say anything. I just looked down at the pan and scrubbed it like crazy. In my peripheral vision I saw him take a few steps forward, and my hands started to tremble.

"So, did he believe you?" he asked.

I stopped scrubbing and turned to look at him. He still had that cavalier smirk on his face and his black eyes were gripping me like a vise. He leisurely picked up the phone from the counter beside him, holding his menacing gaze on mine.

"You bastard," I muttered. God, I was furious. I dumped the sponge in the sink and tore out of the kitchen. I went straight into the bedroom and closed the door behind me.

"How could you let him come into the kitchen?" I demanded.

"What? Oh, Salt, I'm sorry." Mint shoved his tennis racket into his duffel bag, and then he reached for me and pulled me into his arms. "I'm really sorry. I forgot you were still in there. I'm in such a rush I didn't think," he said, kissing me on the forehead. Then he let go of me, zipped up his duffel, and grabbed his suitcase on the bed. "Would you open the door, baby."

I opened the door and stepped aside to let him pass. He carried his bags into the living room and I went over to kiss him good-bye.

"Have a great show," I said.

"Thanks. I'll call you and let you know what happens. I love you."

Just as Mint pressed his lips against mine, Jori burst into the living room. "Come on, Mint. We've gotta get out of here," he ordered.

Mint pulled away from me abruptly. As he leaned down to pick up his bags, Jori's vicious, almost fiendish eyes shot into mine. I turned around and walked into the bedroom and slammed the door.

Chapter

24

About two days after Mint left, I went to a party at Lola's apartment on West End Avenue. I'd been over to her place a couple of times. It was one of those cozy apartments with soft cream-colored rugs and big fluffy pillows. She had a lot of wooden bookshelves filled with organic cookbooks and little white candles and sandalwood incense. Anyhow, I arrived at about eight and Lola opened the door in a pair of jeans and a white blouse. She hugged me and I handed her the bottle of wine I'd brought.

"Where's your friend?" she asked. She'd told me to bring Minty, and, since he was out of town, I'd asked Dame and a prospective girlfriend of his.

"Oh, my friend Damon's coming a little later with his date. I hope it's okay that he's bringing someone," I said.

"Oh, sure. The more the merrier."

I followed Lola inside. A lot of people were there already. A lot of them were from the soap opera, but there were some people I didn't know. It was one of those nonchalant parties where everybody wears jeans and roams around like buffalo. People were strewn all over the place. They were perched on the kitchen counters, sitting on the living room rug going through Lola's record collection, hanging out in the hallway. I'd just gotten a glass of wine and was coming out of the kitchen when I bumped into Lucas.

"I say, haven't we met somewhere before?" he said in a sharp British accent.

"You think you're rather witty, don't you?" I remarked, smiling.

"Are you gonna play on the team?"

"What team?"

"Our softball team. You don't know about it?"

I shook my head.

"Every summer 'Today Is Tomorrow' goes up against another soap from a different network," he explained. "We lost to 'As the World Turns' last year."

"No one told me about it," I said.

"Will you play? We've only got two women on the team."

"Oh, yeah. Definitely. I love baseball."

"Oh, so you can hit then?" Lucas leaned back against the wall and gazed at me.

"Hit? Can I hit? Just think of me as the Babe in a skirt," I joked.

"Uh-huh. Okay. We'll see," he said teasingly. Then he glanced around. "So . . . is your boyfriend here?" he asked, as casual as hell.

"No, he's in L.A."

"Ahh." Lucas nodded and took a sip of his drink. Then he began to tell me about this play he'd seen, only I wasn't really listening. Ever since Lola had told me what he'd said about me, it was always in the back of my mind when I was around him. As he was talking about the play, I started to look at his goddamn pupils. I read somewhere in a magazine that if somebody likes you, their pupils dilate when they're yacking with you. Only Lucas had dark eyes, like mine, so I couldn't see a damn thing.

"Did you ever do theater?" he asked me.

"Only in high school. What about you?"

"Yeah, I just did stuff in school, too."

"What plays?"

"Oh, God . . . we did *Death of a Salesman*, and—"

"I did *Death of a Salesman*," I interjected.

"No, really? I loved it, but, Christ, was it morbid."

"Seriously. I feel the same way. You have to watch that poor old bastard go bananas, and as if that isn't enough, he has to die in the end."

"Exactly." Lucas smiled and nodded. "We always did dismal stuff, though."

"So did we. The only one that wasn't was *The Importance of Being Earnest*. We did *The Glass Menagerie*, which was absurdly depressing, and *The Seagull*—"

"Oh, God, we did *The Seagull*. All those lovesick Russians running around, shooting birds and committing suicide. It was delightful."

It was fun reminiscing with Lucas. We continued talking for a while until Chad, Lola's boyfriend, came over. Chad was a big, husky guy with a friendly-as-hell smile and a dark frothy beard dabbed with streaks of white and gray. He was a veterinarian over at Mercy Animal Hospital.

"Hey, how are you two?" he asked, flashing his wide smile. "I haven't been able to watch the show lately. Lola tells me you're Lucas's stepmother now."

"Yeah, I'm having his kid and his father thinks it's his," I explained.

Chad raised an eyebrow. "Run that by me again?"

"I'm pregnant with Lucas's character's child, but Lucas's father thinks it's his. It's kind of a nightmare," I said. Chad smiled and offered Lucas his condolences.

A couple of minutes later, I spotted Damon arriving with his date. I told Lucas I'd be back and went over to greet Dame. He actually looked very nice. He was wearing jeans with a white T-shirt, and the T-shirt didn't have any stains on it or anything. He was also wearing a black sports jacket that looked very handsome on him. He'd even combed his hair back so it didn't flop into his eyes. His date was adorable. Her name was Amy, and she was very petite with big, inquisitive blue eyes and a headful of cappuccino curls.

About three seconds after I shook hands with her, Damon told her he'd be right back, grabbed the sleeve of my jacket, and dragged me over to a corner. Man, was he nervous.

"Salt, you can't tell her anything about me being a hot dog. She doesn't know about it," he whispered heatedly.

"Of course I won't mention it. Calm down, for christsakes."

"And she thinks I'm twenty-six and a dentist."

"What!"

"Shhhhh! She's right over there," he said anxiously, glancing around.

"Damon, what do you mean, she thinks you're a dentist?" I whispered.

Dame ran his hand through his hair. "When I met her, she was telling me and her girlfriend how her teeth used to be crooked on the bottom, so I told her I was a dentist."

I stared at him blankly. "Damon, it doesn't make sense. Just because she mentioned her teeth used to be crooked, you thought she'd want to go out with a dentist?"

"Oh, I don't know why I said it. I was nervous and it just popped out. I didn't wanta tell her I was an unemployed actor and a hot dog, for godsakes. You promise you won't say anything, Salt?"

"I won't say anything, but she's going to find out sooner or later," I said.

We went back over to Amy, who was talking with Lola. After I introduced Dame to Lola, we all went into the kitchen to get drinks. I asked Amy what she did.

"I'm studying child psychology at NYU," she told me.

"Oh, I always loved psychology," Lola said.

"You know, I watch 'Today Is Tomorrow' all the time. Well, whenever I don't have a class. You're really good," Amy told Lola.

"Oh, thanks," Lola said, uncorking a bottle of wine. "Jenny's a great character because I get to explore so many different personalities."

"You know, Lola won the Emmy for best supporting actress last year," I said.

"Oh, that's terrific!" Amy exclaimed.

"Thanks. I didn't expect it at all." Lola handed Amy a glass of wine.

We went back into the living room and joined a couple of people sitting near the couch. Lola didn't allow anybody to smoke in her apartment, so I'd brought about ten packs of gum along. I was offering a piece to Amy when Damon blurted out, "You know, four out of five dentists recommend sugarless gum for their patients who chew gum."

Amy and I looked at him.

"I mean, I recommend gum for my patients . . . who chew," he added anxiously.

What a disaster. I was about to change the subject when Lola said, "Oh, I didn't know you were a dentist."

Damon ran a hand through his hair and coughed a couple of times. "Yes, yes. Yup, I'm a dentist."

"What made you decide to go into dentistry?" Lola wanted to know.

I leaned forward a little. I wanted to hear this one.

"Oh, well . . . I've . . . teeth have always . . . since I was a small child, I've always been fascinated with teeth. Incisors, molars, wisdom teeth. All of them just fascinated me. Their structure and enamel and so on. . . ." What the hell was he saying? I glared at him, and he coughed again and drummed his fingers on his jeans. "Um . . . is there a bathroom I can use?" he asked Lola.

She told him where it was, and he stood up and took off.

When Dame returned we were all listening to Audrey Gillian, one of the actresses on the show, tell a story about the time she did a love scene with Peter Garrett and he got into the bed naked. Everybody was cracking up over it when the doorbell sounded and Mick arrived. He was in his battered blue jeans, a white T-shirt, and a black suede vest. His trademark bandana was wrapped around his leg, and his hair was all scrambled with wind. After he said hello to a few people, he came over and sat down next to me and patted my goddamn leg. Mick never did anything in the customary way. He never kissed you hello on the cheek or anything. He'd just slap you on the back or pat your leg or nudge up against you like a mountain lion.

"What's up?" he asked, leaning back on the couch.

"Not much. How'd your interview go?" I asked. He'd had an interview with *Soap Opera Digest* Friday afternoon.

"Oh, it was okay. They always ask the stupidest questions, though. Nobody gives a shit what I eat for breakfast or what my favorite song is."

"Oh, Mick, you know there are tons of young girls out there who are just dying to know what you eat for breakfast," I kidded.

He made a wry face and took a sip of his drink. "So, tell me, what does Minty think of our love scenes?" he asked.

"He won't watch them. He watched some of the first one and told me it was giving him a headache."

Mick smiled, and his eyes got all crunched up in the corners. "My ex-wife used to hit me over the head with stuff when she saw my love scenes."

"I didn't know you'd been married."

"Yeah, we got divorced three years ago. What's this?" Mick

pointed to a bowl of something lumpy and green on the coffee table.

"I think it's guacamole, but I haven't tasted it. So you want kids."

"Oh, yeah. Can't you see me as a dad?"

I studied him, crunching on a celery stick. "Well, sort of. I have an image of you strapping a toddler to a bungee cord."

"Very funny." Mick dipped a corn chip into the green stuff and shoved it into his mouth.

Lucas came over and plopped down next to me on the couch. I always found myself sitting between Lucas and Mick. Not that it bothered me or anything. We all started talking about movies, and then Damon and Amy came over and sat across from us. As Amy was commenting on some film, Damon pulled a goddamn sandwich out of the inside of his jacket. He interrupted Amy to ask her if she'd like it.

"What is it?" she asked, peering at it dubiously.

"It's bologna on whole wheat. But I've got chicken salad on rye, if you'd like that better." Dame reached into the other side of his jacket and pulled out another sandwich. The guy was a walking delicatessen, for christsakes.

At around twelve-thirty everybody started to split. Right before Damon left, he pulled me aside and asked me if I liked Amy.

"Yeah. I think she's very nice," I said.

"Did you notice how she was fondling my knee during the game of charades? She wants me." Dame raised his eyebrows and smirked like a bastard.

"You aren't going to attack her tonight, are you?" I had a feeling, from the goddamn look in his eye, that he was getting ready to pounce on her.

"No, I'm not gonna attack her. I wanta take it slow. I wanta have a relationship with her."

"Okay." I hugged him. "Call me next week."

A few minutes later I went down in the elevator with Lucas and Mick. When we came out of Lola's building, it was as hot as hell and the sky was smudged with mist. Mick and I lit up cigarettes and we all started to walk down the block.

"I like your friend. He's really funny," Lucas said.

"Damon? Yeah, he's a character." I took a deep drag off my cigarette, then ran ahead a little. "Ahhh! We get to sleep late tomorrow!" I said, twirling around on the pavement like a lunatic.

"Holy shit. Tomorrow's Sunday," Lucas blurted out.

Mick playfully smacked him on the back of the head. "Where ya been, kid?"

"I thought . . . oh, forget it."

"You were that kid who always showed up at school bright and early on Saturday morning, weren't you, Lucas?" I said.

"Yeah. Actually, it happened to me twice."

Mick walked over to his bike and straddled it, looking like Marlon Brando with the cig hanging out of his mouth. "Care for a ride, Salty?"

"I'd love one!" He'd given me a few rides on his motorcycle, and I adored it. I darted over and got on behind him.

"Oh, sure! Just leave me here. Just take off, why don't you!" Lucas wailed dramatically. "Boundless impertinence! Young fry of treachery! Let this pernicious hour stand aye accursed in the calendar! Fie, for shame . . ." he rambled, thrusting one finger into the air.

"Take it easy, Luke!" Mick called, revving up his bike.

"See you Monday!" I cried, waving to him.

"Grab on to me, Salty," Mick instructed. I slid up a little on the smooth seat and wrapped my arms around him. It was like holding on to a goddamn boulder. When he took off we were submerged in this great cold breeze. I leaned my head over his shoulder and watched a stream of cars disappear past us. The city was all black and gray, stabbed with white headlights. We went through the park to the East Side. The trees' silhouettes became creatures—dinosaurs, demons. I rested my cheek against Mick's back, smelling the suede of his vest and watching the jigsaw of light between the trees.

As we came out of the park, Mick asked me what street I was on again.

"Seventy-first between Park and Lex."

When he pulled up in front of my building, the cool air was instantly extinguished, draped in the oppressive heat. I hopped off Mick's bike, and his face cocked sideways to look at me.

"How about a smoke before I take off?" he asked.

"Sure." I said.

Mick got off his bike. We leaned up against a parked car and took out our cigarettes. I was looking for my lighter when Mick whipped a match out in front of me. I glanced into his eyes. He was looking at me. His eyes were tinged blue-blond in the light from the flame. Then he gazed down. He lit his own cigarette and leaned back against the car again.

"I miss California," he said, looking up at the sky.

"You liked it there?"

"I liked the space. The mountains. Sometimes I feel trapped in this city. I miss nature, you know." Mick's eyes slid down into mine. I felt a bead of sweat trickling down from the nape of my neck.

"Yeah. I know. I miss it, too."

"You never seemed like a city girl to me."

"No?"

"No. You have this great . . ." He paused for a second and looked down.

"What?" I asked.

"A great natural beauty and vitality. I could so easily picture you in the country somewhere." I smiled and glanced away. I don't know why but I could feel this burning sensation flooding my face and neck. I was sure I was blushing. I was also sweating like a madman. I lifted the hair off my neck to cool it a little.

When we finished our cigarettes Mick started to goof around and act out the ending of one of our upcoming scenes. He wasn't doing it seriously or anything. He was hamming it up like crazy. He pressed his hands over his chest and told me I was his world and that he didn't believe any of the malicious things Andrew was saying about me. I played along.

"I just don't understand why he hates me so," I wailed.

Mick pulled me into his arms then and dipped me backward. We had a kiss in the script at this point. His face was right over mine and we were both smiling and laughing, but then he stopped kidding around. His face got this very serious expression, and my laughter kind of dried up. We just stared at each other for a moment. Then, suddenly, he pulled me up and I stepped back.

"I should be going," he said, walking over to his bike.

"Oh. Oh, right. Um . . ." I don't know what the hell I said. I was a little disoriented.

"Have a good sleep," he said, revving up his bike.

"You, too. And thanks for the ride."

"Anytime, Salty," he called. He took off down the street and I turned and went into my building. As I was going up in the elevator I started to think about what had happened. I was almost positive Mick had wanted to kiss me.

When I got upstairs, I dumped my keys in the dish in the entrance and went into the bedroom. As I was changing for bed, I started to think about what a nice time I'd had. For the first time in ages, I'd really enjoyed myself at a party and hadn't wanted to spend the whole night in the can or something.

When I got into bed it was around one-thirty in the morning. I turned off the light, rolled onto my side, and looked at Mint's empty side of the bed. I started to think about him. I started to imagine what it was like for him in L.A. I imagined the gallery and his hotel room. I get a real vivid picture of places I've never been. So I was imagining Mint's hotel room and it was pink with a lot of vases of flowers and a big white bed. Then there was a balcony that overlooked a lot of movie theaters and palm trees. But then I imagined Mint walking out of the hotel, and it was terrible, because the street was loaded with tanned, blond bimbos in string bikinis and Rollerblades. They all had huge hooters and hard rear ends, and they were all whizzing around him, and I was horrified. I really thought that's what it was like out there on the West Coast, and I couldn't stop thinking about it. It was kind of like when you watch a gory movie late at night and then when it's done you try to go to sleep, but you can't, because your brain's doing a slide show for you. It's got all the really gory parts of the movie stored in the projector and you can't shut the goddamn thing off. So you try to outsmart the bastard. You sneak up behind the projector and dump all these new slides in. You stick in Snow White and all the dwarfs plucking wildflowers beside some sun-kissed pond. The thing is, the brain is no moron. It's a brain, for crying out loud. It knows damn well what you're up to, and it has a plan of its own. It'll show you all your tweeting birds and daffodils until it's convinced you that you've beaten it. Until you think you're pretty damn clever. Then just as you start to relax, *wham*! That's when it gets its revenge. Before you know it, Snow White is revving up her chain saw, grinding off Dopey's head, and punting it into the sun-kissed pond. Now she's galloping through the wildflowers, crushing them under her blood-splattered ballet slippers. She's coming after Sneezy now. She's sawing the poor bastard up into half a dozen pieces. . . . Well, you get the idea. No matter what I tried to concentrate on, all the blond bimbos would come charging through my head like that goddamn Energizer bunny and it was giving me a pain in the ass. I finally had to sit up and watch the tube for a while. I watched "Star Trek," and when I finally fell asleep I had a dream that the

Enterprise crashed onto a hot, tropical planet inhabited by blond aliens with wheels for feet.

❧

Minty called about three days after he left and told me how great everything was going.

"I'm so happy for you, Minty," I said.

"You know Johnny Carson bought a painting?" Mint said.

"Really?"

"He didn't come on opening night. He came during the day and met privately with Sandro and me. He bought *Amalgam*."

"*Amalgam*? The really huge canvas with the pigeons taking off in the rain, and they're all kind of blending into one?"

"Yeah. That's it."

"That's fabulous. Mint, what's all that noise?" There was one helluva racket in the background.

"Nothing—Sandro and a couple guys from the gallery. We're having a few drinks before dinner."

"Where are you?"

"What?"

"Where are you?!"

"I'm in my suite. Oh, Salt, I'm gonna stay out here for a few extra days."

"Why?"

"Because I'm supposed to meet the curator of the Los Angeles County Museum and—"

"I thought he came to your opening."

"What? Oh, no . . . yeah, I mean the curator of the Getty Museum. There are also some important collectors he wants me to meet."

"When will you come back?"

"On the twenty-ninth." I heard Jori calling Mint in the background. "Hey, Salt, I've gotta run. We're leaving for dinner."

"At eleven o'clock?"

"It's eight here, Salt."

"Oh, yeah, I forgot." I heard Jori call Mint again. "I've really gotta go, baby. I miss you. I'll see you in a couple days. Bye."

"Bye, Mint." I put down the receiver and sat there for a minute. I started to think of about half a dozen different ways to kill Jori. But then I knocked it off. I got a little worried God might hear me thinking, and I didn't want to piss him off.

❧

Mint came home from L.A. at about ten o'clock in the evening on the twenty-ninth. I was in the bedroom when I heard the front door open.

"Salt!" he called. I ran out to him.

"Minty!" I threw my arms around him. He smelled like cigarettes and airplane.

"How are you, baby?" He drew his head back and I brushed some of the bangs out of his eyes. His skin was the color of gingerbread.

"Your nose is peeling," I commented.

"Yeah, I fell asleep by the pool at the hotel."

"Is this a new suit?" He was wearing a gorgeous taupe suit.

"Yeah. Sandro and I went shopping on Rodeo Drive. Wait till you see some of the stuff I got." Mint turned around to get his bags, and that's when I noticed the huge Gucci suitcase.

"Is this a new suitcase?" I asked.

"Yeah, well, I needed a bag to put all this stuff in anyway."

He carried his two suitcases into the bedroom. I picked up his duffel bag and followed him. He set his Gucci suitcase down on the bed, and when he opened it I couldn't believe my eyes. It was completely loaded with Versace and Armani suits and shirts and

269

ties. He had gorgeous new belts and this beautiful patterned silk robe.

"Minty, my God . . . you bought all this? It must have cost a fortune," I remarked, holding up the robe.

"Hey, I was celebrating. And here . . ." Mint pulled a pale blue package out of a pouch of his suitcase and handed it to me.

"Tiffany's?" I blurted, looking down at the box.

"Go on . . . open it," Mint urged.

I took the top off the box. "Oh, my God . . . Minty . . ." I held the gleaming gold-link bracelet up in front of me.

"I wanted to get you something really elegant. Do you like it?"

I put the bracelet on my wrist and stared down at it. Jesus, it was the heaviest bracelet I'd ever felt in my life. It could have been a barbell, for christsakes. It was very beautiful and all that, but it wasn't me at all. I didn't want to disappoint Mint, though, so I told him I loved it and gave him a big kiss. He smiled down at me and walked over to the closet.

"How was the fancy airplane?" I asked as I undid the clasp on the bracelet and stuck it back in the box.

"MGM Grand? It was incredible. It's like you're flying in a restaurant. Jack Nicholson was sitting in the compartment right next to us." Mint began to take off his shirt.

"Minty . . . you're so thin." I'd never seen him that thin before. His torso was so angular, so sharp. All his ribs were jutting out and his stomach was completely concave.

"Huh? Oh, I had some kind of stomach thing for the past week, and I hardly ate anything."

"Can I get you something? You should eat something. I picked up some bagels for you. I could toast a bagel and heat up some soup for—"

"No, no, baby, I'm fine. I ate on the plane. I'm just exhausted."

I walked over and hugged him. "Why don't you go to bed? I'll unpack for you."

Mint agreed, and he was asleep about five minutes later. I started to hang up all his new suits and ties. I was putting some shirts in his dresser drawers when something on his bedside table caught my eye. I went over to look, and discovered it was a gold Rolex, exactly like Jori's. I was going to pick it up to look at it, but then I realized I didn't want to touch it. I didn't even want to know it was there.

❧

About a week and a half after Mint got back, I had my first week-day off in months. I wanted to spend the day with Mint, but he was doing a shoot and interview for *Vanity Fair*, so I settled for catching up on some reading and doing laundry. I dragged the laundry basket into the elevator and went down to the basement. When I walked into the laundry room I found Mr. Gooter bent over, looking in the dryer. He was wearing his slippers, a pair of checkered pants, and a striped short-sleeved shirt. His old dog was lying on its side on the dusty floor, its lumpy body heaving with breaths. Something like that—an old man and his dog in a basement—can depress the hell out of me. As soon as I saw the two of them I got very emotional. It's the same thing when I see an old geezer coming down the street with his old dog. I always try to smile at the geezer and compliment him on his dog or hat or something.

"Hi, Mr. Gooter," I said cheerily. He lifted his head and squinted at me. "It's Salty."

"Oh . . . hello, Salty."

"Do you need any help?" I asked, going over to him.

"I can't . . . I think something's wrong. . . . I put these clothes in the dishwasher and they aren't getting wet," he murmured.

"No, Mr. Gooter, this is a dryer. You want the washing machine."

"Who do I want?"

"The washing machine—over there." I gestured to the washing machine.

Gooter looked over at it like he'd never seen it before in his life. "Oh. So we'd better take them out of the dishwasher, then." He started to bend back over and I told him to go sit down and that I'd put them in the washer for him.

"Thanks, Salty. I'm a little pooped." He went over and slumped down in this lousy-looking chair with a plastic seat cushion on it. When I finished unloading all his laundry, I asked him where his detergent was.

"Oh, I forgot to put that in. It's in the basket." He pointed to this haggard-looking laundry basket, and I went over to it. He had a bottle of Wella Balsam shampoo in there.

"This is shampoo."

"Gesundheit."

"No . . ." I walked over and showed Gooter the bottle. "This is shampoo for your hair. You don't have any fabric detergent?"

"You can't use shampoo in the dishwasher?" The poor old bastard was getting worse by the minute.

"No. Listen, I'm going to put my detergent in the machine and then I'll give it to you." I got my box of Tide and began to pour it over his clothes. He kept telling me he couldn't accept the detergent. It must have taken me five minutes to convince him to keep it.

"You know, I was watching this program the other day and I could have sworn I saw you on it," Gooter said.

"You must have seen me on 'Today Is Tomorrow.'"

"No . . . no, I didn't see it today. I saw it a couple days ago."

"No, I meant the show is called 'Today Is Tomorrow.'"

"You're going to be on tomorrow?" What a nightmare. This was turning into "Who's on First," for christsakes.

"No. The name of the show, its title, is 'Today Is Tomorrow,' " I said very slowly.

"Ahhhhh. That's the name of it. You never told me you were on a television show."

"Yeah. I've been on it for a couple months now." I finished putting all my whites into the other machine and turned it on. When I turned around, Gooter was snoring. Jesus. He'd fallen asleep in three seconds. He must have been tired. He'd slipped way down in the chair and I was afraid he might fall off and kill himself. I went over and gently tapped his shoulder.

"Mr. Gooter?"

"Huh? I don't have any corn," he mumbled.

"Mr. Goot—"

"Try the next aisle."

"Mr. Gooter, wake up." I rubbed his shoulder a little harder and his eyes fluttered open. He raised his head and looked at me.

"Oh, Salty. Thank goodness you're here. Some crazy lady was chasing me around the market." He rubbed his eyes with his bony fingers and pushed himself up a little.

"Mr. Gooter, you look so tired and this chair must be awfully uncomfortable. Why don't you go up to your apartment and rest? I'll bring you your laundry when it's done."

"Oh, no. That's too kind of you," he protested. He kept saying no until I finally convinced him to go. When he got up out of the chair, he put a hand on my shoulder and told me I was a nice girl. Then he told Zelda to come along. Zelda opened her eyes and looked up at him. It was so goddamn touching, the way she looked up at him. It practically choked me up. You could see she just adored the poor old bastard. She struggled to her feet, and she was a little shaky but she was okay. She just kept looking up at Gooter with that devoted expression as they shuffled off together out of the laundry room.

After Gooter left, I lit a cigarette and read my book for a while. Then I got Gooter's laundry into the dryer and began to put the rest of mine into the washing machine. I was yanking Mint's black jeans out of the laundry basket when something fell out of them and rolled across the floor. I just stood there, not even moving to see what it was. Somehow I guess I already knew.

2

Mint got home from his interview at about five. He came into the bedroom where I was folding the laundry.

"Hey, baby. You're home early," he said, walking toward the closet.

"I didn't go to work today."

"Oh, right, I forgot." He took out one of his new raw-silk suits and laid it on the bed. "There was this guy at the shoot today, Harley Farell, who—"

"Minty . . ."

"What?" He slipped off his jacket and glanced over at me.

"When I was doing the laundry today . . ." I stopped folding a towel and looked up at him. "You're doing cocaine."

He sighed loudly and looked down at his suit. "I'm not doing cocaine," he said staunchly.

"Oh, come on, Minty. A vial of it fell out of the black jeans you took to L.A. Do you expect me to believe you didn't know it was there?"

"I knew it was there. I didn't do any. Sandro gave me some to hold for—"

"Christ, Mint! Do you think I'm that stupid? Do you think I haven't noticed how wired you've been lately or how much weight you've lost?"

"Okay. So I did a little. It's no big deal. I'm not addicted to it. I don't even like it that much."

"How can you say that? You sound like an insecure teenager who needs to prove he's cool. Does Jori have that much control over—"

"Don't bring him into this!" Mint yelled.

"Why not?! He's the one who pressured you into doing coke—"

"Nobody pressured me into it!" Mint's eyes narrowed and his expression grew stone hard. "You're so fucking naive! Doing two lines every now and then isn't going to kill me!"

"But it's hurting you. How can I just sit back and watch you—"

"It's not hurting me! I'm fine! I feel better than I've ever been. You know, I came home today with this great news to share with you, and you have to lay all this crap on me. I don't need to come home to this." Mint grabbed his new jacket and raged past me.

I rushed after him, but he didn't turn around. He snatched his keys from the dish on the entrance table and left the apartment.

❧

Mint came home at about one in the morning. I sat up and turned on my lamp when he came into the bedroom. He looked at me for a moment, and then he walked over and sat down beside me on the edge of the bed.

"Salt . . . I'm so sorry. I won't do it anymore. I promise." He took one of my hands in his, and I breathed in deeply and looked away from him. "Please, don't be angry. I need you, Salt. . . . I need you. . . ."

I felt his hands tightening around mine. I turned back to look at him. Tears were brimming in his eyes and, suddenly, he was six years old again . . . it was hot, it was August, and he was running toward me with something he had found, his white hair wildly streaming, honeycombed with sun, his cheeks stained russet red. He'd almost reached me when he tripped over something. I remember sprinting to him from the sandbox and kneeling beside his small spread-eagled body. Dirt-streaked tears were winding down from his blinking eyes, climbing over the bridge of his nose, vanishing on the ground. He wasn't making a sound, but I heard him screaming anyway. I heard it in his warped features, in the wincing slivers of his eyes. I looked around for Aunt Christa, but she was still outside the park gate, getting us hot dogs from the vendor. I was only six, but it didn't matter; I loved him and I knew what to do. I leaned forward and helped him sit up. I was only six, but I didn't care about the deep, bloody gash on his knee—a cut so bad that later Aunt Christa had to take him to the doctor for stitches. I didn't care. I held him in my arms like a grown woman holding her child. I smudged his tears away with my little fingers. I pulled his head against the plane of my chest and felt him jerk with the screams he was stifling. "Don't cry, Minty . . . I'm here and I'm not ever gonna leave you . . . not ever . . ."

The memory faded. Minty's mature, strong, white hand was overflowing in mine. I drew him into my arms and felt his tears melt into my skin. "Don't cry. It's all right. I'm here, Minty . . . I'm here . . ."

Chapter

25

One night, in the beginning of August, Mint and I had to go to this party on Central Park South. When we came out of our building I expected him to hail a cab, but he just started to stroll up the block.

"Come on, Salt," he called back.

"We're walking? Mint, I can't walk thirty blocks in these heels," I said, following him. When I caught up with him, he looked down at me with this very sly smile on his face.

"I thought we might drive."

"Drive? What are you talking about?"

He suddenly veered to the left and walked over to the curb. He folded his arms across his chest and leaned back against a gleaming black Porsche.

"What?" I asked.

He kept smiling and all of a sudden I realized what he'd done, and my mouth fell open.

"No. . . . Minty . . . you bought this car?"

"What do you think? Isn't it gorgeous?" He rested an arm on the top of it and stared at me.

"It must have cost a fortune!" I exclaimed, coming over to look at it. Man, you should have seen this car. It was the raciest-looking thing I'd ever seen.

"Don't worry about it, baby. I've got it covered." Mint tossed a set of keys up in the air and swiftly caught them in his hand.

Jesus, was this some car. It had buttery black leather seats and a disc player. After Mint turned on the ignition he slipped in a Psychedelic Furs CD, stuck a cigarette between his lips, and took off like Mad Max. He kept one hand on the steering wheel and one hand on the stick shift, and, I have to admit, he looked as sexy as hell driving the car. He looked like the real James Bond. The one nobody ever knew about. The one who was too busy to audition for the part.

So we got to this building on Central Park South. When we got up to the apartment, Mint rang the doorbell and a maid came and led us into this huge two-story studio. There were about ten people strewn around with drinks. Blair Horning, the guy who was throwing the party, came over immediately when he saw Mint. I'd only met Blair once before. He did leveraged buyouts or something. He was a very spiffy-looking guy with a big Prince Charles nose and dirty-blond hair. From the look of his apartment, you could see he had a helluva lot of dough. The problem was, his decor was a disaster. He had this funky art deco furniture in black and dynamite red. Everything looked very cold and graphic. The artwork was what stood out the most, though. He had all this supermodern minimalist crap all over the walls. He had a gigantic Fontana—this big blank canvas with a knife slash in the center of it. What a piece of crap it was, and I'll bet you it cost a fortune. That kind of thing kills me. When people buy a really expensive piece of crap when they could have used the dough for something really worthwhile. He had a Barnett Newman, too, a large red canvas with one line drawn through it. One line, for christsakes. That pit bull on "Letterman" could have pulled that shit off blindfolded. Over by the long black dinner table he had a Lichtenstein of some blond broad, crying as usual. I didn't mind the Lichtenstein, though.

About five minutes after Mint and I arrived, everybody sat down to dinner. I was next to Saul Somebody-or-other, this big fat guy with a beard, who was a wine connoisseur and world traveler. He was one of those people who never let you get a word in edgewise. He just kept yacking while he shoveled risotto into his mouth.

He was right in the middle of telling me about a safari in Africa when the doorbell sounded and the maid led Jori and the Creature over to the dinner table. I was hoping he wouldn't show up. As soon as they came in, everybody stopped talking and looked over at them. I couldn't believe what Jori did then. He strode right up to Blair at the head of the table, put a hand on his shoulder, and said, "Sorry we're late, Blair. We were at Redford's for cocktails. Couldn't get away."

What a bunch of horseshit. "Redford's for cocktails." You know he wanted everybody to think he meant Robert Redford, and Jori knew Robert Redford like a hole in the head. Besides that, what a rotten excuse, to say he'd just come from a cocktail party.

As Jori said this, the Creature just stood there grinning like an idiot in her exceptionally tight white beaded dress. Something was different about her, and I kept trying to figure out what. She still had those huge Zulu lips, but something was different. Then I realized something was up with her nose. She had fucked up her nose, for christsakes. She had one of those Las Vegas cookie-cutter jobs now. When she walked past me to go to her chair, I turned around and got a good look. Her nose was the size of a jelly bean. Her goddamn Zulu lips were bigger than her nose. What a nightmare.

During dessert, I accidentally caught Jori's eye. He flashed me this predatory gaze while he savagely bit into a fig. I quickly looked away from him and started to jiggle my foot under the table. I was going to try to talk to the guy on my left, but he was too absorbed in the dame on his left. He'd been putting the moves on her all night and, man, you should have heard the load of crap he was feeding her. He kept telling her she reminded him of a Botticelli. Then at one point he started to rave about her complexion. He told her she had skin so pale and glowing, like freshly fallen snow. Like freshly fallen snow, for christsakes. What a poetic guy he was. A real Lord Byron.

I couldn't stand it. I had to get out of there. As soon as dinner ended I went up to Mint and told him I was leaving.

"You're leaving now?" Mint thrust out his arm and looked at the gleaming gold Rolex on his wrist. "It's only a quarter to eleven, Salt."

"I know, but I have to get up so early, and I'm just beat," I said.

"Oh, you're leaving. What a shame," Jori said in his phony-as-hell voice. "I was hoping you'd come along to MK later." What temerity he had. I didn't say anything to him.

"Sandro's having a party at MK tonight. I'll be home a little late," Mint told me.

"Okay. I'll see you later," I said.

I thanked Blair for the evening and walked out the door. When I got outside the building I started to walk toward the Plaza. It was very mild out, like eighty degrees or something. When I got down to the Plaza, I decided to hail a cab. The cabby's name was Luther and I know that 'cause he kept turning around to tell me every two seconds. Every two seconds he'd crank his head around and say, "Hello there, my name is Luther and this is my cab." At first I thought it was very nice of him to turn around and introduce himself, but when he kept doing it, it started to get on my nerves. He didn't say one other thing for the whole ride, either. He didn't talk about the weather or the ball game or anything. He just kept repeating, "My name is Luther and this is my cab." Even when I handed him his fare he said it. I have this theory that the city gets half its cabdrivers from the insane asylum. I think they must go there and get 'em cheap.

※

The following Saturday I went up to Gooter's to give him these old sweaters Mint didn't want anymore. They were really very nice sweaters, but Mint kept saying he needed more room in the closet and that he wouldn't wear them again. When I went up to Gooter's he wasn't there. I figured he was out walking his pooch or something and decided to come back later. When I came back later that day, he wasn't home yet. I went up again to his apartment late Sunday afternoon, and when he still wasn't there I started to get a little worried. I thought the poor old bastard might have mistaken the subway for the elevator or something. I went down to the basement to ask Manuel, the super, if he'd seen him. I found Manuel in the laundry room standing on a dryer, changing a light bulb on the ceiling.

"Hi, Manuel," I said.

He stopped twisting the light bulb and looked down at me with this terrible expression on his face. "Oh, no, ees you. Don' tell me you flush somethin' else down the toilet."

"No, no, the toilet's fine."

Manuel's expression relaxed a little, and he asked me if I needed to use the machines.

"No. . . . I was just wondering if you've seen Mr. Gooter, by any chance. I've been knocking on—"

"Mr. Gooter pass away seeks days ago, Salty."

"He—he died?"

"Yes. I deedn't know you knew him or I would have tol' you."

I leaned back against a washing machine and looked over at

the ratty-looking chair Gooter had sat in the last time I saw him. I couldn't believe he was dead. I felt this awful sensation. Like I'd been slapped across the face.

"What happened to him?"

"His seester came from Florida and she had him cremated."

"What about Zelda? Did she take his dog?" I asked.

"No. She no can have pets in her apartment. I took the dog to the ASPCA on Wednesday."

Oh, God. He took Zelda to the ASPCA! I couldn't bear the thought of that poor old dog at the ASPCA, not knowing what was going on, losing her best friend. He'd brought her in on Wednesday. Four days. They might not have killed her. I rushed upstairs to get my handbag and went to get her.

When I got to the ASPCA, I raced up to the front desk and told the receptionist what I was there for. She went through some files and then picked up a phone and called somebody.

"You're lucky, miss. She was due to be put down tomorrow morning," the woman said after she got off the phone.

"Then she's alive!"

"Yes, she's alive. You see that man in the red sweatshirt? You tell him you're here for Zelda, and he'll take you into the back to get her."

"Oh, thanks. Thanks a lot," I said.

Nothing could be more dreadful than what I saw in the back. It was a prison, only none of its inmates were guilty of anything. They were alive and they were all being punished for it. One after another the cages lined the halls. Horror-film light from single bulbs on the ceiling flooded frantic eyes. The painful barking and howling wasn't even as loud as the raging despair in those eyes.

Finally the man in the sweatshirt led me into a small room where more cages were heaped on top of each other. When I entered, all the dogs in those cages leapt to their feet and struggled to get my attention. They all poked their noses through the cramped, rusting bars and tried so desperately to get me to come to them. But I couldn't come to them. I had to find Zelda.

I found her at the end of the room. She was the only dog who hadn't stood up when I'd approached. Instead, she crouched in the back of her cage, her head buried in her chest, her tail tucked fearfully beneath her. It brought tears to my eyes to see her like that. She was just like me when my parents had died and I lay on the bottom bunk of Mint's bed, my child's body wound into a shell of misery, my head tipped down in bitter, brutal confusion. Like an animal, I didn't understand, I was too young to understand. All I knew was that my mama wasn't there anymore. The only thing in the world I depended upon for safety and security and love had vanished. I felt every drop of Zelda's terror because her terror had been mine.

The man opened Zelda's cage for me. When I picked her up, she was trembling so fiercely it made me shiver. She was so old and scared and her coat was so dusty and matted. "It's okay, Zelda," I whispered. "It's going to be okay."

2

When I got home it was around a quarter to six. I was just carrying Zelda into the kitchen to get her something to eat when Mint appeared outside on the fire escape carrying a canvas. He slid it through the open window, resting it face up on the wooden table, then leapt down into the kitchen.

"Minty?"

He raked back his shimmering bangs and looked over at me. "What the . . . what are you doing with that dog?"

"It was Mr. Gooter's. He died, Mint. Manuel took her to the ASPCA and I had to go get her."

Minty scratched his forehead and squinted his eyes at me. "What do you mean, you had to go get her?"

"Just what I said. They were going to kill her. That's what the ASPCA does, it—"

"I know what it does, Salt. I'm asking why you felt responsible. That dog has nothing to do with you," Mint said brusquely.

"What difference does it make? People give money to the starving children in Ethiopia and it doesn't have to do with them. They don't know the children, they just want to help."

"Yeah, well, they don't bring the children back to live with them. I've gotta be honest with you. I don't want a dog around."

I stopped stroking Zelda's neck. "Why?"

"Because we're not gonna live in this dump for much longer and I don't want to have to deal with a dog. It's just gonna piss all over the carpets and stink up the apartment."

"God, how can you be so insensitive!" I didn't understand what was happening to him. Every day he did something that . . . that just wasn't him. "You're becoming so goddamn materialistic!"

Mint shoved a chair aside so forcefully that it fell over backward. He tore around the table and came toward me. "We're not poor! We've got money now, so what do you want to do? Keep it stuffed under our mattress? Send it to all the children in Ethiopia? I worked damn hard for this money and I don't think there's anything wrong in spending some of it!" Mint yelled. "And I'm not going to live with this animal. I want you to take it back tomorrow." He glared down at me with furious eyes. "I'm going to the Pigeon."

He brushed past me then and I just stood there. I just stood there for five minutes with Zelda trembling in my arms and Minty's words still lashing at my heart.

At around eleven that night I finished studying my lines and got ready for bed. After I came out of the bath and got into my night-

gown, I got a blanket from the linen closet to make a little bed on
the bedroom floor for Zelda. She wasn't trembling anymore, but
she'd hardly eaten anything, and she looked so unhappy. I was
just arranging the blanket for her when I heard the bedroom door
open. When I turned around, Mint was standing in the doorframe with a bouquet of white roses.

"Salt . . ."

I stopped fixing the blanket and stared at him.

"I'm sorry. I've been thinking and, look, if you really want the
dog, it's okay." He moved toward me and bent down on a knee
and handed me the roses.

I was so mad at him. I wanted to slap him across the face like
those feisty, husky-voiced broads in the movies. But I didn't have
the balls. I just set his roses down on the floor and started to fix
up the blanket again.

"Salt, I said I was sorry. What more do you want? You can keep
the dog." I still didn't look at him. I kept my eyes pinned on the
blanket. "Salt? Salt, will you say something? . . ." He grabbed my
shoulders and twisted me around to face him.

"I can't believe the way you spoke to me! How could you treat
me like that?!" I jerked away from him, stood up, and stalked out
of the bedroom. I'd gotten halfway through the living room when
I sensed Minty behind me. He grabbed my arm and yanked me
up against him.

"Don't! Let go of me, Mint." I tried to free myself, but it was
useless. He dug a hand into my hair, gripped a fistful, and tilted
my head back.

"I'm not going to let go of you," he said severely, and then he
kissed me. God, did he ever kiss me. Like Rhett Butler kissed
Scarlett when Atlanta was going up in a blaze of flames. My entire body went limp. Like I'd just been shot point-blank through
the heart, that's how limp I went. That's how deadly his kiss was.
Minty swept me up into his arms and carried me back into the

bedroom. He made love to me so violently and fervidly that tears began to streak down my face and curve over my jaw. I could barely breathe. I don't remember breathing. I remember suffocating at his open lips and drawing my fingernails down his back. When it was over, he leaned his head against my chest. His breath was quick and warped with exertion, and every time he exhaled I felt it burn into my skin. Then, suddenly, he looked up at me.

"I love you, Salt," he said quietly.

I held my eyes in his, searching for him. For the small blond boy I trusted and recognized. I wanted to tell that boy how desperately I loved him, but I couldn't find him, so I didn't. I just closed my eyes and hoped I'd see him in the morning.

❧

About two weeks after I rescued Zelda, I got together with Damon and went to Central Park to take out one of those goddamn rowboats. The park was loaded with people. That's because it was a Sunday and it's always loaded like that on Sunday. On my way to meet him I started to walk down the little hill that leads to the statue of Alice in Wonderland, and I noticed a bevy of teenage girls strewn all over this hunk of gray rocks. They were all trying to get a goddamn suntan. It was probably fifty-eight degrees and they were lying out in their bikinis as if this were Saint-Tropez or something. They were doing their best to act very chic, taking these Marlene Dietrich drags off their cigarettes, and you could see they just wanted everybody to drop dead at the sight of them. I remember I used to do the same thing when I was a teenager, thinking I looked incredibly sophisticated, when I really just looked like a moron.

So anyhow, as I walked past them I saw that two of them were staring at me. I ignored them and kept walking. About ten seconds later I felt a tap on my shoulder, and I turned around and the two girls were standing there. Seeing them up close like that, I knew they couldn't have been more than sixteen.

"Yes?" I asked. I figured they had something to say to me, but they just stood there, smothered in goose bumps, staring at me. "Is there something—"

"You're on 'Today Is Tomorrow,' right?" blurted out the one with the frosted lipstick.

"Yes. I'm on the show."

"We watch it all the time. We love Laura. You're really excellent," the brunette said.

"Yeah. You're a really good actress," the other one remarked.

Jesus. I was incredibly flattered. "Thanks. Thanks, that really means a lot to me," I said. It did, too. It meant a helluva lot to me.

Then I couldn't believe what they did. They asked me for my autograph, for christsakes. They wanted me to sign the backs of their notebooks. No one had ever asked me for my autograph in person before and I got all flustered. I almost dropped the pen, and as I signed my name I sort of mashed all the letters in Salty together. I guess it didn't matter, though. When I finished signing their notebooks, they thanked me about a thousand times and went back off to the rock. I started walking again with a big smile on my face. I felt kind of proud of myself. I mean, I really felt like I was doing a job.

I started to climb up this little hill until I got to the road where all the bikers and joggers and Rollerbladers are. I must have waited a whole five minutes to cross the road. Every time I tried to go across, some guy on a bike would come along and I'd have to leap back up on the curb. I have terrible judgment about how long it'll take me to cross the street. I also never know which way to go. You know how when you're walking toward someone on the street and that person starts to swerve left, so you start to swerve right to go around them? Well, I'm that moron you run into who can never figure out which way to swerve. I'm the one who keeps swerving in the direction you're swerving. I don't know if that means I'm dyslexic, or just plain stupid.

Finally I just ran across the road to where the boat pond was and started to look around for Dame. Of course, I found him in the little snack-shack thing by the side of the pond. He was in there buying french fries. When he came out into the sunlight, I got a good look at his outfit. He was wearing army pants. They were those green camouflage jobs, and they weren't especially attractive. He also had on his baseball cap and his big Lakers sweatshirt.

When he spotted me, Dame came over and dropped his knapsack on the dusty ground, placed his french fries on top of it, and gave me a huge hug.

When he released me he said we should hurry and get on line for a boat.

If you've never been to the boat pond, it's quite a nice-sized pond, and you can take out these rowboats and row around in there. The rowboats are mostly full of lovers. Dame and I must have been the only two guys on line who weren't slobbering all over each other. There was one couple directly ahead of us and they were driving me nuts. They kept talking in that lovers' baby talk, you know? They were just nauseating. They must have been in their early thirties and they were both wearing the same color sweater. You should have heard the charming name he had for her. He called her Poo-Poo. He kept saying, "Does Poo-Poo wanta cookie?" Poo-Poo, for godsakes. What kind of a name is that? If Minty had ever tried to call me Poo-Poo, I'd have smacked him over the head. I tried to ignore them and asked Dame about Amy.

"Oh, things are great. I finally told her I wasn't a dentist."

"Well, it's about time. What has it been—two months?"

"Yeah. About that. Anyhow, she told me she knew I wasn't a dentist from the start. She said nobody who eats as much garbage as I do could be a dentist. Besides, she followed me to work one day," Dame said.

"Oh. She knows you're a hot dog?"

"Uh-huh. But she doesn't mind. She's really amazing." He crammed about ten french fries into his mouth.

In front of us the guy was helping Poo-Poo into the goddamn boat. She was one of those wishy-washy dames who can't even step into a goddamn rowboat without assistance. When the couple got in, the guy who was in charge of everything shoved their boat off. Dame and I got in a boat about five minutes later. Of course, we got a rotten boat. Practically all its paint was chipped off and the whole bottom was tracked with muddy water and leaves. When we got in, Dame insisted on rowing. He sat down on the little bench and started to row like a bastard. For such a skinny guy, he had quite a lot of strength. We tore right by Poo-Poo and her boyfriend, and they had a five-minute head start.

When we got to the middle of the pond, Dame set down the oars and we looked around for a minute. It was very nice out there 'cause it didn't feel like the city at all. It certainly wasn't the Riviera or anything, but it had a lot of charm. I wouldn't recommend bringing your fishing pole, though, 'cause you'd probably just reel up a beer bottle or a homicide or something. I took my pack of smokes out and lit one up while Dame pulled a giant bag of Doritos out of his knapsack. As I was staring at the water, I started to think about Minty and I got really depressed.

"Hey, what's wrong, Salt?" Damon asked.

"Oh, it's nothing."

"Come on. I know you, and something's wrong."

I took a deep drag off my cigarette and looked up at him. I started to tell him about how Mint had reacted when I brought Zelda home.

"He wouldn't let you keep it?" Dame asked.

"No, later he came home and told me I could keep her, but I was . . . I was so upset by the things he'd said. He's not the same person, Damon. Ever since he met Jori he's changed, and I just don't feel the way I used to about him. You know I used to worship him."

"Yeah. I know," Dame said quietly.

"My whole life used to revolve around him, only it's different now. I have a separate life of my own." I looked at Dame. He just sat there, staring at me for a moment.

"What are you going to do?" he asked.

"Oh, God, I don't know. I just don't want to give up on him. I've been with him my whole life, and I *know* this isn't him. I think it's really been hard for him to handle the kind of success he's had, and Jori hanging around him all the time and everything . . . I'm just hoping he'll calm down. I want . . ."

"What?"

I gazed up into the sky and watched a group of pigeons swerve and dive down into the trees. "I just want him to be like he was."

Chapter
26

Early in October, Mint came home from the Pigeon around midnight one night and woke me up. When I sat up, he started to pace around the bedroom like a lunatic.

"What is it? What's going on?"

He stopped pacing and looked at me. "Sandro came to the Pigeon tonight with Rex Wurst. Rex is giving me three hundred thousand to do a mural in his new home in Santa Barbara. God! Three hundred thousand dollars, Salt! I can't fucking believe it!" Mint rushed over to me, lifted me up off the bed, and twirled me around in his arms.

"Minty, that's wonderful!" I said as he set me down.

"It's more than that. Do you have any idea how important Wurst is? He's a billionaire and he's got a world-famous collection and he wants me to paint his living room! God, this blows my mind." Mint started to pace around again, and I backed up against the bureau.

"This means you'll have to go back to California, right?"

"Well, I can't very well paint his living room on the West Coast from the East Coast, baby. Three hundred grand, I can't—"

"When will you go?"

"Huh?"

"When will you go to California?"

"In a month or so. I want to throw a party for Sandro at the restaurant before I leave." Mint went over to his bedside table, picked up his black date book, and started to riffle through it.

"Why?" I asked.

"Because he got me this deal, Salt. Without him, none of this would have happened. I owe him."

I climbed back into bed and got under the covers. "Do you mind if I don't go? I mean, I'd feel . . ."

"No, I understand." Mint turned around and looked at me. "You don't have to go." When he turned back to his date book, I curled up on my side with my back to him. I watched his enormous shadow on the wall in front of me until I fell asleep.

❧

On the night of Mint's party for Jori, I stayed home and decided to clean out the storage closet. I got into a pair of old sweats and rummaged through boxes filled up with old, useless crap. Old warped hats, old jars of paintbrushes, lousy shampoos, expired cold medicine, gold lipstick from 1980, Mint's deflated high-school football, and a couple of pairs of disgusting shoes. It was a nightmare, because everything was tossed all over the place. I'd find some horrible-looking shoe stuck in a rust-covered toaster oven, and inside the goddamn shoe I'd find a Michael Jackson *Thriller* tape. It was the most fucked-up storage closet on the face of the earth.

Anyhow, I was right in the middle of cleaning it out when I came across the old boot box with all the pictures of Minty and me as kids in it. I hadn't seen those pictures in ages, so I decided to take the box down and go through it. I sat down on the bedroom rug next to Zelda. She was lying on her heating pad, and she had one eye open and it was looking at me. She was doing much better now. She was eating and she didn't have that horrible expression on her face.

I patted her for a couple of minutes before I started to look at the photos. There were some of Mint and me going off to camp, some of us in the playground. There were pictures of Minty drawing on the floor in the bedroom in his pajamas, and there was one of him sitting on the john. He must have been four or five and he was just sitting there, smiling like a bastard for the camera. Kids are crazy. They don't even care if somebody snaps a picture of them on the john. My favorite picture of us was the one taken on Christmas morning. We're standing in front of the Christmas tree and Mint's hugging me. He's mashing me in his arms and we're both laughing. You can see one of my front teeth is missing and Mint's got a piece of tinsel around his neck.

As I was looking at that picture, I started to get kind of depressed. I started to think about how things had been lately with Mint. Suddenly, I just wanted to go to the Pigeon and be with him. I wanted to show him I'd stand by him. That no matter how much I despised the people he was with right now, I'd endure them for him.

I got up and looked at the time. It was already ten o'clock. I went over to the closet and grabbed my plain black dress and black shoes and changed as fast as I could. Then I went into the bathroom and swiped some blush over my cheeks and put some goddamn lipstick on. I didn't have time to style my hair so I just stuck it in a ponytail.

When I walked into the Pigeon, it was around ten-forty-five. Everybody had finished dinner and they were all milling around with glasses of champagne. There were a helluva lot of people. I started to wind around looking for Minty. I ran into Blair Horning with that actress who played the *Playboy* bunny. What's her name? Hemingway. The blonde. Horning was flirting with her like nuts. I ran into Helmut Huldheinz. He was standing between the Creature and some guy I didn't know. Just as I came up to them, the creature, who was staring up at Helmut, blurted out, "Ohh! You're from Berlin! I thought you were from Germany!" What a nightmare.

About two seconds later she spotted me and flung herself all over me. When she untangled her arms from around my neck, I asked her if she'd seen Minty. "Minty? Um . . . um . . . um . . ." Her eyes started to dart around and she began to chew on one of her long ketchup-red nails. You would have thought I'd asked her to calculate the velocity of neutron accelerations. Finally, she said no.

I wandered off and asked a few more people, but nobody seemed to know where he was. I was about to ask this woman with soufflé hair when I spotted Jori near her, and veered away. I went over to Johnny Vane by the birdbath, and before I even opened my mouth he criticized my goddamn outfit. He said, "Oh, my." Then he started to click his tongue against the roof of his mouth. "I see we've been shopping at the Gap again." Then he had the nerve to tell me that polyester was all the rage in Paris these days. The woman standing next to him was practically chuckling her stupid head off. I ignored both of them and asked Vane if he'd seen Mint. He took a puff off his cigarette and said, " 'Fraid not, darling."

I walked off toward the kitchen. When I poked my head in, I asked Tony, Minty's partner, if he'd seen Mint. "No. Sorry, Salty."

Ah, shit. How could he not be here? He was throwing the goddamn party. I went back out and scanned the room once again.

As I was about to go over to a group of people to my right, I felt someone grip my arm. When I turned around, Jori was standing there. I yanked my arm away from him and looked at him with an ice cold expression.

"I see you've come out of hibernation," he said. What an ass he was. I turned around and was about to walk away when I heard him say, "Are you looking for Minty?" I gazed back over at him. He took a serene sip of champagne and raised his arched black eyebrows.

"Yes," I said, frosty as hell.

"He's down in the wine cellar."

I stared at him skeptically. I had a feeling he was up to something. He probably wanted to get me down in the wine cellar so he could attack me again. I didn't say anything to him. I turned around and walked off into the swarm of guests.

I went around the whole goddamn room two more times, and when I still couldn't find Mint I decided I *would* try the wine cellar. Jori was way over by the birdbath talking to Vane, so I felt a little more at ease. When I opened the door, one of the cellar lights was on. I walked down a few steps and was just about to call out Mint's name when I heard his voice.

". . . want to be with you. I'm trying as hard as I can."

"I'm tired of meeting you in the middle of the night, Minty! I'm tired of hiding."

"Look, it's hard for me right now. I've got my hands full. But I want you to come to California with me."

I couldn't move. I couldn't breathe. I clutched the banister and closed my eyes.

"When are you going?"

"In about a month. I was commissioned to do a mural and Salty doesn't know how long it will take. We can have like three months together, baby."

"Oh, Minty . . . I always think of our time in California. Let's go back to the beach house. Can we stay there?"

"I've already asked Sandro, and he's giving me the keys."

"I can't stop thinking about you. Today during the shoot, I couldn't even concentrate because of you."

"I can't stop thinking about you, too. God, I love you, Sabina. . . ."

I closed my eyes and for one fleeting moment I was five years old again and tears were rushing down my cheeks and I was gasping and terrified because my mother was dead. Only it wasn't my mother now. It was Minty. I opened my eyes and quickly turned around, but I could barely get my balance. I was so weak all of a sudden. I started to step up the stairs, when I felt my shoe hit something hard, and I looked down to see a wine bottle tilt and plummet sideways off the stairs. Minty ran out from behind a wine rack seconds after the sharp crash tore through the cellar. He looked down at the shattered bottle, and then his eyes lifted up into mine.

When I came out of the restaurant, I ran out into the street and hailed a cab. Just as I got into it, I saw the restaurant door burst open, and Minty rushed out and screamed my name. I ducked down in the backseat and told the driver to step on it. I was so dizzy, I felt like I'd been physically beaten. I pressed my face up against the cold glass of the window. I just wanted it all to go away. To go away forever. I wanted quiet. I wanted innocence. I wanted that first night back, the one when Minty really kissed me for the first time in my old bed. I wanted that first touch, that first ache, the one that tears through your gut like a steam engine and blurs everything else in the world.

When the cab pulled up in front of my building, I paid the driver and went upstairs. In the doorway to the bedroom I stopped, and leaned up against the frame. My eyes were burning, over-flowing with tears, and I couldn't stop the mangled sobs from welling up in my throat. I don't know how long I stood there. At one point I glanced down and saw Zelda approaching me on her old fragile legs. She came right up to me and gazed up at me with her wet black eyes. I knelt down and gently held her in my arms.

Finally, I got ahold of myself. I wiped my tears with the palm of my hand, and went over to the closet to get my suitcases. I laid them down on the bed and started to fill them with my clothes. While I was in the bathroom loading up some cosmetics, I heard a door slam. When I came back into the bedroom, Minty was standing in front of the bureau, staring at my suitcases on the bed. He looked as though he was in a trance. Just standing there, motionless, with his mouth slightly open and his black trench glistening with drops of rain. I didn't speak. I walked right past him and shoved my cosmetic bag into a suitcase.

"What are you doing?" His voice was so soft and tremulous I hardly recognized it.

I turned to look at him. "I'm leaving you."

He stared at me and swallowed. His eyes were shuddering, sud-denly gleaming, melting. "Please . . . Salty . . . you can't leave. Please." He started to shake his head, and I turned away and walked over to my bedside table to clean out my drawer. He came over and grabbed my arm and twisted me around to face him.

"Salty, wait . . . please, I'm so sorry. I won't see her anymore. I swear!" he said frantically.

I wrenched my arm away and stormed to the other side of the room. I stood with my back to him for a second and then I turned to look at him.

"You think that's it? You think that's going to make everything fine? This isn't even about Sabina, Minty. For months it's just been one thing after another. Sabina was just the last straw. God,

I was so stupid. All this time I was forgiving you and making excuses for you because I wanted so desperately to preserve the Minty I knew. But he doesn't exist anymore."

Minty looked at me, his eyes shattered with tears. "He does. He does exist," he said fervidly.

"No . . . no, he doesn't. I watched you disappear, and I—I don't know who you are anymore," I said quietly.

Minty bowed his head and closed his eyes. When he looked back up, the tears ran down his cheeks and I had to look away from him.

"Just give me one more chance. Please. I can't lose you, Salty. You belong with me." His voice trembled toward me.

I felt tears stinging my eyes, but I wouldn't let them fall. "We're not kids anymore. We're totally different people, and I don't belong here."

Mint didn't say anything. He just stood there, staring numbly at the floor. After a few moments he asked me where I was going.

"I'm going to get a hotel room and then find an apartment."

Neither of us said very much after that. Minty just sat there on the bed and watched as I finished getting ready. When I'd packed as much as I could, I asked him if he wouldn't mind helping me with the suitcases. He was very somber. He didn't speak or look at me, but he picked up the two bulky bags I'd packed. I put Zelda on her leash and followed him out to the elevator.

When the elevator door opened in the lobby, it felt so strange. It felt like I was dreaming. Nothing seemed real. I would have been sleeping now. . . . I was supposed to be sleeping beside Minty. . . . I was supposed to be hopeful, believing he might change. Believing in our future together. But instead I was walking through the lobby with its dim watery light. It was almost two in the morning, and I was walking out into the windy street with Zelda at my heels and with Minty, who didn't say a word.

Mint hailed a cab. After he put my suitcases in the trunk, I walked over to him. He was standing about five feet from the back of the cab, his trench coat thrashing and rippling in the wind.

"I'll come back and get the rest of my things when I find an apartment," I said.

He still didn't look at me. His head was bowed down, staring at his shiny black shoes, which were beaming in the streetlight.

"I think . . . it would be better if we didn't see each other any-more. I don't think I could handle it. I need to get on with my life, away from the past. . . ." I said.

I was shivering suddenly. Only, I don't know if it had anything to do with the dampness or sharp gusts of wind. I didn't know what else to say. My mind was blank with exhaustion, with the pain that everything around me was real. That it wouldn't over-expose, magically contort or dissolve in the morning. I was living this and it would never dissolve.

I waited for him to say something . . . to look at me . . . but he didn't. I couldn't stand there any longer, so I turned around to get in the cab. I'd only taken two steps before I felt the strength of his hands on me and my body was yanked back. All I wanted to do was slam my fists into his chest, but I couldn't. I couldn't because somewhere buried deep inside this stranger was a child I loved so very much, and I needed to feel his arms around me just one last time. I don't know exactly how long I stayed there, enveloped in his arms, my head crushed against his chest. Finally, the taxi driver called out that the meter was running. As I was pulling back from Mint, he gripped my arm.

"I'll get you back, Salty. I know I'll get you back. We've been through too much together," he said forcefully.

I stared at him. His eyes were squinted against the wind, blaz-ing with certainty. I didn't say anything. I walked away from him and got into the cab with Zelda.

I told the driver the address of the hotel and turned around to look back at Minty. He was standing exactly where I had left him, in the haunting downpour of street light. He was paler than diamonds against the russet leaves and asphalt sky. He looked at me fiercely, tragically, and suddenly I felt the engine quiver and the cab plunged forward. Minty grew smaller and smaller, fainter and fainter. Soon he was nothing. He was gone.